ACHILLES

ACHILLES

THE DEEP SKY SAGA

BOOK ONE

GREG BOOSE

DIVERSIONBOOKS

Diversion Books
A Division of Diversion Publishing Corp.
443 Park Avenue South, Suite 1008
New York, New York 10016
www.DiversionBooks.com

For more information, email info@diversionbooks.com

First Diversion Books edition September 2017.
Hardcover ISBN: 978-1-63576-054-5
eBook ISBN: 978-1-63576-053-8

Printed in the U.S.A.
SDB/1708
1 3 5 7 9 10 8 6 4 2

To Veronica and Juliette,
my two moons.

CHAPTER ONE

Jonah rocks his shoulders up and down, struggling to free his long arms from his sleeping container. The thing is like a cocoon, warm and moist and suffocating, unwilling to separate from the sixteen-year-old boy who, for the third straight night, has officially given up on sleep. His arms finally escape, and in frustration he plucks out his earplugs and rips away the tiny pillow strapped to his head, and he lets it all float away in the darkness.

He takes his time opening his eyes. Since the wormhole—the time jump—he's been dealing with vertigo, migraines, and nausea. The hallucinations, though, they started yesterday: the classroom floor slithered like snakes, and his plate at dinner separated into a dozen pieces that spun around and waved at him like little hands saying goodbye. Still, he considers himself lucky that this is all he's dealing with.

Over half of the ship has been afflicted by the wormhole. Some have it worse than others: a cook woke up yesterday and suddenly couldn't use her legs, a demic biologist lost his ability to speak, and a girl from Module Nine—a quiet Second Year cadet from Kansas City—couldn't stop scratching herself or shouting out the names of all the bones in the human body. The doctors have her restrained in the sick bay, next to a senior navigator who constantly bites at the air in front of his face. Insomnia, Jonah realizes, is nothing.

His eyes open and he stares at the half-circle of light glowing twenty feet below, outlining his sleeping level's only exit. Between him and the exit are four cadets sound asleep, one snoring loudly, all of them slightly rotating in the air like the hour hands on antique clocks. Five more cadets float above Jonah, a clique of seventeen- and eighteen-year-old guys who only just recently stopped talking and fell asleep.

Jonah blindly waves his arm to his left where his sheaf sticks, but he has drifted too far away. His fingers find the cord that tethers him to the inflatable module wall, and he slowly tugs himself along, yawning. The instant the paper-thin rectangle touches Jonah's skin, the sheaf releases itself from the wall and the screen comes to life. The device curls inward and expands, doubling its size to sixteen inches. The date and time float in front of his face in three-dimensional figures: 19 OCT 2221, 0108 GMT.

Jonah blinks, rubs his face, and looks again. It's only one o'clock. Six more hours until the lights come on. Six more hours until he's free to roam the Mayflower 2 and get something to eat. The only thing that keeps him from screaming out in frustration is the fact that after these six hours, it's only twenty-four more hours until they land on Thetis. It's practically over. It's almost here. After thirteen months aboard this ship, trapped with one hundred seventy-seven people who still somehow remain strangers to him, it's almost over.

He waves his hand in front of the sheaf, and it flashes to the home screen where week-old news from Earth—from before the wormhole—scrolls along the top and bottom: "Support for President Louise Cruz at All-Time High." "65% of Cubans Want to Secede from the United States. Back to 56 States?" "Rebel Forces Take Back London."

A sharp noise suddenly breaks Jonah away from his screen. He rolls up the sheaf and tucks it into his shirtsleeve, and he holds his breath. Behind him in the darkness, the inflatable wall flaps once, twice, and then repeatedly, sounding like a row of flags caught in a storm. And then below him, something metallic whines, the eerie noise echoing up and into Jonah's mouth. For over a year he's slept inside this module, barreling through outer space, and the walls have never made a sound. Ever. Until now.

He's hallucinating, Jonah tells himself. It's just the insomnia and the wormhole effects. The walls aren't really flapping. There isn't a leak. The module isn't going to rip apart. He's going to make it to Thetis safely in less than thirty hours. And then he'll sleep for days.

The flapping and other noises, just as suddenly as they started, stop. Jonah takes a quick breath. And then another and another. He counts to ten, twenty, thirty, and the noises never return. The hallucinations are getting worse, he thinks. He'll talk to Dr. Zarembo after breakfast. Perhaps she can help.

Jonah pulls back out his sheaf and unfurls it, catching a quick reflection of his dark brown face with deep half-circles under his eyes in the glowing screen. His thick black hair is uneven from his pillow, and he half-heartedly pulls at it with his giant right hand while his brown eyes study the rest of his image. Jonah's mouth is straight, his lips full. His nose, wide like a newborn's fist. He stares at the bones of his cheeks that point out like wings ready to take flight. He sighs, wondering if his dad ever looked this strange and awkward at sixteen.

His image disappears when the sheaf begins to project a hologram inches away from his nose: A hazy blue and green planet slowly rotates on its axis. A radiating yellow dot hovers above the southern coastline of the planet's one continent: the Athens colony. Rising slowly from behind the planet, the word THETIS appears in all capitals, and the name circles around the globe twice before fading away.

He watches the planet that's twice the size of Earth and a smile cracks across his lips. *This is going to be good,* he thinks. *No, this is going to be great.* With only one hundred thirty-four humans living on Thetis, he might actually get his own room. Hell, maybe he'll even get his own yurt with a view. He needs some space. It's amazing that he actually misses something from his time living on the streets and under the bridges of Cleveland: that ability to be alone.

He touches the northern pole of Thetis and the planet immediately stops rotating. Jonah then double taps the same spot and a tiny red dot appears, just where he left it, and a second later, a long document fans out horizontally in front of the screen. He runs his exhausted eyes over his classified state file, a document he's not supposed to have.

He scrolls to the section of the document detailing his time in five different foster homes. Mr. Nora, the father of his third foster family, called him, "An all-around awful kid to be around." He said, "Jonah was filthy, too quiet, and a goddamn thief. I once found him stealing food right from my daughter's plate. I made sure he never did that again." Jonah unconsciously rubs his chin. That's where the man's fist had landed. He was only eight years old when a tiny piece of bread had fallen off fourteen-year-old Amberline's plate, onto the floor. She didn't even notice it. Jonah, having finished his minuscule portion of scrambled powdered eggs, still hungry, drowning in thoughts on how to survive the day's endless supply of bullies, waited several minutes before reaching down to put the crumb in his mouth. Amberline shrieked. Mr. Nora swung.

"He seemed smart, and we liked having him. For a while, that is," Denise Pacsun, his fourth foster mother, said. "But then he stopped obeying me and my husband. He tried to run away several times. It caused quite a disruption in our strong family unit, and that's when we felt it was best he lived somewhere else." Images of the Pacsun twins flash before Jonah's eyes. His mind goes to the night the boys stripped Jonah's clothes off and held him down and placed scalding rocks on his back and legs, creating silvery scars that still cover his skin like a school of fish. He ran away the next morning, blood soaking his shirt as he stumbled through the neighborhood.

Finally, Jonah scrolls to the seventh paragraph of the document, inhaling deeply as he reads the two sentences that haunt his entire existence: "Austin and Flora Lincoln, both twenty-four, were killed in the Los Angeles earthquake of 2205. They are survived by their son, Jonah Lincoln, five months." He reads it twice, and when the tears form in the corners of his eyes, he drags an icon from the desktop to the center of the screen and nods. A photograph appears. A handsome, extremely tall black man smiles at the camera. He leans over a hospital bed where an exhausted woman holds her newborn baby to her chest. Jonah stares at the photo, at his dad, his mom, himself. He stares at the large window in the background full of sun, at the stack of pillows behind his mom's back. Tears blur his vision, and he pushes the photograph back off the screen.

The rest of the document is the ugly story of how Jonah escaped his final foster home at the age of fourteen after old Mrs. Hoyt died of a heart attack in her bathroom. How Jonah found her lying on her face and didn't report it to the police. How he survived on the streets of Cleveland for five months—where he slept, what he ate, what petty crimes he committed—before finally agreeing to enter the academy, after much coercing from his social workers. The first month at the school was brutal. Fights. Missed homework. No friends. Failed tests. But with time, he found his way.

"His grades and attitude have soared, relatively speaking," wrote the academy's counselor after Jonah's third month. "He spends a lot of time in the exercise room and in the swimming pool, becoming somewhat of an expert at the high dive. Jonah has yet to make many friends." He puffs out his chest as he thinks about the swimming, the training, his newfound love of history and art. And his chest only grows larger when he thinks back to that sweltering November evening two years ago, the night he was selected to join the crew of the Mayflower 2 and help re-establish the colony on Thetis. When news reached Earth that all those kids died in the avalanche on their field trip to the Polaris Mons, it consumed everyone for months, including Jonah. He never thought that tragedy, so far away, would lead to an opportunity. No one ever really chose him for something before; he was always forced one place or another. But suddenly the academy wanted him, and then Thetis wanted him. It was a strange and uncomfortable feeling, but he was thrilled to avoid what was happening in London and start over.

Eighty kids were chosen for the Mayflower 2: forty military cadets—like Jonah—and forty kids from the academic sector in Northern California. The demics, as the cadets call them.

Finally feeling tired, as if sleep is actually near, Jonah closes the document. He attempts to shut the sheaf down but accidentally opens another program. Suddenly a video pops up, a half-watched film from Thetis featuring the academy's brightest star, Armitage Blythe, a passenger from the first ship. The cadet is huge, with the head of a pumpkin and arms like tree trunks. In the video, Armitage pulls a large section of bark away from a twisted gray tree, revealing a nest of white, bat-like creatures that take flight in a misty cloud of ink. A caption runs along the top, but before Jonah can read it, a boy's voice comes from below.

"Turn that shit off, J."

Jonah closes his fist and the device shrinks in half and goes blank. He then wings his sheaf at the wall and it sticks audibly in the dark. It takes him a second to realize the voice belongs to Manny Ucedo, another First Year cadet like himself. The thirteen-year-old boy is the closest thing he has to a friend at the academy, which isn't saying much. Jonah doesn't know a lot about him, aside from the fact he has seven brothers and likes surfing, two things Jonah knows nothing about.

"Sorry," Jonah whispers. "Can't sleep."

Manny yawns. "Yeah? What's new?"

"I know. But I'm going to go try again right now, though. See you in the morning."

There's a soft crinkling of a wrapper.

"Well, if you're hungry, I have a crystal orange here I was saving," Manny says.

"No, I'm okay." As soon as Jonah whispers it, he immediately wishes he hadn't. Not many people offer things to Jonah, unless it's an older cadet proposing a fight or offering some type of criticism. "I'll just wait until breakfast. But thanks. It's just one o'clock, you know."

Another yawn from Manny. "Damn. Well, I have about five or so nappies and a couple of dozers if you want them. Either will knock you right out. Just ask Blaire over there."

"I don't do pills, actually, but thanks."

Jonah reels his arms back inside his sleeping container. He finds the temperature knob next to his hip and turns it a couple notches to the right. As his legs warm, he tries a doctor's recommended deep-breathing routine. In his nose, out his mouth, then reverses it. He concentrates, clears his mind, and after a few minutes, Jonah feels sleep beginning to coat the back of his skull. For the first time in days, he feels nearly at peace, ready to rest.

But then something leathery brushes Jonah's cheek. His eyes snap open, and a rush of liquid heat shoots throughout his body. He rips his arm out of his container, ready to snatch one of the Pacsun twins' hands to bend it backward over his wrist, but to his surprise it's just the module wall. He takes a deep breath and uses his neck to push away from the material. *The ship must have altered its direction,* Jonah thinks. They could be closer to Thetis than he thought.

The module walls start flapping again. Jonah freezes and waits for it to stop, but instead the metallic whine returns, too. Then, there's a pinging that mixes with the flapping and the whining. It's coming from outside. It's as if a wave of sand washes over the ship. It has to be another hallucination.

"Manny?"

He doesn't respond.

The pinging gets louder and louder, and Jonah rams his fingers into his eyes, pushing them this way and that, and he starts to hum, hoping to distract his brain, but when he stops and his eyes and ears adjust, the pinging is still there. And then objects all over the room begin to rattle and buzz in their cabinets.

The foot of Jonah's sleeping container swings left and gently bounces off the wall, spinning him completely around.

"What the hell is going on?" someone moans from below.

Another boy coughs. "The ship is changing direction or something."

"Shut the hell up down there," a Fourth Year barks from the ceiling, "or I'll kick your asses."

Jonah's feet hit the wall again, spinning him. More boys feel it and wake up, groaning, complaining.

"Are we taking evasive maneuvers?" Manny asks. "Are we entering an asteroid belt, trying to get away?"

"There's no asteroid belt, asshole," the Fourth Year says. "Not in this part of the Silver Foot."

"It's been going on for a while," Jonah says so quietly that no one seems to hear him.

"What time is it?" a Second Year asks.

"Time for everybody in this fucking room to shut the hell up and go back to fucking sleep," snaps an eighteen-year-old. "Christ. Bunch of fucking babies."

The walls begin to flap violently, as if there were a hundred men outside, slapping and clawing, dying to get in.

"What is that?" Manny shouts.

Everyone spins in their containers, bouncing off each other and the walls. The ship is not only changing directions, but it's doing it too fast. Every cadet in the sleep level wakes up, and they shout, groan, and complain. A needling panic spreads under Jonah's skin. The noises are too much; Jonah bursts out of his sleeping container like he's exiting an escape hatch.

"Who the hell is that?" a boy shouts as a frantic Jonah swims upward in the darkness. He doesn't answer and rows himself along the ceiling. He floats past a boy who is surprisingly still asleep, and he slaps his fingers against the opposite wall, feeling for the window. He needs to see outside, what's causing all this noise. He needs to see the stars.

Without warning, bright white lights swamp the level, causing the boys to howl and cover their eyes. Jonah finds the window and presses the tiny square under the black glass, and it loses its tint. Jonah gasps at the sight: There, taking up his entire view, is a giant brown, green, and blue ball enveloped in a thin layer of white. They're entering its atmosphere.

"We're landing early!" Manny shouts.

A Third Year pulls himself past Jonah, slamming his palm under each of the other four windows, exposing everyone to the sight. This planet doesn't really look like the image of Thetis on his sheaf, but it *is* familiar.

"Everyone just shut up for a second!" the Third Year yells. "Something's… Something's wrong!"

"We're coming in too fast!" a boy shouts.

The module walls stop flapping and start contracting and expanding around the windows, ballooning in and out like an exhausted lung. The noises outside grow even louder, and Jonah thinks he feels the truss, the network of metal bars that holds all nine of the giant cylindrical modules in a row, twist and bow. Outside, blue and purple flames appear and disappear like ghosts. The boys grow silent with fear. They know that at any moment the truss is going to open like a flower, and each of the modules will parachute to the ground.

A recording of a woman's voice bursts out of the ceiling's speakers: "Attention. Attention. This is an emergency. All persons must secure themselves into their launch seats immediately. This is not a drill. Prepare for an emergency landing."

Red lights abruptly replace the white ones, flashing in rhythm with a new, bleating siren. Jonah turns from the window and watches the cadets bat their hands along the walls as they descend to the floor.

"Jonah!" Manny shouts from below. A launch seat rises from a thick ribbon of metal at the base of the room, and Manny falls into it, holding his arms out wide, allowing the belts to connect around his body. "Get to your seat, J!"

The rest of the seats unfold from the floor in a perfect square, sliding along thin grooves, locking into place as compressed air hisses from their bases. Bulbous helmets climb over the seats' shoulders, connected to three gray tubes. Jonah eyes his seat and starts downward, but something stops him. On the other side of the level, stuck to the wall at an odd angle, is his sheaf.

The siren suddenly goes silent, and the speakers in the ceiling pop and fizz with static. Jonah keeps waiting for the captain's voice to come through, to tell them to prepare for deployment, that everything will be okay, but it never does.

Down below, a Fourth Year punches the intercom panel: "Hey! HEY! What's going on? What's happening?"

"Try Module Seven!" a Third Year named Daniel cries. "Check on Ruth! My sister! My twin sister! Please!"

"Shut up!" the Fourth Year yells over his shoulder.

"We're going to die!" another boy wails.

Out the window, the ball is much closer. The ghostly flames outside the window change color, grow longer, and begin to shoot away.

Everyone else secures their helmets over their heads while Jonah swings his feet behind himself and plants them on the wall. He crouches like a snake about to attack and launches himself at his sheaf. He sails through the rumbling air, batting away three empty sleeping containers with his huge hands. As soon as he reaches the wall, Jonah grabs his sheaf and rolls it up. Then he springs toward the floor, where a few of the boys actually raise their arms, cheering him on.

Jonah is just a few feet from the ground, floating downward like a balloon with a small leak, when gravity is suddenly restored in the ship. He crashes onto the corrugated metal floor and a bolt of pain shoots across his shoulders. He wobbles to his feet and bounces off a few boys before falling into his seat. He extends his arms, and belts shoot out above his shoulders and between his legs, attaching in a series of clicks. He's strapped in tightly, and after securing his helmet, he looks over at his right hand to be sure he's still holding his sheaf. Once he sees it's still there, he stares up at the ceiling and waits for the ship to rise out of its decline, or for the truss to spread open and drop the modules, but neither happens.

Then, to everyone's relief, the ship begins to level out, as if someone has finally taken control. Jonah holds his breath as everyone's seats automatically compensate, swiveling and moving along a series of grooves cut into the floor and walls. Quickly, they're locked along the wall, which has now become the floor. Maybe they won't be deploying after all, Jonah hopes, and they're heading back out into the Silver Foot galaxy so they can come in slower.

But then the ship dives again, and the pinging comes back, more powerful than ever, and everything becomes a blur; nothing has an outline or an individual noise. Their seats move along the walls for a second time, but some boys get stuck along the way. Jonah no longer knows which way is up; either he's upside down, or the others are. Tethered sleeping containers ricochet against the walls like horses trying to break out of their reins. The ship keeps diving. It's only a matter of seconds before they crash and die, Jonah thinks, and he clenches the sheaf in his hand.

Something screams along the outside walls, and suddenly the pressure inside Jonah's helmet disappears. Oxygen is sucked out of his body so fast it feels like his lungs have been turned inside out. He rips off his helmet and finds the level filled with screams. The ship changes direction again and Jonah's head is forced to his left shoulder, and it's then he notices the chair next to him is empty. He struggles to look back up and after a few seconds sees a boy named Blaire, a Second Year, unconscious and tucked deep inside his sleeping container. His long brown hair peeks just over the edges of his blankets. *Sleeping pills*, Jonah thinks.

"Blaire!" he shouts.

The ship hits the ground. There's a deafening roar of metal scraping rock, and the boys empty their throats, lungs, guts, everything. There's an explosion, and the ship bounces back into the air, high and in a gradual arc, and then all is eerily still and quiet. The screaming stops. No one makes a noise; they just look at each other in disbelief. It's like they're headed back out to space and everything has been fixed, that this was all a dream. Upside down, Jonah almost laughs, believing again that it's just one of his hallucinations. But then they descend once more, and this time when the ship hits the ground, metal grinds and pops and something explodes in the module below or above. The craft violently stops as if it's rammed something immovable, and the truss outside snaps. Jonah's module is released from the metal network, thrown high into the air, and the cadet adjusts his grip on his sheaf while he watches this new world flip over and over and over outside the windows.

The module slams into the ground, and a jagged black boulder tears through the wall just below Jonah's feet, barreling inside like a shark attacking a school of fish. The tip of the boulder cuts right through Daniel, severing his torso clean from his legs, and then it bites its way through the opposite wall. Suddenly the module is in two separate pieces. As the other half rips away, Jonah sees a cross section of the other ten levels of his module: several demic girls, still in their seats, spiral out into the ether; some already dead with their helmets on, some alive and screaming. A young boy sails out of the first level, his arms swinging at his sides as if he's trying to fly. As the other half of Module Six spins off in a different direction, Jonah watches Blaire's tethered sleeping container whip outside and slam against the outer wall, knocking him halfway out. Blaire's eyelids burst open, and a second later, he's crushed as the module section rolls over him and then out of sight.

A wave of rocks sprays Jonah's face, choking him, stinging his eyes and cutting his cheeks. Something hits his nose and he feels the bones shatter. Clumps of soil attack his ears, clogging them, and something sharp drives along his neck. His module tears apart some more and a rush of wind blows over him, and then, in an instant, Jonah's seat comes to an abrupt, violent stop. Jonah jerks forward, ejecting debris from his throat and mouth. He takes a deep breath and coughs and coughs and coughs. When he blindly brings his trembling hands to his face to carve the dirt from his eyes, Jonah begins to cry. Not because of the crash, or because of what happened to Daniel or Blaire or the young boy who tried to fly, but because he realizes he no longer holds his sheaf.

CHAPTER TWO

Jonah rubs his knuckles into his eyes, grinding stone and soil into their corners. His eyes burn and fill with water, and he can't keep them open for more than a split second, catching just blurry images of whites, browns, and reds. He takes a deep, quivering breath and instantly smells his own blood, and the last two minutes of chaos catch up with him.

He just crashed. The Mayflower 2 just crashed and people died. *Kids* died. Blaire was smashed. Daniel was cut in half. Those girls spiraled into the air, screaming. But he's not dead. Somehow, he's still alive. The moment Jonah understands this, he goes stiff in his seat, and his body begins to talk to him, radioing in injuries from his face and left elbow, his shoulders and neck. Everything seems to hurt. And something feels wrong with his forehead; pressure and blood pool together in the front of his skull—just below his hairline.

Among all the aches and throbbing pains and the jarring flashbacks from the crash and the thick layer of dirt coating his throat, Jonah realizes there's an odd pull to his arms. It's like they're floating. His knees and feet feel strangely weighted, too. He finally dares to open his eyes for more than a second, and the sight immediately makes him vomit. The mixture of bile, dirt, ash, and crystal orange doesn't shower down his chest, though; it strangely and softly floats to the ground in a fuzzy orange cloud.

Jonah is fifty feet above the ground, hanging horizontally in what's left of his sleeping level. The back of his seat is to the sky, his arms and legs swaying beneath him in pain. Directly below him stands a gnarled, charcoal-black tree with long skinny branches that are as pointy and sharp as spears. A few tips stop just inches from the toes of his bare feet, daring him to fall. Jonah coughs, spits, and gasps for a good lungful of air, and in between, he prays his belts stay together.

Tears help clear his eyes, and soon he can keep them almost halfway open. The seat to Jonah's left is empty, its belts ripped apart, and two seats over, a Third Year hangs crushed and bruised like a piece of rotten fruit. The boy's right arm is missing at the shoulder, the tip of his tongue blue and bleeding between his broken front teeth. Most of his face is scraped away, showing bone and purple muscle. Jonah knows the boy can't still be alive, but he keeps staring at him anyway, waiting for the Third Year to catch a gasping breath or throw an insult his way.

He screws his index fingers into his ears, clearing away what he can, and then excruciatingly shifts his body so he can look to his right. Manny. Manny hangs just like him, but he's a dozen feet higher up on the wall. Gray dirt coats his black hair, and the bottom half of his face is covered in blood. His arms dangle below him, swinging in opposite directions like pendulums.

"Manny?" Jonah wheezes. He waits more than thirty seconds before catching enough breath to say his name again. The oxygen is different here on Thetis.

The fingers on Manny's left hand twitch and curl inward. Jonah doesn't want to, but he laughs. Then he sobs gratefully. He's not the only survivor. He's not the only one. "Manny, wake up. It's J. It's Jonah. Wake up."

Gray sheets float off Manny's hair as he raises his head. His eyes remain shut, glued with soil and blood.

"Wake up. You have to wake up."

A stripe of saliva falls out of Manny's destroyed lips. It stays connected for more than ten feet before it separates and drifts onto one of the sharp branches below.

"Manny. Can you hear me?" Jonah whispers. "Manny? We crashed. We're alive, though. We have to... Can you hear me?"

Manny's arms stop swinging; they slowly rise to his chest, his neck, his chin, and his lips. Somewhere, far in the distance, there's an explosion and several people scream. Men, women, and kids, all calling out at once. These noises were always out there, Jonah realizes, but they've just now taken hold of his brain. There are more survivors. Some yell for help, others yell names like Franklin, Olivine, Brooklyn, Roberto. A woman wails for a doctor. Another woman yells for a knife.

"People are coming," Jonah says as he watches Manny's hands slide over the belts on his seat. "We're going to be okay."

Manny's hands continue to touch his belts. Soon he finds the release clasp, and his fingers begin to circle it.

"No!" Jonah looks down at the tree branches. They look like they're made of half wood, half rock, and they stick out in all directions like quills on a giant porcupine. And between the razor-sharp tips and the massive trunk, each branch is lined with giant clusters of spikes, baby porcupines clinging to their mother. "Manny, stop. Don't touch your belts, okay?" The boy doesn't listen. His fingers keep digging into the clasp. Jonah's voice gets stronger. "Jesus! Stop moving your hands! You open that clasp and you're going to die, Manny! Just—come on! Wait. Someone's coming. Listen to me!"

Someone *is* coming. A man shouting for survivors sounds like he's just on the other side of the module wall.

"Help us!" Jonah calls, bargaining with his shredded throat. "Module Six! Level Ten! Hurry!"

Manny's thumbs burrow under the tip of the release clasp. In horror, Jonah shouts, "Stop! Don't open your belt!"

The boy groans and drops his head, but his thumbs get leverage, and their curling knuckles start to lift the clasp.

"Help us!" Jonah cries, his voice now sharp and loud. His eyes are glued to Manny's moving thumbs. "Hurry!"

A dark bare foot appears under a crooked rip in the module piece, far down on the left. A man calls, "Anyone in there? Anyone alive?"

"Hurry, please!" Jonah shouts. The foot disappears, and Jonah hears the man circle the module, looking for an opening. Near the base of the tree, Jonah eyes a large hole. "On the other side! Keep going to where the trunk is!"

But it's too late; when Jonah looks back up at Manny, the boy's thumbs pull up on the clasp. There's a *click, click, click*. The belts break away, zipping up over Manny's shoulders and down between his legs.

"No!" Jonah screams.

A black man in a red Mayflower 2 jumpsuit ducks through the hole the exact moment Manny leaves his seat. In what feels like slow motion to Jonah, Manny's upper body sags and then he falls. Jonah roars and reaches for him, his long arms stretching, popping away from his wrecked shoulders, but he's just too far away. His fingertips barely brush the boy's passing leg.

Manny's chest hits a nearby branch, and he immediately flips backward. A gaping red hole, wider than Jonah's outstretched hand, appears under the boy's neck, and it pumps out three large clouds of blood like a smokestack. Jonah watches in disbelief as the First Year falls farther down the tree, his body snagging and tearing along the cluster of spikes like a bag of sand. Manny flips again and again until finally his stomach slams into a baby porcupine. Tiny tips go right through him and out the boy's back, pointing up at Jonah, maroon with blood.

All Jonah can do is stare. His insides churn with a black mass of heat, his throat stiffens with adrenaline, and his brain clears of any thought, but his eyes just stare at the cluster of bloody branches sticking through Manny's back.

The man below roars like a wounded lion, pulling Jonah's eyes away from the cadet, his one friend. Jonah and the man look right at each other, neither saying a word.

"Okay!" the man finally says in a shaky voice. "Okay, kid! What should I do? Tell me what you want me to do here!"

The man below runs and leaps over a splintered edge of the trunk, and Jonah thinks he must still be hallucinating because it looks like the man jumped more than ten feet high. The man then stands directly below Jonah and holds his arms out wide. "You okay? I don't know what to do here, kid. How do I get you out of there?"

"I don't know," Jonah whispers. His seat begins to whine and creak. It leans forward a few degrees and then there's a *pop*, like a bolt coming loose. He freezes every muscle, keeping his stare on the man below, pleading with himself not to look at Manny. He finally recognizes the man as the quiet computer engineer from the Progress Support Module. Jonah opens his mouth to say something is wrong with his seat when the base pole slips past a notch with a resounding *clunk*, and the seat begins to slide down the metal grooves of the wall, right toward the tree.

"No, no, no, no!" the engineer yells.

Jonah glides helplessly down the curved wall. A branch grazes his left knee and the tip of his nose. New tears blind his vision. After ten feet, though, the seat catches in a slot and stops abruptly. Manny is off to his left; when he wipes away the tears, he can see him out of the corner of his eye. Jonah is now forty feet above the engineer who curls his arms, ready to catch him. Between the two of them are dozens of razor-sharp branches, each lined with several of the clusters. The tree is so thick that Jonah can only find one small opening free of branches, but reaching it would require him to leap more than ten feet to his right, which means it's impossible.

"Don't move," the man says.

"I won't. I can't," Jonah answers.

The man sweeps his eyes over the massive tree. "Maybe I can climb to you? What do you think about that? Should I climb?"

Before he can respond, Jonah's seat begins to swivel. The backrest rotates, and in a few seconds, Jonah faces upward. He's almost directly below the one-armed Third Year.

"Whoa, okay. Things keep moving. Things are moving, huh? Um, hey. Hey, my name's Garrett. What's your name, kid?"

"Jonah Lincoln," he calls over his shoulder. His voice doesn't sound like his. Nothing feels real anymore.

"Okay, Jonah Lincoln. I'm looking at this tree here, and I don't think I can climb up there without killing myself, so I'm going to go get some more help. I'll be right back, I promise, and we'll get you down. We'll find something to break all these branches away, and we'll get you down. So, just hold on. Hold. On."

The seat whines some more, and the seat begins to tip backward. "No!" Jonah shouts. "I think…you have to catch me. I think I have to jump."

"No way, kid. Don't even try," Garrett says. "Just stay put. I swear I'll be right back."

Something then shifts in Jonah, and his brain starts firing. He pushes away the trauma and the panic, his cadet training kicking in. "Look to my right. There's a clear spot to my right." He steadies his trembling hands long enough to pull on the belt clasp at his chest. His belts zip away, and he grips the sides of his seat so he doesn't slide off.

Garrett sounds terrified. "Right now? We're doing this right now?"

"I don't think I have a choice." Things come even more into focus, and Jonah carefully brings his knees to his chest and rolls onto his side. Every muscle feels bruised and weak. The seat creaks and tips downward a little more. Jonah scrambles to his feet and peers down at Garrett. "Here I come."

The man sees the tunnel through the branches that Jonah plans to jump through and shuffles underneath it. "You can't jump that far. That's too far. I'm telling you, just wait."

Jonah's mind flashes to a scene on a rainy playground at the age of seven, when his foster father said he would catch him at the bottom of a slide. Jonah slipped right through the man's fingers and hit the back of his head on the asphalt. Instead of scooping him up, the man just laughed and told him to get up and stop crying like a girl. Jonah looks down at Garrett, knowing he can't trust this man to catch him, but he takes a deep breath and tells himself he *can* make it. If he really wants to, he can make the opening. He kicks back his right foot and prepares to jump, but the distribution of weight is too much for the seat, and it breaks away before he can. He sidesteps onto the thin base pole at the last moment, barely catching himself from falling. The seat crashes through the tree, flipping and bouncing until it comes to rest on a huge cluster. Garrett covers his head as wooden shards fall, but they don't seem to come. When he looks up, the shards float almost like feathers, and he bats them away with ease. Things are moving at an odd pace, Jonah thinks, but he doesn't have the time to dwell on it. His bare feet cup the freezing pole, and he flattens his palm against the wall.

"Here I come," Jonah says again, bending his knees, holding both arms high above his head. He pictures the academy's pool of blue water below him. *This is just another dive,* he tells himself.

"Okay," Garrett says. "Okay, okay, okay. You can do this, kid. You just have to jump far, though. Really, really far."

The cadet's long legs spring and extend, sending Jonah through the tree in a long, graceful arc. He sails through the branches without being touched, and to his shock, he covers the ten feet with ease. When he finds himself over the opening, he pulls his legs to his chest and plummets. Jonah drops through the wooden tunnel, tipping backward halfway down toward the imaginary pool. His shoulder is pierced, and his back is scraped—he screams in agony—but he doesn't open his body until he's clear of the last branch. Then he whips his hands above his head and swings his legs to the sky, and Garrett's arms meet the cadet's upper back and thighs. The man grunts and wobbles backward, and together they fall to the ground in a cloud of black dust.

On his stomach, Jonah reaches for his shoulder. He didn't think he could be in any more pain than he was in five minutes ago, but here he is, feeling as if a pack of wolves were pulling and feasting on his back.

Garrett pushes himself to his feet. "That was a hell of a jump, kid. I mean... Holy shit. You okay?"

Jonah pulls his arm back to his chest and curls into a ball, trying anything to lessen the pain. He finally spits a glob of dirt and blood. "Not really."

"I bet. But hey, you're alive, all right? You made it. Not a lot of people can..." Garrett trails off and walks a couple circles around Jonah as the cadet rolls onto his side. "Not a lot of people are alive, you hear me? I need to get back out there and see if anyone else needs my help. I need...I *need* to keep moving, or I'm going to fall apart. Okay? You understand me? I'm about to fucking fall apart here."

Jonah nods and wrenches his neck up to look up at Garrett, embarrassed but grateful. From his first memory, from his first foster home and first classroom, he's hated asking adults for help. A suffocating blanket of humiliation covers him from head to toe as he watches Garrett walk toward the opening.

The man stops and rubs his neck. "I don't want to go back out there." He turns with quivering lips, his hands in shaking fists. "Why me, you know? Why us?"

He's not sure if Garrett means the crash landing or the fact they survived. Neither makes any sense to Jonah, and so he just whispers, "I don't know."

Garrett closes his eyes and takes a few breaths, and then smiles briefly. "That was a hell of a jump, Jonah Lincoln. I don't know how you did that."

"Me neither," he admits, struggling to his knees. "It looked impossible."

"Yeah, well, pay attention. Gravity is definitely different here."

"Can't believe we made it to Thetis."

Garrett walks over and offers a trembling hand covered in dried blood. His face is small and creased with wrinkles and sadness. "We didn't make it to Thetis, kid. We're on Achilles, one of the moons." The man pulls Jonah up with ease—almost yanking the cadet completely off the ground, sending lightning bolts of pain through his shoulder. They stare at each other another moment, and then Garrett solemnly walks back toward the hole in the wall, this time without stopping.

Achilles? Dumbfounded, Jonah limps after him, but before ducking through the opening, he stops to look back at his destroyed sleeping level, the shredded tree, his fellow cadets. The guilt of not being able to save Manny has already set up camp in his mind, and Jonah knows nothing will ever uproot it. Somehow, he thinks, this is all his fault.

The sunlight is blinding, and at first all Jonah sees are fuzzy blobs of whites and yellows, browns and blues. He covers his eyes with his arm and a rich, pungent smell rushes up his one clear nostril—a mixture of fire, sulfur, soil, and burning plastic. Shapes begin to separate and appear, and within seconds, he sees his toes are just a few yards from the edge of a sharp, hundred-foot cliff. Below stands a lush jungle that waves with neon colors and twisting columns of smoke. He instantly takes a few steps back.

Jonah stares in disbelief at the gigantic red and black trees towering high above the rest of the jungle. From their thick bases to their spindly, crooked tops, fat yellow leaves the size of parachutes ring their trunks like floppy shirt collars. The outer edges of the leaves curl upward, holding gallons and gallons of what Jonah thinks must be rain. A strong gust of wind blows over the jungle and thousands of the leaves bend and spill their water into the thick canopy below.

A large group of skeletal brown birds—or maybe they're bats or bugs or something like dinosaurs—launch their drenched bodies out of the wet trees and fly off into the horizon, spinning around and around as they go. Jonah's eyes follow them until they're nothing but specks, and then he sees that beyond the trees is an ocean or a sea or a giant lake, a bright blue body of water so wide it seems impossible their ship didn't crash into it. A few miles straight out, there's a faint outline of an island. Way off to his right, a wide red mountain range looms so incredibly tall that Jonah can't see the peaks, even on this cloudless day. They terrify Jonah, and he turns in the other direction to see an almost barren plain of ankle-high brown grass and a few porcupine trees. The air is hot and sticky, and standing there before it all, Jonah has a quick moment where he thinks he's been sent back in time to a prehistoric era on Earth. But he's on Achilles. No one's ever been on Achilles before.

"Jonah!" Garrett yells behind him. He spins to see the man shifting nervously from foot to foot near the module, still unwilling to rejoin the chaos. "Your face… It's a mess, all right? Try to find one of the doctors, okay? I saw one walking around in a yellow coat. Find her."

Garrett jogs away without waiting for a response. Jonah turns back to the cliff's edge. Below, a dense flock of small green discs glides in from the left, slapping their flat bodies hard against the tree trunks below with a resounding chorus of *thwaps. Thwap, thwap, thwap*. Jonah backs away and follows Garrett's tracks around the module.

The sight punches Jonah in the stomach. Among the thousands of flaming pieces of the Mayflower 2, dozens and dozens of mangled bodies lie spread out as far as he can see. Men, women, kids. Classmates. Strangers. Cadets and demics. Military officers, crew members, and teachers. Jonah's gaze bounces from a severed arm to a headless man to a pile of four young girls. Blood and oil soak the brown grass of the plain. Twenty yards away, a woman with a dripping head wound pulls herself through the chaos with one arm. A tall, pale boy with bright blue hair shuffles close behind, hugging his shoulders.

Jonah falls to his knees as he watches the injured try to separate themselves from the dead. Many of these kids were recruited solely to replace the ones who died on that field trip on Thetis, to improve the morale of all those mourning adults, to be the next generation. Now, someone is going to need to replace them.

Like exploded eggs, shards of the white modules lie every which way. Fifty yards ahead, a man and a woman pull several dead cadets out of a smoking corner of Module Five. The back of one boy's head is missing. Stumbling out of the same corner and holding his left elbow is a muscular kid named Griffin, a Third Year, who has the face of a lion shaved into the side of his orange hair. A demic girl sobs as she helps an older professor sit down in the shade of a tree, and next to them, a bearded man drags a large orange cylindrical piece of equipment away from a rushing fire. He moves quickly, lugging the orange tank right over a dead girl, pulling her along for a few short feet. Something detonates to his right, spewing blue-gray flames and debris high into the air, rocking Jonah onto his hands.

Jonah orders himself not to cry. He grinds his teeth, pushing a loose incisor sideways, focusing on that pain instead of the blackness that claws at his insides. His eyes refocus on the wreckage, bobbing from body to body, eventually settling on Garrett, who staggers into the middle of the madness, unsure which way to go. He finally jogs to the left, toward a woman cradling a young boy under a warped piece of the truss.

The giant truss once looked like the big brother of the original Eiffel Tower in Paris: an intricate, narrow work of metal that widened at its base. It was supposed to be indestructible. It was also supposed to open and drop the parachuting modules safely to the ground like they were the seed heads of a dying dandelion. Now, though, it lies twisted, charred, and split open, and where there were previously nine inflatable modules tucked inside, only the front two remain. When the Mayflower 2 was launched over a year ago, sixteen land vehicles clung to the outer frame, all with their own parachutes. Only four vehicles remain attached and intact: three are rugged electric cycles, and the other is a tank-like truck with yellow treads and a mounted gun on top. Jonah looks over his shoulder, and in the distance, he can barely see where the ship originally made contact with the ground, discarding and destroying the other vehicles, leaving a trail of debris until it twisted and opened like a dying patient on a surgeon's table.

Smoke billows throughout the plain. A bloody man sprays

blue foam on a smoldering module piece while two older cadets help a small girl out of its cloud-filled belly. Jonah orders himself to get off his knees, to help, to find the doctor in the yellow coat, to do something, anything, but he's paralyzed from the view.

He's not the only one, though; on the periphery, several other kids and a few adults stare blankly at the carnage, trying to wake up from his or her nightmare. Something under the truss bursts into flames. Patches of grass fizz and detonate like firecrackers. A man screams for help, for anyone to please just help him, and it's only then when Jonah focuses on this one voice that he finally moves. It's as if he has no choice, and the man is yelling only for Jonah. He numbly gets to his feet and scans the wreckage. There. Right there. A short arm in a torn blue sleeve sticks out from under a piece of the truss, waving frantically. Jonah stumbles toward the arm as everything else fades away. It's just him and this arm now. He locks in on it and keeps moving, but when he's just ten feet away, a thick patch of grass near his feet begins to sizzle and pop, and before Jonah can run, it explodes, rocketing an empty launch seat into Jonah's side.

It's as if he's been blown to pieces, and he falls over like a tower of toy blocks. His head feels like it's a hundred miles from his shoulders when it lands on something sharp and hard, and then he sees only whiteness, hears only a dull ringing. His mind bubbles with heat, and then the ringing disappears, replaced with the screams of everyone around him, including the man he never reached. Jonah rolls onto his back and tries to call out for help, but his mouth doesn't move. A foot-long insect, a fuzzy yellow thing with red-tipped wings, circles his head and lands on his lips. Jonah tells his arms to swat it away, but they are lifeless, stuck to the ground like anchors. The bug stings his lips, crawls to his cheeks, and stabs him twice, and then it flies away, and all Jonah can do is let the throbbing pain radiate throughout his face until his eyes close and he's asleep.

CHAPTER THREE

A RED BEAM CRAWLS OVER JONAH'S LEFT PUPIL, WAKING HIM with a jolt.

"Don't move," a woman says. There's a hand on his forehead. It's small, cold, and trembling, but still it comforts Jonah, steadies his breath, and keeps him from sitting up. The red beam seems to shoot right into his skull, bouncing around his brain and into his throat. He tastes it. It's metallic and gritty. Or maybe, he thinks, that's blood and dirt. A second later, sounds rush into his ears as if someone has flipped a switch: fire rages somewhere nearby, an older boy sobs and kicks something plastic, and someone chants, begs, cries for someone to wake up. A man far off shouts for more water, and before Jonah can decide to help, the woman's hand presses his head firmly to the ground. "You're okay, Jonah, but just don't move."

He tries to ignore the man sounding more and more desperate for water, but it's impossible. *Someone get him some water*, he thinks. *Please. He needs water*. The red beam seems to carry weight on his eye, and as it crawls slowly downward, it drives Jonah's eyeball gently to the top of his socket. The hand leaves his forehead and he hears an electrical whirring, and then something begins to suck debris out from under his bottom eyelid. The pain is barely tolerable and he locks his jaw and begins to count; it's as if tiny hot forks dig and scrape the bottom of his eye. The woman seethes and sighs as she pushes the machine deeper under his lid. The pain doubles, and Jonah screams and pounds his fists on the ground. The man still yells for water. Jonah can't believe no one has brought him any water. He rips handfuls of dirt up from the ground and tries to close his eye, but the woman pleads with him not to.

"I know, I know. It doesn't feel good, but just give it a second. Give it another second. It'll feel much better then, trust me," she says as the beam pushes his eyeball in the opposite direction. The top and the corners of his eye are suctioned, and he gets used to the pain. When the same attention moves to his right eye, the man finally stops shouting. Jonah just hopes that means he received some water, and not that he doesn't need it anymore. "Jonah," the woman says, "your nose is broken."

"I thought so." He smacks his lips and wobbles his jaw back and forth, and then he remembers the fuzzy yellow insect that stung him before he passed out. To his surprise, his face doesn't hurt. Much.

The beam and suction finally end, and when Jonah closes his eyes, he's amazed they're relatively pain-free. The woman's fingers crawl over his cheeks, behind his ears, and then around his neck. While her hands fumble the top of his spine, Jonah finally looks into the face that's been hovering over his head. It's Dr. Zarembo, or Doctor Z, as everyone calls her. Streaks of black dirt and dried blood cover her gaunt cheeks, perfectly outlining her thin, pale lips before continuing down her slight chin. Dark maroon hair falls from behind her ears, the ends black and melted.

"Thank you," he whispers.

She smiles wearily. "You're welcome."

His eyes drop to Dr. Z's shoulders. She is wearing a yellow coat. The sight of it brings Garrett's distraught face to his mind, and then Jonah remembers the blue sleeve sticking out from under the truss, and he sits up, knocking the doctor onto her heels.

"Whoa. Wait," she says. "Hold on. Just hold on. You're still a mess."

He says nothing and looks past the doctor. The arm is no longer there, and a pit of regret and shame swells inside Jonah's chest. His eyes sweep back and forth in hopes of finding a sliver of the blue sleeve when he sees Vespa Bolivar. The tall Fourth Year cadet struggles to walk backward between two fires as she drags three small boys across the dirt by their wrists. They're dead. Like so many others, they're dead. Vespa pauses midstride and wipes her cheeks with the back of her sleeve. He watches in complete awe. Vespa is one of the toughest cadets at the academy, and here she is crying, too.

Jonah stares and thinks of the moment he first met her. It was his second week at the academy, and as a hazing ritual, the squibs—pre-First Years—were matched against Thirds in hand-to-hand combat. He remembers how Vespa stood barefoot before him—seemingly coming out of nowhere—wearing all black, the sides of her head shaved, with the rest of her black hair tied high above her head in a wild, uneven fountain. Her face was a perfect V, punctuated with an intense pair of deep-set green eyes. The other cadets began to chuckle and whisper, and Jonah just stood motionless, dumbfounded, paralyzed with intimidation. Vespa was shockingly beautiful, but at the same time frightening, and he'll never forget how she looked him up and down and then laughed, right in his face. A whistle blew and she pounced like a tiger, twisting him around in a blur, slamming his face to the floor while locking him in a searing arm-bar. He can still feel his cheek pounding that sticky gym mat, the girl's sharp knee digging into his lower back. That day, when she finally released him, when all the laughing died down and the instructor barked at him to get up, all he could do was cough a weak congratulation up at her. She just walked away without looking back, and that was the last time he spoke to her.

Dr. Z says something and taps him on the shoulder, but he continues to stare at Vespa holding the boys' wrists and how the white sun shines off her black hair. He closes his eyes and pictures her grabbing him by his wrist, pulling him somewhere safe. He tells himself to get up and help her, but he just sits there in some deep-seated shame and anger he doesn't quite understand, peeking over the doctor's shoulder like a toddler at a zoo. Vespa turns and walks forward, her back now to the bodies. This seems to make her stronger, and her bare feet hurry along the brittle grass.

"I didn't help anyone," Jonah whispers, lying back down. "There's something wrong with me. There's always been something wrong with me, but now…Manny's dead and Blaire's dead and all these people are dead and people were yelling and screaming and that guy wanted water so bad and I just…" he trails off. His thoughts fade and blur. Words come slowly. He feels like he's back at the Pacsun home facing the twins, and they're telling him to take off his shirt, *or else*. "There was a man who had an arm up and he was…I was hit by something and there was an explosion and I'm…I don't even know." Tears flood his eyes and stick to his temples. He hides his face in his hands.

Dr. Z stands and exhales. "Look, don't be hard on yourself right now. Come on. Not right now. First of all, you're pretty damn injured, Jonah, and secondly, what you and I just lived through was an extremely, *extremely* traumatic experience. You're in shock, just like everyone else."

Jonah sits up again and looks at Vespa. "Not like everyone."

"I need you to listen to me for a second. And then I have to go help some other people. Jonah, I think there's something going on with your eyes, something bad. I need to run some tests, if I have the time and can find some working equipment. But, look, if you want to help, if you honestly feel up to it, then we all could use you. Especially your height."

Dr. Z extends her small hand, and Jonah grabs it, pulling himself to his feet. "Thanks."

"There are some kids still trapped in a piece of Module Three, I know that. A few people are trying to help them out, but maybe your long arms could be of some use. Don't strain yourself too much, though. I gave you a shot, but the numbness of your shoulders won't last long."

He takes a deep breath. "Where is it? Module Three?"

She points to the top half of a module up the plain, beyond the main wreckage. A bright white vapor billows out of its base. Jonah squints to see two men, including Garrett, circling it while a shirtless cadet with a shaved head points up at a small girl sitting on top of it. The cadet climbs onto Garrett's shoulders and reaches for the girl, but he's still several feet shy of touching her hand. Another girl sits behind her, rocking back and forth. The white vapor grows thicker, hiding them from Jonah's view.

Jonah thinks of Vespa and how easily she was able to change direction and find new strength, and he steels his jaw. Then he runs as fast as his bruised legs and bare feet allow. The difference in gravity is instantly noticeable, and to his surprise, he begins to cover seven to eight feet with every stride. It's almost like he's hovering over the ground.

He circles around the edge of the wreckage, jumping high over items discharged from the ship: a computer console, an exercise bicycle, and a stand-alone shower. He gains speed and jumps higher, farther, blowing past a huddled group of demics crying under a porcupine tree. The module piece up ahead is almost completely invisible inside a cloud of white smoke. If there's anyone inside, they don't have long.

"Maybe I can reach her," Jonah wheezes as he comes to a stop. His lungs are still adjusting to the atmosphere.

A gust of wind blows in the opposite direction, taking the white cloud with it. Everyone turns to face Jonah, and the boy on Garrett's shoulders slides to the ground. It's Paul Sigg, the highest-ranking Fourth Year on board the ship. He's solid with muscle and sweating profusely, and there's a deep yellow and purple bruise running from his armpit all the way down to his waist. Jonah doesn't know what the boy hit, or what hit the boy, but it's a wonder he's able to stand up. A jagged scar pulses with fresh blood around his neck.

"Just get out of here, Firstie, we got it. Go collect the dead or something. Find some medical supplies."

Jonah takes a step back and looks over his shoulder, unable to hide his disappointment. He's supposed to follow orders from higher-ranking cadets, but does that apply here? He stares at the two girls on the top of the module who are trembling with fear. One of the girls screams as her head lowers a few inches and then stops. The top of the module is collapsing. There isn't time to follow orders.

"Garrett," Jonah says, stepping forward. "Let me up."

Paul growls and puts a palm on Jonah's chest, but Jonah avoids his eyes and pushes past him. Garrett crouches, and the other man, a bearded engineer with a gaping gash on his leg, helps push him onto Garrett's shoulders. Jonah stretches his long dark arms over his head toward the first girl, doing his best to ignore the pain crossing his back.

"Come on!" Jonah yells. "Jump!"

From below, Paul shouts, "No, you asshole! They need to pull you up! Up! Someone has to go inside and help get the demics out of there!"

Shocked, Jonah looks down at Garrett's upturned face. The man nods.

"There are four girls inside," the first girl says. She has the pointed face of a bird. "They can't get their belts off. They can't get out of their seats. Hurry. Please."

Jonah swallows hard and then looks down at Garrett and says, "I need you to jump, and then I'll jump, too." Without hesitation, Garrett squats and then springs up. Jonah's feet push off the man's shoulders and he sails upward as if launched by a trampoline, traveling far past the edge of the module. He peaks at thirty feet and then begins to descend.

"What…the…hell?" Paul drones.

Jonah circles his arms wildly at his sides as he awkwardly lands on top of the module. He slips and falls and then rolls past the birdlike girl, toward the middle where it's flimsy and collapsing. He finds a jagged hole just big enough for the small girls to fit through, but there's no way Jonah will be able to get inside this way. He needs to find another way in, or make the hole bigger.

Below, Paul yells for the girls to jump, and over they go. Jonah scrambles to the edge to see the demics hugging each other.

"I need something hard!" Jonah shouts. "I need to break away some of this metal if I'm going to get inside!"

Paul finds a black stone the size of a fist. He tosses it up to Jonah, but it sails far over his arms. The Fourth Year quickly finds another rock, this time underhanding it gently. Jonah catches it and moves back to the hole. For the first time, he hears a girl crying inside. Jonah holds the black rock high above his head and slams it down on the jagged edge of the hole. It shatters in his hand as a plume of white smoke envelops him.

"Shit," he whispers. The center of the module then creaks and sinks several more inches. The girls inside scream and cry, and Jonah's about yell for another rock when he notices the bleeding gash on his palm. The rock cut him. He fans away the smoke and looks over the pieces scattered around his knees until he finds a particularly long shard, with a sharp, almost serrated edge. It's a perfect blade. He places the shard against the edge of the hole and tries sawing at the metal. Sparks fly, and to his surprise, the metal peels away. Within twenty seconds, he carves away three or more feet, and then he sticks the rock blade into the waistband of his pants and lowers himself inside.

It takes a moment for Jonah's feet to find something stable for his 6'5" frame, and when he does, he lets go of the smooth lip of the hole. His head passes through two thin layers of metal before entering the sleeping level, where four girls hang upside down in their seats. He thinks of Manny and panics, his chest heaving with doubt. Far down below, five or more girls lie in a motionless pile, their limbs tangled and broken.

Only three of the four girls strapped into their seats are awake. When they see Jonah crouching on a cabinet, they all start talking at once until the oldest, a redhead with a constellation of freckles blasted onto her face, raises her voice to say, "Our belts won't come off. The mechanism is broken, and I'd say at the rate the vapor is seeping in, we have about four or five minutes before we suffocate."

"We'll die just like them," a tall brunette cries, pointing to the bodies below. "They're dead. Look at them. They're dead and we're going to die, too. You'll die, too, now."

"Rosa, just shut up," says the girl closest to Jonah. She's small, and her skin is darker than his. Her giant brown eyes brim with tears. "I can't move my one leg. It's stuck."

Her left foot is pinned against the backrest of another seat knocked from its base. Jonah shuffles to the edge of the cabinet, and to his relief, it doesn't fall. He hangs his right leg over and then bends his knee.

"Okay. Try to keep your ankle loose," he says, studying the angles of the backrest. And then, with held breath, he thrusts his heel at the seat pinning the girl's foot. The seat goes spiraling down and lands on the bodies below. "Now," he says, showing her the rock blade, "I need you to hold on to me with one hand and cut away your belts with the other hand. You're going to fall, but I'm going to swing you over to me, okay?"

She reluctantly takes the blade.

"No, no, no! Help me first," Rosa interjects. Tears and sweat soak her face. "Please. I can't take another second. I'm going to freak out. I swear. I'm about to die. I can feel it!"

"You're next," Jonah says. "I promise. But she's first."

"I'm going to die!" Rosa screams. "Don't you hear me?"

Jonah clasps the small girl's hand as she saws at the belts. Her body starts to slide away from the seat, and when she slices through the last belt above her left shoulder, she falls. Jonah sees Manny's face as he plants his feet and digs his fingernails into her wrist. She swings in a perfect half-circle, and the moment she's below Jonah, he yanks her upward. She grabs his knee with her other hand, and a moment later, she's lying facedown on the cabinet.

"Thank you, oh my god, thank you," she says.

"You're welcome." He shoves the small girl through the hole in the ceiling, but not before retrieving the blade.

"My turn, right? It's my turn," Rosa says. "You said it was my turn."

"Yeah, it's your turn. Let's go." He takes a quick second to gauge his options. She's fifteen feet away. The only things to hang on to are the other seats, and to get to Rosa, he will have to get past the unconscious girl still belted in.

The redhead sees Jonah looking at the other girl and says, "She's dead. She's been dead for the last two and a half minutes."

Rosa begins to sob.

"Okay," Jonah says, sighing, refusing to let it sink in. "This is what we're going to do. Rosa, I'm going to climb over to that other girl and hold on to her belts, and then I'm going to swing over to you and hand you this." He holds up the blade. "Then you're going to do exactly what that other girl did. You're going cut away the belts, and then I'm going to swing you over so you can climb out the hole. Okay?"

Rosa sniffs and nods. Jonah leans far off the cabinet, whispers to himself that he can do this, and jumps. His right hand catches the belt over the dead girl's shoulder, and he swoops toward Rosa with the rock out. Rosa reaches and misses the blade, but before she can start crying all over again, Jonah swings back over and slips the rock between her leg and her belt.

"Just start cutting," Jonah groans. His shoulder begins to throb from the activity, and he knows he has to hurry if this is going to work. When Rosa saws through three of the four belts, Jonah kicks himself away from the dead girl and grabs Rosa's hand just as she cuts through the last one.

They swing together, and as they make their way toward the cabinet, the wound on Jonah's shoulder rips open and speeds across his upper back like a fault line. His scream echoes inside the module, inside his broken nose. He releases Rosa without knowing where she'll land. Jonah peeks through his tears to see her fall on top of the cabinet. She sets the blade at her feet, and without looking back, she jumps, grabs a piece of metal, and scrambles up the hole. All Jonah can do is slide his wrist between the dead girl's body and her belts and watch Rosa's feet disappear.

"Are you okay?" the redhead asks. "What can I do? Tell me what I can do."

Jonah pulls himself up a foot or two with his other hand, trying not to cry out in pain. Sarcastically, he asks, "Go for help?"

"I'll be right back," she responds in the same tone.

He aims his mouth at the hole and shouts for Paul and Garrett. Below, the chair he dislodged from the small girl's foot shifts and rolls over the bodies. A leg moves, and the white vapor comes up stronger than before.

"That's not good," he says.

"No, it's not," the girl says quietly. "I just can't believe this. I just can't believe I traveled three hundred eighty days, through a *freaking* wormhole, basically through *time*"—she then pauses to cough and hack from the incoming vapors—"and I survived a crash landing, and now here I am about to die *upside down* from suffocation? That's bullshit!"

Jonah opens his mouth to tell her that neither of them is going to die when a pair of long legs descends from the hole. A second later, Vespa Bolivar drops onto the cabinet. Her green eyes flash from the dead girls below to the redhead stuck in her seat, and then to Jonah who hangs helplessly by his wrist. By the alarmed and exhausted look on her face, it appears she's on her third wind. Every graduating cadet is supposed to be able to reach an almost impossible fifth wind. After that, it's respectable to rest.

"I need some help." Jonah coughs. He's ashamed to be hanging there like this, caught against a dead girl he couldn't save. He was supposed to be the hero, to make it up to Manny and the man with the waving blue sleeve, but now he finds himself saying, "I'm stuck, and my shoulder is all messed up. I can't really move."

Vespa turns to the redhead and asks, "Who are you?"

"Aussie," she says. "I'm an academic."

"No shit you are," Vespa says, studying the vapor pooling above their heads.

The ceiling creaks and Vespa springs into action, moving toward Jonah while calmly saying, "Aussie, I'm just going to help this lanky kid first, and then I'm going to get you out of here." Vespa drops to her stomach and reaches Jonah's wrist. As she releases him from the dead girl's belt and swings him directly below her, she says, "People are gathering outside, appointing duties, and some are trying to eat. I think it would be for the best if we all try to get something in our stomachs." She hoists Jonah onto the cabinet with ease. He can't believe how calm she seems, or how strong she is. "Night's falling, and we're going to need to create some decent shelter. Who knows how cold it gets here."

"Thanks," Jonah says, but Vespa ignores him and turns to Aussie. He hides the burning pain zigzagging across his shoulders and back, and bends down to pick up the rock blade. He holds it out in front of him and is about to offer it to Vespa when she turns, jumps off the cabinet, and catches Aussie's belts. The girls are quickly face-to-face, nodding at each other.

"Here, catch," Jonah says. He tosses the piece of rock to Vespa, but she doesn't even try to catch it. The blade slowly falls to the floor, twisting and turning until it lands flat on the cheek of one of the dead girls below. Vespa doesn't even notice; she digs her fingers into Aussie's belt clasp and pulls, pulls, pulls. The white cloud thickens around them, blocking Jonah's view.

"It's just stuck!" Aussie shouts. "I've tried, but the mechanism is—"

An invisible Vespa grunts, and then there's a click and someone is overcome by a coughing attack. Jonah waves his arms in front of his face to dissipate the cloud, but it's too thick. Suddenly Vespa comes into view, sailing toward him with a gagging Aussie on her back.

"Move, Firstie!" Vespa yells.

She lands right next to him on the cabinet and immediately shrugs Aussie into Jonah's open arms. Vespa slips her hands under one of Aussie's feet and orders Jonah to do the same. Together, they hoist the redhead halfway through the hole. "Now," Vespa says, coughing, putting her hands on Jonah's shoulders, shoving him down into a crouch. She sits on his left shoulder and says, "Stand up and I'll push her the rest of the way through."

It's painful, but Jonah slowly straightens his legs. The vapor has completely taken over the module, and he holds in what little breath he has left. Vespa rocks on his shoulder, and then one of her hands grips the top of his head. Her feet move quickly up his body. And then just like that, she's gone, and the ceiling bows from her weight. Jonah begins to waver from the fumes. He doesn't have the strength to pull himself out. He tries not to but starts to sit down.

Vespa's voice booms from above: "Jesus, Firstie! Grab my hand already!"

He stands and extends a palm straight up into the cloud. A hand clasps his forearm. Jonah uses his last breath to jump. His knees hit the lip of the hole, and then Vespa flings him to the edge of the roof of the module, where he lands flat on his back. The sky, through the blowing white smoke, is a greenish-gray.

"Come on," Vespa says, kicking him a little too hard in the side. Her shiny black hair frames her stoic face, and in the setting sun, her cheeks, nose, and lips glow a vibrant white. "Get up!"

"Cadets!" Paul calls from below. "Let's go!"

Vespa jumps over the side. She says something to Paul, and then Paul shouts, "Firstie, we're walking away in five fucking seconds! With or without your ass!"

Jonah flips over and crawls past the column of smoke streaming out of the hole. He lowers his head and holds his breath. And as he reaches the edge of the module, he can't help but think of his parents trying to escape the earthquake that killed them. And he asks himself the same thing he always does: In the chaos of that earthquake, did his dad shove him under that dresser on purpose, or did fate send him rolling to the only safe spot in the bedroom? He swings his legs over the edge of the module, seeing only his dad's bright white smile from his photo. The roof whines and moans behind him, something shifts just below its surface, and it starts to cave in. Jonah pushes off, Garrett and Paul catch him, and then Vespa herds them all away as the giant half cylinder collapses in on itself, releasing a monstrous white cloud into the air.

CHAPTER FOUR

Fire from the wreckage rages in all directions, feeding on a sea of brittle grass and weeds that mysteriously sparks and explodes. Two adults and several kids stand in a crooked line, their mouths working on a found box of crystal oranges, their clothes torn and melted and not warm enough. They're taking a break from searching and collecting and crying and panicking and looking for personal belongings. Jonah cautiously steps into the group as the landscape below burns and spreads its fiery wings. He can't find his sheaf. He's looked everywhere.

A stout, silver-haired man in his fifties shuffles past Jonah in the wildfire light. He falls to his knees and uproots a weed. He uncurls one of its leathery leaves, examining its filleted edges before cracking it in two. A black powder covers his fingers, and he brings the glistening pieces to his nose.

"Well, now that's pretty damn interesting. This thing's filled with methane, for one," he says before licking the powder from his fingers. "And this… Huh. It might be…it might be a close relative to the saltpeter we have on Earth, or could it be some kind of charcoal-sulfur mixture? I'm sorry, but that's really pretty interesting to me." His tongue crawls over the fronts of his teeth. "And there's something else here, something…must be a natural flash powder? I guess that would explain why these things explode like they do." He stands and twists around at the wreckage behind them. "So it looks like we basically crash-landed on a minefield."

"Well, now that's pretty freaky," a boy says from the shadows.

A hand grabs Jonah's wrist from behind. He spins and wrenches his arm out of the grip, ready to fight like he's back in Cleveland. He's relieved to see it's just Dr. Z.

"Jonah, I need to talk to you. Wait. What's all this blood on your back?" She pulls down his collar. "*Jesus.* Come with me, hurry up. We found two cases of medical supplies, and we need to clean this and sew it up. And how's your nose?"

Jonah stretches his lips and tries to wiggle his nose. The disconnected bones rub against each other painfully. "Definitely still broken."

"I'll try to set it."

It's been five hours since the crash. On Jonah's left, four men, two women, and several cadets dig shallow graves for the dead, their sweaty clothes shining in the fiery glow. Dr. Z guides him another hundred yards to a makeshift hospital, which is nothing more than a circle of sleeping containers and a few launch seats, all softly lit by three electric lanterns. When Jonah arrives, a shadowy man kneels over a sleeping container. He pulls a sheet over the head of a small body, and then he places his palms on his face and steps away, slumping into the darkness.

"How many are we?" Jonah asks with a lump in his throat.

"How many are we? You mean, how many of us are alive?"

Jonah watches the man stagger and disappear into the shadows of the evening. "Yeah."

"From my last count, there are sixteen adults and forty-four kids left. Total." Dr. Z circles around the wounded and kneels next to the newly covered body. She peeks under the sheet and closes her eyes. She then picks up a rock and chucks it into the night air.

It takes her a few seconds before whispering, "Forty-three. Forty-three kids. Forty-three k—Jesus."

"That means one hundred and eighteen people are dead or missing," comes a whisper at Jonah's feet. He looks down to see a demic boy sitting up in a sleeping container. He's sixteen or seventeen years old, tall, with tight blond curls pulled behind his ears and a perfect oval face. His right arm hides inside a hastily made sling. "That's about, what? Sixty-seven percent of us?"

The staggering figures run down Jonah's throat, choking any words that pop into his mind. A movie of faces from the ship plays behind his eyes. Different run-ins and passersby. Table mates. Teammates. Manny. His math teacher. The two older demic girls who invited him to game night the day before the wormhole. The navigators. The captain. *The captain.* The moment Jonah sees Captain Tolivar's drooping cheeks and his friendly brown eyes, he stops the movie. "Wait! What about the captain? What about him and the first officer and the others? Where are they? Are they—?"

"They're dead." Dr. Z sighs.

"But are you sure? Because I saw the Support Module, and it looks like it's still in really good shape. They could still be alive in there."

The doctor pulls Jonah away from the others. "Listen to me. What I am about to tell you is very sensitive, Jonah. Do you understand me?"

Her voice scares him, and he's not sure if he really wants to hear what she is about to say. "Yes. I understand."

"Most of the senior cadets know this already, so it's just a matter of time before you hear it from one of them or somewhere else, but we're trying not to incite any more panic tonight than there already is. We'll have a meeting tomorrow morning and tell everyone then. The thing is, Jonah, that the captain and the first officer, and two other flight officers… They were shot. They were killed. Somebody shot them and we're pretty sure that's why we crashed."

Jonah stumbles backward, his eyes stuck on her cracked lips. "What do you mean? Why would somebody shoot them?"

"We don't know. A few people are in there right now, in the Support Module, trying to figure it out. They're looking for clues, treating it as a crime scene." Dr. Z sets her slight jaw and flares her nostrils before continuing. "It's truly unbelievable. It's absolutely despicable and really beyond words. All these kids... And *right* before we got to Thetis. A day away. I just don't get it. This whole place is a crime scene."

Jonah staggers past her into the makeshift hospital, a hospital that wouldn't exist if someone hadn't shot the captain and his crew. He figured they crashed from a mechanical failure. He just guessed something was wrong with the ship and Captain Tolivar had done his best to keep them alive, a hero in a time of emergency. But now, in crashing waves, it hits Jonah that someone aboard the ship, someone he has lived with for over a year, has killed 67 percent of one hundred seventy-seven people. There are only fifty-nine of them left.

"Are you okay?" the doctor asks.

He turns to say that he's not, but his knees begin to shake. It's barely noticeable at first, and Jonah thinks he's merely giving in to the day's events and the fresh news of the murders, but then one of the electric lanterns tips over and a few people scream out in the darkness. The boy with the sling stands up and cries, "Earthquake!"

Jonah freezes at the word, *the* word, his parents' word, and he grabs the nearest empty seat and steadies himself, desperately trying to push away visions of his parents being crushed by a falling ceiling. Dr. Z stands over the wounded, her arms up and out like a mother bird shielding her eggs.

The shaking gets more violent, and a thunderous rumbling comes from Jonah's right. He squints into the night and the wildfire beyond, and soon a dozen kids, Garrett, and the silver-haired professor sprint toward them, all of them screaming, most with their hands behind their heads.

"Run!" shouts Garrett. "Run! Get out of the way!"

A blur of something large and black suddenly bounds past Garrett like a ghost. Another blur flies past, just missing him. Garrett then changes direction and darts right through the hospital, jumping almost thirty feet over the wounded, calling for everyone to get out of the way.

Two big black shadows charge up the plain, side by side, chasing after a thin crowd of kids who stumble in every direction on the shaking ground. The shadows separate and dart around a pair of demic girls holding hands. The girl on the left trips, yanking the other girl down, and a huge black beast jumps over them at the very last moment. In the faint light, Jonah catches a glimpse of the thing's powerful back paws and whip-like tail. Another one comes into view: It's as tall and as large as a moose, but it moves with the agility of a jungle cat. A thick blanket of black wool hangs from its haunches and from under its belly, and as it jumps over the two fallen girls, its coarse hair sweeps along their backs. The two demics jump to their feet still holding hands and run for the hospital lights. But when they are just steps away from Dr. Z, a beast comes out of the darkness and rams into the girl on the right.

She's blonde and petite and she goes airborne like a dead leaf in a tornado. She lands somewhere in the dark, out of sight. The other girl shrieks, dives into the dirt, and then claws her way behind Jonah, who pulls the launch seat between him and the action.

Dazed by the collision, the beast backs up a few feet and swivels its shaggy neck toward Jonah and the girl. Its head is double the size of a moose's, and its face is all nose, a jet-black, pebbled mess of wet skin. Out of its one nostril drips a thick stream of yellow liquid. More beasts and people charge by, but all Jonah can concentrate on is the domed, percolating section of skin on top of this beast's nose. It slowly rises in the shape of a mushroom. The stem of skin underneath is beet-red and inflates like a balloon. It gets to the size of a basketball, and just when Jonah thinks it's going to pop, a dozen tiny holes flap open, sending gusts of air in every direction. The air blasts the wool off the animal's face, revealing four milky white eyes and several hollow stumps of bone. The beast steps in Jonah's direction and growls.

Dr. Z pulls a syringe out of an open kit. "Just hold on."

The stem on its nose empties, and the wool falls back over the muddled eyes. Jonah steps backward, and the beast lowers its hind legs. The mushroom on its nose begins to inflate again, and thick yellow bubbles froth and fall out of its nostril. The animal unhinges its lower jaw, and two rows of rotten teeth drop more than two feet and bounce into place. Some rise into ten-inch spikes.

Dr. Z comes in from the side on her toes, the needle in her right hand. She gets close, and all she has to do is jump, stab, and run away, but the animal dips further down, and then pounces at Jonah.

The demic boy with the blond curls sends an echoing, haunting scream into the air as Jonah throws his arms up over his head. The beast's front paw crashes into his elbow, spinning him backward. He falls on his stomach, crawls a few feet, and then flips himself over to find the beast standing directly over his legs. The mushroom on its nose deflates, and to Jonah's horror, its milky eyes begin to rise out of its skull on dripping yellow sticks. The animal sets a paw on Jonah's chest, pinning him to the ground. Somebody yells for him to move, to spin away, but he's absolutely paralyzed with fear; all he can do is stare at the jaw of rotten teeth rocking back and forth under its head. The air turns sour.

A burst of adrenaline finally pumps through his body, sending him into action. He swings and punches at the paw. Once. Twice. Three times. The beast raises its head and then slams its other front paw onto his chest. The impact empties Jonah's lungs, waters his eyes, finishes the short fight. The animal doesn't waste any more time; it swings its jaw toward Jonah's throat.

A blue beam of light zips in from the left, slicing right through the beast's neck. Its severed head flips in the air and then lands on Jonah's heaving stomach. With a thud, the beast's massive black body falls on its side, where its paws jerk wildly and claw into the dirt. In shock, Jonah bats the head off him and takes a gasping breath of air.

"You're *such* a Firstie, man." Jonah whips his head to see Paul holding an LZR-rifle at his side, its long gray barrel glowing with tiny white lights.

As quickly as the adrenaline arrived, it also disappears, and Jonah drops his head back to the ground in trembling relief. He almost died. Again.

Dr. Z rushes over and places a hand on the headless beast's chest. "Damn it, cadet! You didn't have to kill her!"

Paul laughs. "You serious? That snout was about to eat my little First Year here. And it was either that thing." Paul then nods his head at Jonah. "Or this thing. And as the highest-ranking cadet alive in this awful, horrific fucking mess of a moon, I'm going to need every cadet I can get. First Year. Fourth Year. Whatever year."

A couple more beasts thunder past, and Dr. Z has to shout to be heard. "You could have tried to scare her first, you know! You didn't have to shoot her head off! She was just running away from the fire. That *we* started. We probably destroyed her home."

Paul picks at his teeth with his thumbnail. "That snout was about to stomp on top of every single person in this sickbay, including you. I should be hearing some gratitude instead of some attitude. I *had* to kill it."

Dr. Z points her finger at Paul's chest. "No, you didn't. So stand down, cadet, and get that gun away from my patients."

"Why do you keep calling it a snout?" Everyone turns to see a woman sitting up in a sleeping container. The left half of her thick black hair has been shaved off, and a perfect line of stitches holds together a bloody section of skin. She raises her hands over her head in exasperation. "How do you already have a name for it?"

Paul runs a hand over his smooth head and then touches the cut around his neck. "It has a long ridiculous Latin name that some demic asshole on Thetis came up with, but I can't recall what that is right now. It's easier to just call them snouts because that's their fucking nickname. Didn't you read your Achilles report?

These things are pretty high up on the old food chain here. I'd say this pretty little lady was about four years old. Maybe pregnant."

A girl standing on the perimeter gasps.

"Oh my god," Dr. Z whispers.

Jonah gets to his feet and wobbles to the empty launch seat. He's lightheaded, working on autopilot. He doesn't care about the snouts or the food chain that he's not on top of; all he wants to do is sit down, breathe, and get away from everyone.

"I said, 'Maybe.'" Paul then walks around the corpse of the beast, examining its belly. "Or maybe not. Probably not. But snouts produce about two calves a year, if I remember correctly. So what? *Nobody* read the Achilles report they put together on Thetis? Because if you did, it shows where the snouts sleep, what they eat, who their natural predators are, everything."

The boy with the sling clears his throat. "Who are their natural predators?"

Paul wheels around. "Roopers, mostly. These little monkey-rat-devil things that live high up in the trees. They hunt the snouts for breakfast at the break of dawn. Drop down in swarms as thick as blankets. Gnaw the snouts right to the bones in a couple minutes."

"I thought you said snouts were high up on the food chain," Dr. Z snaps.

"They are. They're still pretty high up there. Jesus Christ, people. We were just on a spacecraft for three hundred eighty days and you guys didn't read the report on Achilles?" He marches over to Jonah who turns his head away in embarrassment. "What about you, Firstie First Year? You read it, right, cadet?"

Before Jonah can come up with an excuse, the woman with stitches saves him. "Oh, get off it. That file is over twelve hundred pages long, kid. I didn't get to every animal. So calm down and stop acting like you're running the show here."

"I *am* running the show here!" Paul barks. "There's not one officer still alive, so I'm the one who's going to keep all your asses safe."

"You're a kid," the woman says, sighing. "You're not in charge of shit."

Paul leans his rifle onto his shoulder and pats it silently, staring the woman down. Jonah looks for an escape route. Dr. Z can stitch him up in the morning, he thinks.

"But how do they even know what animals are on this moon? I didn't know they flew up here and scouted this place," the boy with the sling says. "I didn't know they explored Achilles."

Paul drops the rifle into his arms and sweeps the barrel back and forth over the plain, eyeing a few straggling snouts lumbering by. Paul says, "They *didn't* fly up here, ya moron. They scouted Achilles and Peleus from down on Thetis. They have that Woesner Telescope down there. Heard of it much? They can practically see everything that goes on up here, *and* on Peleus, *and* on a couple of the other planets in the Silver Foot. That thing's so powerful they can see little bugs shitting out turds up here and then watch even tinier bugs eat 'em up. You're a demic, kid, how the hell did you not know that?"

"I spend a lot of time in the lab," the boy mutters. "But now that I think about it, yes, I did know about that. About the telescope. I'm just a bit discombobulated, considering everything."

A thought springs into Jonah's mind. If they can see bugs on Achilles, surely they can see them. He stands up, knocking his seat over, and waves his hands up at the sky and rotates in circles, still feeling the beast's weight on his chest. "So they can see us right now? They should be able to see me?" He yells and waves his arms wider. "Hey! Hey! We're here! We're right here!"

"Fucking stupid-ass Firsties." Paul covers his face. Jonah grows red but continues to wave his arms. He doesn't care how foolish he looks. He just wants to get to Thetis and away from this mess.

"Sorry, Jonah," Dr. Z says. "Not possible. We're on the wrong side of the moon. We probably won't be visible to Thetis for at least two months or so."

"Forty-one days," the boy with the sling says. "I mean, judging by the time that the sun set today. That's when both of our rotations would make it possible. That's when they'll be able to see this spot. This exact spot right here. But I could be off by a day or two."

"You could be," Paul sneers. "And you probably are."

Humiliated, Jonah slumps back into the chair. Could he make *any* more mistakes today? His eyes hurt. His legs and shoulders hurt. And after the close call with the snout, his stomach has been in pulsing knots. It's been over eighty hours. He needs to sleep.

"But can't we just call them?" The girl who gasped from the perimeter walks halfway into the light. She has long brown hair that reaches her waist.

"Now *that* would be nice." The silver-haired professor enters the group from the opposite direction. He's out of breath, hands on his hips. "That would make things a bit easier, right? We could just call them up and ask them to swing on by and pick us up?"

"Yeah," she says. "Let's do that. Exactly."

"*Exactly*. The only problem is that our communication system is totally one-hundred percent down," the professor says, sighing. "For the time being, anyway. And the crash site is so huge, it'll take us days to find everything we might need to fix it. Hell, we still don't know where Module Eight is."

"*What*?" Paul yells. "How the hell is that possible?"

"How the hell is it possible? It's just gone, kid. We think it may have bounced down into the jungle. *That's* how that's possible. And have you seen how large that jungle is down there? A couple of guys stopped looking at nightfall. The team got too spooked."

Paul kicks the dead snout's belly with a resounding thump. "They stopped looking? Because it was *dark* out? That's insane! That's unacceptable. There could easily be survivors down there. Maybe dozens of them." The cadet takes a deep breath and licks his purple lips. "Okay. All right. I'll organize a team right now." Jonah flinches at the vision of stomping through the jungle at night, especially with Paul. All he wants is to find a tree and sleep under it until someone comes up with a plan. The Fourth Year looks him up and down before scoffing. "Yeah, right. I think I'll take a couple Third Years. Cadets who can handle it."

"But Thetis is expecting us in twenty-four hours, right?" the boy with the sling asks. "When they can't come in contact with the ship, they'll just track our last position and see we're on Achilles and come and pick us up."

"Distress beacons are dead. All of them." Paul spits. "Whoever killed the captain and the rest of the flight crew *also* sabotaged a lot of other stuff. The navigator and that Garrett guy just checked it all out. Totally worthless."

"Wait. What? Somebody killed the captain?" the long-haired girl asks.

The woman sitting up in her sleeping container stares at Paul. "Say that again, kid. What happened? Who was killed?"

The professor quickly makes intense, unexpected eye contact with Jonah, causing the boy to look away into the darkness. "Before the crash, it seems the flight crew was shot and murdered. That's why we crashed."

Everyone conscious in the makeshift hospital, save for Dr. Z, Paul, Jonah, and the professor, blurts out questions with no answers. Paranoia creeps up Jonah's back and wraps itself around his shoulders. He wonders if any of these people could be the traitor, putting on a show of how surprising this news is right now. How can he trust anyone?

After a moment of silence, the girl says, "If the distress beacons are broken, they should let the academics take a look at them. Some of us are actually really good at repairing things, if you didn't know. Maybe we can fix one."

"Be my guest," Paul says. "I'm telling you, though, it's hopeless."

"Well, still, I'd like to see," she says.

Paul clicks on the flashlight attached to his rifle and walks toward the truss. "Follow me, then. I'll show you, and then I'll go assemble my team to find Module Eight."

"I'm coming, too," the boy with the sling says. He limps after Paul and the girl, and the professor follows.

Dr. Z picks up the launch seat and wipes it clean, then motions for Jonah to sit down. He hesitates, but Dr. Z takes him gently by the arm and looks into his eyes. "You okay?"

He looks down at the snout. Of course, he's not okay. None of them are okay. Someone hijacked the ship and killed over half the passengers, and there are wild beasts with mushroom noses and two rows of teeth. "Yeah," he whispers. "I guess."

"It just doesn't stop, huh?"

"Not yet, I guess." He's exhausted and shuts his eyes as the doctor begins to disinfect his wounds and injects him with a local anesthetic. Jonah tries to clear his mind, to bury the vision of those swinging teeth coming at his throat, to forget the beast's sour breath, but he can feel his skin being pulled this way and that way by the stitching needle, and it constantly brings him back to reality.

Some of the wounded at his feet moan and beg for water or drugs, and Jonah peeks open an eye to watch Sean Meebs, a muscular Second Year cadet wearing rectangular night-vision specs, attending to their different needs. He works diligently, pouring water in a young boy's mouth while touching the forehead of a babbling Third Year girl nearby. Sean skips over each and every adult to help the kids first. A man grabs Sean's ankle, but the cadet kicks and shakes the hand off violently so he can get to a boy wheezing and mumbling in his sleep.

When all the kids have been attended to, Sean drags an empty seat over and sits right in front of Jonah, facing him. He doesn't take off the thin specs, and their green shimmer gives the fifteen-year-old boy a ghoulish look. Jonah squirms from his closeness, from the colors of his specs, from the lack of sleep. He's never had a problem with Sean. Back at the academy, he was the only cadet who seemed to work harder than Jonah to get to Thetis.

"This is pretty much like a nightmare, huh?" Sean asks.

"It's worse," Dr. Z says from over Jonah's shoulder. Jonah nods, hoping she's almost done.

"Well, right." Sean runs a hand through his wavy blond hair and spits through his two front teeth. "Because it's real and we're not just all asleep dreaming some stupid dream together. But damn, it's almost like we were all dreaming this amazing dream where we were all *this* close to living in this *supposed* paradise, on Thetis, where everything is supposed to be all great and shit, and then *BOOM*, we're in a nightmare, dropped in some kind of hell."

Dr. Z draws the needle through Jonah's skin and then pulls until edge meets edge. "This place is the furthest thing from hell," she says. "I *have* read some about Achilles. There's fresh water. There are beautiful plants and mountains. Exotic animals that are absolutely harmless, not to mention gorgeous. But what we just went through, this moment right here, this is definitely some kind of hell. But it would be hell on Earth, too."

Sean moves his chair even closer to Jonah. "If it's so great here, then why didn't we colonize Achilles or the other moon Peleus instead of Thetis?"

Jonah is about to ask him to leave them alone when Dr. Z says, "Good question, cadet. You'll have to ask the Powers That Be when you get the chance. And hopefully, that will be possible very, very soon."

"Whatever. I bet Thetis isn't even that great. Probably run by a bunch of asshole adults who order the kids around like slaves." Sean removes his specs and sticks them into the collar of his shirt. His left eye socket is yellow and purple with bruises, and a cut runs across the top of his nose, as if he's been punched or met a snout head-on.

Dr. Z places a hand on Jonah's neck and pulls another stitch through. "If you feel that way, why did you volunteer, cadet?"

The Second Year plucks the specs from his collar and puts them back on. With straight lips, he says, "Kind of hate my family, doctor. At least those that were left, I guess. What more can I say, other than my life was *majorly* depressing on Earth and that I was looking for the exact opposite thing? It sounds lame, maybe, but I was kind of hoping that I could maybe be happy in another galaxy, on another planet."

The doctor laughs. "No offense, cadet, but I think that is the most ironic thing I could hear right now. No one is happy in this galaxy right now, I assure you. Everyone on Thetis was counting on our supplies. They're in a lot of trouble without us."

Jonah actually perks up on hearing Sean's explanation, and he offers the cadet a quick smile. Sean's sentiment is one of the driving forces behind Jonah's interest in Thetis, aside from dodging the war in England. To have the exact opposite life in this galaxy is his plan, too. Maybe here he could have a family and study to be a biologist or even a painter. He hears the snipping of scissors, and the doctor dabs at his wound with something soft.

"That takes care of that." She sets both hands on Jonah's shoulders, pats him, and then moves to one of the open medical kits. "But there's more to do and something I really need to talk to you about, Jonah."

"Sure." He's completely depleted of energy and it's hard to sit up, but he's grateful to be taken care of.

"He going to make it, doctor?" Sean asks.

Dr. Z squeezes some solution on her hands and then dips her head in front of Jonah's. She gently prods the bones of his nose with her fingers. Jonah growls; the pain is excruciating, and he pounds the armrests with his fists, completely awake again. "Well, you won't need surgery. Which is great because I don't have the equipment, or the team. You *will* have a lot of swelling, though."

When Jonah opens his eyes, tears spill just an inch down his cheeks and then stay there.

Dr. Z moves to another medical kit. "The gravity here is pretty interesting, huh?"

Jonah exhales through his mouth, trying to regain some composure. "Yeah."

Sean adds, "From what some dorky demic told me earlier, it's a little less than a third of the gravity on Earth. So, I'm like, sixty pounds here or something. And if you could jump, like, two feet high off the ground on Earth, like me, then you could now jump, like, six feet. Which, considering everything else, I think is pretty damn cool."

Dr. Z grumbles, "*Pretty damn cool.* I need to talk to Jonah about something. Cadet, would you give some privacy?"

"Sure," he says, adjusting his specs. "I'll see if I can find any more blankets for the kids."

Once Sean leaves the light, Dr. Z spins Jonah away from the rest of the patients. "Jonah, when I was cleaning your eyes earlier, I saw something I didn't like. Something I've seen before, unfortunately." He sits up straight, pushing sleep away. "The backs of your sockets were rimmed with a bluish color." She clicks on a small flashlight and tugs on his upper and lower lids. "Right. They're still like that. To me, it looks like you have what is a relatively new blood disease called Sepsis Bimorphyria, or Sepsis B."

Jonah tries to focus on the name of the disease, but all he can picture is his eyes turning blue, from back to front, until they look like marbles. Why would they turn blue?

"Are you listening to me, Jonah? This is very serious."

"Yeah," he says quietly. "I might have a blood disease. My eyes are turning blue. But that's still okay, right?"

"I was able to find a blood meter in one of these kits and I tested some of your blood from before. I hope you don't mind. You have what I *think* is Sepsis, but it's not regular Sepsis, and it's *not* Sepsis B. It's something else, something that isn't good."

Jonah just stares at her, his mouth open. He thinks about running away so he doesn't have to hear whatever else she is going to say.

"You might have a newer, mutated form of Sepsis B. Either that, or my blood meter is broken. But I have to say, with the blue rims and the results I've seen from some of the others...Jonah, I'm sorry."

He thinks back to his recent vertigo and nausea. "Is it from the wormhole?"

"That's my first guess, yes."

Jonah doesn't mean to ask the next question, but it slips out: "So, what? Am I dying?"

Dr. Z pulls back her maroon hair. Her face grows grim. "Without antibiotics, intravenous liquids, and a few other things that I don't have with me, or things that were destroyed in the crash, I would say, in my professional opinion, that you have about a week until you start to feel sick, maybe sooner. And then you have less than thirty days until you go blind and things become irreversible. And yes, then you would most likely die." She pauses. "I'm sorry."

Jonah slips off the chair and lands on his knees. His fingertips circle around his eyes while Dr. Z apologizes further. What is she talking about? He's dying? And not from hunger or a street fight? Not from the crash or an earthquake or from some abusive foster family?

"Now, the good news is that if the guys on Thetis are able to find us and take us to the Athens colony, then you should get everything you need and you'll most likely be fine. So let's just pray Thetis finds us."

"What about the homing beacons? They're destroyed," he says.

"Well, let's pray for that, too. That they can fix one."

"Help me," groans a man behind Jonah. "Doctor. Please."

"I have to help the others, Jonah. We'll talk more about this tomorrow morning, okay? I have some ideas I'd like to try. Maybe I can stop it. But try to get some sleep tonight, and I'll see you in the morning." She moves toward the man and peels back his blanket. He has no legs.

Jonah stares at the man's two stumps wrapped in bloody bandages and can't comprehend what he's looking at, or what he just learned. Then, after a few seconds, he floats to his feet and walks clumsily to the perimeter of the light. He doesn't know which way to walk. He has a fatal blood disease and might die in thirty days, and he doesn't know which way to walk.

"Where are you headed?" a voice in the darkness asks.

Frightened, Jonah turns to see the green shine of Sean's specs. "I don't even know. It doesn't even matter."

"Well, if you want to sleep, follow me."

At first, Jonah doubts he'll ever be able to sleep again, not after what Dr. Z's just told him, but then it's as if he's been run over by a truck. He needs to lie down.

"Grab my arm," Sean says. The two walk quickly across the dark plain. Jonah feels a sense of relief to be blind at this moment; he doesn't want to know if he's walking on stones or bones, if what's sticking to his foot is blood or oil.

"Let's hurry up," he says.

"Thirty seconds away. Calm down, Firstie."

Jonah moves his hand to the back of Sean's shirt and allows the boy to lead him through an opening in a broken module. A young girl with a terrified voice asks who it is. The cadets don't stop moving until they're lying next to each other on the cold soil. Finally, Sean says, "It's Sean and Jonah, two badass cadets. We're going to sleep, so don't worry about it and shut up."

"That's it, then. Nobody else. Getting too damn crowded in here." It's a different girl's voice; it's Vespa's, and it's the last thing Jonah hears before he falls asleep.

• • •

Vespa's voice is also the first thing Jonah hears when he wakes. She's upset, whispering loudly in his ear, her spit covering his cheek. Jonah tries to focus on her, but his foggy mind can't make out what she's saying. Then she's silent. Then she boots him in his shins and growls, "Cadet. Get up. Get the hell up right now, Firstie. It's an order."

He opens his eyes. He feels nauseous. His body begs for him to go back to sleep. "What time is it?"

A beam of light hits his face, and then a fist bunches the front of his shirt around his neck. He's pulled viciously to his feet and shoved into someone else's arms, but he's too tired to resist. Jonah wobbles a few feet forward before a hand pulls him back and holds him in place. Normally, he would fight back. Normally, if someone touched him like this, he would panic and swing blindly until he got his bearings. But not tonight. Tonight he's just too tired. He opens his eyes just as Vespa kicks a sleeping Sean in the ribs.

"I said, get up, cadet," she seethes.

Sean groans and spits, and finally Jonah turns to see that it's a Third Year named Portis who's holding him up. Beside him stands a stocky girl cadet named Steph, with a close crop of bleached white hair. Jonah's never cared for either of them.

"It's still night out," Griffin says with a yawn. He stumbles to his feet and then purposefully slams his thick shoulder into Jonah's, knocking both him and Portis back a few steps. "This is horse shit. Just let us sleep."

Sean finally rolls onto his knees. "Please tell me we're not doing some kind of night training exercise. Because that would be pretty stupid."

Vespa leans down and growls in his face, "Just hold on, cadet." She then turns to the six cadets who grumble and sway around her. "Follow me. Right now." Vespa ducks out of the module, and the cadets file after her. Jonah notices that one of them, a blond boy with a short red beard, a seventeen-year-old Third Year named North, is trembling with absolute terror. Tears cover his cheeks and sweat clings to his beard. He is mumbling incoherently, letting everyone exit before him.

"Over here," Vespa orders in a loud whisper. "We have a major situation."

"That's an understatement," Sean mumbles.

"No, this is something new. Something worse."

The cadets all stand up straight at the same time. Even Jonah is fully awake now.

"How major? Like, can we deal with it in the morning?" Griffin asks. "I feel like death, man."

Vespa's voice lowers an octave. "No. I don't think this situation can wait until morning."

"They're all gone!" North bellows and then covers his mouth with his dirty fingers. He wheels around and stumbles a few feet into the darkness before falling to his hands and knees.

"Who's all gone?" Sean asks.

Vespa rubs her neck, and Jonah notices she actually looks scared, like a helpless little girl. Her light falls on North's back. "North was in Module Two last night, still in the truss."

"I couldn't sleep," he whispers. "I just couldn't, you know. My head's all messed up from the crash."

"He says there was a meeting called by some of the adults a couple hours ago…" Vespa trails off. "I think maybe you all should just see this for yourselves, like I did. North, I need you to get the hell up right now. *Right now*. Lead the way. Let's go."

The boy pushes himself off the ground and a small flashlight appears in his shaking hand. He scratches his beard. "This way."

"Wait," Steph says. "Stop. You're freaking me out. Just tell us what's going on first. Where are we going?"

Vespa shoves Steph in the back, harder than Jonah thinks is necessary. "Shut the hell up and just move."

The girl snaps her body upright, and then she marches after Vespa and North. "Screw you, *Vespa*. You're not my commanding officer. I don't have to take orders from you."

"*Yeah*," Sean mocks. He tries to slap Jonah in the stomach with the back of his hand, but Jonah's on high alert. He didn't like that shove from Vespa. He doesn't like the look in North's eyes. Something very bad has happened. His reflexes tighten and he blocks Sean's hand before dropping down into a fighting position. Sean and Griffin burst out laughing, and his skin grows hot. He feels like a fool. He straightens up and follows Vespa, not caring where she's headed.

"Well, I don't," Steph mumbles.

Portis walks next to Jonah with his wrist in his teeth, chewing on his skin. He drops his wrist from his mouth just long enough to shake his huge head of black hair like a wet dog and says, "Shut up, Steph. Jesus Christ."

Vespa wheels around. "I don't want any more chatter from any of you. Okay? All right? This is serious. We need to move as quiet as ghosts, cadets. And if you see anything you can use as a weapon, I suggest you pick it up."

Why do they need weapons? The group moves faster, and Jonah jogs to catch up. But should he catch up?

North sweeps the ground in front of his feet, and they zip along the perimeter of the crash site. Jonah keeps his eyes open for anything of use: a weapon, a shoe, food, his sheaf. He scoops up an L-shaped piece of metal with a fist-sized bolt sticking through one end. Steph finds a heavy wooden chair and stomps off its legs, distributing them.

They change directions and push through a thick patch of grass that's chest high and stiff like bamboo. The blades clap and clatter around Jonah, and he has to force himself to breathe through the adrenaline pumping in his body. North leads them single file to a cliff and points his beam down into the jungle.

"Down here," he says as he takes a hesitant first step down the cliff. A chorus of howling squawks rains down from the tallest trees, and then there are the sounds of wings flapping and branches bending in the distance. And then there's silence. Everything about this feels wrong to Jonah. He stares down into the darkness, his heart pounding in his ears.

"Wait. North, you went all the way down there? By yourself?" Steph asks. "Why would you come down here?"

"Yeah, seriously," Griffin grumbles.

"Because I heard them screaming," North says. His voice is completely stripped of emotion, and Jonah can tell the boy has pushed beyond some kind of intense fear he has of this place. North runs on body mechanics now, telling his feet each time when to move. Jonah's been there many times in his last few foster homes. Whatever happens, happens at this point, you think. It's out of your hands.

The closer they get to the jungle floor, the tighter Jonah's hand grips the flat end of the metal. Is this a trap? How well does he know any of these cadets? Is he the only one not in on something? At the tree line, everything is cloaked in shadows; the pale moonlight from Peleus can't penetrate more than a few feet inside the jungle. Jonah wants to stop, but he's like North now, and he concentrates solely on keeping his feet moving.

Vespa points to a low-hanging tree branch covered in wet, bubbling fungi, and after they all duck past, she produces a small blue handgun. Jonah eyes the gun and grips his weapon so hard this time that it cuts into his palm. It takes everything in him not to turn and run. Vespa grabs North's flashlight to illuminate a row of giant purple flowers with six-foot-tall petals, and says, "We're on our own now. You'll understand what I mean in a second. But listen to me. I need you to remember your training and that we *will* get through this. I promise. North and I will stand sentry right here, so take a look around, look for clues, but don't touch anything. And do *not* scream. Do *not* panic. Just come right back here, and we'll regroup and strategize."

"Holy shit. Enough already," Griffin says, snatching the flashlight out of her hand. The lion shaved into the cadet's hair turns away from Jonah as the boy marches confidently toward the flowers. He swipes a jagged chair leg across a closed purple bud that's as big as a football, knocking it to the jungle floor, where it smokes and disintegrates. Steph, Jonah, Sean, and Portis march after him.

They enter a small circular clearing and Griffin whips the flashlight all around. Jonah slowly spins as he walks, hoping to see whatever there is to see, then get out of there. There's a sickly smell in the air, and it hangs over Jonah's head like a net. He doesn't see anything, and just as he's about to call out to Vespa to just tell them what they're supposed to look for, Griffin sucks in a wheezing lungful of air.

"Holy shit. Holy shit, holy shit, holy shit. What the—"

Jonah follows Griffin's flashlight. It's pointing up into the trees, and when Jonah sees what it's landed on, his breath sweeps out of his body. His chest heaves for air, but nothing comes, and little white explosions begin to float over his eyes. Still, he can't look away.

Steph sees it, too, and she shrieks and rams her bleached hair into Jonah's chest, pushing him into a thicket of thorns. The sharp points drive into his skull and neck, but the pain isn't enough for him to move closer to the clearing. Steph pushes and spins away, and Jonah just leans there, staring.

Portis begins to gag, and then he chomps down on his wrist and runs, crashing back through the flowers, past Sean, who takes off his night-vision specs and squints up at the trees. Griffin grabs Steph's wrist, standing perfectly still, his head stuck at a rigid forty-five-degree angle. When he touches his face, Jonah finds himself doing the same thing.

Griffin's flashlight stays in one trembling place, and every few seconds, a man's bloody face twists and swings into its light. He's dead, bloated and purple, hanging from a black vine around his neck, twirling like a toy. It takes Jonah a moment to realize the man has no legs. It's the same man from the makeshift hospital, the one whose groans took the doctor away from him.

"That's—I think that's Professor Eck," Steph finally whimpers. "He's a demic teacher. Benjamin Eck. I know him. Oh my god."

"Holy shit," Griffin whispers again. When it seems they've all had enough time to process the legless dead man hanging from the tree, Griffin lowers the beam to the ground, and when he does, they all jump backward in horror at the discovery of a new body. Sitting directly below the professor is the woman with the half-shaved head who had asked about the snouts. The one who had fought with Paul. Her feet are straight out in front of her, her arms tied behind her back. A white piece of clothing sticks out of her mouth, falling below her chin. Her pale green eyes are lifeless, but they're wide open and aimed right where Jonah stands in the thorns. He steps out of the bush, drawing in for a closer look.

Steph falls to her hands and knees, crying, sucking wind.

Griffin keeps his flashlight right at the woman's face. "This is what's-her-name, the cook."

"Mrs. Perlman," Steph wheezes. She stands up and immediately begins to backpedal. "Let's go. Let's go, let's go."

Vomit shoots up Jonah's throat and hits the back of his teeth. He doubles over, but then he's suddenly afraid to show any signs of weakness to whoever did this, and so he swallows the bile and makes himself stand straight up. He tucks the emotions into the dark corners of his mind to deal with later, when he's alone and safe. He steels himself, hacks, spits, and concentrates on his breathing.

With his eyes still on the ground, Sean asks, "What do they say? On their shirts. It says something."

"What?" Steph asks.

Griffin lowers the beam to the cook's abdomen, and clearly written in mud, it reads: *RUN.*

"Run," Griffin whispers. "Holy shit. It says, 'run.'"

Jonah's skin prickles and rises off his body as if someone has caught him with a thousand fishing hooks. *Run*? He feels his joints locking, his muscles and tendons shrinking around them. He stares at the muddy word and his focus goes to the dark jungle around him. He listens. At the slightest movement, he's leaving, he's gone. He *will* run.

Steph grabs Jonah's arm. "Let's just go."

The legless man above them then rotates, and when Griffin lights him up again, Jonah pays attention to his shirt. He now sees it's smeared with muddy words, too. He squints and reads: *KIDS ARE FREE NOW.*

"Screw *this.*" Steph lets go of Jonah and backpedals out of sight. "Screw this! Screw *all* of you!"

"I can't even look," Sean whispers. "What does the other one say?"

"It says, 'Kids are free now,'" Jonah whispers. The words fall from his mouth like heavy rocks, dropping on his toes, pinning him in place. The little pinpricks of the thorns stuck in his clothes scrape over his skin, but they do nothing to distract him.

Vespa's voice sounds like a gunshot in Jonah's ears. "Okay. You've all seen it. Now let's go. Hurry. Now."

The cadets crash through the jungle. Those shirts and their warnings, statements, or threats stick to the roof of Jonah's mouth and replay over and over on his silent lips. *Run. Kids are free now. Run. Kids are free now. Run. Kids are free now.* He had just seen these two people. The man was about to die, shivering in a sleeping container. Now he's dead, hanging from a tree branch. *Kids are free now.* And the woman, Mrs. Perlman, she had just been asking about the snouts and telling Paul to calm down. She was going to be fine. And now Jonah realizes none of them will ever be fine again. *Run.* He should run. Should he run? Where?

At the bottom of the cliff, Vespa clears her throat. "Now listen to me. We'll talk about all that crazy shit in a second, but there's something else." She pauses, and then in a cracking voice, she says, "They're all gone. All the adults, they're gone. They're missing. They left, or they were taken away."

"What the hell are you even talking about?" Griffin asks. "What do you mean, they're all gone?"

Jonah steps forward in a daze. "No, they're not all gone. I just saw Dr. Z about—"

"She's gone," Vespa interrupts. "For the last hour, North, Paul, and I have been in every shelter, every module, the sickbay, under the truss, *every-freaking-where*, all over the wreckage. Every adult is missing except for *that* man hanging from his neck and *that* woman gagged on the ground."

"They're just all gone," North whispers. "We can't find any of them."

Griffin swallows a lump in his throat and says, "Run. Kids are free now."

CHAPTER FIVE

DARKNESS CONTINUES FOR ANOTHER TWELVE HOURS. JONAH spends most of it sitting in the farthest corner of Module Five, his back flat against the shredded wall. His head bobs high over the sea of kids like a weathered buoy, and he starts to memorize faces. He pays attention to who huddles with whom before the accusations start. Then he pays attention to who turns on their friends, and how fast.

As Vespa paces back and forth on the opposite side of the room, Jonah fingers the melted holes in his shirt. He tries to ignore the tiny burns on his chest and neck, but they throb and itch and remind him how useless he's become.

After leaving the professor and cook down in the jungle, Griffin demanded to see the Support Module to conduct his own murder investigation of the flight crew. Vespa agreed, and Jonah followed silently up the cliff in a terrified stupor, deciding it was better to stick together—at least for the moment—than to wander into the darkness and run. *Run*, he thought. *Run.* He said the word over and over in his head. Where was he supposed to run? Did the adults run? And did he even have the energy to run?

Jonah's mind was lost in images of Dr. Z, Garrett, and the dead bodies in the jungle when a flickering orange light appeared over the cliff's edge. He smelled smoke and burning plastic. Soon, he heard the crackling of fire. The cadets shouted and doubled their efforts up the cliff.

"What the hell?" Griffin yelled. "WHAT THE HELL!"

Far in the distance, the Support Module was consumed in an orange and purple fireball. Thick white smoke billowed off it in blankets, and neon sparks shot out in every direction. The messages that had been repeating in Jonah's head slammed against the back of his skull, ricocheted down his spine, and bit at his toes, and before he knew it, he started to run. He charged straight at the fire, covering several feet with each long stride. *Run*, he thought. *Just run.*

He heard footsteps close behind him, and then Vespa's voice: "Firstie! Damn it! Stop!"

They were thirty feet away when Jonah dug his bare heels into the dirt and stopped. He had just run into a large cluster of the landmine weeds, and they were starting to spark and hiss like storm clouds. Jonah backpedaled and whipped his arm behind him to hold back Vespa, but she had too much momentum and pushed right past. She jumped high into the air.

"No! Get out of there!" Jonah shouted.

She landed on a narrow strip of dirt between the plants and the module. A weed off to the right exploded, blasting up a geyser of dirt and fire. Jonah covered his head and yelled again, but Vespa ignored him and stepped closer to the flames. The Support Module was collapsing. There was a creak and then a pop, and then Jonah thought he heard a voice, as if a woman was crying for something. It was faint, and he wasn't sure if he actually heard it, but then Vespa shouted over her shoulder: "Someone's inside! I think someone's in there!"

"You have to get out of there! The plants!" Jonah shouted.

Two weeds blew up on his left, blasting debris and flames high overhead. "Vespa!"

She stepped closer and closer to the module, trying to peek inside its windows. Jonah wanted to jump after her, to throw her over his shoulder and carry her to safety, but his feet were suddenly cemented to the ground. His knees shook. Acid rushed up his throat and coated his tongue and teeth. He was falling apart. Again. And this time Vespa would suffer for it.

He heard the cry again, faint but clear. It *was* a woman. And she needed help. Who was it, and where was she? Was it Dr. Z? Was she trapped inside the module? Were *all* the adults trapped inside? Jonah stared at the inferno and couldn't believe anyone could still be alive in there. Vespa raised her hands helplessly.

That was when Jonah's feet started to move again. A patch of weeds on the left ignited, sending fiery debris everywhere, but he just put his head down and kept going. He took two long strides toward the module and saw a clear spot in the middle of the burning weeds to launch from. He raced into it, planted his right foot, but just as he was about to leap, a weed a few feet in front of him exploded. White and green sparks blew against his chest like birdshot, bouncing up to his neck and chin. He screamed in agony as his flesh burned and his shirt melted to his skin. He stumbled backward, slapping at his chest, dousing the flames. Through tear-soaked eyes, he looked up and saw Vespa pacing in front of the module. He knew he should run away, but he couldn't; if just a few more plants went off and there was a chain reaction, Vespa would be blown right into the fire.

Jonah took ten steps back, clenched his teeth, and then sprinted forward. The cool air soothed his burns, and he jumped just as a weed exploded at his heels, its shrapnel punching Jonah in the back and legs. His feet hit the narrow stretch of dirt and he fell onto his hands, then he pushed himself up and tore toward Vespa.

"Come on!" he screamed, reaching for her arm. But just as his fingers touched her shoulder, a dark shadow came in from his right and rammed him like a train. The impact left him breathless, unable to hear or think. His feet left the ground as he went horizontal. Jonah's fingers still tried to grab Vespa, but she was no longer there. Everything was black and gone.

His hearing returned just as the weeds started to detonate in large groups, booming in unison. Jonah found himself floating over the ground as fire, dirt, and scalding hot rocks showered his left side. He tried to turn over, but whatever rammed him held on tight and wouldn't let go, pushing him farther and farther away from the fire and Vespa. He had to get back to her, he thought; maybe it wasn't too late. He struggled against the shadow and howled in pain when he couldn't move, and then a moment later, it all stopped. He was thrown to the ground, where he rolled onto his back in a daze. Next to him, coughing and swearing, was Vespa. And standing above them both, the shadow turned into Paul, his bald head gleaming in the firelight.

"The hell were you two doing?" Paul asked. "Starting fires? With everything going on?"

Jonah looked over at Vespa, who spat at Paul's feet. "Asshole! It wasn't us. And there was somebody in there!"

"There was nobody in there, cadet. I assure you."

Vespa pounded a fist on the cold dirt and dropped her forehead to the ground in defeat. Jonah didn't know what to say. There was a woman somewhere—he was sure of it—but if she was inside the module, she was dead by now.

"I heard a voice, too," he finally said. "There was a lady. She could have been inside, I don't know. Maybe they all were."

Paul looked over his shoulder, and Jonah followed his gaze. The module was flattened, charred, and unrecognizable.

"I was all the way at the other end of the wreckage when you idiots showed back up. Made it here as fast as I could, and I didn't hear anyone but *your* little voice, Firstie. You know, you're becoming a hell of a liability out here." And then Paul said, "I'm starting to wish you'd died in the crash and I was left with someone a little more competent." That cut so deep into Jonah that he lay there for a full minute, letting Vespa and Paul walk off into the darkness before he took North's dirty hand.

Now, from his vantage point in the back of Module Five, Jonah watches Vespa pace in the lantern light near the only exit. Steph and North flank her, all three holding spears ripped from one of the porcupine trees in the valley. In Vespa's side pocket, he sees the bulge of her blue gun. He stares at her pocket enviously while picking at the melted holes in his shirt. Everyone's a suspect; everyone in here, and everyone in the other module with Paul. Paul's the biggest suspect of them all, Jonah's decided, arrogant and aggressive, arguing with the cook at the makeshift hospital, disappearing to find Module Eight in the middle of the night. Hours later, two adults are dead and the rest are gone. Jonah hears Paul wishing him dead over and over in his mind, and when he closes his eyes, he sees images of the professor twirling above him from the vine. He wants a gun. His whole life he's been the pacifist, the boy who throws the second punch—if he throws a punch at all—and now Jonah wants a gun. *Kids are free now. Run. Run, run, run.*

"When the hell is daylight already?" Portis yells and then leans back and puts his palm between his teeth.

A lean demic boy with long, straight brown hair jumps to his feet and blinks his eyes several times. He speaks rapidly: "Yeah. Hi, um. I'm Michael, and I was doing some calculating earlier and I believe that here on Achilles, at this exact point on its calendar, judging by the time it took for the sun to set this evening, night and darkness lasts just over twenty-four hours. Twenty-four hours and seventeen minutes, to be exact. And daylight is just nine hours and forty-three minutes. To be exact."

Portis stops chewing on his hand and finds Jonah's eyes above the crowd. It's as if he's talking right at him when he says, "Well, that's shitty."

Jonah stares Portis down until the Third Year looks away with a grin. He's never liked Portis, and he likes him less and less as the hours crawl by. Could he have done all this? Could Portis have slipped away at night and killed those two people and led the rest of the adults away? Is he working with Paul?

Michael sits down and puts his pointed chin in his hands. Jonah notices he doesn't sit with anyone, and he tucks this information away in his memory, right next to the haunting voice of the faceless woman inside the fire.

The demics grow restless when day finally breaks. Many of them demand to use the bathroom. More than a few want to comb the wreckage for personal items.

A tall demic girl tries to walk past Vespa. "I don't know why we have to be on this 'lockdown' of yours, but I need to see Dr. Z. I have a really bad headache. I feel awful."

"Okay," Vespa says as she steps in front of the exit. "We'll start having bathroom breaks in a little bit, okay? There are just some things you need to know first before you, before we..." Vespa trails off as she looks into the faces of the twenty or so kids at her feet. "Here's the deal. Last night, one of the cadets was trying to sleep in Module Two when he overheard the adults calling each other to a meeting. An all-adult meeting, apparently. The cadet didn't know what the agenda was, or where they were going. All he knew was that he wasn't invited, so he tried to go back to sleep, like I'm sure all of us would. A short time later, he heard people screaming down in the jungle."

Rumblings rise from her audience. Two girls start crying. Jonah picks at his shirt and watches the kids huddle together. He feels sorry for them, that they're about to hear it all for the first time. After all, he's a trained First Year cadet, and he's still paralyzed by the news several hours later, barely able to dive further than the surface of the situation.

"What kind of screams?" the redheaded, freckled Aussie asks from her knees.

North lifts his eyes from the ground. "It was a man's scream at first. I don't know what he was saying. And then there were more. But I was half-asleep, you know, and they sounded pretty far away and I..."

Vespa takes over. "The cadet grabbed his flashlight and ran after the voice, or voices, and followed them down the side of the cliff."

"They weren't just screaming, though. They were yelling about something. People were arguing, but I don't know what about." North's voice cracks. "I thought I could handle it. I'm supposed to be this fearless Third Year, you know. That's my training. I should have brought someone with me. It was stupid."

Aussie stands up. "Who was screaming? Who was it?"

"I—I guess it was a demic guy. A professor."

There's silence, and then Rosa, the hysterical girl Jonah saved from the collapsing module with Aussie, stands and asks, "Which one? Who? Are they dead? They're dead, aren't they?"

North nods. "Yeah, he's dead."

Rosa crumples to the ground, and the sea of kids churns with fear. Michael jumps to his feet again. "Who? Who was it? Who died?"

Vespa raises her voice, trying to take back control. "We're pretty sure it's Professor Eck. And there was a woman down there, too. The cook with the bushy black hair. Mrs. Perlman. She's dead, too."

The demics cry out with questions. Some of the older ones point fingers at the cadets, demanding that North tell them everything from the beginning, and the younger demics simply cry, shiver, and hug each other, begging to go home.

"But what does Dr. Z say?" a girl yells. "Maybe they're *not* dead and she can save them!"

"Dr. Z is gone!" Portis shouts from the other side of the module, his big mouth cupped by his dirty hands. "They're *all* gone. And those two down in the jungle are definitely, definitely dead. I saw them myself."

A wave of silence crashes down on the children, all of them turning and bobbing as this new current moves through the group. Vespa gets a syllable out before Portis calls, "Did you hear what I just said? All of the adults, *every single fucking one of them*, they're gone. Out of here. They're not here anymore and we're on our own."

Next to Jonah, a walrus of a boy—a clumsy, oafish eighteen-year-old with terrible acne and huge bushy eyebrows—rolls onto his knees. His right arm bends oddly above his giant head, his palm twisted up and out as if shielding his eyes from the sun. The boy tries to pull the arm down with his left hand, but the arm surprisingly springs back in place. "Why would they leave us?"

No one has an answer. Three demic boys are accused of driving the adults away with their on-ship antics, hacking into the gravity controls too often during meal times. Rosa says that one of the dead girls in her module was flirting with Professor Eck too much and he and the other professors were tired of it, and tired of all them by association. The tall girl who tried to get past Vespa marches over to Rosa with tears in her eyes, demanding Rosa take back what she said about her dead friend.

One of the boys from the hacker group, a lanky teen with a birdlike face and long black bangs twisted in front of his eyes, yells matter-of-factly, "Looks like we're *all* going to die!"

"That's highly unlikely," Michael says. "Statistically speaking, I mean."

"Shut the hell up, Michael!" the hacker yells back. Jonah notices a faint, thin mustache above his lips. "Just shut up, Pissy! Go piss your pants somewhere and just shut up!"

The other two hackers snicker at this, the middle one catcalling, "*Pis-say*! *Pis-say*!"

Jonah's insides bubble with rage, and he almost jumps at the group of hackers, but he lets it go on without saying a word. He doesn't want to draw any attention to himself. Even at his height, he knows it's possible to go unnoticed. And that's just what he wants right now.

"Are you freaking kidding me?" Aussie yells. "You're picking on Michael right now? *Right now*? With all that's going on?"

"Pis-say," the middle boy says with a cough. The other two bounce with held-in laughter.

"Enough! Everyone just shut up!" Vespa barks.

And then, just like that, Jonah is outside, barreling past Steph and North. *So much for staying unnoticed*, he thinks. But he can't listen to the fighting and crying anymore. His temples throb and he feels dizzy. He leans hard against a burnt tree trunk, remembering he's sick and going to die regardless. If some maniac hijacker doesn't kill him in the middle of the night, then his disease will take him in a month. He checks his fingernails to see if they might be blue, and when they're not, he studies his toes, feet, ankles. *Not yet*, he thinks. *But maybe soon*.

The plain is wet with dew and everything glistens, even the bloodstains and charred debris. He looks at the remains of the Support Module; a couple cadets sifted through the ashes last night and found just the four bodies of the flight crew inside. The adults are still missing. Whoever was crying last night is still missing.

Vespa's voice carries out of the module as she goes over the details of last night, asking if anyone saw anything. Nobody has an answer, and then the hackers start laughing about something. Someone exits, and Jonah spins around to see Michael. Tears sit in the corners of his eyes.

A bolt of empathy shoots down Jonah's spine. "Hey. Um. You okay? I mean, can I help...with anything?"

"It's just ridiculous, you know? It happened five years and two months and thirteen days ago, and they still won't let it go," Michael says, parting his long brown hair with shaking fingers. "*Pissy*. That's all they say, and I don't know how to make them stop."

"It'll stop."

"Yeah, when that tough cadet girl is around, sure."

"When I'm around, too," Jonah says softly. He's surprised to say it, to promise something to someone he hardly knows, but it feels good. And it's nice to feel something good for a moment.

Michael doesn't respond, but his head lifts toward the pale gray sky.

North, Vespa, and Steph exit the module cautiously, and the rest of the kids cluster behind them. Vespa gives Jonah a suspicious look and he feels his face grow hot. Maybe she thinks he could be the traitor. He's angry with himself for putting even the smallest target on his back.

Cadets and demics emerge from the module piece across the way, and Vespa meets Paul in the middle of the valley, alone, while both their camps look on. Sean waves at Jonah and he nods back.

The two unofficial leaders separate, and when Vespa returns, she pulls the cadets aside. "Your mission is to find weapons and food while the demics try to piece together a working communication device. Paul and his cadets are focused on finding some kind of energizer, like a battery or generator thing, so we can have some power around here. We're going to stay in pairs, or in threes. That way if someone around here is a killer, if anything happens to someone's group, then our list of suspects grows *very, very* short. So whatever you do, do *not* let any member of your group out of your sight. And keep your eyes on these demics. They're smart enough to surprise you and all of us. Who knows what they're capable of? So use your heads *and* your training. Two of Paul's cadets—that Malix kid and Christina—are already hidden at both ends of the wreckage, watching for suspicious behavior, and for any signs of the adults."

"Whatever happened to Module Eight?" North asks.

"No one knows yet," Vespa says.

"What happens if we find weapons?" Steph asks.

"You bring them to me, and before nightfall Paul and I will figure out the lucky ones who'll go down into the jungle to help us bury the professor and the cook and look for some clues. The weapons were supposedly locked in the lowest level of Module Three, but Module Three is absolutely everywhere. So the weapons could be anywhere."

The demics surround Vespa the moment the cadets set out. Jonah walks off with Steph and Portis, and when he's not busy keeping track of everyone in the valley, his eyes search for his sheaf. He could really use a moment with his parents' photo right now.

Jonah's group heads for the very tip of the crash site. A carpet of rubble lies underfoot: cooking pots, vent coverings, and a shattered fish tank with several suffocated tropical fish amongst the glass. Jonah climbs into a crushed land rover that's missing both its axles, but it's empty. Its dashboard dangles from wires, as if someone has ripped it apart. Fifty yards away, another rover sits helplessly upside down.

Most things they come across are broken and charred beyond recognition, and yet Jonah finds a shining ten-inch kitchen knife. And by the time they reach the farthest part of Module Three—the first two-and-a-half levels on its side, black with smoke damage—he finds a mismatched pair of sneakers he can wear.

"I'm telling you guys, I think that North kid did all this," Portis mumbles before taking a quick bite at his forearm. His skin is pocked with red circles and teeth marks. "I don't know what it is, but there's something really off about that guy. And seriously, why the hell would he go down there by himself? I'd be scared shitless and bring every cadet I could wake up."

"Who set the fire while we were down there, then?" Steph asks. "If he was with us, who started the fire?"

"Maybe it started on its own." Portis shrugs. "Or maybe it was one of the adults."

Steph overturns a refrigerator-sized container. Its doors are still closed, its corners dented. "What do you think, Jonah?"

Jonah wants to say it could be her. It could be North or Portis or Paul or Vespa or the hackers. Or the adults could have just simply left them behind, killing the two that rebelled. "I have no idea," he mutters.

"You're such a Firstie," Portis says, laughing. "Grow a pair and have an opinion. Christ."

Jonah's skin grows hot as he listens to the boy laughing. "Screw off, Portis."

A smile crosses Portis's face. "What did you say to me? What was that, Firstie?"

It suddenly hits Jonah. Just because they didn't make it to Thetis and he's about to die, it doesn't mean he can't still start over.

It doesn't mean he has to wait to earn anyone's respect. *Shit*, Jonah thinks, *I'm dying. I don't have time to be pushed around anymore.* He marches over to Portis and stops inches from the boy's huge nose. Jonah has over eight inches on the Third Year. "I said, screw off."

Portis blasts Jonah backward with two open hands, causing him to trip over a bloodstained launch seat. "Now *that's* what I'm talking about, kid. Get pissed! Show me. Show me what happens when the Firstie gets pissed."

Jonah grinds his teeth and marches back over, ready to throw his customary second punch, when Steph sticks her spear into one of the door handles of the container and stomps on its other end. The door flies open and she gasps.

"Guns?" Portis walks away from a fast-approaching Jonah, who is both relieved and disappointed the confrontation seems to be over. He stands there and lets the adrenaline drain. He's proud of himself. For a change.

"No," Steph says, digging around inside. She pulls out a thin box wrapped in gold foil. "But we have food."

"Excellent." Portis grabs one and rips the foil away with his teeth. A burst of steam blows in his face; the meal has just been cooked. He sits with his back to the large container and stuffs his mouth with warm tofu and black beans, broccoli, corn nibs, and a vanilla cupcake. Steph and Jonah watch for a second before they tear open their own boxes.

"You know what I *really* think?" Portis asks between bites. "I think we're all dead and this is like, the in-between. Like purgatory. Or maybe *I'm* just dead, just me, and this is a bunch of bullshit I have to work through to get to heaven or hell or whatever. Those who died are innocent, and they've already been yanked up into heaven, and those I see as still being alive—like you two assholes—are the souls still trying to figure some shit out."

"You're an idiot," Steph whispers.

Jonah takes a large bite of veggie lasagna and considers Portis's idea; he never thought that this might *actually* be hell, like Sean had said to Dr. Z the night before.

In the distance, groups of demics jump out of module pieces and sift through the rubble. Two cadets stand high up on top of the truss with their hands shading their eyes. Paul's head pokes out of a module and he motions for Sean and someone else to join him. It takes a while for Jonah to locate her, but he finally spots Vespa standing directly under one of the rugged electric cycles still attached to the truss. She's looking up at its wheels.

"Who am I kidding? We're not dead. We're not that lucky," Portis says with a mouth full of broccoli. "We're just screwed." Then, after a moment of silence, he asks, "But we'll get out of here, right, guys?"

"Maybe," Steph answers. "Probably. I mean, I hope."

Jonah opens the other two doors of the container, and to his relief, there are hundreds of meals and dozens of jugs of water and synthetic milk.

"Jackpot," Portis says, pulling out a water jug. He places it to his lips and takes a long drink before passing it to the other two. As Jonah sips, he watches Vespa leap almost ten feet high and grab a rung of the truss. She pulls herself up, and after a series of acrobatic jumps and twists, she stands above the cycle. Then she stomps twice, and the vehicle plummets to the valley floor, where a giant blue and yellow parachute blasts out of its back and falls limply to the ground.

Before anyone else can touch it, Vespa is back on the soil, cutting away the parachute lines. Sean helps her pull the cycle onto its wheels. She then swings a leg over its back, and after fiddling with its controls, a headlight comes on. The three cadets hear applause, and then Vespa is off, heading straight for them.

Jonah raises a jug of water as Vespa gets near, and she pumps her hand in response. He sighs a breath of relief. *She must not hate me completely*. Vespa skids to a stop and turns the engine off. Steph runs a finger down the length of the black cycle before slapping Vespa's open palm.

"Now, if we can get the other two down, plus that big tank thing, we'll be in some sort of business," Vespa says.

"Want some breakfast?" Jonah offers her one of the foil boxes, and with it, a dozen unspoken apologies for being such a pain in the ass.

Vespa nods and takes the meal. After ripping open the foil and smelling the steam, she says, "What's your real name again, First Year?"

"Jonah Lincoln."

"Good to know, Firstie."

Jonah breathes a little easier. And he makes a vow never to hesitate again when she needs his help.

"And now what?" Portis asks, before chewing on the webbing between his fingers.

Vespa balls up the foil and throws it over her shoulder. "Now we get everyone some food. Immediately. Get morale up."

Portis takes his hand out of his mouth and climbs on top of the cycle. A grin stretches across his big brown face. "My dad used to have one just like this. You mind if I round up the troops?"

"You're goddamned lucky I'm hungry, cadet. Otherwise, I'd beat the shit out of you for the way you were acting earlier." She puts a steaming turkey leg in her mouth and sits down. "I still might."

• • •

Almost half the day passes. Everyone hopes for a ship from Thetis to somehow arrive, and they eat and drink until Paul tells them to stop, to ration and get back to work. A group of demics gathers clothes, and soon everyone finds a moment to change. To his surprise, Jonah finds one of his old green jumpsuits in the pile, and he's glad to be rid of his burnt shirt and torn pants. Griffin discovers a large cache of weapons wedged under the end of the truss, and each cadet now carries a long LZR-rifle. The other two cycles are dropped from the truss, but only one comes to life. Vespa works diligently on the tank-like truck for over an hour, but she can't get it to budge from the metal. They locate another large container of food. A couple of Second Years are put in charge of guarding everything they've found.

Like Jonah, Paul is growing increasingly restless. The Fourth Year and his team can't find the energizer, which Paul explains is an extra power supply for one of Thetis's smaller spacecrafts. Sean seems just as determined as Paul to find it, if not more so, and when the sun starts its descent, the two cadets become accusatory and pull in more kids to aid in the search, even recruiting some demics from Vespa's camp.

Jonah keeps thinking about the professor and the cook, Dr. Z and Garrett, the fire and the woman's voice. *Kids are free now*. Free from what? Sanity? And *run. Someone wants us to run and we're all just standing here, and night will be here soon.* Then what's going to happen? Is tonight Phase Two if last night was Phase One? He's crazy for just waiting around, isn't he? Shouldn't they be running?

While Paul, Sean, and the demics hunt for the power supply, Vespa calls all the nearby cadets in for a meeting.

"Nope. Sorry. No way. We're not doing any more of those," a girl's voice says from behind the huddle. Jonah and the other cadets spin around to find a thin demic girl scratching the underside of her chin with the barrel of a blue handgun. Her face is long and bronze, and her dark lips pull down in the corners as if they were attached to her stiff shoulders. The girl's hair is black and hangs in a messy ponytail. A bright white shirt, much too large for her, hides everything to her knees. There's no way she's older than fourteen.

"Where'd you get that gun?" Vespa asks.

"Same place you got yours, I guess."

"Demics don't get guns."

The girl shrugs and examines the weapon. "Well, I don't see how that's fair, so I'm keeping this little guy. And anything else you cadets lay claim to from here on out, I'm getting some of that, too. *And* no more of these meetings with just the cadets. The academic crowd needs to be informed of all plans from here on out, and we get a voice in what we do as a group. That all starts right now. So make room."

Vespa marches toward the girl and opens her hand, demanding the gun. They stare at each for a moment, waiting for the other to back down, and then Vespa lunges. The demic angles herself and steps backward, snatching Vespa's wrist with her left hand. There's a blur of white, a sharp cry from Vespa, and the circle of cadets is dumbfounded as the girl slams the Fourth Year onto her chest. A knee falls onto Vespa's back, her wrist still secure in the girl's hand.

"Get off me!" she screams. "Get this little shit off me!"

Jonah is so surprised he almost laughs. Steph and North move toward them, but the girl simply twists Vespa's wrist until the cadet yelps and tells them to back off.

The girl moves her knee onto the back of Vespa's neck. Calmly, she asks, "So, can I keep the gun? Do you mind? Or can I keep your wrist?"

"You can have the gun, all right?" Vespa spits a mouthful of dirt to the side. "Now get off me before I get pissed off."

The girl releases Vespa. She takes the barrel of her gun and scratches the back of her skull. "You guys itchy? I've been *super* itchy ever since the wormhole."

"What's your name?" Vespa growls, rubbing her wrist. Her cheeks are maroon with embarrassment.

"Brooklyn," the girl says.

"And you're a demic?"

"Sure. But you know we don't really like that term. Don't try to demean us because we're supposedly not as strong physically."

"But you're not. Well, most of you aren't, at least," North says.

"Where did you learn to fight like that?" Vespa asks.

Brooklyn releases the magazine of her gun into her palm and then locks back the slide, ejecting a single bullet from the chamber into the air. The bullet glides slowly in the low gravity, and she catches it with her other hand. Examining her weapon closely, she says, "My father was in the military."

Vespa looks on. "Oh, yeah? Which branch?"

The girl reloads her gun and says, "That's classified."

"You're still a demic to me," growls Ruth. It's the twin sister of Daniel, the boy who got sliced in two in front of Jonah's eyes when they crashed. This is the first time Jonah's heard her speak since they landed, since she found out her twin didn't survive.

Jonah likes the small girl's attitude, and ignoring Ruth, he asks, "If you were to join our meeting, what would the academics propose we do?"

The cadets wheel around, disgusted at his offer of inclusion, but he doesn't care anymore. Vespa grumbles audibly.

"Well, everything is pretty much useless here, if you haven't noticed," Brooklyn says. "We've been searching for specific parts to fix the communication devices, but they're either crushed beyond use, or missing. Some things are suspiciously missing, actually."

"So what? Are you saying people are stealing stuff?" Portis asks. "That the adults took them?"

Brooklyn watches the demics hustle about under Paul's direction. "Maybe. Probably. Or it's you and me and everybody else. It's survival of the fittest, right? Do anything you can to survive? And to some people, that means lying, cheating, and *most definitely* stealing. It doesn't matter if you're a genius or the toughest kid here. Everyone wants an edge. I can see it happening already, which isn't surprising. I'm sure some of you stole extra food rations and ammunition, not to mention the best clothes." She pulls at the sides of her huge shirt. "It's not going to be long until we smart kids revolt against the cadets, by the way. And if you were *half* as smart as we are, which I doubt you are, you'd start treating us as equals. Or at least pretend to. Otherwise, we'll leave you behind to fight each other for scraps while we're waving from a window on our way to Thetis."

"Just shut the hell up, kid," says Griffin.

"So, what do you think we should we do?" Jonah asks, receiving fewer stares this time.

"We've had our own meetings. Thetis, as you might know, has a telescope that monitors its moons closely. By our calculations, we're about forty rotation days away from being visible. Now, some of the academics, like myself, are taking the warning to run pretty seriously. I mean, you don't up and kill a couple people, take the time to write something creepy like that on their shirts, and then *not* get pissed when people don't respect your warnings. So some of us have decided to avoid tonight's sure massacre and move west, taking what we need from the crash site with us. We'll be able to close the visual gap by twenty or so days. Whatever it takes to double our chances. It's all about the numbers. It's *always* about the numbers."

Jonah's mood lifts higher than the mountains behind him. Twenty days? If they could flag down Thetis after twenty days, that would give him just enough time to get the cure Dr. Z talked about. He might just make it after all.

"And the rest of the demics?" Steph asks. "What do those geniuses think?"

"It doesn't matter what they think. They're too scared to go ten yards from where they are now. Couple of them haven't stopped crying since we got here. *I* voted to go in the direction that we've determined to be the west. I voted to run, like the shirt says. And I'm telling you, when you get a warning like that, you have to take it seriously."

Griffin kicks a charred spoon. "Yeah, *that's* real smart. There's a killer out there. We'd be walking right into a trap."

"Or there's a killer right here," Brooklyn says. "Maybe I'm having a conversation with the lion-headed asshole killer right now." Griffin touches the side of his hair. "Regardless, if you're not the killer, then you're nothing but a sitting duck right here. At the rate people are dying and going missing, no one is going to make it forty days. That's why I like twenty. Numbers, people. I'm telling you."

Jonah exhales a lungful of hope. He knows what he's going to do before anyone even asks him. Not that anyone will.

"Maybe the adults come back tonight, and they have a better plan," North says.

"Kids are free now, remember," Portis says. "Get it through your gross beard, man. They're not coming back. They're never coming back."

"Don't say that," Steph warns.

They all spin around at the sound of Paul yelling at a group of demics: "There's just *no way* it's not here!" Slowly, each kid in the search party breaks away to talk to the cadets guarding the food and water.

"We've got these now," Vespa says to Brooklyn, picking up her rifle. "We're not exactly sitting ducks."

Brooklyn waves over a small group of demics. "It's a long night, cadet. You're going to have to sleep sometime. Too many kids to watch over. *I'd* say you're a sitting duck. But hey, that's just my opinion. And I'm taking my opinion west. In like an hour."

As Vespa looks to be mulling things over, four demics cautiously approach: a handsome, tall boy with the sling; the freckled Aussie; an awkward, pale boy with an upturned nose and bright blue hair; and a tiny Korean girl holding a bandage over her one eye.

"Hey," says the boy with the sling. His blond curls are stuck to his sweaty forehead. "So, um, do we have a plan yet?"

Brooklyn looks at the cadets. "Screw these guys. We move in less than an hour. Find a bunch of bags and backpacks, stuff them with food and whatever else we can use, and then let's start for the wild, wild west."

"Hold on, little girl. Let's wait until tomorrow morning before anyone does anything. We haven't even found Module Eight yet," Steph says. "And I'm going to keep looking for stuff. It would be totally stupid to leave at this time of day, anyway."

Paul and Sean march in their direction, arguing and pointing fingers at each other. "We've looked all day and found what we can," Jonah speaks quickly. "I know this sounds kind of crazy, but I think I'm with Brooklyn. I say we move while there's still a little light. We'll take lanterns so we can travel at night, and one of the cycles can lead the way while the other one takes up the rear."

"The sooner we move, the sooner the telescope can see us and Thetis knows where to send a ship," says the boy with the sling.

"*If* they have a ship," Griffin says.

"They're supposed to," Brooklyn says.

Paul shoulders his way into the middle of the meeting. "Can't find the energizer thing anywhere, which is ridiculous because we've found all of Module Nine. There's no way it could just disappear... So, what are you all talking about? What did I miss?"

The demics shy away until Brooklyn twirls her handgun on her index finger. When it stops, the barrel points up at the sky, and she squints up the length of it. "We're talking about moving west, son. Soon. In under an hour. Pack your shit."

Paul laughs. "Yeah, right. *Stupid demic.*"

"She's talking about moving into Thetis's visual range," Vespa says. "If we can't find a way to communicate with Earth or Thetis and they don't know where we are, then we have about forty days until we're seen. She says we can cut it in half and they could find us in twenty." After a pause, she says, "I don't know, Paul, some of us don't think it's a terrible idea."

Paul looks incredulous, as if each kid just spat in his face. "I'm the highest-ranking cadet here and *I* say we stay right here. I'm sure Thetis already knows where we are, and they're just a day away from getting here. It's what, a twenty-six-hour flight for a smaller ship, right? Plus, all the last-second preparations. We take off now, then we miss the lifeboat. You're all fucking idiots. I hope you know that."

"That's true," the Korean girl says. She takes the bandage away from her face, revealing a festering green wound under her right eye. "I was thinking that if they were really coming, then they would have already shown up by now. But I didn't think of some of the outside variables. Why didn't I factor in the outside variables? Maybe they'll still come."

"See?" Paul asks. "Even a brainy demic nerd like her agrees with me."

"They would have been here by now," the boy with the sling says.

The Korean girl dabs at her wound. "Not if they needed time to prepare a ship. That could have taken them three to ten hours, depending on the readiness of the crew and if there were any technical problems to address before launch."

The boy throws up his one good arm. "Then that means they would show up well past nightfall, and maybe you don't remember that somebody's out there killing people. Somebody told us to run. Aren't you guys scared yet?"

"Let's just hedge our bets, then," Brooklyn says. "Some stay and some go. If the ship comes here, those kids send it off in the direction of those that head west. And vice versa. I think we can trust each other that much."

Jonah watches the eyes of everyone in the group, trying to read each of their minds, when Paul speaks up: "Listen, assholes. It's suicide to head into that jungle, then to try to deal with that huge lake or ocean or whatever's between the jungle and the west, not to mention what's beyond. You all saw those snouts last night, what kind of damage those dumb bastards can do. If you've read the reports, then you'd know there are *much much much* worse things out there than those clumsy things. Wait until you come face-to-face with the roopers, or the giant white mountain spiders and the jellyfish things with talons that just float around wherever they want, slicing shit up. This place is *not* friendly. It's much more hostile than what they've encountered on Thetis. And what if this traitor killer is in *your* camp? He'll be able to pick you off so easily down in the jungle. Once you're away from the safety of shelter and numbers, he'll strike immediately, I guarantee it. I'm the highest-ranking cadet, and I insist that we all stay."

"You don't speak for me. And your rank means absolutely nothing to me," Brooklyn says. "I've read the same reports and I'm packing up and leaving in an hour with however many kids—academics *and* cadets—want to join me."

"You're dead out there!" Paul barks.

"You're dead here," Brooklyn says matter-of-factly.

"You're not taking any of the food."

"Like hell I'm not. I'm taking my portion, and anyone who chooses to come with me will take their portion, too."

Paul slams his palm into Brooklyn's left shoulder. She spins like a tornado and then falls on her face, her gun bouncing away. Without considering the consequences, Jonah jumps in between them, pushing Paul backward, offering a hand to Brooklyn. His feet are suddenly swept out from underneath him. His cheek meets the black soil, and then Paul drops a knee onto the back of his head, and it's driven downward with all the Fourth Year's weight. Furious, Jonah swings his arms under his chest to push himself up, but they're slapped flat and helpless.

Before Jonah can try to get up again, he hears soil crunching behind him, and a second later, Paul's face lands just inches away from his own. They stare at each other for a moment before Paul's head is jerked upward by a small set of hands, and his neck is craned further back than it should ever go. Brooklyn, sitting on top of Paul's upper back, winks at Jonah, and Jonah can't help but laugh. And then she pulls back just a little bit more.

Paul wails in agony. His limbs whip every which way. North leaps over Jonah and wraps a huge arm around Brooklyn's neck. He chokes her off the cadet, and Jonah, again without considering what anyone will say, gets to his feet and delivers a crushing right hook to North's red beard. The boy whimpers and tips backward, releasing Brooklyn. The girl runs and stands beside Jonah, who prepares himself to keep fighting.

By the time Paul gets to his feet, sides have already been chosen. Behind Paul stand North, Steph, Griffin, the Korean demic, and the blue-haired boy. Vespa, Sean, Ruth, and Portis fall in next to Brooklyn and Jonah, with the boy in the sling hiding in their shadows.

CHAPTER SIX

Vespa negotiates for one of the cycles by letting Paul's camp keep the excess weapons, a fairly even trade in Jonah's eyes. Five more demics join their westward crew, plus Malix, an athletic black fifteen-year-old cadet with a square jaw and small ears, and Christina, a girly but tough Third Year with long sandy blonde hair. About three hours of daylight remain when they stand on the cliff's edge saying their goodbyes.

"I guess we'll go ahead and bury the dead for you then," Paul says to Vespa. Jonah stands just out of Paul's vision as he studies the jungle below, trying to map a route through.

Vespa frowns and pushes her shiny black hair out of her face. Her voice is soft. "Sorry to leave you with that, cadet. I guess with everything going on I forgot it was on today's agenda. Be really careful down there when you do it."

Their hands meet and pump, and then to Jonah's surprise, Paul yanks Vespa close to his chest. She wraps her arms around his waist and buries her forehead under his chin. Jonah looks on with shock. Vespa slowly pushes away, composes herself, and then offers her hand again.

"This is the stupidest thing you could do, cadet," Paul says. "Completely and totally and insanely stupid." Then, he almost whispers, "I only told you a little bit about what I saw last night. Looking for Module Eight. It was so messed up, Vespa, I can't even…I can't explain the rest of it, what happened. There's something horrible out there. There really is. Don't go."

"Don't *stay*. And it sounds like what you saw was just your head messing with you, Paul. Don't you get that someone *really* doesn't want us around for whatever they're planning? How do you not get that? I still want to get to Thetis. I really do. So I'm going to ask you *one more time* to come with us. Right now. Pack some shit up and let's go. Take the lead on this one."

He lets go of her hand and rubs the heels of his palms into his forehead. "*Damn it, V*. You're going to die out there. The shit I saw. You go down there and you're walking into the lion's den. Just stay here, we'll all bunker down and cover each other's backs, and if things get any worse, if one more major thing goes wrong, then we'll all march out of here together."

"Things *are* going to get worse up here. I can feel it. We all can feel it. I'm sure you can feel it, too. All I smell is death here. I'm going to survive all this shit and find my way to Thetis. One way or another."

Jonah wishes Vespa would stop asking Paul to come along. The guy would prefer it if Jonah were dead; he'd said so. He wouldn't have Jonah's back. But what's really on Jonah's mind is what Paul could have seen in the jungle that has scared him so much. Paul's never scared.

"Just stay alive and I swear we'll see each other in twenty-odd days," Vespa says. "You promise to send help west if it arrives?"

Paul spits over his shoulder—the glob floats away like a bubble—and tries to smile. "I'll think about it. You promise to swing by and pick us up on your way to Thetis if it shakes down like that?"

"I'll think about it," Vespa says. She then drops a leg over the cycle, revs the throttle, and tears away into a looping circle around her group. At Paul's feet, a cloud of dust hangs eerily in the air. Jonah can't help but notice the Fourth Year's hands are shaking.

"I *really* hope all that marine layer down there stays put and doesn't move any further east." Jonah turns to see Brooklyn in her huge white shirt. Her black hair is no longer in a ponytail, and she scratches the back of her head violently with both hands. "You see the marine layer? That cloud over the water? Hope it settles right where it is. We don't need that."

Far beyond the jungle, a thick greenish-gray blanket creeps over the blue sea. The horizon is hazy, and Jonah doesn't see the island he noticed the day before. "What are we going to do once we get to the water?"

Brooklyn stops scratching and shrugs. "I think we'll figure it out when we get there. By the time we're at the beach, with all the nerds we're traveling with, we should have a couple good plans to work from. I hope so, at least. But we should definitely be able to get to the beach and set up camp by nightfall."

Jonah keeps looking for the island. "You think that's possible?"

"Sure. Even if we make twenty-minute miles, there's no reason we shouldn't reach the sand by sunset. From what I can tell, we're about three and three-quarters of a mile away from the water. Those are my calculations."

"And that's why you're a demic, and I'm not." He cringes before adding, "I mean an academic. Why you're an academic. Sorry about that."

"Oh, right. Ha. I was actually just kidding about that before. We don't mind the nickname. Who cares, you know? I was just giving you guys shit because you were being such jerks. We call you ca-dicks behind your backs, by the way. Or at least I do."

Jonah tries not to, but he laughs, and the sound hangs over the cliff like a cloud. Dozens of kids, including Paul, eye the two of them. Brooklyn whistles and rocks on the balls of her feet while Jonah composes himself. He likes this girl, and he thinks they could maybe, possibly, be friends. The thought makes him want to walk away. Things don't go well when he makes friends. They usually get bored of him, or join another crowd and gang up on him. Or they die like Manny. Still, he stays there next to her, enjoying her company.

"So, anyway," Brooklyn says. "We should hit it before that marine layer stuff comes over the trees and blocks what little sunlight we'll have."

"You still think this is a good idea?"

"Man, don't be such a wuss."

They walk past Ruth, her long naked toes dangling over the edge of the cliff, an LZR-rifle strapped to her back. The cadet's pale face is empty, completely devoid of emotions, and it drops to her left every few seconds as if someone speaks to her. To Jonah, it looks like she's looking for Daniel. She rolls her neck and clenches her fists, cracking every knuckle in her hands. She then drives a single fingernail down the back of her neck, leaving a long beading trail of blood. Jonah wishes she'd stayed behind at the crash site.

Vespa stops the cycle and looks over the kids who wait for her to drop her front wheel over the cliff: there's the long-haired and bullied Michael; Bidson, the big walrus boy with his arm stuck above his head; two of the girls from his botched module rescue, Aussie and Rosa; the boy with the sling, Brian; and, unfortunately, the three hackers, all of whom steer mostly clear of the cadets, whispering amongst themselves. The youngest hacker, a chubby boy with faded pink hair, jabs his finger in the air like he's working out a calculation. It's an odd group, peers Jonah thinks she wouldn't associate much with, or at all, if the circumstances were different. She nods at Jonah and Brooklyn, and then, with the toes of her newfound shoes, she pushes herself past Ruth. Jonah waits for her to look back and search for Paul in the crowd, but she doesn't. Then over she goes with her fingers pumping the brakes. The group heads west.

• • •

Three hours later, just minutes after sunset, the kids stagger out of the jungle onto a silver beach that stretches for miles in both directions. The mountains to the north loom black above the valley. Jonah's arms ache from hacking through the trees with the small kitchen knife, his legs wobble from the bogs of hot water and freezing cold grass, and after a few steps onto the sand, he falls to his knees in gratitude for making it this far. Whatever spooked Paul the night before left them alone. Or watched from a distance. Or went after somebody else.

As Jonah picks himself up, he notices hundreds of shallow lines in the sand, all in pairs, all leading out of the water and up into the jungle. The lines are about five feet apart, and in between, the sand is perfectly smooth.

The cadets nervously gather wood from the lip of the jungle, and a half hour later, they sit around a raging purple fire, passing out foils of food. Vespa and Malix flank the group, rifles drawn and ready. Everyone is on edge, and hardly anyone has spoken since leaving the wreckage. It's on all their minds: Are the kids who stayed behind getting slaughtered? Are they hanging from trees? And are they next?

Rosa rips open her dinner, and it immediately falls upside down in the sand. She lets out a lone, haunting sob before kicking the food into the fire. "I hate it here so much. I don't deserve this. I really don't. I wish I were dead."

"As if you're the only one here who wants *you* dead," mumbles the second-oldest hacker. He has bushy brown hair and a gap between his teeth.

"Hey, demic, what's your name?" Vespa asks.

"Didn't I tell you?"

"No," she says.

"Then it must not be any of your fucking business."

Jonah cringes, awaiting Vespa's retribution. Quickly, though, Bidson says, "It's Shelly. His name is Shelly."

"Shut up, asshole," the boy says, kicking sand in his direction. "Who asked you, ya elephant? Seriously? Everyone calls me Richter, my middle name."

With her eyes glued to the jungle, Vespa backpedals until she stands directly behind the hacker. "Well, little Shelly, how about you stop being such a dick?"

"I'll think about it," he grumbles.

"That was an order, not a suggestion."

Richter sticks his tongue out and mocks being scared. Christina tosses a new log into the fire, sending up a column of sparks. Jonah watches as it turns to smoke. He wishes they hadn't stopped for the night. His time is running out.

Brian clears his throat. "Excuse me, Ruth? I just want to say that I'm just really sorry about your brother. What happened to him, I mean. He and I used to play that game Skyler Bomb 3 a lot. Like every morning after breakfast. Daniel was my friend. Maybe he mentioned me..."

Ruth doesn't look up, but her jaw flexes, and Brian trails off. She has a ticking clock, too, Jonah thinks, but hers will be much more violent, much more unpredictable than his blood disease. He's actually grateful it's dark; he doesn't want anyone to see his eyes in case they're nothing but solid blue marbles.

"Hey, you know, maybe we should go around in a circle and introduce ourselves," Bidson offers. "That way everyone can—"

"Go for it, fatty," Richter says. "Do it up. Seriously. You first. Wow us with your shitty life."

The oldest hacker with the black bangs laughs. "And holy shit, put that big ugly arm of yours down already. You're freaking me out with that fat meat hook."

"I can't," Bidson whispers. He yanks down on his arm, but it pops right back up. "Ever since the wormhole, it's been like this. The muscles...they've fused or something. I wish I could put it down, believe me."

"Well, I'll remember to use you as a clothesline if I get my shirt wet," Richter says, laughing.

Jonah opens his mouth to defend everyone else affected by the wormhole when Bidson stands to address the group.

"Sure, fine, I'll go." His arm bounces as he rotates. "My name is Bidson Woods. I'm from Long Beach, California, and I play the piano. That's something I've been doing since the age of three and something I hope to do again someday...if my arm ever relaxes... Um. I have one older sister who lives with my parents. Her name is Alice, and I miss her a lot right now. My main area of study at school was evolutionary biology, and I was aiming to get my degree in environmental law for a career in conservation science, but then this opportunity came up, to join the Athens community on Thetis, and..." The boy looks around to see if anyone is still listening. He eventually settles his eyes on Jonah, and the two of them stare solemnly at each other as he says, "I just couldn't turn it down. How could I turn it down? But now here I am. On Achilles. With all of you guys. I should have turned it down."

"And I bet you're very, very hungry," Richter adds with a smile. Vespa smacks him in the back of the head.

"Ouch! Screw off! Seriously!"

"I'm Aussie, if you didn't already know," the redhead says, shooting to her feet. "I'm originally from a small town outside of Cincinnati, in Kentucky, but we moved to Pasadena when I was ten. Next week is my seventeenth birthday. I'm an artist, a painter. I like math a lot, too. I was on track to be valedictorian. Um. What else?"

"You forgot to say that you're really super hot," the oldest hacker says. "Like, super duper."

Aussie's cheeks turn maroon, and she falls silent.

The boy smacks his lips, laughs, and then pushes his bangs away from his dark eyes. "Hell, I'll go. I'm Hopper. *Hi, Hopper*. I'm um, well I'm a human being from the planet Earth. Male. Caucasian. Gemini? No, wait. Shit. I'm a Libra or something. Whatever. I really like computers *and* girls, in that order. But only sometimes, Red. Only sometimes. For fun, I enjoy crashing on uninhabited moons in galaxies far, far away, and *then* if there's enough time, I like to be hunted down by maniacs who write creepy messages on the shirts of their victims. It's kind of an expensive hobby, though, so I might find something new to do. Checkers, maybe. Fashion?"

No one speaks. Jonah thinks he can feel a pair of eyes on him, but when he looks around, he finds everyone staring at Hopper, who smiles and sits back down. Sean then tosses a log in the fire and coughs.

"I'm Sean," he says. "That's it."

"And I'm Brooklyn from New Boston."

"Her dad was in the military," Vespa adds sarcastically.

"You know it, girl." Brooklyn smiles.

"My name is Portis, and I have four older sisters, one of whom is waiting for me on Thetis. She's one of the few survivors. And I'm telling you guys right now, I plan on seeing her again. Soon. So let's get my ass to Thetis for a heartwarming reunion, okay?" The boy then solemnly puts his wrist in his mouth for a second before adding, "And I can't stop biting myself since the wormhole. I just can't."

Jonah then stirs and gains a few people's attention. Barely audible over the fire, he says, "I'm Jonah Lincoln, and I'm from all over Ohio. I'm a cadet. And nothing else really stands out about me."

No one else volunteers; either they don't care or are too tired. Jonah had hoped to hear some of Vespa's backstory, even just where she's from, but she moves away from the group before Jonah can finish his last sentence.

Ruth, Christina, and Brooklyn take up the next watch while some of the kids fall asleep. Jonah just lies there, staring at where the cliff and the wreckage should be.

Vespa sits with her back to the water eating a boxed meal. She catches Jonah looking at her and asks, "How sure are you again, Firstie? That you saw the other side out there?"

"Pretty sure." He keeps his voice flat and distant, acting as if he doesn't care she just caught him staring. It's frustrating it's on his mind with everything going on, but he'd really like to move and sit right next to her. Maybe touch her shoulder with his. "I saw land out there. Maybe it was an island, or maybe it was the other side. It was the first thing I noticed after the crash."

"Maybe it was a mirage, though," Sean offers. He lies on his back, looking up at the stars of the Silver Foot. "Like your mind playing tricks on you under all that stress. Or from the wormhole."

"That's definitely possible. But if it's clear tomorrow morning, we should be able to see it. Otherwise, I don't know what we're going to do," Jonah says.

With a jug of water between his long legs, Hopper says, "I just wish I had a sheaf with some GPS action, ya know? Then at least we'd have a map. Think about how much help *that* would be. We're blind out here."

Hearing the words "sheaf" and "blind" gives Jonah a pause, causing him to close his eyes and hug his arms around his waist. He can't tell anyone about his disease. That is, until a ship from Thetis arrives and he can beg for some medicine.

"I just wish I had my other glasses right now," Sean says. "The ones with all the movies on them. They were locked up in Module Eight's media level."

Hopper puts the cap back on the water jug. "We all lost a lot of things, bro. Some people are pissed they lost their friends or their lame-ass teachers, but *I'm* pissed I lost my Mini Sheaf X13. That's what I really want right now, you know, to keep myself entertained on this stupid hike."

"Why? What does it do?" Sean asks.

"Man, it does everything. *Everything.* It's the most powerful piece of equipment I've ever tooled around with. I jail-broke that bad boy in seconds and then spent five months adding my own software, my own codes, codes I stole... Damn, you know, I bet I could probably contact Earth with that thing, from right here on this freaking beach. I could probably hack into Thetis's system and just talk, talk, talk away with some hot chicks on Earth. Hear about how much they miss me, or just what's going on in the war."

Vespa sits up. "Are you telling me that we're down here, and *instead* we could be combing the wreckage site for your sheaf and maybe talking to Thetis or Earth?"

"Man, I already found it with the other busted-up sheafs. It's burnt to a crisp. Not one piece of it was salvageable. Worst tragedy so far, if you ask me."

Those listening remain silent, including Jonah. *All* the sheafs were destroyed? Good thing he grabbed his, even if it is missing amongst the wreckage. There's still a chance he could somehow get it back, as slight as it might be. The hacker wipes some sand from his clothes, twists in his seat, and opens his backpack. "But I *do* have something else y'all might like. Sneaked it out of the tank the day of the crash."

In the boy's palm sits a square piece of black metal. Several clear tubes circle it, pulsing red and yellow.

Sean immediately gets on his hands and knees and crawls over. His face drains of color. "Wait. Is that a—"

"A homing device? A mother-fucking homing beacon?" Hopper asks. "Yes, ladies and gentlemen. Yes, it is. And it was the only one I could find in all that mess. All the other ones from *all the other vehicles,* and from all the modules, were missing. But whoever stole them missed this little guy."

"I can't believe you found that," Sean whispers.

Hopper smiles, brings the device up to his fuzzy lips, and kisses it.

CHAPTER SEVEN

After sixteen hours, most of the kids are hard at work with full stomachs. The sky is a dark gray that's two or three shades from black. An hour ago, just off shore, hundreds of arm-sized fish leaped high above the water, crashing together, wrapping their long tails around each other's abdomen, emitting red flashes. The noise and lights woke anyone who was sleeping, and Vespa officially called it a night.

Jonah didn't sleep. Not for a second. He just lay there, reliving the crash over and over and over. And when he wasn't reliving the crash, he kept telling himself that if he's going to survive, then he has to commit to stop being this passive, quiet Firstie who hesitates first, acts second. He needs to be aggressive, confident, and loud. As the others slept around the dwindling purple fire, Jonah studied their faces, the way they breathed and where they placed their hands, and he realized that none of these kids were going to save him, not even Vespa. It was up to him.

Hopper's homing device brought new energy to the group, but it also brought an intense anger from Vespa and a few others.

After all, he held a key to being rescued, and he kept it from everyone. Vespa got right up into his face.

"Listen," he said before stuffing it back into his bag. "I got a really, really bad vibe from some of those cadets. That Paul guy, holy shit, he was a little *too* intense back there, don't ya think?" Jonah flinched and waited for Vespa to punch Hopper in the gut, but she didn't bat an eye as the boy continued: "The way that guy wanted to find that power supply and wouldn't listen to anyone else? Like, anyone at all, as if he knew *exactly* what was going on? He was getting *real* buggy, real freaky, and I didn't trust him, *and* I didn't trust that idiot Griffin and his stupid lion haircut or that Steph chick. I wasn't going to tell anyone about my little find until we were far enough away from those freaks."

"And so what? You trust *us*?" Vespa asked.

"I *used* to. Until you started going bat-shit crazy all the time. I mean, what's your problem, anyway?"

Vespa opened her arms. "Are you insane? Look around, asshole! Take your pick! How many problems do you or I possibly need?"

"Well, now you have one less problem." Hopper patted the backpack. "If Thetis starts looking for the tank that was on that truss, well, they'll find you and me and everyone here on this beach. Bingo bango."

"They'll find *all of us*," Vespa said. "Everyone back at the wreckage, too. Plus, any adults we can find." After a deep breath, she turned to the rest of her camp and asked, "Anybody have anything else on them we should all know about? Anyone have a tiny spacecraft in their back pocket? Maybe a portable wormhole that opens up right on Thetis? Because that would be helpful right about now."

Nobody answered. And then they started to sleep.

Now in the gray morning, on his third wind, Jonah drops a long red sapling a dozen feet from the fire. Brian and Michael drag it to Rosa, who works vines strategically around the wood, connecting it to the others. Jonah turns and looks up the beach, hoping to see the cycle's square headlight, hoping to hear from

Malix and Sean that they don't need to be building these two rafts because they've found a way around the body of water. The rafts are supposed to be a distant Plan B.

The demics work much faster than Jonah anticipates. They argue over calculations and weight requirements, wind and the length of the paddles to be cut. Richter and Aussie direct Portis to cut the wood into even lengths with his rifle. After each raft has thirty-five pieces across, Michael requests two thicker logs to be attached underneath as crossbeams. Daybreak is almost upon them as eight oars are carved to Richter's demands.

Jonah, sore and with nothing more to do, sits with his feet in the water and waits for sunrise.

A square white light appears up the beach, cupping the tide line, and Jonah rises, clenching two handfuls of silver sand. *Here we go,* he thinks. Vespa is the first to reach Malix and Sean, just out of earshot of Jonah. Her shoulders slump, and she looks west out over the water. He releases the sand from his hands.

"So?" Jonah asks, approaching with Hopper, Portis, and Rosa. The first hints of white and purple appear overhead. The sun is about to rise.

"So, nothing," Malix says. He looks disheveled and shaky. He kills the engine and slides off the seat. "The beach just keeps going and going and going. But when we got about a mile up, there were some, um—"

Sean interrupts: "There were some ugly zombie dog things that chased us around for a while. Really vicious bastards. But then the beach just keeps going and going in the same direction."

"*Son of a bitch,*" Vespa says, sighing.

"How are the rafts coming along?" Sean asks.

"They're done," Rosa says. "But it's suicide to just start rowing into nothingness."

Jonah watches Malix dig at his fingernails. Something's wrong. Something he's not telling the rest of them. He's about to ask the cadet what else they saw when Hopper sticks his head into the huddle. "But it's not nothingness, ya freaks. Look west. Our soldier boy Jonah was right. There *is* something out there."

They turn to see a piece of land straight ahead—no more than a mile wide—illuminated by the rising sun.

Jonah exhales. "I knew it. Thank you."

"Thank the gods," Vespa whispers.

"But shit, what is it? An island?" Portis asks.

"Maybe," Hopper says. "That, or the tip of a peninsula."

Vespa's eyes go wide. "Wouldn't that be nice?"

"*That* would mean our luck was changing," Hopper says.

The kids pull the two rafts to the water's edge, and Christina drops the eight oars in a clanging pile. Vespa swings a leg over the cycle's back and pushes it toward a raft with her toes.

"Wait. Whoa. Hold on," Michael says. "How much does that thing weigh?"

"I don't know," Vespa says. "But not much on Achilles with this kind of gravity. I'd say—"

"By the looks of it, I'd say it weighs about a thousand pounds, maybe less, on Earth. Which means it's probably about three hundred and thirty-four pounds here. Rounding up, of course," Brian says.

"Of course," Portis mumbles, gnawing on his shoulder.

"Shut up," Brooklyn says. She grabs her stomach and looks like she's going to be sick, and then she stumbles away. Concerned, Jonah follows her, but she waves him off and takes some deep breaths. Then she furiously scratches her head.

"It's still too heavy to put on the rafts," Michael says. "Plus, we wouldn't be able to move it around if we need to distribute our weight to keep from tipping."

Vespa laughs. "Well, too bad, because we can't leave it behind. It's much too valuable. So somebody help me get this on board one of these things."

"Michael's right," Brian says. "The rafts are specifically designed to get just the fifteen of us across the water. We put that cycle on one of these, and it's going to throw it off. We encounter any kind of waves, it'll either sink us or crush someone. You have to listen to us. We know what we're talking about."

Ruth snorts indignantly and chuckles.

"We're serious," Michael says.

"I'm with Vespa on this," Jonah says. "That cycle is way too important to just throw away."

"Maybe we build another raft and tether it behind, then. We'll tie it down," Vespa says. "I'm sure you demics can whip that up in a couple of minutes. I'll help. We'll all help. It'll be easy."

"Sure," Brian says. "That, we can do. Okay. Fine. We'll need roughly sixteen trunks to start with and then..."

Sean rubs his chin. "Or *maybe* what we do is have some of us stay here and take the cycle in the other direction, *down* the beach this time. And if it's a dead end, we make another raft and catch up with you."

"Hell no," Brooklyn says. She looks green in the face. "Are you kidding? No splitting up. No way."

"Of course not," Vespa agrees.

"You okay?" Jonah whispers to Brooklyn.

She stands up straight and forces a smile. "Yeah, yeah. Just dehydrated."

"Well," Sean says. "The thing is...I'm not a very good swimmer. If I fall off, or the raft flips over, I'm pretty much dead."

"I can't swim at all," Rosa says.

"Me neither," says the youngest hacker.

"Well, big deal. We'd jump in and grab whoever falls off. I'll grab you. I'm actually a really good swimmer," Jonah says. His body grows hot and stiff, as if dipped in wax, as it always does when he talks about himself.

Vespa turns toward the island. "Absolutely! We'd jump in and help anyone. No big deal."

Sean sits on the sand. For the first time, Jonah notices a scared look in his eyes. "I'm sorry, guys, but I'm not going."

"*Sean.*" Jonah offers him his hand. "You don't need to know how to swim. Seriously. I have your back."

The cadet lets the hand hang over his head and says, "Look, I have a thing about water, okay? I'm not going. None of you guys can make me go, either. You're not my commanding officer... And remember, we're free now to do whatever we want, as morbid as that sounds. Right? And this is what I want. We haven't even looked at the one other viable option, to go *down* the beach. So give me the cycle, and if one or two more people want to come with me, then we'll check it out. Or, hell, I'll just go by myself."

"Hey, man," Malix says. "Just because we saw th—"

"Shut up, Malix," Sean snaps. The two of them share a look until Sean buries his face in his shoulder.

"Hey. Whoa. What else happened this morning?" Jonah asks. "Something's wrong with you two. There's something you're not telling us. No secrets. Not now. What'd you guys see?"

"Just some zombie dogs," Sean says.

"Zombie dogs," Malix repeats.

"If you two are putting us in any more danger than we already are," Vespa threatens, "I'm going to tether you both to the rafts by your wrists. What happened out there? What did you see? Cadets, *now*."

"You have to tell us," Rosa whispers.

Sean squints into the horizon. "We didn't see anything but a hell of a lot of sand and a bunch of weird dogs that scared the absolute shit out of us. That's it. I swear."

"I just want to hurry up and go." Malix looks over his shoulder. "Let's just go. Let's get on the water."

Rosa's chin quivers. "Please don't lie to us."

The cadets don't say another word. There's a new, unspoken urgency within the group to move, amplified by Malix's jumpiness.

"We should go," Michael says. "If there's someone hunting us down, we should go."

"Yes," Aussie agrees.

"That's it. We're leaving right now." Vespa stands over Sean. "And you're coming with us."

"No, I'm not."

"*Asshole*. How would we even meet up again or know what's going on with you?" Brooklyn asks. "We don't have any ways to communicate."

Sean swings his rifle around to his chest. "If I'm in trouble, I'll shoot this straight up in the air, two shots. Over and over in twos, and I'll wait for you to answer me. If I find another way west, and if I think you should come to me, I'll shoot in threes, and if I'm coming your way because I've come to a dead end, I'll shoot in fours."

"I'll go with him." Everyone turns to see Ruth standing with her toes in the water. Sean cringes but doesn't say a word.

"Good," Hopper mumbles. "Awesome. I'm *totally* on board with this plan."

"No," Brooklyn says. "You guys, we're not doing this. Pull your shit together and have some faith."

"Man, faith is for suckers." Hopper laughs. "Faith is what the uneducated cling to."

Ruth responds by sitting next to Sean and hugging her knees.

Vespa runs her hands through her black hair. "Fine. Do what you want. I'm not your mother. That it, then? Does anyone else want to go down the beach? I can't afford to lose any more cadets, though, so don't even think about it."

Everyone looks at Rosa, but she says, "I trust you guys if I fall in. But we should go soon because I don't want to be out there when the sun sets."

"I agree," Brooklyn says. There's something off about her stare, Jonah notices. She looks like she might faint at any second, and he stands beside her, waiting to catch her in case she does.

"You lose that cycle and you're a dead man. I want it back," Vespa says to Sean before looking back over the horizon.

After a few minutes, the cycle leans in the soggy sand as Ruth climbs behind Sean. The kids say a round of goodbyes, and Jonah wonders how many more times this will happen. Sean's right; everyone's free to do whatever he or she wants. If a demic wants to stay right here, on this very spot and make sand castles for the rest of his or her life, then what can the rest of them do about it?

Jonah approaches the cycle and waits for Ruth to look at him, but she just stares at the back of Sean's head. "Take care, Ruth." He then offers his hand to Sean who takes it and pulls him in surprisingly close.

"Run," Sean whispers. "Keep running."

"I…am. I will," Jonah says, stunned. "You should, too. You shouldn't leave the group."

"I know. But there's something I need to check first."

"What did you see this morning, Sean? Tell me. What do you need to check?"

"My sanity, man. My sanity."

They share a serious, confusing moment of eye contact until Malix comes in for a long, awkward handshake.

Sean waits until the rafts bob on the almost nonexistent waves before turning the cycle on. Everyone wades in with their packs and guns held high above their heads, and once they struggle to climb aboard and everyone settles in, Jonah waves to Sean. The cycle speeds down the beach, Sean's right hand out, his two fingers making a peace symbol.

"We'll never see them again," Brooklyn says over Jonah's shoulder. Color has come back to her cheeks.

Hopper clutches his backpack to his chest. "Screw 'em."

The oars are distributed to the strongest on each raft. Jonah rows with Brooklyn, Bidson, and Christina, and the other boat moves under the direction of Vespa, Portis, Malix, and Michael. Everyone falls into a rhythm, pushing west on the crystal blue sea. Below them, fat green objects—like giant gumdrops—pulse up and down and dance in circles around dark red boulders, emitting thick yellow clouds of goo from their tops. Vertical gray discs claw along the bottom in packs of a hundred or more, shark fins with feet, Jonah thinks, and they change direction like birds, sweeping over large sections of rocks in seconds. There are translucent rods here and there, reflecting the rising sun, diving to ram the backs of the gray discs, where they then split in two and disappear. The demics are fast to point out every new species, every color, the interesting way something moves. Jonah looks when he can, but he tries to keep his eyes on the brightening horizon. They're moving slowly, but at least they're moving. Everything can still be okay as long as they keep going west.

Sitting cross-legged in the middle of Jonah's raft, Hopper cups his mouth and yells, "You okay over there, Pissy? Good news! If the water gets on your pants, no one will know if you pissed them or not!"

Michael steels his jaw and refuses to acknowledge the calls. Jonah hears Richter on the other raft cackle and whoop.

"I said," Hopper yells, "You can piss your pants if you want and—"

Jonah bats his oar sideways, drenching Hopper's back with a slow-moving swath of water. Brooklyn doubles over in laughter.

"Dude!" Hopper cries. "Watch it! What the hell!"

"You make fun of him again, and I swear I'm going to grab you by your hair and throw you in," Jonah growls. Everyone is silent. The sentence feels warm and tingly coming out of his mouth, not because he threatened someone, but because it's something Vespa would say.

"You almost got the homing device wet, ya dipshit!" Hopper shouts.

Jonah catches Brooklyn's blue eyes. He can tell she wants Jonah to pounce, to teach this kid a lesson. But that's not who he wants to become, not some hothead. He merely wants a bit of the illusion that he is.

"I'm just going to say this once," Jonah finally says. "You call Michael names again, if I hear you make fun of him just one more time, I'll break your damn teeth."

"And I'll hold you down when he does it," Brooklyn adds.

Hopper rolls his eyes and hugs his pack closer to his chest.

"And tell your two punk friends that I said that," Jonah says loud enough for the other hackers to hear, his skin cooling from the ocean air.

"I'll make it a priority, Captain Dipshit," Hopper mumbles.

The rafts stay close together, bobbing and pushing, and once they are a few hundred yards from the shore and can no longer see the sea floor, the rowers take a five-minute break to pass around a water jug. The sun is hot on their shoulders, and the demics complain to each other about not thinking of building a shelter on board.

"Whoa!" Aussie yells, pointing at the water in front of her raft. She twists and follows something that heads in the other direction, "Holeeeeee... Anyone else see that? Wow!"

"See what, Red?" Hopper calls.

"That black thing? It was like ten feet long!"

The kids all look overboard. Within seconds, Jonah spots one. It's black, gray, and longer than the raft. It has stubby arms and legs, and he counts two or three dorsal fins running down its back. At the end of its tail is another pair of feet, totally different from the others, plate-like and webbed, with long white claws. And then the creature is out of sight, heading toward the beach. Jonah bobs up and down, mesmerized, smiling but scared, hoping it's friendly.

In a few more seconds, everyone's spotting one or two, and then a herd swims underneath, body-to-body, racing to get somewhere first. The water churns with greasy foam all around them. The rafts rock up and down; the crossbeams are scraped and thumped. Jonah and the others work hard to keep themselves from tipping over, following orders from Michael and Aussie on where to move to maintain balance.

"Look!" Christina yells, pointing at the shore.

The creatures launch themselves at the beach, arching high in the air before flopping onto the sand. The kids can hear their soft bellies pound against the surface, one after another, until more than a thousand gather all along the shoreline. After a short congregation, the animals scurry up the beach, disappearing into the jungle.

So that's what all those lines on the beach were, Jonah thinks. "We should start naming things."

Brian laughs. "Um… Hoppers, maybe? Seems appropriate."

"I like." The hacker laughs. "We're distant relatives, obviously."

A large thump on the crossbeams sends Brian gently rolling into Jonah's legs. "My apologies," he says, sighing. Jonah helps shove him back to the middle, worried about how aggressive the creatures are becoming. That was the biggest bump yet. He dunks his oar back in the water just as two of the creatures breach the surface like rockets, arching thirty feet or more until they land on their long sides with a huge splash. They look like dinosaurs.

"Freaky." Hopper laughs.

"So cool!" Richter calls.

Vespa says, "Just watch out!"

Jonah finds himself actually enjoying the show, but as more and more breach the water and some fight under the surface, he senses a roiling panic. Not only in the other kids and himself, but also in the hoppers. Up and down the coast now, the creatures leap high out of the water, flopping and splashing. *That's enough,* Jonah thinks, and he whips his head at the island in the distance. His heart sinks when he sees how far away it still is. One of the creatures lands just a few feet away from Jonah's corner of the raft, covering him with water, knocking him toward the middle.

"I think something's going on!" he yells.

"I'm done with this shit!" Malix shouts from the other raft, which has spun completely around. It drifts farther and farther away, no matter how hard they paddle. "It's starting to get—Holy shit!"

Between the rafts, something monstrous blasts high out of the water with one of the hoppers thrashing in its teeth. Jonah falls backward onto Brian in a wordless stupor. Rosa screams.

The creature is over sixty feet long, with side fins that stretch into the air for what seems like miles. It looks like a living airplane, with hubcap-sized eyes and translucent skin. When it finally twists and nosedives back into the water, Jonah can see its small blue brain, a network of veins and arteries, and a curving dark skeleton of bones. On the peak of its spine, there's another mouth of teeth, opening and closing at a great speed, eating the air and whatever hopper bits fly past. The creature slams back into the water with the bloody hopper howling and kicking, creating a strong, rippling wave. Jonah's raft rises and then dips at a sharp angle—too sharp—and not many can hang on to the slippery wood. Jonah's arm gets hooked under Brian's leg, and they somersault and crash into Hopper. Then the three of them enter the warm sea, tangled together and upside down.

Jonah twists away and swims for the surface, his mind racing with a white, popping panic. *Get out,* he thinks. *Get out before that thing finds you.* Just as he's about to get a lungful of air, someone from the raft falls on his head, bending his neck backward. He sinks with his eyes closed. A body tumbles over him and he reaches out, snatching the person's wrist. Without thinking, he yanks upward and releases. He opens his eyes to see it's Christina, and he swims after her, refusing to look anywhere but up. When he breaks the surface, he finds Christina and Bidson pawing at the side of the raft, trying desperately to climb back on. Rosa lies flat in the center, her face frozen in horror.

"Help!" Hopper splashes nearby. With the airplane fish still on his mind, Jonah pulls the hacker toward the raft. Malix shouts and leaps from the other raft onto the deck of Jonah's, and he yanks Christina up, flinging her on top of a shrieking Rosa.

With Vespa and Richter and everyone else from the other raft shouting above him, Jonah helps push Bidson and Hopper out of the water. *Where's Brooklyn?* He scans the water around him, and then her hands appear on the opposite side of the raft. She climbs on board and crawls over the wood to grab Jonah by the elbow. But just then, something below barrels against his shins, pushing him away from the raft with a jolt. Brooklyn falls face-first, and they both go under.

When he opens his eyes, the first thing he sees is Brooklyn looking over his shoulder, a string of bubbles shooting out of her mouth. The shock in her eyes tells Jonah what's coming, and before he can even make a guess of what he should do, Brooklyn plants her hands on the top of his head and pushes. She goes up, he goes down, and the back of his skull is rammed with what feels like a metal girder. He completely flips over and finds the scarred belly of one of the translucent monsters an inch from his nose.

Jonah twists away, right into a maroon patch of water, and he keeps his eyes on the beast until it disappears. But before he can gather his thoughts, another one finds him. It's bigger than the last, and it speeds out of the murky blue water flashing several rows of sharp teeth. As it gets nearer, its big yellow eyes roll back into its head and glow bright green. Instincts take over and Jonah draws in his long legs; he's on autopilot, his only thought to be ready to kick, and to kick hard.

Brooklyn suddenly appears above him with her LZR-rifle in her hands. She aims at the monster and pulls the trigger. A white current sparks and crawls along the barrel of the gun, but it doesn't fire. The creature keeps coming, its long fins swooping at its sides, and it draws back its lips to reveal a wall of thick silvery gums. Jonah thrusts out his feet the same time Brooklyn slams down the butt of her weapon. They both hit the fish's upper lip, stunning it, and then Brooklyn slams the rifle down again, knocking two long teeth out of its gums. The beast jerks away, but not before its second mouth grazes Jonah's forearm. He screams a muddled scream and several hoppers speed off in the other direction.

His lungs burn and ache. He grabs Brooklyn's hand, and they swim upward. They're one foot from the surface when the water all around them lights up with flashes of blue. Jonah spins to see two mouths of teeth coming right at him, and then there's a burst of light, and the beast explodes into a mess of bone, blood, and green guts. They push their heads above the surface and enter a roaring wall of noise of shouts and rifle fire. There's a hand in front of his face and he takes it, and a second later, he and Brooklyn heave and cough on the surface of a raft.

"Where's Brian?" Rosa jumps on Jonah's back and pounds on

him until he rolls over into the blinding sun. His forearm throbs and bleeds.

"Stop. Please stop," he says, almost choking.

"Jonah!" she screams in his face. "Where's Brian?"

"What?" He's confused. There's too much noise. The sun is too bright. His arm feels like it's on fire. "Brian?"

Rosa pounds her tiny fists onto his chest. "He's still down there!"

Jonah pushes her off, trying to comprehend what she's saying while still seeing all the mouths of teeth coming at him. Brian with the sling. Brian with the sling is missing. He's still down there. *He's still down there.* His brain snaps to life and he staggers to his feet, tripping over Brooklyn, falling back on his hands and knees. On the other raft, Vespa stands with her legs wide apart, aiming and shooting into the sea. Portis stands next to her, laughing maniacally, his finger glued to his trigger. Aussie, Michael, and the other two hackers scan the water, pointing out targets for them to shoot. Around their raft, five of the giant airplane fish float dead on their sides, their green guts and blood fogging the water. Their severed fins float like surfboards.

"Where is he?" Aussie screams. "Brian! Where is he?"

"Anybody see him?" Michael shouts.

One of the monsters then launches out of the water directly in front of Vespa, a shiny black hopper escaping its front teeth. The cadets open fire, blasting pieces of the monster in several directions. The hopper lands on its back and swims away.

"Come on, Jonah! Save him! Go get him!" Rosa shouts, pushing Jonah toward the edge of the raft. "Save him! You said you'd jump in and save him! Go! Go, go, go!"

Without hesitation, Jonah crawls over the boards, his own voice echoing in his ears: *We'd jump in and get you. I'm actually a really good swimmer. I'll grab you.*

The water shimmers and bubbles in front of him. A monster's severed head floats to the surface with its glowing green eyes and rotates in the current. *I'll grab you*, Jonah hears himself say again. He takes a deep breath and tears off his shoes. Right before he's about to dive back into the water, Vespa's shouts reach him: "Jonah, no! Don't you dare!"

"Go, Jonah!" Aussie cries. "Go find him!"

Jonah stares Vespa in the eyes and then leans forward, thinking this might be the last time he sees her, the last time he sees anyone. She aims her rifle right at him, and then a hand snatches Jonah's wrist and he's twisted back to the middle of the raft. Malix pins him down and says, "Do *not* go back in that water. You won't come back up, man. You won't. Listen to me."

Jonah tries to get back up, but Brooklyn lays her rifle across his neck. Then Bidson's left palm drops onto his chest.

"Just stay here," the big demic says. "He's gone. Don't be stupid."

Rosa leans over the water, waiting for someone to dive past her to find her friend, but no one does. She spins around to stare at Jonah, her eyes brimming with tears, and then, to everyone's surprise, she pinches her nose with her fingers and jumps overboard. Hopper and Bidson scramble to the edge, with Jonah and Brooklyn close behind, and together they gasp as one of the giants swoops over and snatches Rosa in its back jaws. On the other raft, Aussie knots her long red hair in her fists and screams. Everyone's lasers are too late; the beast dives and disappears into the darkness with Rosa. A trail of blood rises to the surface and then spreads and fades.

Both rafts fall silent; the sloshing of the water sounds like thunder in Jonah's ears. The kids wait for Rosa to surface, for Brian to heave himself over the edge of the wood, but no one appears. Christina sees something in the water in the other direction, and she fires until muttering, "You guys are too late. Lunch is over."

"We have to keep moving," Vespa finally says. "Grab your oars and watch the water. You have my permission to shoot anything bigger than you."

"I don't need your permission for anything," Malix says, leaping back onto her raft.

"Wait. We're just going to leave them here?" Aussie asks.

"Leave them where, demic?" Vespa answers. "Where are they, exactly? Do you see them? They're gone. I'm sorry. I'm really sorry, but they're gone."

"Brian?" Michael shouts with his face dangerously close to the water. "Come on, Brian!"

"We're just going to keep going?" Aussie asks.

"What else are we supposed to do?" Brooklyn asks.

Jonah stares numbly at the water, his eyes scanning for any kind of movement. They can't be gone. They can't be dead. After another minute, he sits back and stares up at the few wispy clouds overhead. Their luck hasn't changed.

Everyone except Hopper gets back into position to move west again. Vespa looks over and screams for Hopper to sit away from the edge and go back into the middle. He doesn't move; he just keeps staring into the water.

"Demic! What the hell are you doing?" Portis yells.

"*What the hell am I doing*?" Hopper snaps back. "I'm looking for my freaking backpack, asshole! All right? I lost it!"

CHAPTER EIGHT

It takes three hours to reach land. What was once a speck of brown on the horizon is now a mile-wide stretch of gray beach that wraps around the corners to the unknown. A bright yellow jungle spreads left and right, and above it, in the middle, squats a small mountain like a fist rising out of the sand. Jonah drops his feet into the water and stands up to his waist. The sea is colder than it was before, instantly waking him from his exhaustion.

Vespa jumps into the water and pulls the other raft toward the sand. They don't have the homing device, but through some miracle, no one else is lost. The two cadets look at each other briefly and then twist around to a huddle of sunburnt kids. No one cheers. In fact, no one speaks.

An hour ago, they watched as smoke blanketed their campsite on the beach, consuming the entire coastline in purple flames. Up at the crash site on the cliff, flashes of whites and blues shot in every direction like fireworks. They immediately began to row faster, convinced not only that those who stayed behind were dead, but also that they themselves were being followed, possibly hunted.

They carry the rafts to higher ground, hiding them under a tangle of vines while Malix and Christina dart ahead with their rifles ready, scouting to save the group from another animal attack. Jonah dabs at the wound on his forearm and wonders if he'll ever see the cadets again. Just like he won't see Rosa again.

In his mind, Rosa pinches her nose and jumps into the water. She does this over and over. Pinch, jump. Pinch, jump. Pinch, jump. He then sees the airplane fish snatch her in its back jaws and swim away. He can only imagine a similar fate for Brian. The guilt in Jonah's stomach is nauseating. He can't turn it off. How is he ever supposed to pull it together? How is he supposed to be this new, aggressive Jonah when everything keeps pulling him down?

Dark clouds come from the west, and the scouts leap out of the jungle the exact moment thunder rumbles overhead.

"We didn't go all that far in," Christina says, swinging her rifle to her back, "But we found something, we think."

Malix smiles and points over his shoulder. "There's a path in there. Some kind of path. It winds around to the left, and then it looks like it goes up the side of the mountain. Someone's been here. People."

"Definitely," Christina adds.

Jonah stares at the yellow jungle. Maybe Dr. Z went through there, or maybe Garrett, and soon they'll catch up to them and find out what the hell is going on.

"Are you sure?" Vespa asks. "Both of you are sure?"

"Definitely," they say.

Aussie collapses onto her knees and lets out a short laugh. "We found them? We actually found the adults? I can't believe it. Oh my gosh."

Jonah stumbles toward the jungle in relief, a smile slowly spreading across his face. They found them. They actually found them. Dr. Z can look at his eyes. She can help him. She can tell them all what to do. It's a miracle.

"No," Malix says, "No, guys, I don't think so."

"Yeah, the path is pretty well worn. It doesn't look like it was just made in the last twenty-four hours," Christina says.

Jonah stops in his tracks. The news drops his head to his chest. Why did he even get his hopes up?

"But it *could* be them," Aussie says. "You don't really know that. You didn't see anyone, so it could totally be them."

Another thundercloud groans and Jonah turns to see Brooklyn tuck her rifle under her arm. "Well, let's go find out, shall we?" she says. "Somebody's hot on our trail, so let's just move already. Get to higher ground on that mountain and scope out the situation."

Portis stops chewing his wrist long enough to pat his rifle and say, "We'll shoot the asshole right off his raft. Blast him up."

"But I don't understand. We're running," Aussie whines. "That's what they wanted, for us to run. So why don't they just leave us alone if we're running?"

"Good question. Maybe they want Hopper's homing beacon," Michael says. "Or maybe we have something else that they want."

"Or some*one*," Vespa says, sighing.

They all look at each other for a moment. Jonah's eyes fall on Richter; he's standing oddly stiff and upright, and his face is empty of emotion, including fear. Soon, though, everyone pads toward the jungle as one.

Malix and Christina were right; there is a narrow path nearly clear of vegetation, and the kids run through it as fast as they can. With his rifle ready, Jonah brings up the rear, following Michael and Portis.

"What do you think, Firstie?" Portis huffs over his shoulder. "You think we're about to ruin the adults' fun by showing up like this? Crashing their little party?"

"I'm more worried about whoever's behind us."

A thundercloud claps close by, and a flash of lightning lights the thin strip of darkening sky above them. Hopper begs everyone to slow down, but soon they reach the base of the small mountain. The clouds open, releasing fat raindrops that float slowly to the ground like snowflakes back on Earth. The drops bounce off the kids like soap bubbles before popping and soaking their clothes and skin. Malix points to a worn line on the mountainside, where jagged rocks climb all the way to the top. "Higher ground! Right there! That's where we need to go!"

"Move!" Vespa shouts above the thunder.

Malix leaps straight up, rising more than ten feet. He catches an edge of a rock and easily pulls himself up. Jonah follows, stepping where Malix steps, grabbing what Malix grabs, all the while nervous to reach the top. They'll either see they're on an island and he'll be to blame for the wasted day and two dead demics, or they'll see they've reached a peninsula with an easier passage to the west and Jonah will be a hero.

Vespa finds a slightly different path and bounds past Jonah and Malix, scaling the wet mountain with ease. She stands alone on the ridge with her back to them, holding a hand over her head, blocking the rain. One by one, the kids join her and each drops their jaw. On the other side of the ridge is a canyon almost a half-mile in diameter. Its edges curve in and out like a ribbon, or a half-open clam shell. Thick bands of bright rock—yellow, orange, red—interchange every couple hundred feet down the sides, but then after what Jonah thinks must be another half mile, it's a black hole. It looks bottomless.

"What is it? A volcano?" Christina asks.

"I've never seen a volcano shaped like this," Malix says.

Vespa stares into the abyss below. "What do the demics think? Michael?"

Everyone turns to Michael, who pushes his long, wet hair out of his eyes. "I don't know. Maybe? Probably? Or it could just be a huge asteroid crater."

"An asteroid that lands directly in the middle of an island? And one shaped like that? You idiot, those odds are so staggering I'm not even going to bother calculating them," Hopper says.

An island? Jonah looks straight ahead and runs a hand over his face in defeat. Sure enough, blue sea sits a couple miles beyond the far ridge. Because of the way the crater's edge rises on the right, he can't see every inch of the beach, but it's pretty obvious they've landed on an island. Spinning on his heels, he sees Portis looking through his scope, scanning the beach behind them.

"Hey, I'm looking at the water down there and I don't see anyone coming!" Portis yells. "No one's tailing us!"

"Are you sure?" Vespa asks.

"All I can say is that I don't see anyone. But that doesn't mean they're not coming."

"Or that they didn't already make it to the beach," Brooklyn growls.

"We have to keep moving then," Malix says.

A thundercloud cracks so loudly overhead that it brings all the kids to their knees. Several bolts of lightning swirl in the sky like tornados, and then one shoots into the yellow trees below with a blinding flash. The wind picks up significantly.

"We have to find cover!" Brooklyn yells, her huge white shirt flapping like a sail.

Vespa grabs Brooklyn's arm and flattens her against the rock, seeming to realize at the same time Jonah does that if a strong enough wind were to pick up someone as light as Brooklyn, he or she might never be seen again. "Everyone lie down!" Vespa scans the crater and then points. "Look! There are ridges along the inside, and wait, I think... There's a cave down there! See it? That's where we're going!"

They squint where Vespa points. Jonah sees the dark opening. In fact, he sees several caves punched into the layers of colors. That's when he notices that one side of the canyon lip is charred black, as if torched by something. What caught fire all the way up here?

"Go down there? You're crazy! We'll die!" Richter shouts.

Portis swings his rifle onto his back and lays a scarred hand on the hacker's shoulder. "There's nowhere else to go."

"On the count of three, we hold hands and slide on our backs down the edge!" Vespa shouts. She sits up and everyone does the same. "When we hit the ridge, run to the right and get in the cave! It'll work! Trust me!"

Vespa grabs Aussie's hand, and Aussie takes Jonah's. "Here we go! One!" Jonah takes the youngest hacker's hand. "Two!" The rest of the kids hesitantly connect, and then Vespa screams, "Three! Now!"

Together, the chain of demics and cadets scoots to the crater's edge. Jonah looks into the black hole below, hoping to see its floor so that he knows it isn't just some bottomless abyss. He doesn't find it, but something in the middle of all the blackness, just where the light fades away and everything goes dark, catches his eye. It shines for just a second, like a magnifying glass catching a reflected hint of sunlight, but then Vespa plunges downward with Aussie, pulling Jonah over the edge.

The First Year yells and yanks down the hacker who pulls Christina, and soon all eleven kids scream as their backs scrape and bounce along the inner bowl of the canyon. With the lesser gravity and the blasting wind, they travel slowly, but it only makes the descent more terrifying as they have too much time to think. A swirl of lightning shoots into the opposite side of the crater, severing off a large chunk of red rock that plummets like a wounded bird. Then the soles of Jonah's mismatched shoes suddenly hit a ridge and he stops descending. He pitches forward, wobbling on his sore knees, until Aussie and the hacker pull him back against the wall.

"Now run!" Vespa shouts. She twists and runs along the crooked, narrow path, her left hand holding onto Aussie, her right always touching the wall in front of her. Jonah squeezes the boy's wrist and runs as fast as the girls in front of him will allow. His lungs feel like they are about to explode. A gust of wind slams them all into the wall, and the raindrops no longer bounce off; they explode against the kids like tiny bombs.

Vespa dives into a jagged cave entrance, whipping Aussie inside. Jonah slams his knee into the rocky frame but safely rolls inside and out of the way of the incoming train of kids.

One by one, they enter the cave. After the pink-haired hacker goes in, Christina, Bidson, Michael, Hopper, Brooklyn, and Portis dive into the shelter. Then Malix comes into view. As soon as the cadet sets a toe inside the cave, he breaks off from Portis in front of him and Richter behind him. A rain-filled gust of wind sweeps across the entrance, picking Malix's legs off the ground. He falls onto his chest and claws his way toward Brooklyn's outstretched arms, but Richter doesn't make it; he's sucked away from the cave with horrified brown eyes that instantly burn themselves into Jonah's memory. Just like that, he's gone.

Hopper staggers forward. "Richter!"

Vespa runs over and snatches the back of Malix's shirt, pulling his face up to hers. "You let go! Why the hell did you let go?"

Malix's face changes from relief to shock, and he looks over his shoulder and then around the cave. "What?"

"He's gone!" Aussie screams. "You killed Richter!"

"You let go!" Vespa shouts. She pushes his face into the cold stone floor and then moves to the entrance, grabbing the upper curves of the frame, anchoring herself with a wide stance.

"But I didn't let go!" Malix yells. "I swear! I had him the whole time!"

"You *did* let go!" Hopper shouts. "We all fucking saw you let go! You just killed Richter, man! You killed him!"

Vespa marches back inside the cave, stopping to kick Malix in the ribs on her way past.

"But I had him," Malix groans. "I'm sorry. I'm sorry, I'm sorry, I'm sorry."

Aussie holds her head in her hands and walks in a small circle, stumbling over Michael. She then turns to the whole group and screams at the top of her lungs: "This is a disaster! Can't you see how much of a disaster this is?"

Jonah curls into a ball and stares at the cave's mouth. At this rate, they'll all be dead in another couple days.

• • •

After an hour, once the storm lessens to a devilish howling, Brooklyn and Christina quietly volunteer to explore while the others eat and rest. The cave, fifteen feet tall at its highest point, twenty-five feet at its widest, runs deeper than any of them could have imagined. When the two girls return to offer a tour of the tunnels they've found, no one moves, so they disappear again into the maze.

They agree to rest for an hour or two, that whoever is following them would never find them in this cave. At least not right away.

Malix sits near the opening with his head against the wall. No one asks him to isolate himself, but everyone seems happy he does. He punishes himself every few minutes by walking out along the ridge to look for Richter. Portis sleeps nearby, facing the wall.

The demics huddle together behind an orange rock in the shape of an hourglass. An electric lantern sits at their half-circle of feet, casting shadows on the wall that, to Jonah, look too much like gravestones.

Next to Jonah, on the opposite side of the cavern, Vespa hugs her arms around her shoulders. She pretends to sleep but opens her eyes every time Malix gets up, then again when he sits back down.

"I think we should go back," Jonah finally says to her.

She doesn't open her eyes, but her nose twitches.

"I know you're awake, Vespa. Listen to me. Aussie is right. This is a disaster, and I think we should go back to the crash site before anyone else dies." He doesn't believe a word of what he says next, but he says it anyway. "Maybe everyone's okay back there."

The cadet raises her lids and stares at Jonah for a few seconds before saying, "They're dead. You and I both know it. There's nothing to go back to. And if we go back, then all our kids died for nothing."

"If we don't go back and see what happened up there, then the *rest of us* are going to die for nothing. We're going to die. Can't you see that?"

"I thought you were sick. That you're going to die unless we don't get off Achilles in, what? Twenty days?"

Jonah is speechless.

"Right? You're sick? You're dying?"

"How did you know that?" he whispers.

"Sean told me," she says. "He said he overheard the doctor telling you the other night. You have some kind of blood disease."

At the makeshift hospital, Sean must not have gone very far, Jonah realizes. He heard everything.

Vespa sits up and then shuffles over until their shoulders touch. When Jonah doesn't respond, she sighs. "All right, Firstie. Talk to me. About something. About anything, I don't know. Tell me why you're here. Why were you going to Thetis?"

"It doesn't matter," he whispers.

"I want to know. Humor me."

Jonah looks down and picks at the rips in his green jumpsuit.

She cracks her neck and says, "Well, fine, I'll tell you why *I* volunteered to go, and then maybe you'll enlighten me." She lowers her voice and faces him. "I haven't told anyone this before, so fucking keep your mouth shut. This is between you and me. So, when I was eleven years old and they said they discovered Thetis, my dad went crazy. He got *obsessed* with it. And when I say he went *crazy*, he literally went crazy. He's actually in a mental hospital right now, and that's where he'll probably always be. He doesn't even know I was on the Mayflower 2, he's so nuts." She waits for a response from Jonah, perhaps some sympathy, but he keeps his lips sealed. If his father were alive, even if he were in a mental hospital, at least he could visit him. Vespa continues: "My dad was this super religious guy. A Jesus freak. My mom was, too, before she died."

Jonah nods at her, hoping to indicate he knows how that feels, that his mom is dead, too. She nods back.

"My dad went to church every morning, prayed before every meal, and he even—*man*, this shows you just how insane he was—he had my sister and me baptized on five different continents in case we ever traveled to one of them when we were older and died. We had crucifixes in every room, in our car, sewn into our clothes, and on top of all that, look. Look at this stupid thing."

To Jonah's surprise, Vespa hooks her finger in the collar of her shirt and pulls it down to the top of her breasts. In the faint light of the lantern, Jonah draws his embarrassed eyes along the curves of her skin, from left to right and then from right to left, pausing each time at the smooth, dark area between the tops of her breasts. It could be an attack from the sepsis, but he suddenly can't breathe. He doesn't want to breathe. A burning sensation appears between his shoulder blades and rages down over his torso. Then with her other hand, Vespa points to a faded blue tattoo over her heart. It's a small crucifix.

"He did this. Personally. To me *and* my little sister." She releases her collar, and with it, Jonah's lungs. "Hurt like hell."

"He did that?" he manages to say.

"Yeah. My little sister had hers removed a few years back, but I… Well, anyway, my dad put so much faith in God and how God created the Earth and all that was good and bad on it and all the other stuff, that he was absolutely *floored* when they discovered Thetis. Another planet just like Earth? *Not created by God?* After hundreds of years of satellites and space probes and the Iranian mission to Ceres and, what, the launching of the Gilpin Telescope, they found the wormhole, and then twenty years later, on my eleventh birthday, they hit it *just* right to shoot out near Thetis."

"And Achilles," Jonah mumbles.

"And Achilles. Right. And Peleus, and the rest of this whole stupid galaxy. At first, though, when they brought back pictures from Thetis, my dad said they were fake, that God created one Earth, and blah, blah, blah. A few weeks later, after more and more pictures were released showing all the animals, he *slightly* changed his tune and said we weren't meant to explore outside of God's kingdom, that Thetis was Satan's playground and a bunch of other stuff. That's when he tattooed us, during all that. And then one night, out of the blue, he up and renounced God completely and said he's an atheist. A month later—and here's where he started to go really crazy—he told people he was *from* Thetis. *And* he said he wanted to go back. That he'd collected the information he was after on Earth and it was time for him to go home."

"Soooo...your dad said he was an alien?"

"Affirmative," she whispers, stretching a few black strands of hair into her mouth. Jonah can see she's nervous, that she's rethinking the conversation altogether.

"So why did you come to Thetis then? After all that, I mean, why would you volunteer?"

The hair falls out of her mouth. "To prove something to my father, ultimately. I've had a lot of time to think about it, and I've come to terms with that part. I mean, yes, exploring and colonizing another planet is an incredible opportunity, a once-in-a-lifetime kind of thing, but aside from my little sister who lives on the other side of the country with our aunt, there was nothing for me back home. Life was kind of shit before I got a scholarship to the academy, as you can imagine. But I think I volunteered for this mission so quickly, so fast, because I wanted to see with my own eyes the *one thing*, the one discovery, that ruined my dad's life, *and* mine *and* my sister's. I wanted to see if it was all worth it."

"Nothing's worth having your family broken apart," Jonah says.

"Yeah, well, I wanted to be sure."

They fall silent for a few minutes. Aussie leans out of the demic huddle and takes a long drink of water. The others look to be asleep. Even Malix has nodded off at the entrance, his head balancing on his knees.

Jonah stares at Vespa and gains some confidence. He clears his throat and his eyes shift upward. He finds a small hole in the wall high above Bidson and studies it as he finally speaks: "I'm a coward. That's why I'm here. I volunteered for all this because I was scared to join the military at eighteen. Because that's definitely what my future held before I got offered the Thetis trip." In a low, shaky voice, he continues, "I don't have any family. I don't have a mom or dad, they're dead, and I don't have siblings or anybody else. Not even any real friends. Once I graduated from the academy, I couldn't think of anywhere I could go, or anyone whom I could go anywhere *with*, if I could think of a place to go. And the thought of shipping off to England to fight in a war I don't really understand or agree with, I just couldn't do that. So I volunteered and was somehow—I don't know how or why—selected. But I ran, you know, just like I'm running now. I'm just a coward with nothing going on, and I was hoping to reinvent myself on Thetis. Be someone else, as stupid as that sounds."

"When did your parents die?" Vespa asks. She drapes a hand over her knee. His eyes flash from the hole up on the wall to her hand to her beautiful green eyes, and then, for some reason, back to the wall. There's something magnetizing about the hole near the ceiling. It's perfectly symmetrical, like a five-pointed star with circles or bubbles at its tips.

"Jonah?" Vespa asks.

"Hold on," he says, standing. Like a broken dam, regret rushes through his veins with every step he takes away from her. *This is why you don't have any friends,* he thinks. *This is exactly why.*

"What are you doing?" she whispers.

Jonah picks up the lantern and holds it high above his head. The light hits the star directly, and it seems to glisten as if wet, and then he thinks he sees a quick flash of green at its most northern point. He moves closer and practically stands on top of Bidson's legs; the demic's floating right arm pushes against his stomach, but he doesn't care. The star flashes green again.

Bidson and the other demics grumble and wake up, shielding their eyes from the lantern.

"What the hell, man?" Hopper groans.

"I need you to move. Sorry," Jonah says to Bidson.

The oafish boy squints and complains that he just got the spot warm, but he rolls away so that Jonah can get to the wall.

"What are you doing?" Michael asks.

"That's what I want to know," Vespa says. She leans against the opposite wall. Jonah feels terrible for walking away from her when she was at her most vulnerable, but the star…

"Don't you guys see it?" Jonah asks, pointing at the hole twelve feet up. "There's a star or something up there. That can't be natural, right? Someone must have made it, carved it out?"

Hopper circles around. "Well, now *that* is pretty freaky."

"Maybe the adults did it?" Michael asks. "Maybe they're leaving clues for us. Maybe we're supposed to know what it means so we can find them. Like a code we have to crack."

"I somehow doubt they wouldn't just write us a note or draw us a map," Vespa says.

They all gather around Jonah, leaning back and forth to get a better look. Malix and Portis stagger over silently.

"Why is it wet?" Bidson asks.

"I have no idea," Jonah says. Then, without thinking, he crouches, leaps, and touches the star's southernmost tip. The rock is slimy and soft, like a sponge. As soon as his feet touch the ground, he hands the lantern to Michael and turns to Bidson. "Do you think maybe I can stand on your arm so I can get a better look? If it'll hold me?"

"Let's give it a shot."

Hopper laughs, but no one else says a word as Jonah climbs up Bidson's back and pushes the boy's arm down, testing it. It pops right back up. Gently, Jonah stands on it like a swing, and Bidson's arm dips for a second before the fused muscles raise Jonah to the perfect height.

It's as if someone has stamped the wall or carved it with a precision laser; the edges of the star are sharp and perfect, and its depth is the exact same at every inch. The whole thing is no larger than Jonah's hand, but staring at it face-to-face, it feels as if it were bigger than the sun.

"So?" Hopper asks. "You going to make out with it, or what?"

"What's it look like?" Bidson asks.

"Like a star with circles on its tips, I guess," Jonah says. He extends an index finger and touches the exact middle. The rock gives and depresses like a pillow, and slime coats his nail. The middle section pulses white for a second and then his hand begins to tingle. He balls his fingers into a fist and looks down at the kids below, wishing he knew what to do.

"Jesus. Let me up there," Hopper says. "I'll figure this shit out."

But Jonah looks back at the star. He's oddly drawn to it, as if he was always meant to find it. The tingling in his hand intensifies, and it only feels better when he stretches his fingers wide. It's then he notices how exact the sizes are; his open hand and the star couldn't be a better match. He doesn't think about it; he just does it: he pushes his fingertips into each of the five circles, and when the rock starts to suck on his skin, he pushes them deeper and deeper until they touch something hot. It burns and he yanks his hand out, and then something inside the star clicks.

"Let me down!" Jonah yells. "Now!"

Bidson pushes away from the wall, and Jonah jumps, landing on Portis, who shoves him off as if he were contagious. The star keeps clicking, getting progressively louder, and the cadets whip out their guns. Everyone backs away, but no one knows where to go.

"What do we do?" Michael asks.

"Brooklyn! Christina!" Vespa shouts over her shoulder and into the tunnels. "We're leaving! Now!"

Suddenly the star glows green and it begins to shake inside the wall, sending dust and rock to the floor. Jonah beats his tingling hand against his thigh and puts the star in the middle of his scope. He's ready to shoot, but knows he won't. Something in his chest tells him this is what's supposed to happen. And he can't wait to see what does.

The star shoots a green beam across the cave, landing directly above Vespa's head. She dives and rolls into Bidson's legs, knocking him onto his stomach. Michael runs for the ridge outside, and Aussie shrieks and yanks on Jonah's arm. He lowers his weapon, captivated, waiting patiently for what's next. Suddenly the star itself blasts away from the wall in a rocky explosion, trailing a thin metallic tube behind it. The star punches through the opposite wall with such force that the cave shakes and Jonah falls onto his back.

A crooked fissure crawls up and down the wall, and slowly the rock begins to separate. A few seconds later, Jonah sits in front of a doorway.

"Duuuude," Portis moans.

"What the freaky fuck?" Hopper asks from a corner of the room.

Vespa touches Jonah's back. "You okay?"

The opening is dark, and the cool air rushing out of it rolls over his skin like water. Vespa turns on the light of her rifle and aims it inside the opening. They see something long and white and shiny stretching the width of the floor.

Jonah ducks into the room, getting in front of Vespa's light. His long shadow paints the domed ceiling like a ghost. All around him, lining the walls and up above, there are hundreds of the same circle-tipped stars, but there are also double squares and stacked Vs, repeating dots and sectioned boxes, and dozens of other symbols that remind Jonah of ancient Egyptian hieroglyphics.

Someone brings in the lantern and the room brightens just in time for Jonah to sidestep the long white object on the floor. It's about four feet wide, connecting the western and eastern walls, and it shimmers like milk.

"Nobody touch anything," Vespa whispers.

"Am I the only one who thinks this is the coolest thing any human being has ever seen?" Michael whispers.

"I do," the youngest hacker says. "Absolutely."

"Should we even be in here?" Portis asks. "Like, seriously? I don't think we should be in here."

"I'm thinking the same thing." Malix runs his fingers over the symbols on the wall. And then, out of nowhere, the cadet stops in his tracks and almost falls over. His face grows white, and then he spins around to run, only to charge right into Bidson and land on his back.

"We have to go!" Malix shouts. "Get out of here! We have to get out of here right now!"

"What's wrong?" Vespa shouts.

Malix crawls toward the door. "Just run! I'm telling you!"

Jonah doesn't feel the same panic. He doesn't want to leave. This room feels like the only safe place he's ever been. "Malix, just wait."

Malix doesn't listen. He gets to his feet and barrels past Aussie. But when he tries to dive out of the room, he bounces backward and screams as if he's been shocked. That's when Jonah sees the faint curtain of white light covering the doorway. Malix then runs into the light at full speed and again bounces back into the room. He grinds his forehead along the ground and begins to sob.

"Dude, what's going on? What's wrong with you?" Portis asks.

"Guy's freaking flipped." Hopper sighs.

"It's a force field," the youngest hacker says at the doorway. "Incredible. I can't believe we're actually seeing stuff like this."

Vespa kneels and carefully places a hand on Malix's back. "Cadet? Talk to me."

Jonah makes eye contact with Vespa and then turns to examine the room. The ceiling is twenty-five feet high, and the way the walls curve at the top and then at the floor, it's almost like they're all standing in a sphere with a few feet of dirt on its floor. The sense of comfort is almost overwhelming to him. Why does all this feel okay?

"We're going to die," Malix whispers, lifting his head. "We're next now."

"What do you mean?" Vespa asks.

"The signs. They're the same ones. The ones near the door with three circles inside the letter C. *Shit*. Shit, shit, shit. We have to get out of here."

"What about them?" Jonah asks, spotting several of the symbols here and there along the curved wall.

"Are you saying you know what they mean?" the hacker asks.

"The night when Sean and I went off on the beach," Malix says, sitting up. His breathing intensifies. He closes his eyes. "We were maybe a mile away. We came to all these huge rocks and we couldn't get by, so we got off the cycle and climbed up to see what was on the other side." He grinds his teeth and opens his eyes, staring right at Jonah. "We found four of the adults from the ship. Dead. Lying there on the rocks. And they looked tortured. Their faces were all torn up."

Bidson falls to his knees. Aussie stuffs her hair into her mouth and begins to cry. Jonah doesn't know what to say.

"Who was it?" Michael asks.

"I don't know," Malix says. "I have no idea. But they had stuff on their shirts, too. More messages."

Vespa stands. "What did they say?"

"Two said, 'Keep Running.' Another one said, 'We're Always Watching.' And then the last shirt said, 'Tell Anyone and You're Next.'" Then Malix points to one of the symbols: three circles inside a C. "And they all had that symbol up and down their arms. Burned into their skin. All over them. I'll never forget it."

Jonah spins on his heels, taking it all in. His blood runs ice cold while his skin pops with heat. But then it all washes over him. Calmness returns, and again he finds that he doesn't want to be anywhere else. Even with the news.

"Okay. Okay, okay," Vespa says. "Nobody touch *anything*, especially those circles in the Cs."

Malix wipes his face. "But how are we going to get out of there? We have to get out of here, or we're next. *I'm* next, aren't I? It's me. They're coming after me. Oh, shit."

No one responds. Aussie picks up a rock and tosses it at the curtain of light in the doorway. It ricochets back at her feet.

It's suddenly obvious to Jonah. "The only way out of here *is* to touch something."

"He's right," says the hacker.

"So then, Captain Dipshit," Hopper says. "When are you going to touch that big white thing over there and kill us all?"

"*Nobody's touching anything*," Vespa says. "Let's just think for a second."

"This is so messed up," Bidson says.

The hacker walks into the middle of the room, right next to Jonah, and rotates with his young face skyward. "There are a lot of patterns here. Lots of them. The way all the symbols are laid out, it's saying something or painting a picture or telling us how to get out of here. I'm just trying to figure it out." He jabs his chubby finger at different points at the ceiling, his pink hair glowing in the lantern light. He mouths numbers to himself until a scowl appears on his round face. "They're not prime numbers, for one thing, and they don't seem to have a noun-verb sentence structure, which makes sense, but I don't—"

"And it's not map of any solar system I've ever seen," Bidson adds.

"Maybe it's…" Michael drones.

Hopper shoulders Michael out of his way. "Hold on, people. I got this."

The cadets watch silently as the demics look for a code, each of them starting and stopping sentences, pacing, counting, arguing and shaking their heads. Suddenly the hacker with the pink hair runs to the eastern wall and touches a hollow diamond with a square inside. It takes him a second before trying to twist the square. When he does, there's an audible click.

"No," Malix moans.

Vespa points a finger at him. "I said don't!"

Jonah considers stopping the boy but doesn't. He wants to see what happens.

The hacker ignores the protests and runs across the room and twists the squares inside two more diamonds. Without stopping, he jumps over the white object and does the same to three more of the diamonds stacked vertically on top of each other. More clicking fills the room.

"Now! Someone needs to jump up and turn the one at the top!"

Everyone looks at the ceiling, and directly in the middle is another hollow diamond with a square. Jonah crouches down, but just before he's going to leap, Portis darts in from the right. "Stand still, big guy!"

"No! Don't!" Malix yells.

Bidson stiffens a second before Portis runs up his back. The cadet launches himself off the demic's shoulders and flies toward the ceiling. He reaches the diamond and twists its square, hanging for a moment by his fingers, and then Portis falls and catches Bidson's floating arm before hitting the ground. Everyone waits for another door to open, for the white object to transform into a giant demon, for the adults to show up and congratulate them on passing some sort of test. But nothing happens. Just more clicking.

Then Jonah sees them. He darts toward the door and the four diamonds next to it, and turns their squares while Malix yanks back on his shoulders, begging him not to. All the clicking stops. And then the entire sphere begins to shudder.

Immediately, every touched diamond begins to glow green, and a moment later, the long white object on the floor comes to life. The milky material has begun to flow from east to west, like a moving walkway. A faint white energy field appears at the ceiling.

"Jesus. Now what?" Portis asks.

"Let's just stop touching stuff for one goddamn second," Vespa growls. "Let's get Brooklyn and Christina and slow down. We have no idea what we're doing."

But Jonah thinks that he *does* know what he's doing. He has some sort of déjà vu, as if he's been here before. He picks up a large stone.

"*Stop*," Vespa warns him.

He doesn't listen to her, running to the eastern wall and throwing the stone into the moving material. As soon as it touches the milky surface, it shoots across the room. When it reaches the other wall, it doesn't bounce back; the stone just disappears.

Hopper runs over to Jonah. "Hell no."

"A portal?" Michael whispers. "That's like—"

Suddenly the stone falls from the energy field at the ceiling and bounces quietly on the floor. Vespa and Jonah make eye contact, and he can see she's starting to lose it. They were never trained for something like this.

"Whoa," Bidson says, laughing.

"Where do you think it went?" Aussie asks.

"Um, the ceiling," Portis says. "Pay attention."

"I mean, where did it go before it came back?"

No one has an answer. Hopper drops the stone back onto the white material and they all watch it do the same exact thing, disappearing at the wall and reappearing at the ceiling. Malix catches it and turns it over in his trembling hand.

"I don't get it," he says.

They try bigger rocks, smaller rocks, rolling them this way and that on the white material. The same thing happens over and over, and the curtain of light at the doorway doesn't leave. They're still stuck there. Frustration takes hold, and Hopper tries touching other symbols on the walls, but nothing changes.

Finally, the pink-haired hacker walks over to the eastern end of the white object. He then turns to the room with a look of desperation on his face. "From the moment I heard the adults were killed down in the jungle, I've been waiting for my turn. To be killed. To die. It's all I think about. I've actually been waiting for *all of us* to die. It seemed…inevitable. And it still seems inevitable, with the way things are going. So, as a man—or a boy, I guess—of science, I can't just waste an opportunity like this."

Before anyone can react, he steps on the white object. His feet are swept out from underneath him, and he shoots across the room on his back.

"No!" Bidson shouts.

Jonah breaks into a sprint, trying to cut the boy off from the side. This feels wrong. Everything else has felt right, but this feels terribly wrong. He moves quicker than he thought possible, and he dives just as the boy zips in front of him. But he's too late. His arms close around nothing.

Everyone runs to the middle of the room, their heads up and waiting for the boy to appear and fall. A second passes, and then another one.

"Come on," Jonah says. "Come on!"

"Where is he?" Aussie asks.

"This isn't good," Vespa whispers.

Ten more seconds pass. The hacker doesn't fall. Malix runs over to the eastern wall and drops the stone onto the white material. It shoots halfway across the room and then stops. The whiteness goes still. The energy field at the ceiling pulses and then disappears. The doorway is clear, too. They can leave. The kids are free now.

"Start it up again! Hurry!" Vespa yells.

Jonah bolts for the nearest hollow diamond to turn it on again, but to his shock, it's not there anymore. There's just a flat section of rock.

"They're gone," Bidson says from the other side of the sphere. "Those symbols are gone."

Jonah looks up at the ceiling. The diamond in the center is missing, too.

"Find another code, then!" Vespa shouts. "One of you demics figure it out! Now!"

The demics study the walls and ceiling in panic, but no one finds anything. Michael digs his fingers into any star he can find. Jonah claws at the walls, pleading with the stone to give. Still, nothing happens.

"I didn't even know the kid's name," Portis says as he runs his hands through his thick hair. "Jesus. How did I not know his name?"

"It was Kip," Hopper says.

"Kip." Jonah repeats the name several times. The feelings he had about the sphere five minutes ago have faded. He no longer feels comfortable or safe in there. "Where the hell did Kip go?"

Shouts sound outside the sphere's door, and they all stop and look at each other. Then, as a group, they sprint through the opening, hoping to see Kip and his pink hair.

They see no one, but then Jonah hears Brooklyn shouting from the back of the cave.

"Just go! Move!" she barks.

A gruff, unfamiliar voice answers her, and Jonah and Vespa pull up their rifles.

"Brooklyn?" Vespa shouts.

"Yeah!" Brooklyn yells back. "We're coming around the bend! Get ready for this shit!"

Michael aims the electric lantern into the dark recesses of the cave. Christina appears, backpedaling with the barrel of her LZR-rifle lit, raised head-high.

Then they all gasp.

"What the—?" Malix asks.

"Whoa. Holy shit," Hopper whispers.

A tall, shirtless man no older than twenty walks into the light with his hands up. He's thick with muscles, from his navel to his neck, and his copper skin is dirty and covered in scratches, some new, some old. His hair is a fountain of blond matted coils that explode in every direction. He wears torn, grime-covered shorts, a small green sack hangs from his hip, and his feet are bare and gray. His dilated green eyes bounce all over the cave. A long, scraggly beard curtains his cheeks and chin, and as he continues to eye the group before him, his jaw moves constantly, like he's chewing gum. Then he fumbles his fingers over his lower lip, bows deeply, and spits a glob of white liquid to his left.

Jonah readjusts his rifle, unable to breathe. It's no one from their ship, he's sure of it.

"Who the hell are you?" Vespa asks. "And where's Kip?"

Still in his deep bow, the young man whips his arms out wide and rubs the tips of his fingers together. "Who am I? What's my name? Right, right. I have manners, I assure you. Call me Tunick."

"I don't care what your name is," she barks. "I want to know *who* you are, what you're doing here, and where you're from! How can you be here? And what happened in that room and where's the boy?"

Jonah is dumbstruck, waiting for his brain to catch up with his heart rate. The man starts stomping his left foot. "Of course, of course, of course. I come in peace, I assure you."

"We found him in a nearby tunnel," Brooklyn says, entering the cave with her gun aimed at the man's back. "Bastard was walking right in your direction."

Tunick stands up straight and touches the ends of his dirty dreadlocks. A sadistic grin appears on his cracked lips for a second, and then he stuffs a finger in his mouth, biting on his nail. His voice is manic, alternating between mumbles and loud, drawn-out words. "That's because I was coming to meet you. You were here, and I was coming from back there. You crashed and I saw it. I'm Tunick. I live here. Well, not here, in these caves, because that would be crazy." He twists around, and the cadets tighten their grips on their rifles. "Spider-y things live in these caves. Giant white ones. No, I wouldn't sleep here. I don't live here. I'll show you where I live."

"Where's Kip?" Aussie asks.

"Kip? Is that your dog?" Tunick laughs. "You brought a dog? Good, good. Let me take the good dog home with me. We'll give him bones. I have so many bones at home."

Jonah steps forward. "We're supposed to be the only humans here. Where are you from?"

"Originally? Originally, I'm from Dallas, Texas. Grew up there. So hot in Dallas. Waaaaay too hot. Not like in these cool caves. It's nice in here. But there are spider-y things. Big white ones. They'll bite ya. Gobble ya right up."

"How is this possible?" Michael asks.

Jonah breaks his stare, lowering his gun. "You came from Thetis, didn't you? From the Athens colony. You were on the first Mayflower ship."

"Ha! I was!" Tunick laughs. "You're a smart boy. That's exactly what I'm looking for. I was hoping you were smart kids. I'll show you where I live. I can show—"

"Shut up for one second, damn it! How did you get here?" Vespa demands.

"I crashed, too." Tunick flattens a hand and sways it over his head like an airplane. He then juts his hand straight down into a nosedive. "One year ago. Or has it been longer? Two years? We stole a ship, we stole a ship. Me and a bunch of other smart kids from Thetis. We stole a ship and we crashed here."

"That's not true," Malix says. "All the kids died in that field trip accident. On that field trip to the Polaris Mons. It was reported all over Earth. None of the kids survived. That's why *we're* here."

Tunick laughs and spits another white glob into the darkness. His face falls and his voice grows grave and low. "There was no accident. The kids, we *escaped.* And Thetis, you should know, is a *very* bad place to be."

CHAPTER NINE

JONAH STARES AT THE MAN. "WAIT. IS IT *YOU*? DID *YOU* DO ALL this? Did you kill... Where are the adults from our ship?"

"Oh shit," Malix whispers.

"Shoot him," Hopper whispers. "Shoot him in the face."

The camp forgets Tunick's last statement about Thetis, and the cadets readjust their weapons. The demics push back against wall. This unhinged man could surely be the killer, Jonah thinks. And now they have him. It's over. Is it over?

Tunick rattles his head back and forth before gnawing on the skin between his thumb and index finger. "What adults? Adults? I haven't seen any adults. I watched you kiddos in the jungle. No adults."

"Kids are free now?" Brooklyn seethes. "You want us to run? Is that what you want?"

Tunick spits and turns to look at her. "We don't need to run, tiny one. We can walk. Unless you want the exercise. I like to stay in shape myself. I'll show you my little gym. But we don't have to run. And we'll bring your dog, Kippy, too."

Heat courses over Jonah's skin as he thinks back to what just happened in the sphere with Kip. His trigger finger sweats.

"I'm going to ask you this just one time," Vespa says. "Did you hang a man in the jungle and write on his shirt?"

"And on the beach!" Malix barks. "You killed four people and cut up their faces!"

Tunick playfully bats his cheeks in rhythm. "*What*? Oh, no. No, no, no. That must have been *Zion*."

"Who the hell is Zion?" Vespa roars.

"I'm the good guy and he's the bad guy. He doesn't like outsiders. No, he'll kill you. With his big, big hands. Can you put your guns down now? I'm nervous. I'm *so nervous* now."

"What do you know about that room back there?" Malix growls, jutting the barrel of his rifle at the sphere's opening. "The one with the conveyer belt and the portal and all the shit on the walls? What is it?"

Tunick sidesteps and peeks inside the door. When he looks back, his face is twisted with an intense look of grief. "You guys...you guys *are* smart. Next time wait for me. My turn next time, okay?"

"One of us disappeared in there and hasn't come back," Aussie whispers. "Where is he? Where's Kip? Please tell us."

Tunick cracks a fake smile and takes a deep breath. "I don't know, I don't know. Too bad you lost the dog, though."

Portis marches forward with his gun aimed right at Tunick's face. "He's not a fucking dog! He's a kid! Where did he go?"

Tunick snaps his fingers next to both his ears and then bites the air next to his mouth. "I don't know."

Portis presses the rifle into Tunick's forehead, pushing the man flat against the wall. "Tell us what the fuck is going on."

"You're a dead man," Vespa seethes. She presses her rifle right next to Portis's. "Answer us. You've been setting fires, chasing us and killing us. And now you're going to answer us."

Tunick puts his palms up in surrender. "I just live here. I saw you crash and I came to find you. I don't know where your Kippy went. You never know where you'll go inside one of those rooms. But as regards the other stuff—the killing and the chasing—well, you must have made Zion angry. What did you do? *What did you do*?"

Jonah wipes his sweaty hand on his jumpsuit and then aims at the man again. He wishes he would just give them a straight answer.

"We didn't do anything, ya freak," Hopper says.

"Nothing," Aussie says from behind a blank-faced Bidson. "All we did was crash here. We're just trying to get rescued."

Portis presses the gun harder into the man's skull. "Where are the adults? Are they all dead? Did Zion kill them all? Is he going to kill us, too?"

"What do all the messages mean? Why do we have to run? Why are kids free now? That's what was written on their shirts," Brooklyn says.

Tunick scratches his beard hard and struggles against the two barrels against his head. "Weird, weird. Straaaaange. I don't know. You must be free now. That sounds so nice, right? You can do what you want. You can take anything. Anything, anything. Verve, verve, verve. But you must be smart about it, though. You're free, but be smart. Zion will like you if you're smart. Then he can trust you. Then you can be with him."

The kids stare at each other in confusion.

"Where does he want us to run to?" Jonah asks.

"I don't know, I don't know," Tunick says. "Run there? Run here? Run everywhere? Maybe he wanted you to run here, so you should come with me now, and I'll introduce you to my sister, and I'll show you my collections, and you can rest and we can talk, and I'll show you Achilles because it's the most *beautiful* place you'll ever see, and say, uh, do you have any food I might have? I haven't eaten anything synthetic in over a year. Chocolate, maybe? Do you have chocolate?"

Without checking with Vespa or anyone else, Bidson opens his pack and tosses one of the thin boxes to Tunick. Vespa and Portis back away with their guns raised. The man rips open the gold foil, and when the steam hits his face, it's the first time that he stands still. He inhales the fumes and instantly saliva coats his lips. Tunick then hawks up a bright white seed or stone out of his mouth, and it pings into the darkness. The rest of the foil is torn away, revealing thinly sliced roast beef, mashed potatoes, carrot sticks, a bread roll, and a thick chocolate brownie. Tunick buries his face into the brownie and then moves the tray back and forth until everything is gone. He wipes his face with his arm, barely removing any of the food mess, and then belches.

Hopper laughs. "Um, that was kind of awesome, dude. You're like a vacuum."

The man smiles and belches again, and then he wings the tray over his shoulder.

"How did you get here?" Jonah asks. "Did you swim or did you make a raft or what? We didn't see you following us."

"No, no, no, no, no. Swim? Ha! Are you mad? Are you crazy? I used the reef. If you were smarter, you would have used the reef."

"What reef?" Malix asks.

Tunick dips a hand into the small green pack that hangs from his hip and pulls out another white seed. He stuffs it into his cheek and says, "I'll show you the reef and then my home. Come, come, come." The man turns and nods at Brooklyn as he squeezes past her. "You, too. Come to the reef!"

"Wait!" Vespa calls after him. "What about our friend? We have to get the white thing in there started again so we can get him back! Right now! Come back here!"

"Those only work once." Tunick turns around. It looks like he's in pain. "Your Kippy dog friend won't be coming back. My turn next time, okay?" Then he starts down the tunnel again. "This way to the reef!"

The group looks at each other and then back at the door of the sphere. Jonah doesn't know what to say. Can they just walk away? Every couple hours, someone else is left behind. How long until it's him? And when are his eyes going to give him away?

"We need to go west!" Brooklyn shouts.

"Yes! West! We'll go west! Yes, west! Yest! Wes! This way to the reef, hurry. There are white spider-y things. They're hungry. They..." And his voice gets softer and more distant until it's nothing more than a faint series of mumbles.

"What do you think?" Brooklyn asks Vespa.

"We can't let him get away," Vespa says.

"I think we need to move anyway. Whoever is following us, this Zion guy, could be up on the edge right now trying to figure out which cave we're in," Michael says.

"I agree," Christina says. "We have to stop stopping."

"But that doesn't mean we have to follow *this* guy! He's freaking nuts!" Portis yells.

"He scares me," Bidson mumbles from under his arm. "And we can't leave without Kip."

"Hate to say it, but it sounds like he's a goner, which totally sucks, guys. I mean it, he was my friend," Hopper whispers. He swallows hard and then grabs the lantern out of Michael's hand. "But we *have* to follow this guy. How else are we going to get out of here? Ya freaks want to climb up the sides of the crater? Especially if this Zion guy is up there waiting for us with a knife between his teeth?"

Vespa looks toward the cave's front entrance, her eyes blank as paper. She then asks, "What do you think, Jonah?"

Jonah stares at the floor and then up at the star high on the wall. "Let's follow him."

"You heard the man. Let's go," Vespa says.

• • •

The tunnels wind like snakes, and Tunick jogs too far ahead at times, but he always runs back laughing, apologizing, urging them to move faster. Jonah keeps his eyes open for more symbols, anything to try to get Kip back. He thinks he's made a mistake, leaving instead of trying harder. But Tunick could have answers. Jonah jogs behind Brooklyn and tells her what happened in the sphere.

She listens, asks questions, and tries to keep up with Tunick, but she loses her cool after a few minutes and demands the man slow down, that she's feeling sick. Tunick just picks up more speed.

Cool air shoots past them after another twenty minutes. Soon, Jonah hears water lapping on the beach, and then over Brooklyn's shoulders, he sees a pale triangle of Peleus moonlight. They spill out of the base of the mountain and find themselves at the foot of another path through the vegetation, just like the one Christina and Malix found on the other side. Tunick waits impatiently as the kids stop and drink water; he hops around giggling for a few seconds before lunging to put Michael in a quick headlock, and then he begins to shadow-box the air. He moves furiously, his arms whipping back and forth like pistons. His energy amazes Jonah. It seems as if the guy could run straight up one of these trees and jump to the top of the next one, top-to-top, top-to-top, all the way around the island.

Tunick boxes his way over to Jonah, and when no one seems to be looking, he snatches Jonah hard by the elbow and whispers, "Do you want to see the reef now, smart boy? Are you feeling limber? Are you feeling…light on your feet?" His breath is sour and suffocating, a cloud of rotten flesh. Jonah gives a nervous laugh and tries to back away, but Tunick only pulls him closer, his fingers tightening around his elbow. His voice turns serious. "Soon, smart boy, you'll be very light on your feet, I guarantee it. Ooh, boy. You're going to like it."

Jonah wrenches his arm away. He places his hand on the strap of his rifle as a warning.

"All right." Brooklyn squeezes between Jonah and Tunick. "We're ready when you are, madman. Just don't lose us."

Tunick keeps staring at Jonah and then spins away, laughing and clapping his hands. He opens the pack on his hip and tosses two more white seeds into his mouth. He then stops suddenly as if he's seen a ghost, and he waves his arms wildly over his head, like he's communicating with something in the sky. He screams nonsense at the air above his head and then pounds his fists against his temples. Before Jonah can ask what he's doing, Tunick relaxes with a smile. "Okay, okay, okay. They're gone. They'll leave me alone for a while. This way, ladies and gentlemen. To the reef with us!"

"Just wait!" Jonah shouts, but Tunick runs down the path. Jonah gives chase with the rest of the kids close behind, and he worries about where this man will actually lead them, if they're headed for a reef or some kind of trap. He can still feel Tunick's fingers around his elbow and taste his breath in his mouth. Tunick ducks between a couple of partially uprooted trees and then skips into an open stretch of tropical flowers and wispy black weeds. Then the man hits an all-out sprint. Jonah's legs feel surprisingly strong, and he pumps his arms, clearing ten feet at a time. Soon, he's only a few paces behind. Tunick makes a sudden left and speeds through a line of trees. They reach the gray beach in no time.

As they stop to catch their breath, Jonah turns to see Brooklyn rocking back and forth on her heels. She looks nauseous, her throat tightening.

"Hey," Jonah asks. "What's going on with you?"

She squints and forces a smile. "Think I have some kind of flu or something. I'll be okay."

"You sure?"

"Of course, *ca-dick*. Relax."

Tunick scoops up an armful of sand and attempts to dropkick it. "Good, good! You guys are *so* good! I'm so glad you're here. Oh man! It's been a long time, a long time. Okay, the reef now. I want you to meet my good friend. He's the best."

He runs toward the water, and once his feet get wet, he darts right, parallel with the sea line. This time the kids are hot on his trail, even Bidson and a struggling Brooklyn, all of them seemingly invigorated by Tunick's energy and the possibility of leaving the island without getting back on their rafts. Off on their left, the shadowy mainland looms with mountains, surprisingly just half a mile away or less. The shore curves right, and around the bend, Jonah sees a winding white shadow stretching through the water.

"Look, look!" Tunick points to the sea, his dirty index finger jutting back and forth so fast it's a blur. "It's not so bad. You just have to keep moving, and be mindful of the zims, 'cause they'll bite ya! They'll bite ya right in the neck. Look at my neck." He leans his head to the side, showing Jonah a cluster of tiny welts that remind him of the school of silvery scars lining his own back. "They're like piranhas but meaner, and they feed on the reef, right at the surface of the water. But just follow me and you'll be fine." Tunick spits a sticky white line of saliva over his shoulder and then spins around so he can address the group. "Just follow me, step where I step, do as I do, keep moving and dodge the zims."

"What are the zims?" Michael asks.

"They're like piranhas, but meaner." Jonah shrugs. He makes eye contact with Vespa and Brooklyn, the two of them displaying the same look of apprehension.

Tunick pulls back and puts his finger to his lips to shush them all, but no one is speaking. He rolls his big green eyes from side to side and then pounds the heel of his palm against his temple. "Okay, they keep talking to me, but I need to focus on the reef. We ready to focus?" Then he's off like a shot, high stepping into the sea until he dives over a low wave. "Now, now, now!" he yells, standing up to his waist. The reef rises out of the water a dozen feet in front of him, a skeletal on-ramp to an ancient highway.

"That guy is out of his fucking mind," Portis says.

"An obvious case of schizophrenia," Michael says. "Notice the disorganized speech, the paranoia." They all watch Tunick pull himself on top of the reef. The man whips his hands around his knees as if battling a swarm of invisible bees. "And possible hallucinations brought on by social isolation."

"But do you guys trust him?" Jonah asks. "Because I don't. What if he was wrong about that room and getting Kip back?"

"I don't know if I *trust* him, but I think I *love* him," Hopper says. "The guy's a freaking riot. I want him to be like my big brother or my dad or something."

"You're an idiot," Vespa says.

"Let's just get back to the mainland and reassess things. Decide if we want to follow him any farther," Brooklyn says, clenching her eyes in pain. "If he tries anything, we lose him, one way or another."

"I like what I hear," Vespa says, draping her arm over the demic's shoulder.

"I bet he knows this moon inside and out," Michael says. "He could be indispensable. He could even be our ticket off this place somehow."

"Sure, he could, maybe, but this dude could also be our demise. Look at him out there," Malix says, nodding at Tunick who gnaws on his elbow like a dog with a new bone. "He's obviously messed up."

Vespa checks her rifle. "I just want him to introduce us to this Zion guy. Then show us how to get west. And quickly." She nods at Jonah, acknowledging his secret disease and its ticking clock. He blushes and then nods back, even though he doesn't feel like it.

Aussie begins to walk toward the water. Her voice is frantic. "We have to keep running. We have to run. We have to keep running. We have to run. We have..."

Soon, all the kids are in the dark water, swimming for the reef with prayers that whatever's below them—be it zims or the translucent airplane monsters from the day before or something else—won't feast again until daybreak. Tunick jumps farther down the reef, and when Vespa says they're ready, the man claps his hands and then rubs his fingers together over the ends of his dreadlocks. "Watch me, watch me. There are some places that are a little—"

A piece of coral breaks under the man's bare foot, and Tunick tumbles into the water with shrieking laughter. The kids gasp and Aussie yells about the zims, but it's not a second before Hopper reaches down and offers Tunick a hand. "Thanks, partner. Thanks, mate. What's your name, Mr. Mustache?"

"Jules Hopper. But just call me Hopper like everyone else."

"Hopper Hoppy Happy. I'm choosing you, Hopper Happy. I'm choosing you, too." The man then yells up at the stars: "I'm choosing this one, too! Mr. Hoppers!"

"Okaaaay, man." Hopper laughs. "Sure thing."

"You've been chosen now."

"You're choosing him for what?" Jonah asks. "What are you talking about?"

"You, too, smart boy. You have some legs. I've chosen you, too. I already told them about you. Now, okay, let's go before we wake the zims. Come on, Happy Hopper. Hop this way!"

Tunick spins and hustles over the reef. Jonah tries to keep up, running over the skeletal structure like a kid during the first five seconds of recess. He runs and attempts to open his mind, wanting that feeling from the sphere back, before Kip disappeared. Something was happening inside him. He just wishes he knew what it was. Maybe Tunick will know.

They go a hundred yards, then two hundred, three, four, and the kids start to relax. The sea on either side of them remains smooth and quiet, and there are no signs of zims or any other forms of life. Third in line behind Tunick, Jonah calls over Hopper's head a couple times to again ask Tunick questions, but the man just speeds up, crossing the rest of the coral reef like a cheetah zipping over a line of grass.

Aussie falls in the water, and so does Bidson, but they're back on the reef in seconds without incident. Peleus continues to shine overhead, and it stays with them all the way to the mainland's silvery beach on the backside of the mountains. There's smoke in the air. But Jonah can't see where it's from.

While some of the kids drop to the sand in exhaustion, Tunick cartwheels around them, asking if anyone wants to race.

"Hell no," Hopper wheezes. "What I want is to get some real sleep. Where's this camp of yours?"

Tunick dislodges a few white seeds from his mouth and skips them out over the sea. He immediately replaces them with three more from his green hip sack.

"What *is* that? What do you keep eating?" Michael asks.

"Oh, just a snacky," Tunick says. "You can have some back at my place. It's about one mile east. That way, that way. You can sleep there, and we can have some more of your food, and we'll tell each other our stories and eat those brownies, and we'll talk about the crash and what happens next. I'd take one of those brownies right now if you'll give me one. Will you give me one? Just the brownie, just the brownie."

Vespa and Jonah exchange a look before Vespa turns to Tunick. "Listen, man. We appreciate you getting us off that island, but we can't go your way. We're only going west. But even before we do that, you need to bring this Zion asshole to me. Can you make that happen? He's got major, *major* crimes to answer to."

Malix pats his rifle. "Yeah. Where is this fucker?"

"Zion? No, no, no!" Tunick whispers. White saliva collects in the corners of his mouth. "That's mad! We go east tonight and I'll tell you things. Things that will blow your mind!"

Michael clears his throat. "Excuse me, Tunick? I'm sorry, but… Well, I really want to know what happened to Kip back there on the island and how we can find him. If there's another cave we can try. But also, and I think Jonah has asked you this a couple times, but we've yet to hear the answer. What's so bad about Thetis? Why did you leave?"

Tunick wheels around, his eyes on fire. "What's so *bad* about Thetis? Little boy, what's so bad about Thetis is that they *lie* to you on Thetis. They tell you one thing, and oh, everything is fine and dandy and then you want to do something they don't like and they lock you up and *starve* you. *And then* you say you've seen what they've been trying to hide, you've seen the outposts and the loooooong, scary history of it all, and then they say you can't have any more verve because they say it's bad for you, and then you tell them you're going to live on your own and then—and then they try to kill you! They tried to kill us! Do you understand, little boy? They piled us all in a rover and tried to drive us right off a cliff, but ho ho ho, it didn't work because Zion saved us. We escaped!"

Jonah quietly turns his rifle on as Tunick speaks. The man's entire body flexes as he rants and raves, and Jonah knows that look. He's seen in too many times in too many foster homes. Violence is near.

"So Zion is from Thetis, too?" Christina asks.

Brooklyn asks, "Who's 'they,' Tunick? Jesus. Just slow down."

"And what's 'verve'?" Bidson asks.

Aussie steps forward. "Are you okay? I mean, you've been here for a long time, and I don't know, maybe we can help you."

"And you can help *us* by finding Zion," Vespa adds. "We'll give you all our chocolate if you can get him here. Swear on my life."

Portis stops chewing on his hand long enough to take off his backpack. "Yeah, man, have some of our chocolate and then start from the beginning. Who tried to kill you? What exactly happened?"

Tunick laughs and then rages in a wide circle, pulling on his beard and dreadlocks, mumbling to himself before stopping to point a finger inches from Portis's face. "I get it. Now *you* want to take away our verve? That's why you're here! *You're* from Thetis! What a plan! Oh, ho ho ho. You don't know *what* you're doing, Big Head, working for them. Of course you're from Thetis!" Tunick shoves Portis down to the sand and steps over him.

Jonah raises his rifle. "That's enough! Back away!"

Tunick ignores everyone but Portis. "You're walking a terrible line, boy. Zion will kill you for this. I just showed you my reef and…this is *my* moon, and *I* make the rules, you understand that, Big Head? Do you want to tell me what to do on *my* moon?"

Vespa aims her rifle. "Back off, asshole. Now."

Jonah fans out, and Brooklyn, Christina, and Malix raise their weapons. Tunick smiles and sticks his arms high into the air. He then hawks up a glob next to Portis's head before twisting around, laughing. "Oh, come now. You don't have to do that, everybody. Where did you get all those guns?"

Jonah presses his eye to his scope. He can take this guy out at any moment, but he knows there are too many questions to be answered first.

Tunick puts his hands down. "Okay, my beautiful birds. I was just kidding with the bigheaded one here, okay? I love you guys. You're my favorites so far. Others were my favorites, but now you are."

"Take us to Zion," Vespa says. Her barrel glows white. "I'm not going to ask you again."

Tunick belches.

"Fine," Vespa says. She aims her mouth at the sky and screams, "ZION! COME OUT HERE, ZION!"

"ZIIIIII-OOOOOON!" Malix sings.

"Wait, guys," Jonah says. "Let's not just call for him without a strategy. Maybe put up an ambush first, all the cadets and Brooklyn get in a U-shaped position? Draw him in and then come at him from all—"

"ZION!" Brooklyn screams.

The yelling seems to stir something inside Tunick. He slams his green eyes shut and peels back his lips and bites at the air. Then he chews madly on the inside flesh of his cheeks. *Tunick can't snap yet*, Jonah thinks. *Not until he helps them.*

"Just wait! Vespa!" Jonah says between her shouts. He shuffles toward her. "Everyone stop yelling for a second and—"

"We just want to talk to you, Zion!" Malix shouts.

"Yeah, you piece of shit!" screams Christina.

"ZIIIIII-OOOOON!"

"Shh," Tunick whispers. "Everybody, shh. Please, let's go right now. Back to my camp and I'll show you some things. Lots of things that you'll want to see. Please, let's not yell for Zion. He's not happy right now. Not, not, not at all."

"Yeah, well, you know what?" Portis yells, getting to his feet. "We're not happy either, all right! We're being killed left and right! We're fucking being chased by a lunatic! One of us got sucked into a portal and didn't come back!"

"Zion!" barks Malix. "Zion, Zion, Zion, Zion, Zi-on!"

Jonah scans the line of trees above the beach. The cadets have lost their sense of training and strategy, running on anger and revenge instead. When no one comes, Jonah checks the reef over his shoulder. It's empty.

"Guys," Hopper says. "Forget Zion. Seriously, let's not mess with that freak right now. He wanted us to run, remember? So let's all just shut up and go to Tunick's and get some rest and hear him out. The dude is from Thetis, remember? Think about that. We can use his intel."

"Yes!" Tunick opens his arms. "Jules Hopper! My best friend! Soul mate! A mate made of my soul!"

"ZION!" Malix screams.

"Malix," Jonah shushes. "Stop!"

"Go to hell, Firstie. Get in the game."

"Seriously, let's just get out of here," Hopper says.

"We're not going east, demic, so shut your face and get it out of your head," Vespa says.

Hopper walks between Vespa and Tunick. "Because of Jonah, right? That's why we're in such a hurry to keep going west? I heard you guys talking in the cave, trying to be all hush-hush. Your dad sounds like a real winner, by the way."

Vespa's face turns maroon with rage.

"Who's Jonah?" Tunick asks.

Jonah slowly raises his hand and stares at Hopper. He doesn't know what to say. He still doesn't want anyone to know he's dying; if nothing else, if there were no sympathy or blame for the others dying along the way, it could make him expendable in the group. *Jonah's going to die anyway*, he hears them say in his head. *He should just sacrifice himself so the rest of us can get across.*

"Yeah, Jonah's sick, for anyone who cares," Vespa says. "If we don't make contact with Thetis in twenty days, then Jonah's not going to get the medicine he needs. And then…then he's going to die."

Everyone turns to look at Jonah. The cadet stares straight at a shocked Brooklyn and confesses, "Dr. Z said I have a blood disease and I need treatment in less than thirty days. If not, she said I'm going to…I'm probably going to… I'm sorry I didn't tell anyone. It was my secret to share, and I wasn't ready to share it, Hopper."

Hopper shrugs and walks away.

"Oh, Jonah," Aussie says.

"Damn," says Malix. "Really? You seriously have like thirty days to live?"

"Something like that. About thirty or twenty-eight days until I can't be treated and it's irreversible." Jonah keeps his eyes on Brooklyn's long face. She exhales with twitching lips. He doesn't know if he's ever seen someone feel so bad for him before. At that moment, he realizes he has a real friend. And now he's going to die.

"That settles it, then. If Jonah needs us to keep moving, we keep moving," Brooklyn says with a shaky voice. "Forget Zion for now. Let's stay ahead of him and make up some ground."

Jonah nods, thanking her. "It's not all about me, though. I can't do that to everyone. We should do what's best for the group. And maybe that means going back to the crash site?"

"Hell no," Brooklyn says.

"Well, I'm not going to die for Jonah just because he's already screwed," Hopper says. "And I don't know about the rest of you freaks, but if you haven't noticed, we keep dying or zipping through portals because we're in such a hurry all the time. We'll get west when we get west, all right? Let's chill with Tunick for a while and hear what's going on. The dude has been surviving here for a year now. Bet he's got tons of tricks."

Vespa turns her gun to Hopper's face. "We're going west."

"So it seems, so it seems." Tunick peeks over Hopper's shoulder. "But if you follow me, I can take you to the others. I know where they are."

Jonah immediately puts Tunick's forehead back in his crosshairs. "You know where they are? Are you talking about the adults? Doctor Z?"

Bidson stumbles forward with an open mouth. "Really?"

"Where?" asks Michael. "Where are they?"

"Ah, ah, ah. I'll help you if you help me. Scratch our backs together, if you know what I mean."

"Tell us where they are. Right now!" Vespa rams the butt of her rifle toward Tunick's gut, but the man blocks it with his palm. When Vespa swings for the side of his knee, Tunick rockets an elbow into her eye. The Fourth Year falls to her knees and loses her rifle. In an instant, Tunick has his arm around her neck, the barrel of the gun lodged against her chin.

"Whoa, dude," Malix says. "Relax, relax."

"Let her go!" Brooklyn growls.

"Now!" Jonah yells, circling left. Portis, Christina, and Malix circle, too. Each of them passes up initial clear shots, just as they were trained. Jonah is relieved they're still following some protocol, but he can't stand the sight of Vespa being so vulnerable. He doesn't know how long he can hold out.

"You just made a huge mistake," whispers Brooklyn. "You're a dead man now. You're dead."

"Shoot him." Vespa spits.

In a singsong voice, Tunick says, "Shoot me and you'll never find those adults you love so much." He then gets serious. "If you ever want to be tucked in again and be told what to do and when to do it, then you should listen to me and give me what I want."

Brooklyn takes a step forward. "Screw you."

"Where's the energizer?" Tunick barks. The desperation in his voice sends shivers down Jonah's back. Vespa tries to drop her weight and twist away, but Tunick tightens his hold, choking her.

Michael steps next to Brooklyn. "Where's the what?"

Tunick clenches his face and then spits a white stream onto Vespa's shoulder. "From the ship, from the ship. The ion fuel cell container you were bringing to Thetis. I want it. I need it, I need it, I need it. Trade me for the girl."

"The thing Paul was looking for? It's gone, man," Portis says. "Nobody could find it."

"LIAR!" Tunick screams. "Don't you lie to me, too! I'll kill her! I'll kill you all!"

The cadets change direction, preparing to take him out.

"Shoot him!" Vespa coughs. Jonah sees she's reaching for her thigh pocket and the blue handgun, but she can't reach it.

"Zion will kill everyone. All of us. So stop LYING and just GIVE ME THE ENERGIZER!"

Hopper holds out his arms, circling Tunick and blocking Malix and Brooklyn's view. "Dude, we couldn't find that thing. Seriously, Tunick. Bro, listen to me. Somebody stole it or it rolled into the jungle or it just blew up, because we looked all over for it. There's no power supply."

"You're lying to me," Tunick says. "Just like they lied to me on Thetis. You want to lock me up. You want to tell everyone it was an accident." He backs toward the jungle. The cadets shuffle their wide circle right along, keeping Hopper, Tunick, and Vespa between them.

"Hopper, out of the way. Stop right there, Tunick," Jonah warns. He finally gets a clear shot, and he knows some of the other cadets must, too, but at the last second he thinks about Dr. Z and the other adults. Killing Tunick may mean killing them.

"Dr. Z!" Jonah shouts into the trees. "Garrett! Dr. Z! Anybody!"

"Anybody!" Michael echoes.

Tunick keeps moving toward the jungle, and Vespa keeps reaching for her pocket.

"Stop, man. Just stop right there. What else do you want?" Malix asks. "We don't have that one thing, but we have blankets, fresh water, and food, man. What else do you want?"

They step into the grass, and Tunick finally stops and growls, "I want the energizer. That's it. This is your last chance because I'll kill this girl. I've killed girls before. SO TELL ME WHERE YOU PUT IT!"

"If you assholes don't shoot him right now," Vespa says, "I'm going to—"

"SHUT UP!" Tunick screams in her ear.

Jonah sees it out of the corner of his eye. Up in the sky, disappearing into a cluster of clouds on the other side of the beach, are the blue lasers of an LZR-rifle. They come in tight pairs. Over and over.

"Sean!" he yells, pointing to the lights.

Everyone turns, and Malix shouts, "Cadets in trouble!"

Tunick seizes the opportunity and whips Vespa into Christina.

Their heads collide with a resounding thud, and they stumble backward into a shadow and then somehow disappear.

"Vespa!" Jonah runs. It takes him less than a second to realize the girls have fallen into a shallow trench. When he reaches the shadowy lip, he knows Tunick is already gone, and with him, any chance of finding the adults alive.

CHAPTER TEN

Enraged, Vespa and Christina sit on the edge of the trench; Vespa rubs her throat and grinds her teeth while Christina takes a long swig from a water jug.

Behind them, Jonah and Portis shoot pairs of lasers into the air. Jonah knows it's his fault Tunick got away, and he can't look anyone in the eye. How could he have gotten so distracted? He keeps shooting and looking down the beach. If it was Sean or Ruth sending those distress signals before, they're not responding now. So, it was all for nothing.

Michael, Jonah sees out of the corner of his eye, stands facing away from everyone. But when something squawks in the jungle, the boy spins around, and there's a large wet spot on his pants.

"Whaaaat? *You did not*!" Hopper bellows. "I love it. Wow. Classic pissy right there. Holy shit, that's great. I knew I could count on you."

Something snaps in Jonah. He drops his weapon and charges at Hopper, punching him hard in the jaw. The hacker twists in the air, his long black bangs whipping in the opposite direction, and he disappears into the trench.

"Finally, Jonah. Thank you," Brooklyn says.

"Asshole!" Hopper shouts from the bottom. "I can't believe you hit me! Ass! Hole!"

Jonah is immediately disappointed with himself. Even though it felt good, punching the hacker seems below him. Looking down into the trench and then back at Michael, he wonders what things would be like if an adult were with them. Would he have snapped like that?

Vespa looks up at Jonah, her green eyes filled with venom. "The next time I tell you to shoot somebody, you shoot somebody. Do you understand me? No questions asked, Firstie."

"Tunick knew too much for us to just kill him, especially about the adults."

"I agree," Brooklyn says.

Vespa jumps to her feet. "ZION! TUNICK! DR. Z!"

Hopper climbs out of the trench. The right side of his jaw is bright red. He spits and scrunches his nose. "Fuck you, Jonah. I hope you die soon."

Brooklyn's fist comes out of nowhere, burying itself into Hopper's stomach. The boy drops to his hands and knees and tries to catch his breath.

"Stop it, guys," Bidson says.

Brooklyn can't help herself. She kicks Hopper in the stomach, flattening him.

Bidson shakes his head. "That's enough."

Aussie stands in front of the group. "Guys, let's go! Why are we just sitting here? We have to follow Tunick. He can lead us right to the adults."

"Supposedly," Malix says.

Christina scans the trees with her night-vision scope. "Right. I'm thinking that was all BS. Who knows what that guy actually knows."

"He has a gun now," Michael says.

This fact sinks in for a moment before Vespa pulls out her blue handgun. "Screw him. Let him go. If he were going to kill us, he'd be sniping us from the trees right now, picking us off, laughing like a damn fool. The best revenge would be to just leave him here on this piece of shit moon. We'll redouble our efforts to move west, and after twenty days, we'll set the biggest distress fire signal you've ever seen and Thetis will come right on over. I'm sick of it here. I'm *really* sick of it here."

"Definitely," Brooklyn says. "Let's get ourselves saved. Let's help Jonah."

"But what about Sean? Forget about my disease for a second. Sean must be in trouble, right? Shouldn't we help him?" Jonah asks.

Portis shrugs. "If he's not responding, he's probably dead."

"Ruth, too," Christina says.

"Can we go back to the beach, please?" Bidson asks. "Just standing here near the jungle doesn't feel the safest."

Michael pulls at the front of his pants and then turns to the water and sighs. "Well, if we're going to keep going, it looks like the shore might eventually curve west beyond the island, so I'd say we're actually in pretty good shape." Then, in a quieter voice: "Everything considered, of course."

Vespa straightens the pack on her shoulders. "Fine. Let's regroup on the beach."

They walk silently into the full moonlight. As soon as they step onto the sand, though, there's rustling behind them in the jungle, and everyone spins around with their rifles up.

"What was that?" Christina whispers.

"I don't know," Portis says.

"Zion?" asks Michael.

They all stand silent, listening, until Bidson asks, "Where's Hopper?"

Jonah looks over the line of kids. Hopper's gone.

Vespa shakes her head. "He wants to be with Tunick, I guess. Guy's nuttier than I thought he was."

"He's crazy," Malix says. He cups his mouth and shouts, "Hopper! You're crazy!"

Everyone looks at Jonah, who yells, "I'm sorry, Hopper! Come on back! I'm sorry I hit you!"

"I'm not!" Brooklyn yells.

Malix steps toward the trees. "Do we go after him?"

"Come back, Hopper! I'm seriously sorry!" Jonah yells.

"Should we take a vote?" Portis asks. "Do we really *want* him back?"

"Let him go," Brooklyn says. "He lost the homing device, and he's been an absolute jerk to everyone. If he wants to join forces with that lunatic out there, let him. He'll come back."

"That could be dangerous, though. I mean, Hopper's a genius," Michael says. "And angry geniuses are vengeful ones. Don't you guys read science fiction?"

"Screw him." Vespa spits. "Does anyone else want to leave?"

Aussie raises a trembling hand. "I think…I think I want to go back. I'm really scared and I'm freaking out, and I think I just want to go back to the crash site and see who's still there. We're pretty close to it now, and I think I'm ready to go back to the ship and see if the others are still there and then wait." After a pause: "I'm sorry, Jonah."

Jonah opens his mouth to say she doesn't need to apologize, that it makes perfect sense, and at the rate they're going there's no way he's going to make it anyway, but Bidson clears his throat and adds, "Yeah, me, too."

"I could go either way at this point," Christina says, sighing.

"What? Don't you all remember the cook and the teacher?" Vespa asks. "What was on their shirts? Or on the shirts that Malix found? And the fire just last night up on the cliff? Someone's killing people at our crash site and you want to go back?"

"Yeah, it was an asshole named *Zion*," Malix says. "We know who it is now. We don't have to keep going west. We'll just shoot the fucker."

Vespa throws up her arms. "I want to shoot him, too, *believe me*. That's all I want. But the bottom line is that we have to close the gap and get in the telescope's range as soon as possible. For Jonah. For all of us."

"We keep going west," Brooklyn says. "Absolutely."

"Guys, no. Brooklyn. Vespa. This is ridiculous," Jonah says, blushing from the attention. "If it weren't for me being sick, you know we'd all be heading back to the crash site right now to warn anyone who's still there that Tunick's coming to look for the power supply, and to tell them about Zion. Think about it for a second. When we were in the cave, after we lost Richter and before Kip vanished, I told myself, *and* I told you, Vespa, that we should go back. My life isn't worth anyone else getting killed. How many kids have died since we started?"

"Three," Michael says. "Four, with Kip."

"Five, if you include Hopper leaving," Michael says.

Bidson adds, "Seven, if you count Sean and Ruth."

"Seven. Seven kids are gone. Already, just two days in, seven kids are gone, and three are definitely dead. That's *ridiculous*. I'm going back to the site and you all should, too, to help whoever's left. No one else is going to die for me. My life..." Jonah trails off. Then, after a hard swallow, he continues, "My life hasn't exactly been a good one. It's been shit, to be honest. And the way things are going, it looks like it's either going to keep being shit, or it's just going to end. The rest of you, your best chance is to go back to the crash site and protect yourself there and wait to be saved."

"Jonah, be optimistic," Brooklyn says. "In nineteen days or so we'll be visible to Thetis."

"Be realistic! Do you really think they're going to be monitoring Achilles at the *exact* moment we're visible to them, scanning our *exact* vicinity? If I were a demic and I could calculate the odds, I'm sure they'd be ridiculous."

"That's why we're going to set a fire," Vespa says. "They'll see the smoke. We'll burn a thousand acres."

Jonah stares at Vespa. He knows she's going to see him as a quitter, a coward, and an ignorant Firstie, but it doesn't matter anymore. He'd rather she see him as all those things, than for him to see her die for him. "I've made up my mind. I'm going back."

"Don't be stupid," Vespa says.

Aussie hugs him. "You're so brave. Thank you."

"I think he's right," Christina says. "Our odds are better going back."

"Jonah!" Vespa barks. "You are *not* just going to give up! That is *not* what you were trained to do at the academy! So get your ass in gear, suck it up, *shut up*, and move west."

"No," Jonah says.

"We should all go back, Vespa," says Portis.

Vespa never breaks eye contact with Jonah. "I'm not going back. You can go back and sit around and wait for help to come—*wait to die*—or you can bring the help to you, and live. We're already two days in. It would be idiotic to turn around now."

"I'm sorry."

Vespa's eyes burrow into his so hard he feels she can see the blue behind their sockets. "So, that's how you're going to honor your parents' death? *That's disgusting*."

Her words cut brutally deep, but Jonah doesn't flinch. "If you keep going west, Vespa, *you're* going to die. Is that how you're going to honor *your* dad? You'll never see if his obsession was worth anything."

Vespa charges and everyone scatters. Jonah closes his eyes and waits for the fists to come. After a few seconds, though, he opens his lids to find Vespa standing directly in front of him, the toes of their shoes inches apart. He looks down into her furious green eyes.

"You talk about my dad again, I'll kill you. I'll kill you before any disease has the chance."

"Sorry," Jonah says. "I didn't mean—"

"Brooklyn!" Vespa shouts into Jonah's face.

"Yeah?"

"You staying with these cowards, or are you coming with me?"

Brooklyn doesn't answer at first, and then she whispers, "I

don't want to go back. I want to keep moving. Help Jonah." After a pause, she adds, "Help myself."

"Malix! What about you?"

"It's too crazy out here, Vespa. And with that Zion guy out there, I think we're better off back at the site. Maybe the demics we left behind have fixed something and we're hours from getting picked up. Maybe Kip made it back."

"Sorry, Vespa," Christina says.

Vespa squints at Jonah and clenches her jaw. It still looks like she's going to punch him, and he flexes his stomach muscles to lessen the incoming pain, but to his shock, Vespa pushes onto her toes and wraps her arms around his neck. She hugs him tight, and he loses his breath as he smells the ocean on her skin.

The Fourth Year slowly draws back. Jonah wants to pull her back in and whisper something into her ear, just like Paul, but before he can, Vespa blasts her palms against his shoulders, knocking him five feet backward into the sand. He lies there absolutely paralyzed from both the shove and the hug; he tries to stand up, but his legs and arms simply sink a few inches into the wet beach.

"If you're going to be a quitter, fine." Vespa stands over him. "But I won't be. If you think you're safer back there, *not running*, your disease must have gotten to your fucking brain. And, who knows, maybe you don't even have a disease. You ever thought of that? Have you thought that maybe Dr. Z was lying to you this whole time, and if she's involved with all this, this could be a part of her sick plan?" Jonah takes a deep breath. Yes, he's thought of that, but he remembers her face hovering above his after the crash, the sincerity and concern in her eyes. "People are dying out *here*, Jonah? More people have died back there. That's a fact. Count it up. I'm going to keep running and I'm going to cut the days in half, and I swear to my dad's old god that I'm going to get to Thetis and see what the fuss is about. I'll stop by in about twenty days with a ship from Thetis, so if you're still alive from just sitting around and waiting with your thumb up your ass, then maybe I'll pick you up."

And with that, she turns around and grabs Brooklyn's elbow. The demic in the huge white shirt, his one true friend, nods at him and mouths "Goodbye." And then the two girls start jogging west.

Jonah sits up. "Vespa! Just wait! Brooklyn! Come on! Come back!"

The girls quickly fade into small silhouettes. Jonah takes a deep breath before standing to face everyone. He can't believe Vespa and Brooklyn just left. And that they left for him. After a few seconds, he looks up at the crowd of dirty, hungry kids, and says, "I'm sorry I didn't tell you guys I was sick. And I'm sorry I led you away from the site and so many of your friends got killed. They were becoming my friends, too. Which is kind of rare for me."

"Man, I'd do the same thing," Malix says. "If you're *that* sick and you're actually dying, then it's a race against time. You didn't have a choice, man. Don't worry about it. But I'm surprised you'd *stop* going when those two are *still* going."

Jonah turns back to the beach. His stomach clenches in regret. "I know. I didn't think we'd split up. I thought everyone would go back together. Including them."

"It really does have the highest rate of survival. Going back, that is," says Michael.

No one responds, and after thirty seconds, they all turn and start to walk. Their feet softly crunch the silvery sand, and a water jug gets passed around. Jonah walks in a daze, barely listening to the others.

"Why do you think Tunick wants the power supply so much anyway?" Malix finally asks.

"Maybe he has some type of weapon he wants to charge," says Christina.

"Or maybe he wants to *build* a weapon," Bidson says.

"Out of what, though?" asks Michael.

Portis pulls the jug away from his lips. "Who knows what that asshole has out there? He could have scraps from his ship's wreckage, or he could have stolen stuff from ours. Maybe he has some sort of science experiment ready to go and he just needs some juice. That's why I think we should stay away from him."

"If he has a science experiment ready to go, then Hopper will come in handy," Michael says.

"That's if Tunick hasn't already killed him. Or Zion," Malix says.

With every step, regret moves from Jonah's stomach and begins to spill throughout his body, coating everything. His decision to stop moving west was based on keeping everyone else safe, sacrificing his life for everyone in the group, especially Vespa and Brooklyn. But they left, and he's going to die. *His friends left to save him, and he's going to sit around and wait to die?*

He doesn't say a word; he just turns and runs. The kids behind him call his name and Malix gives chase, but Jonah ignores them and keeps running. He follows Vespa and Brooklyn's small footprints in the sand, but after fifty yards, they veer right and disappear over the grass. Jonah skids on his heels and shouts into the jungle, "Vespa! Vespa! Brooklyn! Wait! I'm coming with you!"

Malix stops next to him and holds his breath, waiting for a reply from the girls. But the boys only hear squawks and leaves and the ocean lapping at the sand.

"Vespa!" Jonah shouts again.

"Brooklyn!" Malix yells. "We're right here! Hold on! Jonah's coming with you!"

There is no response. After a minute, Malix pats Jonah's shoulder and says they're gone, that it's time to go, but Jonah just stares into the dark line of trees.

"Vespa!" Jonah swings his rifle into his arms and shoots into the air, sending a repeating pair of blue beams skyward. Then he tries shooting in threes and fours, but there's still no response.

"They're gone, man."

Jonah can't believe it. He shoots twice more, and then he solemnly pulls the rifle over his back, turns, and walks past Malix in silence. Just like that? They're gone, too? This moon just keeps taking and taking. It can't just keep taking. At some point it has to give something back. Or someone.

"I don't think she actually wanted you to go with them, you know. You could hear it in her voice," Malix says as he slaps him on the back. "She's just trying to protect you if you're so sick. And you're really *that* sick, huh?"

He doesn't answer, picturing Vespa and Brooklyn sprinting through the trees, jumping up the sides of mountains, diving into waterfalls with some sort of snarling creature chasing behind. They've got about eighteen more days of *all this* to go out there. He knows he'll never see either one of them again.

When Jonah and Malix return to the group, Aussie wraps her arms around Jonah's sides, pinning his wrists to his body. It's been a long time since he's been hugged, and that's twice in ten minutes. "I just want to say I'm so sorry you're so sick."

Jonah wiggles out of her embrace and looks over his shoulder one last time, hoping to see the girls returning at full speed, or maybe Kip. Or Brian or Rosa or Richter or… But no one comes.

"Do you need to rest?" Bidson asks him.

"I don't want to stop," he says. "I'm sick, but I don't feel sick, and I don't think I'll feel sick for another week or so. If everyone's up for it, I say we keep going. Get back as soon as we can."

"It might be faster to go back over the reef and then across on the rafts," Bidson says. "There's no way we'll be able to climb those mountains."

"I can't go back on those rafts," Michael says.

"Me neither," adds Malix.

"No way," Aussie says.

"But what about Tunick?" asks Portis. "We set foot in that jungle and that dude will straight up kill us. He'll kill us, and then he'll eat us, and then he'll eat all the chocolate out of our packs for dessert."

"Jonah?" Michael asks.

He squints upward at the mountains. This is a decision Vespa would make, and he wishes she were there to make it. Everyone stares at him, and it's odd; some of them have pity in their eyes, but there's also respect there. It's strange to see, and it feels incredible. "No," he finally says. "Tunick is long gone. Like Vespa said, if he wanted to kill us, we'd all be dead. He's after that energizer—that's all he seems to care about. And he's probably halfway back to the site with all his little roads and paths he's made over the past year. There has to be a fast way to get through those mountains. A valley or a tunnel or something."

"You're probably right," Michael says.

"But what about Zion?" Aussie asks. "It sounds like he's the guy we need to be worried about. What if *he's* in there?"

Christina reaches behind her back and produces a blue handgun. She hands it to Aussie. "Then you shoot him."

"Oh." Aussie carefully turns the weapon over, examining every inch. It's obvious it's the first time she's ever held a gun, and Jonah wonders if it's a good idea.

"Wait," Bidson says. "I want a gun, too."

"Sorry. That's all I've got." Christina holds up her hands.

"Just use your muscles, man." Portis laughs. "Squeeze the shit out of somebody with your good arm."

"So, that's it, huh? We're going through the jungle, then," Malix says.

Jonah sees a look of concern come over all their faces. Like him, they're probably imagining packs of bloodthirsty monkey creatures with glowing eyes, flying jellyfish dragging sharp talons, and a beastly, half-naked Zion carrying an armful of spears, one for each of them. He looks through the night-vision scope of his rifle. Nothing shows up. With a flick of a finger, the barrel glows white. He takes a step forward and says, "Let's just get this over with."

They creep inside the jungle line, their flashlights and lanterns on. Overhead, branches shake and crack, and there's a low chittering all around, but the cadets only find small flying discs and birdlike creatures in their scopes. Jonah has to remind himself to breathe at first, but after twenty minutes, they all fall into a rhythm, and then Malix and Christina hesitantly resume their roles as scouts.

Jonah allows Michael to hold on to the back of his jumpsuit, and he forgives him each time he bumps into him when he stops to listen. Aussie follows closely behind, breathing rapidly, her gun straight out in front of her face.

Bidson stumbles nearby. "I keep picturing the adults are all around a fire at the crash site. They've killed Zion, and everybody else is okay, and they're almost done fixing the communication network. And Hopper has made it back, too, and he is feeling so guilty about leaving us that he's putting together a rescue team to come find us."

"I like that," Portis says. He moves ahead and spins with his eye glued to his scope. When he's satisfied, he aims into the canopy and spins again. This is how he moves, spinning and aiming, spinning and aiming, pausing only to bite a finger or chew on his shoulder. "There's no way in hell Hopper is there already when he has only had a ten-minute start on us, though, but it's definitely possible that the adults are back and they're fixing things. Maybe that fire we saw up there last night was our guys killing Zion. Wait, here comes Christina."

Christina's face pokes through a row of giant orange wildflowers. "You guys have to see this."

CHAPTER ELEVEN

From a distance, it looks as if they've found a bright, twinkling city in the middle of the jungle. Jonah chases Christina into a cluster of trees that appears to be hooked up to a power grid. Millions of tiny white bulbs pulse like winter holiday lights back on Earth, and Jonah's eyes sting painfully, but he refuses to look away.

Michael rotates on his heels. "Whoa."

Malix steps out from behind one of the glowing trees. "But look closely! They're some kind of lizards or something. Check it out."

Jonah cautiously walks to the nearest tree, shielding his eyes from the growing light. He focuses on one of the bulbs, and when it finally fades, he sees a five-inch winged toad creature with a swirling red and yellow design on its back. Two long, floppy ears slide back and forth over the toad's striped head, as if they're licking its scalp, until they seem to pick up Jonah's presence, and then they both point at his face. The design on the toad's back separates, revealing a cloudy white abdomen. A microscopic light appears on the abdomen's tip, and within seconds, the creature glows with such intensity that Jonah has to finally look away.

The lights reach a hundred or more yards to the east and west, pulsing in several patterns. It's like the kids are in a grand hall, or an outdoor mall, and to Jonah's surprise, Malix and Christina lock arms and swing each other around, laughing among the twinkling lizards.

"Why do you think they glow like that?" Portis asks Michael.

"Oh, probably for mating, but it's funny because they don't seem to be moving much. They're not pairing off. But their bioluminescence could also be due to the production of certain defensive steroids that tell their predators they taste bad."

"Right," Bidson whispers.

"So, does this mean they think we're the predators?" Jonah asks. He slows his movements; he doesn't want to scare them off. He also doesn't want them to attack.

"Maybe," Aussie adds. "Or maybe there's something else around that triggered the light show. Maybe Hopper or Tunick was just here."

"True," Michael whispers. "But for all we know, this could be how they sleep."

Then, out of the corner of Jonah's eye, far down the path of well-lit trees, he sees a shadowy figure jump out from between two trunks and hide behind another.

"Hey, hey. We have company," Jonah whispers. His voice remains calm, but his heart immediately turns to fire. He's had enough surprises for one night. He presses his eye to his scope. The glowing toads are too bright, though, and to avoid burning away his vision completely, he rips the scope away from his face. His skin cools with anticipation.

"Is it Zion?" Bidson whispers.

"Where? Where?" Portis asks. He snaps his fingers at Malix and Christina, who stop dancing and jog over. "Jonah saw somebody."

"I saw it, too. Over there." Aussie frantically aims her handgun left and right. She then yells, "Hopper? That you, Hopper? Tell us so we don't shoot you! I have a gun now! Just tell us where you are!"

A shadow explodes out of a group of giant wildflowers and flattens itself behind a twisted tree. Malix charges ahead. "Stop! Stop right there! If you don't tell me who you are in two seconds, I'll shoot you right in the face, I swear to god!"

"It could be Vespa!" Jonah calls. "Don't shoot!"

The toads up and down the line of trees increase their brightness with all the noise, and Christina blindly circles around the opposite side of the twisted tree while Malix shields his eyes in front. A gunshot suddenly rings out. Once. Twice. Bark flies off the tree in front of the cadets, and they dive and roll away. The toads on the tree take flight, zipping toward Aussie, whose gun barrel smokes in her outstretched hands. The toads buzz and swirl together, and then they dive. A tornado of light attacks Aussie, and she screams and fires her gun without aiming, shooting Portis in the thigh. He collapses to the ground, wailing.

Jonah charges and swings the butt of his rifle at the buzzing cyclone of toads, a baseball player with a thousand balls to choose from. He bats several of the creatures to the ground. He can't hit them all, though, and even more descend from the trees to attack Aussie. They cling to her, covering her open mouth. Thousands more appear, first looping upward in a glowing arc, then winding toward Aussie like a school of fish. Jonah watches in horror as they blanket Aussie from head to toe. Suddenly a high-pitched yipping comes from behind the twisted tree, and the toads scatter into the sky. The yipping grows stronger and stronger, and finally the most stubborn fly off Aussie, leaving the girl convulsing with sobs, her skin bleeding with scratches and bites.

"Somebody!" Portis presses his hands tightly over his thigh. "She shot me, she shot me. Damn. *Shit.* I can't believe she shot me!"

With the yipping still echoing through the trees, Malix rips off the end of his sleeve, and he and Christina rush over to Portis. Bidson stands motionless on the side, afraid to move, and Jonah kneels over Aussie, who keeps whipping her hands over her body as if she were still being attacked by toads. He has to grab her wrists and pin them to the ground.

"Aussie, stop! You're okay, you're okay," Jonah tells her. "They're gone. The toads are gone, Aussie. Just stop. They're all gone."

Michael bounces around in panic, repeating Jonah's every word. Aussie sobs and finally opens her eyes, and then lets out a long, reverberating scream. It takes Jonah a moment to realize she has her eyes locked on something over his shoulder. He turns to see a young girl standing just behind him.

The girl slowly backs away. She's small and bony and absolutely filthy. A green vine keeps a wild mop of black hair out of her sunburnt face. In one hand, she holds a long, crooked machete made of black stone. In the other, a cluster of uprooted weeds with circular leaves that drops large clumps of soil with every step.

"Hey," Jonah musters. He keeps his eyes on the machete, which to his relief, is covered in a white liquid, and not blood.

"Great. Now who the *fuck* are *you*?" Portis groans. Christina and Malix reach for their rifles. Michael backs away silently, knocking a lantern over.

The girl twists around and stares at the three cadets, and then she puts a finger to her lips. Her nostrils flare in and out while her large eyes shift back and forth.

"What? Jesus, now what? What do you hear?" Portis asks. Then louder, "Enough with the fucking drama! I've been shot, little girl. I'm bleeding to death. Who the hell are you, and will you please just go away? JUST GO AWAY!"

"Portis," Jonah warns, his hand up to the girl. If she came from Thetis, if she's been on Achilles for over a year, then he wants to talk to her.

The girl clenches her jaw as Portis blathers on, and when it appears she can't take it anymore, she pounces, catching everyone off guard. She thrust-kicks Malix in the chest, sending him several feet backward. In the same motion, the girl spins and knees Christina in the temple, drawing blood. Before Portis can utter a sound, the girl has the machete pressed against his throat.

"Shit," Portis croaks, his hands planted on his leg wound. "I'm sorry. Don't kill me. Please."

Jonah scrambles to his feet. "Wait, please. We're just lost, and we're just trying to get—"

"Shh," the girl whispers angrily. A large chunk of soil falls from the roots of her plant.

Christina rolls onto her side and struggles to aim her rifle at the girl, but the long gun wavers weakly in her hand. "You little bitch."

"Everyone quiet," the girl whispers.

Jonah watches Malix creep up behind her. Before Jonah can tell him to stop, before the girl can react, Malix presses the barrel of his rifle into the back of the girl's skull. "Now you listen to me, you little piece of shit. Back away, drop your weapon and uh, that plant thing you have, and put your hands on the top of your head. Slowly."

The girl keeps the blade at Portis's throat and stares at Jonah. "Please be quiet. He's coming. We have to move. Now."

"Who's coming?" Bidson asks.

"Zion?" Michael whispers.

Aussie sits up and grabs Michael's hand. Jonah presses his scope to his eyes and scans the dark jungle, his heart beating out of his chest.

"Good," Malix growls, pushing the barrel harder against her skull. "It's time we meet."

"No. We have to go," she says. "Come with me."

"Zion! Get your ass out here! I want to meet you!" Malix shouts. He pulls the gun away from the back of the girl's skull and shoots a long blue beam into the air. "Come on out, asshole!"

The girl with the machete curses and spits, and then Jonah sees her whisper something into Portis's ear. The cadet's eyes instantly widen, and then just as quickly as she arrived, the girl disappears amongst the trees.

"Wait!" Jonah shouts after her.

Portis sits there, his mouth open. Then a smile appears on

his face before he clutches his leg and wobbles from side to side in pain.

"Portis?" Jonah asks. "What did she say to you?"

"Zion! ZION!" Malix screams. The few remaining toads circling above fly off, leaving the kids in almost complete darkness, with just slivers of Peleus slipping through the trees.

Jonah clicks on the light of his rifle. "Portis? What did she say?"

"Um, I'm really… She told me that my—"

There's a loud rustling to their left, and Jonah spins with his scope to his eye. Aussie grabs his jumpsuit, and Christina positions herself over Portis. Jonah turns on the night-vision mode of his rifle, and behind a sparse, spiky bush, he sees a bright green figure crouching, rubbing its hands manically together over its head.

"Tunick?" Jonah whispers loudly.

The bright green figure falls to his butt and claps his hands softly. In a low whisper, he asks, "Smart boy? Ooh, hoo, hoo, hoo. You need to run. Are you with Zion, smart boy? Did you meet Zion yet?"

"Not yet," whispers Aussie, her words catching in her throat.

Malix marches over. "Seriously, man? You again?"

Tunick crawls out of the bush. He rolls over and covers his face from the lights with his dirty hands, begging, "Stop, stop, stop. So much light. Don't be so mean all the time. You're so mean to me and I've been nothing but nice."

"Nice?" Christina laughs.

"I should kill you," Malix growls. "I should shoot your head off right here. What are you doing here?"

"Where's Hopper?" asks Michael.

"*Where's Hopper*? *Where's Kippy*?" Tunick asks. "The question is, little boy, where's Zion? Because I can smell him. He's downwind, so smelly. I heard you yelling. Don't yell at night. You'll attract so many things, so many bad things. I thought you were all smart."

Far off in the darkness, Jonah hears more rustling. A branch snaps.

"Uh oh," Tunick whispers. "Come, come, come. We must

run. We'll race, we'll race. Winner gets all the chocolate and the energizer."

"No," Jonah says. He squares himself in the direction of the noise. "We're not running anymore."

"And why the hell would we trust you after you attacked Vespa?" Christina asks.

Tunick draws his knees up to his face and then kicks his legs into the air. He lands on his feet and rubs his fingers together nervously next to his ears. "I'm sorry. I was confused. I was angry. Time is running short if I'm going to show you something. On the count of three."

"I can't exactly move, asshole," Portis whines. "I've been shot. By her."

"I'm so sorry, Portis," Aussie says.

"I'm *not* going anywhere!" Malix barks. "I want to meet this guy already. We've got a bunch of questions. And after he answers me, I'm going to burn a bunch of dots and Cs all over his fucking body."

Jonah continues to scan the darkness. With nothing to shield them but the trees, and no fortified escape route, they're at a complete disadvantage. "I thought you were friends with Zion, Tunick. Tell him we just want to talk to him and that we come in peace. He trusts you, right?"

"No, no, no. Not right now. I stole something."

"What did you steal?"

The noises grow closer. Jonah can't figure out what direction they're coming from. Malix presses his back against Christina's, and they slowly rotate with their rifles up.

Tunick begins to backpedal to the bush from where he came. "He doesn't want to talk. Be smart, smart kids. Come with me and *we* can talk, and I'll show you what I need to show you before it's too late. It's not very far from here. Look, look, look." He springs over to Portis and lifts him up by his armpits. "I'll carry Big Head." Tunick drapes the cringing cadet over his massive shoulders.

Jonah feels the jungle closing in on him, as if they just walked into a trap. He feels the exact opposite of what he felt in the sphere. He looks around at the disheveled, exhausted, and unprepared kids and shakes his head, his confidence gone. "Damn it. I think we should do this somewhere else. Set up a perimeter in case things go south. Get a wall to our back, or lead Zion into a bottleneck. Portis, are you okay?"

Tunick rotates so Portis can look at Jonah. "Man, I'm losing a lot of blood. I need to get out of here."

"Malix," Jonah says. "Let's fall back and find a better location, somewhere Zion can't get the fall on us like this. I want to talk to him just as much as you do, believe me."

Still up against Christina and looking through his scope, the cadet says, "I'm not going any—"

Blue lasers suddenly blast out of the darkness, sweeping back and forth over their heads. Jonah recognizes the lasers as Mayflower 2-issued LZR-rifle fire, and he hits the dirt and shouts, "Friendlies! Stop! We're friendlies over here! Cadets!"

Christina peels away from Malix and drops to a knee, firing back.

"Wait!" Jonah shouts. He pictures Vespa and Brooklyn, confused or in trouble, unknowingly shooting at their friends. "Friendlies! Friendlies! We're just kids! We're just kids!"

The lasers keep coming, shredding the trees all around them. Malix roars and pulls his trigger, sending a barrage of blue light into the shadows. The demics lie on the ground and cover their heads. A large branch overhead cracks and falls on Bidson, flattening him to the ground. Jonah doesn't know what to do, to fire back or retreat. He points his barrel skyward and shoots several pairs of lights, hoping to communicate with those in the darkness. The enemy stops shooting for a second, but before Jonah can call for a ceasefire, the lasers attack from a different angle.

"Over here!" Tunick grunts, tossing Portis high over the bushes. The cadet howls in pain, and Tunick jumps after him.

A beam blasts through Michael's long hair, and he falls writhing at Jonah's feet. This isn't friendly fire, Jonah realizes. That shot was intentional. He places himself behind a charred tree stump. He kills the flashlight under his barrel and yells for someone to turn off the lantern.

Aussie claws her way past Michael, crying and choking. She falls onto the lantern, snuffing its light.

Jonah waits until the enemy fire reappears, and once a few lasers blast in from the far left, he aims and shoots. The rifle bucks against his shoulder, and he locks his arms and tries to ignore Tunick's laughter. Bidson wiggles out from underneath the tree branch, huffing his way toward a row of thick wildflowers, but a laser catches his left wrist, blowing off his hand. The huge demic twirls away into the shadows.

"Fall back!" Jonah shouts.

"Are we hitting him?" Christina yells.

"Doesn't look like it," Malix says, ducking a beam. "The bastard keeps moving. *Stop moving*!"

Jonah can't believe how fast they seem to be losing. "That's it, cadets! Fall back!"

"Oh, come on!" Malix yells. He and Christina kneel and shoot randomly into the night, and Jonah knows it's doing more damage than good. If their body heat isn't giving their location away, then their rifles are.

Aussie and Michael belly crawl toward the bushes. In his night vision, Jonah sees them huddle near Portis and an unmoving Bidson. Tunick dances around their bodies.

"Last chance!" Tunick yells. "YOU'RE ALL GOING TO DIE! On the count of three! One."

"We gotta go, guys!" Jonah shouts at Christina and Malix.

"Two," says Tunick.

"We should split up and flank him," Malix growls.

Christina lets up on her trigger. "Flank him? We can't even see him. We should wait for him to expose himself."

"I'm not going to wait for him."

"Well, flanking is out of the question!" Christina barks.

"Three!"

Another chain of blue zips over their heads. A massive tree on the right explodes, and in what feels like slow motion, the trunk slides away, tipping directly toward the three cadets.

"Run, run, run!" Jonah dashes over and yanks Christina to her feet. Malix jumps up, firing, shouting. The cadets zigzag toward the bushes and barely leap out of the tree's path, and then they all skid to a stop, dodging a sweeping line of blue light. Christina and Jonah bump into each other and trip over a downed branch, tangling their limbs.

Malix makes a break for it—lasers buzzing all around him—and he dives and somersaults into the bushes. Christina pushes off Jonah and scurries after him.

"Jonah!" Aussie screams. "Come on!"

Jonah grits his teeth. He hears Manny's voice telling him to turn off his sheaf. He sees him falling through the trees, the cluster of spikes driving through his back. Then he sees Dr. Z's face and Professor Eck swinging back and forth, legless, vandalized. He whips his rifle onto his back and feels all of it, the loss of these people and all those who died in the crash, and it all festers together inside him until it runs blazing hot up his spine. He is going to kill Zion. He is going to kill Zion before he dies.

A blue beam passes over his head, burning his hair, as he crawls toward Aussie's handgun. He stuffs it into his pocket, takes another deep breath, and then gets up and sprints. A few steps later, a shoelace catches a downed branch, and Jonah falls flat on his stomach. He sits up and yanks hard on the lace, tangling it more.

"Shit!" he yells.

A laser buzzes over his left shoulder, and then another cruises over his right. *This is it,* Jonah thinks as he fumbles with his shoe. *Any second, it's all over.* But the next beam goes back over his left shoulder, and the next over his right. Zion, for whatever reason, is letting him live.

"Come on!" Malix shouts. "What are you waiting for? Come on!"

"Jonah! Run!" Aussie screams.

There's a pause in the fire, and Jonah rips off his shoe and barrels through the bushes, telling himself that Zion just made a huge mistake. Tunick grabs his shoulders and dances. "You made it, smart boy! Now we race. Ready?"

Jonah sees everyone is there, including a sheet-white Bidson, whose left wrist bubbles with blood. He's in too much shock to feel the pain, Jonah thinks, but that will change soon.

A laser punches the left side of a nearby tree, blasting leaves and branches high into the air.

The kids scatter in every direction. Aussie trips and lets out a blood-curdling scream: "Oh my god, oh my god, oh my god!"

"Run like mice." Tunick laughs. He yanks Aussie to her feet and pushes her through a line of trees. "Come, come, come!"

They follow Tunick down a steep embankment, Portis leaning on Christina. The lasers finally stop, and once they turn a couple corners, Jonah orders Tunick to slow down so they can bandage Bidson's wrist. The boy has started to moan incoherently, and he's stumbling left and right, bouncing off tree trunks and boulders.

The large demic clumsily sits on a rock and stares under his bushy eyebrows at the shards of bone sticking out of his skin. Christina rips the hem off her shirt and bandages the arm. As she attends to him, Michael staggers away and vomits.

Malix retraces a dozen steps and crouches behind a boulder to watch through his scope. Behind him, Tunick spits a white seed out of his mouth and tosses two more in from his green hip pack. Immediately, he flexes his arms out wide and whips his head back and forth.

Aussie sets her hands on Jonah's chest and discreetly pushes him away from the group. She's crying. "Up there. I tripped. I tripped and I saw them."

"Saw them? Saw whom?"

"Two adults from the ship. They were dead, Jonah. Their throats. Their throats were cut and..." She begins to shake and cry, and Jonah hugs her close.

"Who was it?" he whispers, hoping she's wrong.

Between huffing sobs, she says, "One was a navigator. A woman with a black braid. I remember her. And the other one was the engineer from my module. The one who helped us get out."

Jonah pushes her away. "Garrett? Was he wearing all red? A red jumpsuit?"

She nods, and he wraps his arms around her again. His chest rises, and he refuses to exhale, holding a huge breath for the engineer, thinking it will somehow bring the man back to life. Garrett's dead. It washes over him like a cold shower, and then all he can think about is the man's bright red jumpsuit. How it looked through all those sharp branches when he was trapped in his launch seat, and then how it looked from across the wreckage as he stood with Paul, the white mist gathering at his feet. It takes a second before Jonah realizes that if Garrett's dead, then Dr. Z is probably dead, too.

"What should we do?"

Jonah puts his lips next to her ear. He knows this news could incite a whole new panic. As long as they were simply missing, the adults were just a moment away from restoring order, from telling everyone it was all going to be okay. "Don't tell anyone yet. Let's wait until everyone's calm or back at the wreckage."

"Okay."

"Let's move," Malix calls over his shoulder. "This is taking way too long, guys."

Tunick bounces over to Jonah and says, "This way, smart boy. Follow my exact steps. Winner gets chocolate and the energizer. Yes, yes."

Bidson is on his feet, his knees buckling, his bandaged wrist hanging over Christina's shoulder, the other bobbing overhead. Jonah looks him up and down and doesn't think he'll make it. Not very far, anyway, and not without Dr. Z. Portis sets a hand on Michael's shoulder, and together they hobble ahead.

"How far are we from your place, Tunick?" Jonah asks, sighing.

"So close. Sooooooo close. You're going to love it."

Jonah looks down at his one bare foot and wiggles his toes.

Another thing the moon has taken. *Vespa*, he thinks. *Please come back.* Not to take over, but to give him the strength he needs to keep his head up.

"Please. Let's just go," Bidson groans. His thick right arm swings back and forth above his pale face.

Tunick skips along the base of the rocky embankment and everyone follows. Jonah ducks under Bidson's arm, giving Christina a break. He needs to think. If two of the adults were found dead up there, Jonah wonders, where are the other bodies? Did Aussie just not see them? Why did Zion let him live when the others were shot so ruthlessly? And what did that girl whisper in Portis's ear?

"Portis?" Jonah asks.

The cadet just mumbles, leaning hard on Michael.

"What did that girl say to you up there?"

He doesn't respond. No one does.

When Tunick gets to a line of trees with trunks no thicker than Jonah's thumbs, he pushes them aside like curtains. Beyond is a narrow valley between two cliffs. Tunick demands they flatten their backs against the right wall and shuffle along the stone. "I have traps. Traps, traps, traps. Traps for the splitters."

"What's a splitter?" Jonah asks as he maneuvers a barely conscious Bidson against the wall.

"Splitters are not the smart kids like you. They turned their backs on the verve. Now follow me ever so carefully." Jonah just shakes his head. It's impossible to figure out what this guy is talking about half the time.

After several more steps, Tunick cautiously jumps over a line of high grass in the middle of the valley and presses his back against the left wall. Aussie follows, then Michael and Portis somehow make it across. Jonah and Christina drag Bidson right through the grass to the other wall. There's an audible click as they cross, and Jonah braces himself for a log of spikes or poison darts to shoot out of the shadows, but nothing happens. Tunick shrugs and keeps going. Malix is always ten steps behind, his eye glued to his scope.

Finally, Tunick holds up a finger, stopping everyone. Then he lifts his leg and releases a roaring burst of gas.

Aussie turns her face away in disgust. "Are you crazy? That was so loud."

Tunick's giggling stops just long enough so he can whisper, "'Twas a verver, 'twas a verver. Nothing I could do. You'll understand soon, soon, soon. I'm sorry. Try not to smell it. It's for the best, I assure you."

"Then move," Christina whispers. "Let's not just stop and stand in it. Come on!"

Malix catches up and shines his rifle light into Tunick's face. "Seriously. Go. We need to find cover."

"But we're here and I won and I win all the chocolate." Tunick ducks down and digs his fingers into a crack in the wall. It takes a few seconds before an outline of a boulder becomes apparent. Then Tunick groans and laughs. "Ohhhhh. I just smelled it, and now I fear *I* might just die. Hold your breath, kiddies. That's a *really* sour verver. Ooh wee!"

"Just hurry the hell up, you stupid asshole!" Malix hisses.

In an instant, Tunick has Malix's throat in his hand. He grinds the cadet's skull into the wall and then presses his forehead to Malix's. Malix tries to kick him, but Tunick pins both his thighs down with one leg, and with his other hand, he holds the barrel of Malix's rifle firmly against the wall.

White spittle covers Malix's face as Tunick says in as clear a voice as they've heard from him all day, "Have some manners, kid. You're about to enter another man's home."

Christina untangles herself from Bidson and aims her rifle at Tunick. "Let him go, or I'll blow your head off. I'm sick your shit."

Tunick rolls his forehead along Malix's and looks hard at Christina. Jonah struggles to keep Bidson up against the wall, fearing he'll land in a trap if he hits the ground.

"Enough, Tunick," Jonah says. "He didn't mean anything by it. Christina, stand down. Everyone just—"

In a flash, Tunick drops his hand from Malix's neck and

snatches the rifle out of Christina's hands. He flicks the weapon upward, and the belt sails over the girl's head so she's no longer attached to it. Then he rips the rifle away from Malix and aims both at the group of kids.

Malix puts his hands up. "Whoa. I'm sorry, man. Tunick, I'm just tired. Listen. I'm tired and Bidson and Portis are dying. Everything's fucked up. Just relax."

Tunick's face twitches wildly, and then he hops up and down, grinning. "Smart boy, smart boy. Give me your gun right now, or I'll kill you all right here."

Jonah whips his eyes to Malix and Christina, who both shake their heads, but Aussie and Michael nod emphatically. He's suddenly aware of the handgun in his pocket, and after another second, he holds Bidson steady with one hand and pulls the rifle over his head with the other.

"Always the smart one," Tunick says, crunching on the white seeds in his mouth. "That's why I chose you. Now you and the rude one." He aims the barrel at Malix. "Put your fingers on the right side of that boulder and pull, pull, pull. Let's go inside and eat and talk and verve."

"What's 'verve'?" Michael says.

"You'll find out soon." Tunick smiles.

Malix sighs at Jonah, and then the two of them swivel the large stone away from the wall. It's pitch black behind it.

"Now go inside, and wipe your feet. I just cleaned up. Move all the way inside to the back. Make room, make room, make room."

CHAPTER TWELVE

The first inside, Malix yanks Jonah to his feet by the back of his collar, and then he shoves the First Year to stand at the other side of the opening. Jonah squares his feet and prepares himself. In his mind, he can hear the deep hoarse voice of the academy's Second Officer, Carlos Dravo: "The farther away you are taken from your point of capture, the more likely you are to never see your mommies and daddies again! Is that understood? And if you *are* taken into a dark room or pushed inside an unmarked vehicle, and you are *not* taken to a government-issued holding facility or a marked military vehicle, *expect* your captor to *try* to kill you! If you want to survive that situation, if you ever want to see anything you love ever again, then you will get the drop on that captor and turn the tables! As soon as possible! Is that understood?"

"Yes, sir," Jonah mumbles in the darkness.

"Shut up!" Malix whispers.

Between Malix and Jonah, there's a faint half-circle of Peleus light on the dirt floor. The rest of the cave is a cold, foul-smelling blackness, and it's impossible to know its size. Jonah steadies his breath and stares at the moonlight, waiting for Tunick to crawl through. Outside, up on the opposite cliff, a hard wind blasts the trees this way and that way, and the half-circle of light appears and disappears, flashing like a broken light bulb in an abandoned building.

The two cadets watch silently as Michael drags Portis through. Soon, Aussie coughs her way inside. When he hears Tunick graciously asking Christina to enter his home, that he would be "most honored," Jonah slides the handgun out of his pocket.

"Malix?" Christina whispers as she crawls through the flashing half-circle of light. "Where are you? Jonah?"

Malix and Jonah don't answer, and no one else speaks up. It's as if they all have their own survival plan, even Aussie, who coughs far inside the cave. The longer he's in the space, the more the smells separate themselves. Jonah tries to ignore the overwhelming stench of blood.

Outside, Tunick asks, "What's your name, big boy?"

Jonah waits for Bidson to answer, but there's just silence. Another one, gone. It's becoming almost routine. A sharp pain appears behind Jonah's eyes, and a headache comes on fast.

"Boy, boy, boy. You don't look so hot," Tunick continues. "You stay here and be my lookout. Good, good. You're a good fella."

Seconds feel like hours as they wait for Tunick to appear. Sweat beads on his wrists and palms, pools on his lower back. His headache worsens. Malix doesn't know he has the handgun, Jonah realizes. He considers leaning forward and letting the Third Year feel the cold, hard metal, but it's too late. Tunick mumbles something just outside the cave opening. Then dirt crunches, and there's the grunt of someone lowering himself to the ground. The leaves flit wildly on the trees above the valley, and the moonlight at the cadets' feet disappears completely. Jonah sees movement and hears labored breathing below, and once there's a flash of light and he can locate Tunick's head, he sets the gun against his skull and barks, "Don't move!"

Malix jumps on top of Tunick, and there's an immediate

struggle. Tunick spins away from the gun and Jonah drops to his knees to secure the rifles, but he can't find them.

Christina shouts, "Get him, Malix! Kill him, kill him!"

Jonah sweeps his hands over the cold dirt floor as Malix turns Tunick over and punches him twice in the face. Malix shouts, "Come on, Jonah!"

The moonlight flashes briefly and Christina jumps on top of Malix, and then Jonah dives into the fray. He twists the barrel of the handgun through Malix's strong arms until it meets Tunick's head. But something is wrong. His dreadlocks are missing. The grunts leaving his mouth are boyish, and when Jonah's other hand finds Tunick's throat, the man's long beard is gone, too.

A spotlight then enters the cave from the outside. Under Christina, Jonah, and Malix is a whimpering and bloody Hopper, his long black bangs hanging limply over the barrel of the gun.

"I can't breathe," Hopper wheezes.

The three cadets roll off the hacker, completely stunned, as Tunick shines the rifle lights around the cave. The kids' shadows loom against the opposite wall.

"Ah, ah, ah. No wrestling without me." Tunick laughs. "That's really not very nice to attack Hoppy Happy like that. The poor boy is scared and cold and just wants to sleep." His voice turns angry. "Now, smart boy, slide your little blue gun out here, and then everyone get against the wall, your backs to me."

"Just shoot him," Christina whispers out of the side of her mouth. "Shoot him, Jonah."

"Do it," Malix adds.

"Tunick, they want him to shoot you," Hopper calls. Malix slams a fist down on the hacker's chest, and Hopper groans and rolls away.

"Your name is Jonah, right, smart boy?" Tunick yells inside.

"Yeah," Jonah says after a beat. His head throbs, and there's a needling sensation in his eyes.

"Shoot him, Jonah," Christina whispers as the demics creep toward the opposite wall. "Remember what Vespa said."

Tunick's voice booms inside. "Jonah Monah, if you want to know what happened on Thetis and what happened to all those people on your ship and why I've chosen you, you, you, then you better not shoot me. You have to be curious."

Jonah rubs his thumb over the gun's pebbled handle. How many times did Aussie fire it? How many bullets are left? He wobbles out of the light and asks, "Who was the girl we saw in the jungle before you showed up? The small girl with the long black hair?"

"Who? Her? She's a nobody, Jonah Monah. I'll tell you all about her when I get inside, but she's an absolute nobody. A nuisance. A splitter."

Malix creeps out of the light, toward the western wall.

"Just tell us from out there!" Michael yells from the back of the cave. "I don't know why you want to hurt us. We're just kids, Tunick! We're innocent and we just want to be sa—"

"NOBODY'S INNOCENT! And how *dare* you tell me what to do inside my own home, little boy! I've been on this moon for over a year, and you've been here for what? Three days? Now, get back into the light where I can see you, or I'm going to shoot the redhead."

Jonah turns to see Aussie shaking against the back wall. All around her are symbols like the ones inside the sphere: hollow diamonds with squares, interlocking circles, three dots inside Cs. Hundreds of them. He also sees a childish drawing of a bat-like creature standing at the bottom of a deep pit, its head and wings sharp and robotic. The angle of the light changes, and he sees that above Aussie's head, hanging on a taut black vine, are thick, fatty bits of animal flesh. The sight makes him nauseous, and his headache intensifies. If he can just make his way to the wall and touch the symbols and trigger something, maybe they can still get out of this.

"Malix," Jonah groans through the pain. He stumbles back into Tunick's light. "The symbols on the wall. We can escape."

Malix immediately starts to dig his fingers into the figures carved into the stone, but nothing clicks. Nothing happens.

"Now, my beautiful smart birdies, I'm not going to kill anyone if Jonah Monah just tosses out that little gun of his. And if there are any other guns in there, slide them on out, too. If I come in there and find anyone else has a gun, then I'm going to shoot them right in the old mouth."

Jonah's headache intensifies, and he can't concentrate. Without thinking, he underhands the blue gun out of the opening. He needs to lie down.

"You just killed us, Jonah," Christina says.

"That it, then? Blades, too. Spears, slingshots, tasers, hammers, bad jokes. Anything that can harm ol' Tunick, you better fork them over," Tunick calls.

No one responds, and then Hopper says, "I think it's clear, Tunick. You scared 'em. Get your smelly ass in here, ya freak."

Malix stops pawing at the wall to kick Hopper's side. "He'll kill you, too! Don't you see that?"

"Traitor," Christina hisses.

"Eat me, cadets," Hopper groans.

"Now everyone against the back, back, back wall. Don't be shy. It's a little cold, but I'll start a fire soon in the back yard. We'll feast and verve and feast some more! I can taste the chocolate now, yessiree!"

Jonah stumbles toward the back, tripping over Portis groaning on the ground. He lands flat against the wall and plants his hands on the freezing stone. He drags his fingers lazily over the symbols, trying to make something click, but he's too weak to grip anything. Tunick's light sweeps over the kids slowly, and Jonah sees that covering the symbols are several different styles of handwriting, all in different colors, but he can't concentrate long enough to read anything they say. Before his vision begins to blur, he takes another quick look at the crude drawing of the robotic bat standing at the bottom of the pit.

Tunick scrambles inside the cave just as Jonah's headache turns into a flashing vertigo. He can't feel anything below his waist. He tips forward and falls to his knees. His hands slide limply off the wall and his sweaty cheek falls against the freezing stone, and it sticks there and feels good. Something warm rushes up from his stomach and coats his heart, and from there it expands and radiates to his arms, legs, and his head, blanketing his muscles, stiffening his neck, pushing on the backs of his eyes. The warmness hardens and it feels as if a pack of wolves were chewing on his bones. With his cheek still stuck to the frozen wall, Jonah vomits. His eyes close, and he can't open them back up. Aussie and Michael call his name, Tunick yells something from the front of the cave, and a second later, he feels Tunick laughing in his ear. Then everything stops.

• • •

Jonah's eyelids flicker open for a second and then close. Water slowly falls over his head, dribbling through his hair, down his forehead, down over his eyelids, nose, lips, neck. The collar of his jumpsuit absorbs the liquid, cooling his burning chest. He opens his eyes again, this time long enough to see a raging purple fire a dozen feet in front of him and a few people sitting on his left. Hopper. Tunick. Michael, maybe. When his eyes fall shut, their faces swirl together in his mind. Michael has Tunick's dreadlocks and Hopper's mustache. Tunick takes on the demic's sloped nose and skinny cheeks. Hopper has long brown hair. More water splashes onto the top of his head.

"Jonah? Hey. You awake, Jonah? Does that feel good or bad?" Aussie asks.

"Smart boy, Jonah!" Tunick shouts. The voice booms in Jonah's skull, crackling his brain.

His mouth tastes acrid, and his lips seem sealed together with glue. Jonah takes his time before whispering, "Feels good. I'm thirsty."

A plastic jug sloshes water against his lips, down his chin. When his mouth is full, he moves his face away. Swallowing takes effort. Jonah's shoulders tingle, and his stomach clenches and cramps. He draws back his legs, one by one, and drops his head onto his knees.

Someone sits next to him and leans into his ear. He can tell it's Tunick by his smell and the sound of the crunching seeds in his mouth. "So, what's this sickness of yours, Jonah Monah? Cancer? I heard on Thetis that cancer was making a comeback on Earth."

"Not cancer," Jonah whispers into his knees. He wants to punch Tunick in the face, but he can hardly lift his arms.

"What is it then? Maybe you're just homesick. Wait! Lovesick? You're lovesick! Oh, *Jonah Monah*!"

He tries to picture the name of his disease, but he can't. His fingers clench. "Starts with a 'C,' I think. Or an 'S.' I don't remember. I need more water."

He hears the jug slide under his thighs, and it takes every ounce of strength to tip it to his lips. He can't picture the word of his disease, the monster that's killing him internally, the cells that are mutating and slowing him down, but he can picture every beautiful drop of water flowing down his throat, coating the lining of his stomach. He pictures Vespa, too. She's running along the beach with the white sun bouncing off her hair. She's alone and smiling.

"Well, I hate to tell you this, but everyone got the grand tour while you were conked out," Tunick says. Jonah smells chocolate on his breath and it instantly makes him nauseous. "You've been asleep for hours. Everybody's having fun, fun, FUN!"

Jonah opens his eyes to the fire and the tall stone wall beyond. Gold foil wrappers are strewn everywhere, and empty boxes of their ready-to-eat meals smolder and curl on the edge of the flames. So much for rationing. On the opposite side of him, past the fire and next to a tall stack of crude blankets, sit Malix, Portis, and Christina. The kids face each other cross-legged, Malix giggling at Christina, Portis whipping his hands over his head, the three of them full of energy, their jaws constantly moving up and down. To Jonah's left, Michael and Hopper seem to be debating the mathematical possibilities of anti-matter, totally oblivious to the fact that Jonah is awake, and they seem surprisingly happy to be together. Michael playfully pushes Hopper's shoulder, and Hopper leaps to his feet and slaps his palm to the curved wall covered with chipped and broken symbols. Jonah looks up for the first time, and he's surprised to see the black sky, Peleus, and thousands of stars. A few tree branches also hang overhead. He's outside, but enclosed in stone circle, or perhaps in a cave missing its ceiling. Then it hits him: he's in one of the spheres, but its top is gone.

"See! And *this* is the proof!" Hopper cries.

"Wait, wait, wait. Let me try," Michael says, planting his hand against the wall. "Whoooaaaa. You're right! That's crazy! You're a genius!"

They both break up laughing. Hopper slaps the wall again and then stumbles back to his seat next to the fire, wiping tears from his eyes. Michael presses his back against the wall and points limply at Portis. The cadet attempts to say something, and as he stutters to get the words out, something white falls out of his mouth. Portis scoops it back up and tosses it in his mouth without wiping it off. Hopper spits a long, floating stream of white saliva over his shoulder, both of his hands moving quickly at the side of his head, blasting themselves open and closed, open and closed.

"They're all on verve," Aussie says. He cranes his head back to see her standing above a smug Tunick, her long red hair tied in a bun on the top of her head. She looks like she's been crying for hours. He wonders if she told anyone about Garrett while he was unconscious.

"Doctor's orders," Tunick declares.

Aussie kicks a stone at the fire. "He forced them. He put a gun to your head and said he was going to kill you if they didn't put it in their mouths."

"And look how happy they are, smart boy. Have you ever *seen* Hopper Happy this hoppy or happy? And those three over there." Tunick points the blue handgun at Malix, Portis, and Christina. "They've been like that for an hour now. Big Head doesn't feel pain anymore, and I think the other two *love* each other. So cute. And now that Mr. Jonah Monah is awake…" Tunick stands and digs a hand into his green hip sack, pulling out two small white seeds. "Now it's time for you two. We'll start slow. They want me to start you slow. And I have to do what they say. I can't disobey."

"Please, Tunick," Aussie whispers. "Just let us go. I really feel sick."

Tunick stands and whips the gun into her face. He presses it softly against the tip of her freckled nose. Jonah wants to tackle him and slam him against the wall, but all he can do is drop the water jug and stare. Tunick leans into Aussie and says, "Well, you are in luck! Lucky for you, the doctor has the cure right here. Please, please, *please* enjoy your first verve. You have no idea how lucky you are. The first time is always the best time."

Tears encase her green eyes. "Please. I don't want it."

Jonah tries to kick Tunick, but his right leg simply straightens out along the floor. The man looks down at Jonah and smiles, and then he pushes down on the cadet's chin with the barrel of the gun. Jonah is too weak to resist; something small and hard lands on his tongue, and then Tunick's dirty fingers enter his mouth and lodge it between the First Year's gums and cheek. As soon as Tunick releases his chin, Jonah spits it out.

Tunick immediately punches Aussie in the gut. The girl crumples to the ground next to Jonah, and laughter comes from all around the room. Tunick fishes Jonah's white seed out of a crack in the floor and says, "You spit that out again and I'll slash her face. I'll take her nose right off and wear it on top of mine. Look around, boy. Do your friends look like they're having such a terrible time?"

Malix walks along the back wall on his hands while Christina hops around him in circles, cheering. Portis lies down, waving his arms back and over in front of his eyes, and Michael and Hopper simply stare at Tunick with wide, goofy smiles.

"Jonah! You couldn't be missing out more, ya freak!" Hopper yells.

"I thought you hated me," Jonah drones. "I thought you hated Michael."

"I don't hate anyone...*smart boy.*"

Michael erupts in laughter. His pupils are so wide that Jonah can't see a sliver of his corneas.

"See?" Tunick says, placing the seed in Jonah's hand. With his shaking fingers, he brings it close to his eyes and examines its pebbled surface. It looks like nothing more than a bleached macadamia nut. "I'm gonna slash her, Jonah. I'm gonna slash her nose clean off if you don't drop that verve back in that mouth of yours."

Jonah takes a deep breath and looks down at Aussie, remembering the look on her face in the smoking module. She blinks hard at him, and then Jonah drops the seed into his mouth.

"Start off with it against your cheek. In the back." Tunick sighs as he shoves a seed past Aussie's lips. "That's where the magic starts. It takes a minute or two, of course. Be patient, grasshopper. I hope you get to see my friends like I do. But that's in time, in time. Don't be scared when they arrive."

It doesn't have a taste. He buries it between his gums and cheek with his tongue, clinking it along the sides of his molars. He closes his eyes and sees flashes of a tiny woman with curly red hair—his second foster mother—who sometimes forced sleeping pills in his mouth. He sees her hair and her wrinkled face and her brown teeth. He smells the chemicals on skin and feels her white vinyl belt come down on his back. Jonah prods the verve with his tongue and opens his eyes. Across the room, Malix hops along the floor on one hand, laughing, telling Christina to try it. Instead, Christina crouches down and jumps ten feet straight up. She grabs the top edge of the wall and hangs there, begging Malix to look at her.

Aussie crawls over to Jonah and sets her head on his outstretched leg. She stares at him for a moment before closing her eyes and switching the verve from one side of her mouth to the other.

"Who was the girl in the jungle?" Jonah asks Tunick as he

sits down in front of him, the fire rising over his shoulders like purple wings.

Smears of chocolate cake surround his mouth. He combs his dirty fingers through his long beard, removing what looks to be mashed potatoes. "What girl, exactly?"

"She had black hair. She was short and small and really fast. The girl we saw just before we saw you."

Tunick crinkles his nose and spits to the side. "Just another splitter."

"What's her name?"

"Must have been Hess. Little Hess and the splitters. I used to really like her. Could tell the hell out of a joke. Hess. Hess, Hess, Hess. I *hate* Hess. Hess lies."

A tingling sensation tickles Jonah's gums. His mouth fills with saliva and he swallows it, gagging at the strong, bitter taste. No wonder Tunick spits so much. "Why did she leave? Why is she a splitter?"

"Ohhhhh, she thinks she's better than me. Better than the verve. Which is *funny* because *she's* the one who got me hooked on it back on Thetis. Hess was 'Ms. Verve 2220,' pushing it on everyone. Irony is, it was Hess who got the adults to try it. She started that whole thing. *What a mistake*."

Over Tunick's shoulder, Christina continues to hang by one hand, and she kicks her feet along the upper wall. The cadet soon spins all the way over, upside down, her feet thrashing in the air for a few seconds before pedaling along the wall again. She's a human windmill. Malix jumps and tries to do the same, but he can't stop laughing long enough to get a good grip.

"What whole thing?" Jonah asks. His voice sounds far away, as if coming from beyond the fire. He feels both relaxed and energized at the same time.

"Give it a few minutes. You'll see, smart boy."

"Portis," he says. It's suddenly difficult for him to form words. "What did Hess tell you? What'd that girl say?"

The cadet stares at Jonah for a few seconds. And then a goofy grin spreads across his face. He opens his mouth to speak but says nothing. Then he bites down on his wrist and draws blood.

The right side of Jonah's face goes numb and stiff. He sucks some of the flesh between his teeth and bites down, feeling nothing but the satisfaction of chewing on something. The flames rising over Tunick's shoulders grab Jonah's attention. Purples turn into blues, blues turn into whites and greens and then back to purples. Yellows appear and turn a hot, blinding white. The colors blend and dance and then they separate from each other in long, thin threads. Jonah wants to stand and touch the fire. But then the threads jump off the very tips of the flames, morphing into swirling fingers of smoke. A face appears in the smoke. It's a man's face. His dad's face? Jonah shakes his head, ignoring Tunick's giggles, and looks down at his own hands. The wrinkles on his knuckles and palms begin to move; they march like ants, moving in slow, constant circles. Then the wrinkles split in different directions and run vertical, disappearing over the webbing between his fingers.

"Oooooh. It's coming on fast for you, Jonah Monah. Don't get sick now. Just some tiny hallucinations to start you out. Nothing your smart brain can't handle. The good stuff will take a couple hours. Then maybe you'll see the sources of all this beauty. And when you work your way up, you'll see whom I see. They're going to like you, Jonah. They tell me they already do. And that's good."

Who's 'they'? Jonah wants to ask, but his lips won't form the sounds. Tunick doubles in Jonah's vision. Left Tunick strokes his beard. Right Tunick twists his dreads in his fingers. Both smile and drool. Both talk and laugh and say Jonah's name over and over and over. And both have the little blue handgun in their laps. Jonah rubs his eyes and tries to control his thoughts that spin off in too many directions. He bites a sliver off the corner of the verve, and it's like an explosion of happiness sweeps up his nasal cavity, electrifying his brain with a million white bolts. This is suddenly exactly where he wants to be. This is better than the sphere. He unwinds for the first time since landing on Achilles. Below him, Aussie rubs an index finger over the cracks in the stone floor. A long strand of white drool separates from her pink lips, covering his pant leg.

"Why is the ground moving?" Aussie mumbles.

The two Tunicks slide together into one cackling man who prods a finger into Aussie's ribs. "You can control it if you try. Try, try, try. The ground isn't moving, girlie. Your mind is expanding, breathing, reaching for new heights. You're *verving*."

Aussie vomits and then laughs. And then she vomits some more. Jonah knows he should jump away from the orange puddle slowly dripping off his leg, but instead he leans back and bites another sliver off the seed. A wave of nausea crashes into the sides of his stomach. Bile shoots up his throat, but he coughs and whips the jug of water up to his lips. He swallows it and imagines the water battling the bile in a massive war in the back of his throat. The water soldiers are more powerful, and they chase the retreating bile back into his stomach where the water battalion declares total victory.

"I don't like this," Jonah manages to say.

"You will," Tunick whispers back.

Christina hollers for everyone to watch her, and Jonah's eyes crawl away from Tunick. The cadet stands on top of the stone before taking a running leap toward the fire. She sails horizontally across the room with her hands over her head like a superhero. She blows right through the top of the fire, separating its flames, and Hopper leaps up and shouts. Jonah sees Christina coming right at him, and he wants to move, but at the same time he wants the cadet to crash right into him. It would be so funny if he were to be bowled over by this girl. At the last second, though, just before Christina's fists are about to plow into Jonah's face, Tunick grabs the collar of her shirt, yanking her to the ground and flipping her onto her back. Christina doesn't seem to mind; she lies there and waves her arms at her sides, a stupid grin on her face.

"My turn!" Hopper yells. He climbs to the top of the wall with ease.

"Do it!" Michael says, laughing.

Aussie flips over and points at Tunick. "Where's your sister, Tunick? You said you had a sister back here at your place. We're here and I want to meet her. Where is she? Maybe we'll be friends."

"Ohhhhh, did I say that?"

"Yes, yes," Jonah slurs. The crackling of the fire begins to sound like music. "Where's your sister? Your sister?"

"I don't have a sister." Tunick laughs, crunching on his verve. He tosses four more seeds in his mouth. "I've been known to stretch the truth as big as the Silver Foot."

Jonah looks up at the planets and stars. They move, bouncing into each other, streaking out of sight. Peleus swoops in an arch, pulsing in a rhythm like the jungle toads. When Jonah blinks, he finds the stars and moon back where they were. And then they move again. Sitting up on the wall, Hopper yells, "Michael, you're totally like my best friend now, did you know that? Dude, I'm so sorry I used to make fun of you! I'm really sorry, ya freak."

"It's okay," Michael says, standing below him. "Just don't hurt yourself up there. I worry about you."

"So, you don't really have a sister?" Aussie asks Tunick.

As Tunick waves his hands over Christina's blissful face, he says, "Who needs a sister? I have a brother, though. Good, good, good kid. Does what I ask."

"I used to have a brother," Christina mumbles.

"Awwwwww. What's your brother's name?" Aussie rolls off Jonah's legs.

Jonah jumps to his feet, full of energy. He pushes past Tunick, toward the fire. His mind is caught in a high-speed chase of colors, and he has to cover his eyes with his hands just so he can concentrate. What did Tunick just say? He has a brother? Jonah drops his hands and stares at the fire that is now pure purple. It's the most beautiful thing he's ever seen.

"So, my birds," Tunick says, turning Jonah around. "Where is the energizer now? That's all we need. If we want to do this again, we need the energizer."

Aussie gets to her knees and vomits again. "Christina has a brother, too."

"I used to. I *used* to."

Tunick slaps Christina hard across the face. "The energizer, goddamnit! It's big and orange! Where did you put it? Why are you so stupid?"

The cadet's face freezes at the insult, and then she begins to sob uncontrollably. Jonah wavers above her. Oddly, it's as if he can feel her tears running down his own throat, and they cascade into a rising pool in his lungs. Christina's sadness is so intense that he begins to cry, too, and he sits and cradles her head in his lap. It couldn't feel more foreign to him, to comfort someone so intimately, but he doesn't want to be anywhere else.

"Jonah Monah? Where's the energizer? Do you hear me, smart boy? I have my orders. They want me to move forward. They want me to move forward *with you*."

Tunick keeps talking, but all Jonah can focus on is the pale yellow light flowing out of Christina's nose and mouth. It moves along the dirt floor, spreading in every direction. "I—I think I can see your soul," he whispers into her ear. He wants to swim in it. He wants to swallow the yellow light like water.

Christina opens her eyes. "My what?"

Something hard slams into the top of Jonah's head, knocking him over. When he looks up, Tunick stands over him with the blue gun in his hand. "You know where it is, so JUST TELL ME!"

Jonah opens his mouth, but the words don't come. The lights. He wants to get back to Christina's soul flowing around him.

"Over here! Hey, ya freaks, look over here!" Hopper dances awkwardly on top of the wall, but he loses his footing, tipping backward and out of sight. Malix backflips up onto the wall and then bows before looking down into the jungle.

"He's fine," he calls down into the room. The branches hanging over the wall begin to shake violently. "Ha! The dumb idiot is trying to kick down this stupid tree and I'm…I'm going to help him. I'm going to help him knock it down. Watch out for our stupid tree because we're going to knock it over!"

Malix goes over the wall into the jungle, and Michael tries to jump up after him. Tunick growls and tosses the blue handgun into the fire, sending up a cloud of purple sparks. He marches toward the wall.

"His name was Eddie. My brother. Eddie, Eddie, Eddie. Edward James," Christina says wistfully.

"I like that. *Eddie*," Aussie says, looking up from her vomit. "Tunick? Tunick, what's your brother's name again?"

Tunick ignores her and grabs the waist of Michael's pants and the back of his shirt, and without warning, launches the small demic over the wall.

"Here I come!" Michael calls.

Over his shoulder, Tunick says, "Verve gives you muscles. Feel how strong you are. And you don't feel pain. Try to hurt yourself if you want. It doesn't hurt. *Much.*"

"But what was your brother's name, Tunick?" Aussie asks.

"Him? Oh, oh, oh. You probably know him, girlie. I bet you know him *really* well. After all, you just spent a hell of a lot of time with him. Almost a year."

Hearing this last sentence brings a crashing moment of clarity to Jonah. A throbbing coolness beats down his neck, and the glowing white light framing everything in his sight fades and disappears. Christina's yellow light vanishes, and the dirt floor is nothing but a dirt floor again. "Who's your brother, Tunick?"

The man doesn't respond. He simply jumps up and over the wall. A moment later, the branches hanging over the stone circle swing wildly above Jonah. There's a sound of the ground ripping, of wood moaning, and as the tree tips away from Jonah and the girls, Tunick yells, "Timber!"

CHAPTER THIRTEEN

JONAH RUSHES TOWARD THE FIRE. THE GUN IS JUST OUT OF reach inside the flames, and even though Tunick has just told them they wouldn't feel much pain, he knows his skin will blister and melt, and he'll feel it in time. He can hear the boys on the other side of the wall laughing and congratulating each other, and he knows he doesn't have much time before they leap back into the room. The cadet is dizzy yet completely focused, and he drops to his knees and scrapes his fingernails into the dirt. As soon as he has a handful, he tosses it onto the gun, driving away the closest flames. Another handful. Another. Then he grabs a nearby rock and digs the gun out of the embers, only to cover it with another handful of dirt. Tunick said that Aussie just spent over a year with his brother. That can only mean Tunick's brother was on the ship. And that can only mean he's involved with all this mess.

Kneeling over Aussie's blank face, Jonah whispers, "Get up. Get up, get up, get up."

The constellations of freckles on her cheeks and nose move and swirl. Jonah blinks and shakes his head, then spits his verve into the fire. He digs his fingers into Aussie's mouth and scoops out the white seed, tossing it against the wall.

"Heeeey," Aussie whines. "What's your problem? I kind of like the—"

Without thinking, Jonah slaps her. "Snap out of it. We've got to go. Now."

Aussie's cheek grows red, but she smiles. "That didn't even hurt. Your slap didn't even hurt, Jonah. That's so weird. Do it again. Hit me again."

Christina props herself up onto her elbow. "Ooh, somebody hit me. I want to try."

"No!" Jonah seethes. He looks back and forth between the two girls, and then he snatches up the dirt-covered gun. The metal isn't too hot. At least, not that he can tell.

"I'll hit you," Aussie says. She gets to her feet and balls up her fist. Christina stands and hops in place, impatient and giddy. "I'm sorry we've never really talked before, Christina. You're so sweet."

"Thanks. I really like you, too. You're *so* pretty."

Just as Aussie swings her arm at the cadet, Jonah grabs her elbow and yanks her toward the wall. "Listen! Both of you grab whatever you can and let's go. How do we get out of here? How'd we get in here? Come on, come on, come on. We have to go right now."

"Somebody hit me already!" Christina barks with her eyes closed. Over the wall, Malix yells for Christina to get over there, that he'll hit her right after they knock over this next tree. Aren't they worried about Zion hearing all this noise? Tunick seemed so worried before, but not anymore.

Jonah grabs Christina's shoulders and puts his face inches from hers. "I'll hit you after we escape, okay? This verve stuff is messing with your mind, Christina. Control it. Remember your training. Remember the academy. Remember Officer Dravo. We're prisoners. We have to get out of here, we have to move. *Now*."

The cadet opens her eyes, frowns, and then goes limp, trying to drop out of his grip, but Jonah holds tight, keeping Christina hovering above the ground. His entire body flexes with agitation. Ten minutes ago, he couldn't lift the water jug, and now he believes he could punch a hole in the wall.

Portis rolls back and forth on the floor; he's in his own world, gnawing on his fingers, blood covering his face. Should he try to take the cadet with him, too? No, he'd only slow them down with his leg wound.

There's a noise on the other side of the wall, and then Michael comes sailing high overhead, screaming like a banshee. At first Jonah thinks the demic is going to land right in the fire, but instead he crashes into the dirt several feet past it. The boy rolls into Jonah's legs and begins to laugh. His front teeth are chipped, and he spits blood without concern.

No one else seems to feel the same sense of panic that Jonah feels, nor do they imagine, like him, what Tunick might do once he realizes they can't help him find the energizer. Or what it might mean that Tunick's brother was on the Mayflower 2. Jonah drops Christina to the ground and wheels around to snatch Aussie's wrist, but to his surprise, she grabs his neck with both hands and tries to choke him.

"No!" she shouts.

"We're leaving," he says, coughing. Her grip is so strong.

Malix's head appears at the top of the wall, and as soon as he and Jonah make eye contact and Malix sees the gun, the cadet whispers something down into the jungle. Jonah snakes his hand between Aussie's rigid arms and slams his elbow down on her wrist. She's forced to release her grip, and Jonah says, "Just stay alive. I'll come back. I'm going to get us off this moon."

"Is there a party going on in there?" Hopper yells from the jungle. "Hey? Jonah?"

"Jonah Monah!" Tunick sings.

Jonah runs along the base of the circular wall in the opposite direction, leaping high over a giggling Portis, trying to find a way out. The floor around the fire begins to separate, rise, and spin, but Jonah knows it's just the verve, and he blinks hard, refocuses, and the floor stops moving. Just when he thinks there's no exit, he catches Michael in the corner of his eye pointing in the opposite direction. He turns and sees it; the wall isn't a complete circle. Two walls overlap, and there's a narrow path between them. Hopper comes into view next to Malix, and when he sees Jonah, he yells, "Tunick! I think your friend Jonah doesn't like it here!"

To his right, Christina and Aussie stand near the wall, arms crossed, eyes dilated. Above the left wall are Malix and Hopper, both of whom flex their jaws in anticipation of a fight. Jonah realizes his only choice is to go straight across. As he pushes away from the wall and sprints forward, Jonah pictures his mom and dad trying to escape their shaking bedroom, and how they somehow had enough time to shove him under the dresser. He's ten feet from the raging fire when he knows he needs another one of those moments right now, as Tunick appears on all fours on top of the wall like an insect. Jonah closes his eyes and leaps through the top flames, bursting out the other side with the taste of ash on his lips.

"No, no, no," Tunick growls, dropping fast into the room.

Jonah doesn't turn around. Something hits the back of his head, but he keeps racing for the passage between the walls.

"Waaaaaait. Where is everyone going?" Portis asks as Jonah blurs by.

Tunick is just a few seconds behind Jonah as he slips through the dark opening and bounces hard from wall to wall with the gun in his hand. Finally, the walls widen and he falls into a cold, pitch-black space.

"Who's going to protect you from Zion? There's nowhere to go, smart boy. Be smarter. BE SMARTER!"

It takes Jonah a moment to see the half-circle of Peleus moonlight on the left side of the room; he's back in Tunick's freezing cave, smelling the foul meat. He flattens himself against the eastern wall just as Tunick barrels inside.

Jonah's fingers feel the carved symbols, and he silently digs his nails inside every crevice, twisting and pulling on every piece of rock. Nothing clicks. Nothing's going to save him, but him.

"Jonah?" Tunick whispers. "Jonah Monah, what's wrong? You don't like the verve? If you don't like the verve, well, then you're a splitter. And I kill splitters, Jonah." After a pause, he barks, "I don't have a choice! I have my orders!" Then, quieter, in a shaky demonic voice, he says, "I can see them, Jonah. If I have enough verve, they talk to me. They've chosen me, and now I have to choose others. And if you don't tell me where the energizer is, I'm going to have to kill you. I'm going to have to kill you all. Those are my orders."

The First Year holds his breath tighter than the blue handgun digging into his palm. Who is Tunick talking about? Traces of the verve creep through his mind again, and Jonah sees a hundred white and green streaks fall from the ceiling. They bounce and circle his feet. A cloud of blue appears around his ankles and grows tall until a faceless figure stands before him. He stares into it, feeling a strange connection to its shape, but when he shakes his head, it all disappears.

"I could go get one of your big guns, smart boy." Tunick is so close that he can reach out and touch him. The man crunches a seed in his teeth. "But maybe... Oh, maybe we should just wrestle to the death in the dark here. That sounds like fun, doesn't it? Me snapping your neck?" Tunick inhales deeply through his nose. "Hand to hand. Ooh wee, I can smell you, Jonah Monah. And you *stink*."

Jonah inches left while his knuckles scrape into the symbols. The floor scratches the bottom of his one bare foot. He raises the gun in Tunick's direction and curls his finger over the trigger. *This is it*, he thinks. *This is when* he *takes something.*

"I know right where you are," Tunick whispers. "I'm just messing with your mind. I'm like your little disease. I am your cancer. I am your killer."

As Jonah begins to squeeze the trigger, he thinks of Vespa sliding down the canyon wall on the island, dragging the chain of terrified kids with her. She never looked up to see who was still following her, and when she hit the landing, she just ran. His finger feels the last bit of resistance, the point of no return where he can no longer look up, and then he shoots.

Click. Nothing happens. He presses the trigger again. Another *click*. The gun is empty. His heart pumps in his throat.

Tunick's laughter fills the cave, and it grows louder and louder until Jonah feels like he's drowning in it. Then he hears a pair of feet scraping across the dirt floor, and before he can brace himself, he's tackled around the waist. His skull bounces hard off the wall, and white rings pop in front of his eyes. Then he's on the ground, his lips kissing the cold floor. The broken bones that Dr. Z set in his nose have dislodged, and they poke into the flesh of his cheeks.

"So boring, so *easy*." Tunick sighs. "Put up a little fight, boy. The older ones fought more than this."

The man kneels down next to him, and Jonah rolls onto his back. *The older ones?* A fist wraps itself around his ear and twists. Jonah instinctively snatches Tunick's wrist and digs his thumb into the back of his hand. Then, with the white rings still attacking his eyes, he swings his bare foot up and strikes the side of Tunick's knee with an amazing amount of force. The fist releases his ear, and Jonah tucks his arms into his bruised body and rolls in the opposite direction.

"Hey, hey, hey! Now we're… *Damn*, that actually hurt, smart boy. Holy moly that hurt. What was that?"

After a furious few seconds, Jonah crashes into a wall. He opens his eyes and finds himself next to the cave opening, right where he stood opposite Malix to get the drop on Tunick. On his hands and knees, Jonah pushes out through the hole. A hand grabs his ankle, but Jonah grips the outside frame of the opening and muscles his way onto the valley floor.

"You're dead!" Tunick barks, crawling after him. "I'm going to string you up like a little snout pup and eat your face!"

Jonah jumps to his feet but immediately trips over something. He twists onto his back to see Bidson slouched against the base of the cliff, his long legs sticking into the grass in a V, his stiff right arm still stuck above his head. The bandage on his other wrist is rusty brown with dried blood. Jonah watches the boy's huge head drop to the side, and then to Jonah's surprise, he opens his big walrus eyes. They look at each other for a second before Bidson rolls his head to the other side.

"Too far, too far, too far. That's too far," Tunick says as he steps over one of Bidson's thighs.

Jonah tries to scramble backward, but his shoulders press up against a jagged tree stump. Tunick laughs and takes another step; his smile is so wide that Jonah can count five white seeds in the corner of his mouth. But in what looks to be the boy's last breath, Bidson's meaty right hand actually moves on its own, and it snatches Tunick's wrist. The man looks down, and that's all it takes for Jonah to get back on his feet.

"Ha! I thought you were done for, big boy!" Tunick says before slamming a fist into Bidson's chubby face. The impact echoes down the narrow valley and rings in Jonah's ears.

The demic, somehow, holds on.

Tunick shakes his head and then hits him again, harder, cutting open his cheek. Bidson's body convulses, his eyelids flitter, and a low groan escapes his lips, but he still doesn't let go of Tunick's wrist. The man begins to pound on the boy's clenched fingers, and Jonah turns and runs, his shoulder scraping along the cliff wall. He jumps over the high grass to the other side of the valley, and far behind him, Tunick's frustrated screams bring a quick, fleeting smile to Jonah's face. And then he runs.

• • •

Jonah crashes through the curtain of thin trees and falls into the rocky embankment, banging his knee into a boulder. He's out of breath. He has no food, no weapons, no companions. He knew it was only a matter of time before he was alone. He staggers along, wondering how all those kids took to the verve so quickly, and how he was able to disconnect himself with just a little bit of determination. Was it a side effect of his blood disease, or perhaps it was just another residual effect from the wormhole?

The jungle is alive with animal calls and shaking leaves, but there's no sign of Tunick. Maybe Bidson's death grip still holds. Bidson saved him. And now Jonah needs to go back to save the others, to somehow convince them to come with him. He'll go after Aussie and Michael first, he decides, and work his way up to Hopper. But first he needs a weapon, and maybe a moment to clear his head of the verve once and for all. He still sees streaks of colors, blues, reds, and yellows, floating and combining into thin clouds that he walks right through. Some colors seem to shoot out of his chest like arrows, trailing long lines of neon that climb the banks and disappear into the trees.

To the south, mountains loom above a wispy level of haze, and that's the direction he heads. He doesn't want to go too far, just far enough to recuperate and make a plan to rescue his friends. He stumbles along the loose stones, his fingers prodding his nose and massaging the back of his skull. Every thirty seconds, he stops and listens for Tunick. Nothing.

Then, out of the line of trees to his left, a giant bat or bird thing, with tentacles swirling out of its belly, swoops low in the embankment and circles the air just ahead of him. It shoots straight back up into the trees, trailing a stench so foul and dense that Jonah collapses, gagging on the toxic fumes. At first he thinks it's another verve hallucination, but the pain in his lungs is much too real. With his collar over his broken nose, he has no choice but to climb out of the cloud and back into the jungle. He's dizzy and confused, crashing into tree trunks with an uncontrollable cough. He can't see anything, but the stench seems to follow him, and he's forced to keep moving. He's making too much noise, he knows, but there's nothing he can do. Then his foot doesn't find any ground, and he falls back into the embankment.

Tunick's voice constantly swirls in his head, talking about the "older ones," verve, the energizer, splitters, being chosen. He mulls it over, but then his mind goes blank when he remembers that

Tunick's brother may have been on the ship. Does Jonah know him? Is it Griffin or Paul or one of the demics? Is it Hopper? Jonah pulls on his hair in frustration; on top of everything, he doesn't know if he can trust a single word Tunick has said so far.

He crawls up the embankment and pulls his legs to his chest. Yellow beams crawl out of his toes and dip into the valley, only to disappear when he shakes his head. Which way is Tunick's cave? His heart shrinks when he realizes he's lost. How far did he actually stumble?

Jonah begins to heave with disappointment in himself. He'll never find his way back to that cave. But maybe he can get back to the crash site and bring reinforcements, if there are any to be found.

He grabs a felled branch; it's four feet long with a sharp point, and he taps it against his ankle as he leans forward to look for the mountains. He's about to slide back into the embankment for a better view when he hears footsteps. His toes grip a smooth rock, and he picks it up. The spear and rock aren't a match for Zion and his gun, or Tunick and his rage, but at least they are something. His only chance is to get the jump on whoever it is, and so he crawls farther back into the shadows and waits.

Then, directly across from him on the lip of the embankment, a round face with a patchy black beard pushes through the top of a bush. His deep-set eyes shine in the pale moonlight, searching back and forth. Jonah stares with held breath, thinking the man looks oddly familiar. Is this Zion?

After a few seconds, the man silently exits the bush, wearing only a tattered pair of black pants, with a huge amber knife tied to his left rib. In his hands are two thick bundles of weeds dropping soil from their roots. Before Jonah can decide if he's friend or foe, two more people step out of the bushes. To his surprise, it's Paul and Ruth, both covered in dirt and looking haggard. LZR-rifles hang from their backs.

"Shit," Paul seethes, sliding down into the embankment. Jonah relaxes, and he's about to ask for help, but he stops himself at the last second. It's slight, but definite; there's something different about Paul's eyes, the way he moves. He looks frantic, even more frantic than when he begged Vespa not to go west.

"Get out of there, cadet. Right now," the man says to Paul. "They might shoot you instead. They're not going to let this kid live for much longer. He's seen too much now."

As soon as he hears his raspy voice, Jonah recognizes him. He's Armitage Blythe, the boy from the videos on his sheaf, the academy's brightest star from the first ship. The last time Jonah saw him, he was pulling a large section of bark away from a tree on Thetis, revealing a nest of white worms that took flight in an inky cloud. And then Manny told Jonah to turn off his sheaf, and then they crashed.

Armitage Blythe was famous for skipping his third year to fight alongside the first wave of US Marines invading England. Jonah never met him in real life, but officers played videos of Armitage several times a semester, boasting how far the recruit had come from being a weak little pacifist to being the smartest, quickest warrior they'd ever trained. Armitage was the first cadet to make the original Mayflower's list for Thetis. And now here he is. On Achilles.

Paul jumps back up into the jungle. "I told you we should have just grabbed the Firstie back there. This is ridiculous. We don't need bait for this."

"Yes, we do. But even if we don't grab the boy, I've got something much better anyway," Armitage says. "Zion is not getting off this moon, I swear."

Wait, Jonah thinks. *Zion is trying to get off the moon? And they want to use Jonah as bait? And why is Ruth here?* He crawls backward and ducks behind a cluster of giant flowers. But then Ruth sees him. He freezes and waits for her to yell. She and Jonah stare at each for a moment, and then she mouths "Go."

He doesn't hesitate and runs without looking. The ground declines quickly under his feet, and he tumbles head over heels down a steep hill, bouncing off roots and saplings and through a thorny patch of weeds. White light pours out of his mouth and nose like water, flooding over the ground before disappearing. He loses his spear, his rock, and his sense of direction by the time he stops moving.

"Down here!" Paul yells from the top.

Jonah hears them scurrying down the hill. He knows as soon as they use their night-vision scopes, he's as good as caught. And what then? Jonah is now convinced that Paul is Tunick's brother, that he strung the professor from the tree and wrote those words on his chest and set fire to the Support Module and caused all this chaos. Didn't he disappear that night to go look for Module Eight? Wouldn't he have the ability and opportunity to overpower the adults with the Third Years he took with him? And didn't he argue with the cook at the makeshift hospital just hours before she was found dead with her neck slit? Jonah crawls over a large boulder and makes himself as small as he can on the other side.

They're close. One person shuffles past, breathing hard. Paul curses somewhere far in the distance, allowing Jonah to take in a lungful of air.

Then, jumping right on top of the boulder he's hiding behind, Ruth surveys the jungle through her scope. "Just be quiet," she whispers. "Listen to me."

Jonah hugs his legs even closer to his chest. He shakes away a new hallucination of lights coming on.

"Sean's gone. Dead. We made a raft and he fell in and I couldn't save him." Something drops onto the back of Jonah's neck. He moves his fingers over it and realizes they're glasses. Sean's night-vision specs. He puts them over his eyes and the jungle lights up in several shades of greens and grays. Fifty yards away, up on the slant of a hill, Paul creeps in the opposite direction with his scope to his face.

"I went back to the site. The place was burned down, and I couldn't find anybody alive, so I stayed in one of the trees until that Armitage Blythe guy showed up last night. He wants to kill somebody named Zion. Hell-bent on it. And I'm going to help him."

"Good," Jonah whispers.

Ruth jumps off the boulder and stands right in front of him. She slowly rotates with her rifle up and out, pretending to be searching for him. "No, not good, Firstie. Zion holds some sort of key to getting off this place, but Armitage, he never wants to leave. And I don't know if I do, either, after hearing about Thetis. If he kills this Zion guy, that threat of leaving is gone. Unless..."

"Unless what?"

"Ruth!" Armitage barks. He's practically on the other side of the boulder. Jonah holds his breath and ducks his head. Should he just stand up and say he'll help them find Zion? He wants the guy brought to justice, too. In fact, he wants him dead. But what if it's a trick?

She steps right up next to Jonah so the toes of her shoes are pressed against his shins. "What?"

"Move already! He's not here."

"Fine."

"You know what? Fuck it. Forget this kid. We're going double back and will flush Zion out ourselves," he says. "So move. Now."

"You know, you're a lot more charming on film," she says, giving Jonah a slight nudge with her toes. She circles around the boulder.

"Watch your mouth," Armitage grumbles.

Jonah watches the three of them bound up the hill and out of sight.

He stands and moves to his left, and then he stops and wanders to his right before sitting down on the boulder. A chill runs across his shoulders. He feels lightheaded and nauseous. Vomit appears in his throat and makes its way up to his molars, but he fights it back for a few seconds before it rises again and explodes past his lips in a cloud of sweet and sour. He watches it dissipate in the air, turning into floating green and gray pixels, and then he tears off the night-vision specs and lies back on the cold rock. He coughs and extends his arms over the sides as if he's been shot in the chest. Small patches of morning sky bloom through the leaves, changing from yellow to blue to purple to yellow again, and as his sweat coats his skin, it sinks in that he can't go back to the wreckage for reinforcements. He's still on his own, and no one's going to help him get back to Tunick's. He should never have let Vespa and Brooklyn go west without him. That decision will go down as the one that ends his life.

He's going to die. They're all going to die. For the first time in days, as his body seems to melt into the rock below him, it finally sinks in. The sky changes to purple and then lightens again, but his mood has never been darker. There was always a glimmer of hope before, but he doesn't feel it anymore. His body stiffens yet feels loose inside, as if his organs swim past each other, attempting to trade spots. His stomach flattens and slides through the spaces of his ribs, his heart swings from the bottom of his spine, and his lungs swell into his shoulder blades. As the verve or his sickness ebbs and flows behind his eyes, the colors and visions keep coming and coming. Rays of neon light shoot out of his chest. Cloudy blue figures float inches from his nose. Globs of orange and red fall from the trees like leaves at the end of autumn. He rolls to his side and tries to get to his feet, but it's like he's a punching bag pummeled off its hook. His promise to never stop moving west shatters all around him.

His eyes close. For the first time he can remember, as sleep approaches, he doesn't worry about what could happen to him, or who might be nearby. If Zion sneaks up behind him and slits his throat while he sleeps, so be it. If Tunick rams a thousand verve seeds into his mouth, that's what happens. And if the Pacsun twins were to miraculously show up with their burning rocks, Jonah would have to welcome the new scars.

"Who cares anymore?" he whispers to himself. "Come and get me."

CHAPTER FOURTEEN

He sleeps for hours, spread out across the boulder as if he's fallen from the sky. The jungle wakes and moves through its morning, and Jonah rolls through a series of dreams until breaking from his sleep like a fish breaching water. He sits up with a jolt, gasping for air, startling a large pack of bright red animals swaying overhead, tall on spindly, twenty-foot-long legs. Their bodies are fat like pigs, but they have rodent faces, with narrow tusks that branch out and curl high above their heads. They stare down at Jonah with beady yellow eyes, leaves stuck in their big mouths, and then they bellow in unison and bounce off on their five thin legs that compress like coiled springs. He watches the last one disappear and then lies back down; his head feels like cement.

After a few minutes, Jonah climbs off the boulder and kneels in a carpet of spidery red weeds. He needs food. He needs water. He needs a plan. His sickness seems to have receded for the time being, and his body feels thick and strong after the hours of sleep. He can feel the verve still buzzing below his skin, but he doesn't mind it; in fact, it gives him the energy he needs to get to his feet.

As he stands, hazy blue shadows rise from the back of his hands and float in place until he tells himself it's not real.

He wobbles on his legs and realizes he no longer feels like waiting and dying. He feels like fighting. But which way should he go? He knows it could be the difference between life and death for not only him, but for Aussie and Portis and Michael and Ruth and everyone else. And that's when he feels the verve gently rising through his body and blanketing his brain, growing hot just below his hairline. And then, on top of the red spidery weeds at his feet, a thick white line flashes in his mind, pointing up and over the hill. It's there and then it's gone. And then it's there again. Jonah doesn't hesitate; he jogs up the hill.

At the top, Jonah stops and concentrates on the jungle around him, and a moment later, another white line flashes in his mind. It dips into the embankment, rises back over the other side, and veers to the left. He shakes his head, and the line disappears. Then he laughs and tells himself he's gone crazy and that this must be the final stage of his disease, that's he's actually still down on the boulder dreaming and dying. With just the one shoe on, he stumbles down the embankment, climbs to the other side, and turns left.

The jungle buzzes with insects, rattles with fat beasts bouncing and fighting on high-up branches, and drips with oozing fungi and tinted water. Jonah runs after the white lines that appear at just the right times, showing him narrow passages and hidden hillsides. Even though he's hallucinating and his eyes hurt as if someone were pulling a needle back and forth behind his sockets, this all feels right. He just doesn't know where he's leading himself.

Finally, after a half hour of crashing through the trees and stumbling over several hills, Jonah barrels into a diamond-shaped clearing dotted with dozens of large black boulders. He slows to a walk, and when he reaches the center, he stops and waits for the next white beam to point him to his destiny. He rotates, heaving for air, his hands planted on the top of his head. Then it comes, flashing for less than a second, a white line aiming at a group of porcupine trees more than a hundred yards away.

Before Jonah can take a step, though, one of the black boulders to his right starts to move. It sways back and forth and then shuffles forward, connecting with a larger boulder. Jonah thinks he's hallucinating again and shakes his head. But the rocks still move. Also, the rocks have hair. Matted, black wool. Suddenly the larger boulder plops hard onto its side and grunts, and Jonah sees the huge, pebbled mass of wet skin and its one giant nostril. His vision tunnels and his stomach drops. Snouts. He's standing in the middle of a sleeping snout pack.

The white flash comes again, pointing at the far-off trees. He backpedals and then takes a few steps forward. Should he go back the way he came and circle around through the jungle, or go straight for the trees and through the pack? Ten feet in front of him, another snout unfurls and drops its long, wet nose onto the ground. A line of yellow froth drips from its nostril, pooling in the sharp brown grass, and then Jonah watches the edges of the cavernous nostril furl and unfurl, furl and unfurl, faster and faster. The beast grunts and flips over onto its lion-like paws, its nose pointed in Jonah's direction. He doesn't even think; he just runs.

He aims straight for the porcupine trees, chugging his arms, flattening his palms, grinding his teeth. He just needs forty-five seconds, forty, thirty-five. But almost immediately the entire pack is on its feet, howling, blindly waking up to his smell. Jonah lowers his head. Grinds his teeth harder. Runs faster. He's just twenty seconds from the trees.

A huge snout appears on his left, running right alongside him, growling and huffing. Deflating on top of its nose is one of those beet-red mushrooms, blowing the long hair from its four milky eyes. Before Jonah can dodge it, the beast gets in front of him and stops, lifting its hindquarters. Jonah's chest and face hit the snout's stiff back, and his fingers get tangled in its wool. He yanks himself backward, ripping out two handfuls of fuzz and oily blood. The snout roars in pain and whips its giant head at Jonah's chest, unhinging its lower jaw. Two rows of rotten teeth rock into place, and they begin to shift along the gums and grow. The beast's muddled eyes rise out of its skull on their dripping yellow sticks like spoiled lollipops.

Jonah turns to get away, but he's rammed hard from behind, blasted right into the first snout's face. His elbow swings down and smashes one of the beast's rising eyes, snapping its yellow stick with a loud *crack*. The white ball drops onto Jonah's bare foot, spraying juice on his ankle. He shouts and jumps backward, and the snout howls and rears up its two back feet in a furious rage, spinning and spinning, kicking the air. Jonah ducks one paw, but the other hits him directly in the throat. He stumbles, gagging, and that's when he's rammed from behind again, sailing right underneath the spinning snout's claws.

Jonah rolls and stands, only to find himself facing five smaller snouts with dwindling mushrooms on the tips of their noses. Judging by their sizes, they have to be cubs. In fact, they're about as big as he is, maybe even a little smaller. The porcupine trees are just thirty yards behind them. He can see the clusters shining on their branches. A faint white beam flashes on the ground, snaking around the pack, directing him there. But how is he going to get past?

Two of the cubs growl and crouch, but before they can leap, Jonah darts to his left, where a dozen adults pace back and forth, smelling and watching and waiting. Jonah twists around just in time to see the two cubs tearing right for him. The quickest one leaps and unhinges its jaw, and Jonah reaches up and snatches its front legs, and they spin in a blur. He lands on top of the beast, his skull bouncing in and out of its teeth. The cub is stunned, but then its back paws kick wildly at his stomach, shredding his jumpsuit, and a few seconds later, he's launched into the air. But he still holds on to its front legs, and as he's rocketed over the beast's head, he pulls its hairy body up at the precise moment the second cub jumps into the chaos. They lock jaws and blindly swipe at each other, and Jonah scrambles in the direction of the trees.

The older snouts—there must be twenty—widen their circle beyond, making his escape look hopeless. The other three cubs stalk him while the first two separate and flank him on either side. Jonah twists and twists, desperately looking for a hole or weak spot in the perimeter. The five cubs close in, each one ready to take the first bite. Their noses rise with the mushrooms, and it's only a matter of seconds before they can see exactly where he is. Jonah twists around again, and his toes slide over something hard and smooth. It's a flat black rock, just like the one he used to rescue Rosa and Aussie in the smoking module. There are hundreds of the rocks poking out of the grass, and he picks up two and wings them at the cub approaching on his right. The first one misses, but the second spins directly at the beast's nose, and it slices its mushroom clean off at the base. Yellow liquid shoots up like a geyser, and the cub tears away in the other direction, shrieking.

The adults howl twice and begin to close the circle. Jonah grabs two more rocks. The cub on his left crouches and shuffles toward him. With the verve still strengthening his muscles, he smashes the two rocks together in his hands and picks up the shards, and now he's armed with several blades. Jonah leaps over the shuffling cub, surprising it, and drags a blade down the beast's spine. As it squeals and heads off for the adults, Jonah rushes toward the other three. Two either smell the snout blood or Jonah's confidence, and they scurry off. The last one, though, deflates the mushroom on its nose and raises its four white eyes on its sticks, circling to the left. Jonah circles along with it, jabbing a blade in front of him, hoping to scare it off. The perimeter gets closer, twenty angry adults upset with the training exercise's outcome. Jonah throws three blades at the enclosing pack, puncturing one in the ribs and another in a back leg. Both gallop off in rage.

The circling cub is defiant, though, and drops its jaw and swings its two rows of teeth into place. The perimeter creeps closer and closer, and Jonah can smell their collective breath. He needs to make more blades; he only has one left. Suddenly there's a loud scuffle right behind him. He turns to see the injured snout with its missing eyeball, spinning and kicking out of control, heading straight for him like a tornado. The cub senses its opportunity and leaps. Without thinking, Jonah drops to his knees and slices his blade back and forth, and then he rolls to his left, barely avoiding the kicking adult. A wet gurgling squeal comes from the cub. Jonah barely has the time to register he sliced its jaw clear off at the cheeks before seeing the adults on the perimeter charging from every angle.

Jonah reaches out at the snout with the missing eye. He times it perfectly; pulling himself onto the beast's back the exact moment the pack arrives. He digs one hand into the beast's wool and twists it, wrapping the hair around and around his palm. The snouts around him snap their teeth and swipe their claws at his legs, but Jonah's ride is too fast and too out of control, spinning and kicking, keeping everyone back. The snout under him slams its injured face into the ground and charges ahead blindly, breaking through the pack. Jonah finally breathes and his mind comes back to him, but his relief is short-lived as he sees they're going in the opposite direction of the porcupine trees, back into the jungle.

"No! Come on!" he shouts, kicking his heels into the snout's sides. He pulls his hand wrapped in its hair in every direction, tearing out wool and flesh, but the beast keeps going as if on autopilot.

The pack catches up, several biting for Jonah, who slices the blade back and forth, injuring each one. Blood splatters his legs and arms. Just as they reach the jungle's shadow, a huge snout leaps and tackles Jonah off the beast's back. His skull bounces off the ground, his vision pops and doubles, and his breath escapes him like a ghost. He loses the blade. Before he can open his eyes, he knows he's surrounded.

His lids separate to the sight of several hairy jaws hovering over his body. There's nowhere for him to go. A thick stream of yellow foam drips from one snout's nose, covering his left leg. The foam is freezing, and his knee trembles and twitches as if trying to escape his body. He tries to sit up, but three paws slam onto his chest. He can't breathe. He can't move, aside from his twitching knee, and he can't see or smell anything but all the wool and the teeth that swing inches from his face.

His stomach and chest tighten as he prepares to be ripped apart. Faces flash in his mind: Tunick, Vespa, Ruth, and Kip. He sees his parents, the professor hanging from the tree, and then he sees Achilles from outside the ship's window, getting larger and larger and brighter and brighter. The biggest snout in the group drops its jaw right onto Jonah's chin and then drags it backward up and over his face, scratching his lips, nose, and forehead with its rough, pebbled skin. When the jaw lifts, Jonah finds himself face-to-face with two of the cubs, and they grunt and hop up and down and slobber and whine with anticipation. They still get first dibs. Their training continues.

The three paws put even more weight on his chest, and Jonah can't do anything but wheeze and bounce his knee and stare up into the slivers of the jungle above. A flash of white appears in his mind but goes nowhere before vanishing. The cub on his right rams Jonah's cheek so hard with its forehead that his neck pops and cracks. He grinds his teeth and waits for it all to end. He stares back up into the jungle, and this time he doesn't see white beams, but instead round black balls, falling like fruit. His knee continues to twitch, and the second cub circles around and snags the flopping leg in its mouth. Jonah closes his eyes.

There's a deafening, awful roar in his ear. Guttural and wet with blood. It's happening, he thinks. They're about to feast. But there's no pain. No crunching of his bones. There's another roar near his legs, and his knee falls out of the cub's jaws. He opens his eyes to see more of the black balls falling from the trees, but they come in blankets now. He shakes his head to stop the hallucinations, but the balls keep dropping, dropping, dropping. The snouts whip their heads to their backs, shrieking and howling. The paws disappear from his chest, and Jonah rolls onto his side in confusion.

As the snouts scatter and some collapse in gushing pools of blood, one of the black balls lands right next to Jonah's face. It bounces away from him and then violently unfolds, popping like a kite catching wind, into what looks like a large wingless bat with a dozen pointy leather ears running across its square head. The creature stands on its two back feet and nods its long, canine nose at him while two tiny transparent eyes roll around and around in their sockets as if unconnected from its head. It rubs its wet front paws together under its chin and then makes a rapid clicking noise with its throat.

Before Jonah can try to shake his head again to make it disappear, a snout cub falls right on top of him, squealing with three of these black creatures attached to its back. Jonah claws out from under its weight and rolls away and gets to his knees, and then he ducks another snout desperately trying to shed the six or so black things that rip at its spine. As Jonah attempts to escape the growing circle of mayhem, he realizes what these little creatures are. The night at the makeshift hospital, Paul called them roopers, little monkey-rat-devil things that live high up in the trees. He said they hunt snouts every morning for breakfast and drop down in swarms as thick as blankets. He also said they gnaw snouts down to the bone in a couple minutes.

Jonah's left knee twitches as he stumbles between two flailing snouts covered with roopers. He falls to his hands and picks up a flat black rock sticking out of the grass. He slams it against the ground, shattering it, picking up the first jagged edge he sees. But then something pronged and sharp plunges into his lower back. He yells and falls forward, and before he can reach behind him with the blade, the stabbing crawls up his spine until a pair of growling teeth sinks into his left shoulder. The pain causes Jonah to collapse into the grass, and all he can do is roll onto his back to try to smash the creature between him and the ground. But he's not heavy enough; he rolls farther into the clearing, and the rooper's snarling wet teeth never leave his skin.

The pain grows and grows, and he cries louder. Jonah whips his blade over his shoulder but hits nothing but air. He sits up and slams his back as hard as he can against the ground. The rooper finally releases its bite. Claws thrash wildly, cutting into his neck and upper arm, and Jonah stabs blindly over his shoulder. He makes contact a few times, but he doesn't know if he's hitting the creature or just digging holes into the ground. He changes his grip and stabs harder, and finally the creature howls, gurgles, and stops thrashing. Jonah rolls away and takes one quick look at the mass of black fur spurting white blood, and then he's on his feet, limping toward the porcupine trees. He picks up rock after rock, whipping them behind him without looking back. Once or twice, he hears a squeal.

He dives between the trees, bouncing off their prickly bark, when a flash of pain pops behind his sockets. White blobs explode in his vision, and then it's as if fire races around his eyeballs. He winces, groans, and falls into another clearing, this one no larger than a module. On the opposite side is a stone wall.

Jonah crawls to the wall and flattens his back against it, squinting left and right, looking for a way out, or for a reason the white beams led him here. He takes a deep breath and tries to focus. The trees and boulders are so close together that there's only one way out, and that's the same narrow space where a faint, scuffling noise has begun. Something is trying to follow him. The roopers haven't given up. Or the snouts. The noises grow louder, and he reaches for the blade over his shoulder, ready to throw, when a small human body squeezes through the gap.

It's Hess, the small girl who whispered into Portis's ear after scaring away the glowing toads. She bounces on the balls of her feet, and her large eyes scan the clearing. A threadbare red T-shirt barely reaches the waist of her blue pants that are much too big and held up with a thick green vine. A crooked black machete bobs at her waist. With her is a tall Asian boy with a shaved head, wearing brown shorts and nothing else. He holds a long spear with white blood dripping from its point.

They all stare at each other for a second before the girl looks high up at the wall above Jonah and smiles.

"You found another one." She laughs.

"Crazy," the boy says.

"What do you want?" Jonah sits back down. He stares at the

narrow space between the trees, waiting for more kids to arrive. "You're Hess, right?""

"How did you know… Whoa, whoa, whoa… What's up with your eyes?"

Jonah's skin grows hot. "Why?"

The boy whistles. "Yuck, man. That's gross."

Hess bends down until they're face-to-face. "They're completely blue. You have like, no corneas. And no white parts. Just the black dots, the pupils or whatever. What the hell happened to you?"

Jonah rubs his palms deep into his sockets, bumping the shattered bones of his nose. This is what he was afraid of. "Doesn't matter. I just need to find Tunick. I have to get my friends back. I need you to show me how to get back to him. Right now."

"Seriously, though, how did your eyes get like that?" the boy asks.

Jonah puts his head on his knees. "I'm dying. Okay? I have a disease. And it hurts like hell. But all I care about is getting to Tunick. Can you help me?"

Hess bends down again. "You're dying?"

"Yeah, okay? I have about twenty-four days until, or… roughly… Shit." It hits him, and his head whips back against the wall as if blasted with a shotgun. When Dr. Z gave him his diagnosis, was she using Earth days, or the longer Achilles days they've been counting since the crash? This whole time, he realizes he's been racing against the rotation days it takes the telescope on Thetis to line up with their wreckage. He's been racing Thetis days. Dr. Z must have been talking about Earth days. He looks at Hess, and his eyes begin to throb again. "If I had thirty Earth days to live, then how many Achilles days is that?"

The girl begins to mumble. "Thirty times twenty-four is what, seven-twenty? Divide that by the thirty-four hour days on Achilles and you get twenty-one… A little over twenty-one Earth days."

He feels so stupid. At the rate they were going, he would have almost certainly died before they could flag down any Thetis telescope. It was all for nothing. "Do you know how many kids I was traveling with that have died over the last few days?"

The boy sighs. "You're really terrible at math, aren't you?"

"Brian, Rosa." He opens a shaking finger with each name. "Um, Bidson probably, or definitely, and Richter and then Sean. And probably Kip. Six? Holy shit. I killed six people. They're dead because of me. And Vespa and Brooklyn are out there somewhere right now, also because of me, probably running for their lives. If they're not already dead. I'm the worst thing that could have happened to everyone. This is why nobody ever wanted to be my friend."

"Well, aren't you a fun guy." The boy laughs. He points his spear high up on the wall and then stabs the ground between Jonah's feet. "And so smart, too. Great with math, overly confident, a real go-getter. You know, I'm kind of surprised someone like you was actually chosen for Thetis. Only the best and the brightest, huh? How'd you slip through the doors?"

The statement stings him more than he wants to admit. Statistically, he thinks, it *was* surprising he was chosen for Thetis. This isn't the first time he's had that thought. Yes, he did well on his written exams and passed all his military exercises, excelling in a few things here or there like swimming and weaponry, but there were far more qualified cadets who weren't offered tickets. And given his background red-flagged with paranoia, extreme issues of mistrust, and a long record of special treatment, it's certainly odd that he was given such a high privilege.

"I tested pretty well," he says finally. His internal answer has always been that they just felt sorry for him. Giving an orphan kid the first break of his life.

"Big deal." Hess laughs. "Everyone tests well. But I'll tell you one thing. If you're going to just sit here and cry over who died and how weird your eyes are, then it looks like that before they let you on the ship, they forgot to check for something major. Your balls."

Jonah can't help but laugh. Pain needles his eyes. "What did you whisper into Portis's ear last night?"

"That ugly Portis Hatcher kid? I just told him I knew his sister on Thetis. And that I know how he can find her. She's here. On Achilles."

Jonah shoots to his wobbling feet, knocking the boy's spearhead from the dirt. "Portis's sister is here on Achilles?"

"She's been on the east coast, exploring and whatnot," the boy says. "We got word just this morning that she's on her way back. But we don't know if we can trust the source."

Jonah feels even more urgency than he did a few minutes ago to get out of here. Not only does he want to save his friends from Tunick before he dies, but now he feels a strange responsibility to reunite Portis with his sister. "You have to get me back to Tunick's cave. Now. Where is it? Where's Tunick?"

"Funny to hear you call him that. But we don't know where he is," Hess says, sighing.

"Luckily," the boy says.

Hess looks high up on the wall. "Who cares about that guy, though? He doesn't matter right now. He's too nuts anyway. What *does* matter right now is that you found another portal."

"Luckily," the boy says again, looking up.

Jonah squints upward. It takes him a moment, but then about fifteen feet up he sees a perfect oval punched into the stone. Inside it sit four squares. The verve wants him here. It wants him inside another sphere.

The boy points his spear at the symbol. "So, how do we open this sucker up?"

Jonah stares at them. He can't trust them any more than he can trust Tunick or Armitage. "I don't care about these stupid things right now. I just want to get back to my friends. Tell Portis his sister is on the way. Tunick has them taking verve and they're all freaking out."

Hess and the boy exchange a look and then Hess says, "If that's true, then there's nothing you can do for them. What you *can* do is tell us how you knew to come in here to find this. We want to find all of them. We have pretty big plans."

He thinks about explaining the white beams, but he just shrugs and asks, "How did *you* find it?"

"Easy," she says. "We followed you."

Jonah throws his hands in the air. "You followed me? You were out there with me while I was about to be killed about a hundred times by all those things out there and you just watched?"

"Can't believe you made it out alive, to be honest. That was pretty awesome," the boy says.

"Fuck you," Jonah seethes. "Show me how to get to Tunick. *Now.*"

"Tell you what. You open this baby up for us, and we'll take you there," Hess says.

"I thought you didn't know where he was."

"I have an idea."

Jonah hesitates for a second before asking, "Who's Zion?"

Hess smirks and traces a finger along the wall. "He's been telling you about *Zion*, huh? Listen, kid, there is no *Zion*. It's something he made up. Like his alter ego or his imaginary friend or whatever. Zion is Tunick, Tunick is Zion. The guy's *absolutely* crazy, if you haven't figured that out yet. There is no Zion. That's him."

The remaining pain in Jonah's eyes shrinks together into a tiny black mass that travels to the pit of his stomach. How can Tunick be Zion? Didn't Zion shoot at him? And didn't Tunick say Zion was the one who took the adults? He's not working alone. The black mass wrenches free from Jonah's gut, and a pool of red-hot aggression fills up his entire body, rising to suffocate his brain. Revenge. Justice. Answers. He knows he's going to need all three if his body is ever to drain this anger.

Jonah grits his teeth. "Do you know how many people he's killed?"

"You pass *any* of your math exams or..." the boy says.

Jonah leaps at him. One hand grabs his throat, the other his spear, and before Hess can reach them, Jonah slams the boy to the ground. He breaks the spear over his knee and aims the point at Hess, who circles them.

"You don't want to do that," she growls. The machete bounces at her side. "Let him up. Now. Or I won't show you where your friends are. I actually know where they are. And they don't have much time if they're verving with him."

Jonah squeezes the boy's throat, feeling something crunch, and then he releases him and stands up.

"That's a good boy," she says.

"Why is Tunick doing this?" Jonah asks.

"I *told* you he's gone crazy," Hess says before pulling a small, crude canteen from around her back. She takes a deep swig, and then says, "Do you know how many seeds he's up to a day now? Maybe fifty. Sixty? The guy's mind is totally fried."

"Totally fried," the boy says.

"Well, is it fried enough for him to kill people? For him to kill people and then hang them from trees and write messages on their shirts for us to run? Is he crazy enough for that?"

"Yes," Hess whispers.

The boy massages his neck. "But his brother could have done some of that for him, I guess. He was on your ship. In fact, he's the one who brought you guys down."

Jonah flattens his back against the wall, picturing himself shoving one of his black blades straight through Tunick's chest. He's going to kill him. And his brother. "Who's his brother? Is it Paul? With the shaved head? Is it that guy?"

"We don't know. We've never seen him," Hess says. "We only know about him because on the day you crashed, Tunick came running into our camp like a fucking madman. He said his brother hijacked your ship. Then he said something about a battery, about a power supply. And then he threatened to kill us for a little while, which is totally normal. And then he ran off. But hey, do you know where that thing is? This battery thing? It's really important that we find it before he does."

"For the last time, no. We don't know where it is. Why does he want it so badly? When we said we didn't know anything about it, he put a gun to my friend's head and almost killed her. We have no idea where it is, but he keeps saying we're lying to him."

The boy picks up a rock and throws it at the oval above, missing badly. "He wants it so he can get to Peleus."

"Peleus?"

"Yup, the *other* moon."

"What? How?" Jonah whispers. "He's...he's crazy."

The boy chucks another stone at the oval, coming closer this time. "Didn't we just say that? But that's what happens to you when you take fifty to sixty doses—*fifty verve seeds*—a day, for months and months. And verve, if you haven't figured it out yet, it ranks pretty high up there in hallucinogens *and* neurotoxins. It would be off the charts on Earth. Our scientists were studying it on Thetis. At least, for a while."

He and Hess share a glance.

She quickly picks up the story: "You take just one or two seeds and you're *gone*. You're gone for hours. You eat fifty seeds a day and you'll be like Tunick, *or is it Zion*? That guy right now is so out of his gourd that he says he can see the souls of Achilles floating around him. Like ghosts or angels, like he can channel the dead or something. He talks to them, and they talk to him."

"He says he can talk to an alien race who used to live here, and they've been giving him orders to create an army. He's nuts," the boy says.

Jonah would laugh if it didn't seem so deranged. "He thinks he can talk to aliens? That he can talk to the ghosts of aliens? So, that's the 'they' and the 'them' he keeps talking about?"

The boy chucks another rock at the oval and it's a direct hit. Nobody breathes for a few seconds, waiting for a click or the wall to separate, but nothing happens. He then looks at Jonah. "Verve is *ridiculously* strong and *ridiculously* addictive, and he's running out of it. And fast."

"How fast?"

"At the rate he's going," Hess says, "he'll be through this area's vervoluptis crop in about two months, which is the last crop he's found on Achilles. That's why he wants to get to Peleus. There's more of the plant up there. Lots more."

Jonah throws up his arms. "But how can he even get there if he found the battery? Our ship is toast, and you guys crashed here, too."

"Right." Hess takes another huge swig from her canteen and then looks up at the oval on the wall.

"None of this makes sense," Jonah says.

"What *does* makes sense," the boy says, "is why he left this area's crop for last."

It takes Jonah a moment. "Because that's where our ship was supposed to crash."

"Exactly. He had it all planned out. Always was a smart guy."

"But you've been here for two years. How could he have planned something like that? I mean, is he able to communicate with Earth? If his brother was on the same ship as I was..."

Hess shrugs. "We haven't figured that out yet. He's definitely hiding something from all of us. Maybe he's built something from the scraps of your ship, we don't know. Keep in mind that we just heard of this whole crash plan idea ourselves a couple days ago."

"Yeah," the boy adds. "We learned about it right as we saw you fall from the sky."

"That's it. I've got to go. Right now. Take me to see Tunick."

"Not until you open up this baby." The boy nods at the wall behind him.

"Forget about the portals!" Jonah shouts. "My friends are going to die!"

Hess shrugs again. "Hate to say this, and I know it sounds awful, but we don't care about you or your friends. We just care about getting inside this thing."

"I'll fight you." Then Jonah says something he didn't think he was going to say. "I'll kill you. I swear."

The boy reaches behind his back and produces a small blue handgun, just like the one Vespa had. Is it Vespa's? "No. *I'll* kill you. *I* swear."

Hess pulls her own blue gun from under her clothing. "Open it. Now. And I promise if you do, we'll take you to Tunick."

Jonah shifts his eyes back and forth between the two of them. "What if I don't know how?"

"I have a feeling you do," Hess says.

Jonah looks up at the oval and then tests his knees. The star in the cave had five points for his fingers, but this symbol has four squares. He has no idea how to get it to work.

The boy raises his gun to Jonah's temple. "Hurry up, blue eyes."

Jonah wants to destroy this kid, to get his hands back around his throat and never stop squeezing, but instead he backpedals to the lip of the clearing and runs at the wall. He jumps, easily rising the fifteen feet. He slaps his large palm against the oval and then plummets back to the ground. The three of them wait for the wall to open, but nothing happens.

"Again," the boy demands.

Jonah runs and jumps again, and this time he focuses on the rock surrounding the symbol. He finds a small ledge to land his toes, and off on the right protrudes a jagged knob that he can hold on to. He wavers, his toes slipping, his fingers losing their grip, but then he steadies himself and turns his head. He can barely see over the porcupine trees and into the clearing streaked with blood and dotted with black bodies, both big and small. Then it's just more jungle. He looks up and considers scaling the wall and escaping, but it's completely flat and too high to reach in a single jump. All he can do is attempt to figure out the oval.

Its lines are perfect and sharp, just like the star's. Jonah digs his fingers into the oval's outline, hoping to feel the sponginess, but it's just hard rock that bites at his skin.

"Come on!" the boy shouts below. "Your friends need you, don't they? Hurry up!"

Jonah tries poking his fingers inside the four squares, but they, too, are nothing but hard rock. He presses as hard as he can, and then he pounds on them. Nothing. He has no idea what else to do, but just before he jumps back to the ground, the bottom left square gleams white for a brief moment, and then just the square's top right corner remains illuminated like an arrowhead. Jonah places a shaking finger on top of the square which is now warm to the touch, and instead of pushing inward, he swipes it up and to the right like he's hiding his parents' photo on his sheaf. Magically, the square shifts along the rock and joins the block in the top right. He does the same to the one carved into the bottom right, swiping it up and left. Jonah holds his breath as the two squares combine.

"You have three seconds!" the boy shouts.

"Hold on! Something's happening!"

The edges of the squares soften and round, and soon they become ovals. Two ovals inside of one. The smaller symbols crawl downward until they're in the exact middle. They look like eyes to Jonah, and without thinking, he places his two blue eyes directly in front of them. Instantly, the ovals blast a series of lights into his eyes, followed by two short gusts of cool air. He's frozen, both mesmerized and physically paralyzed. He loses his grip on the rock and falls backward with his arms and legs open wide. He can't breathe. He can't scream. And when four arms break his fall, he can't wrench himself away.

"I think he…" the boy whispers.

Jonah squints up at the oval and watches it streak downward like the blade of an axe, separating the stone like curtains. A thundering rumble knocks them all to the ground. He wants to run, but still he can't move. The base of the wall rounds and reaches outward, and then it's like Jonah lies in the opening of an ancient teepee. Finally, his legs regain feeling.

"Nice work, kid," Hess whispers, getting to her feet. She still holds the gun in her hand.

"So, should we go get Lark?" the boy asks.

"Not this time," Hess answers.

"Tunick's now." Jonah coughs. "I opened it. Now you tell me how to get there. Your end of the deal."

The boy staggers into the opening and then twists to aim the gun at Jonah. "Not yet. I can never get these things to do what I want. For some reason I bet you can."

"And then what?" Jonah asks.

"And then we'll take you to Tunick," he says. "Promise."

CHAPTER FIFTEEN

As soon as all three are inside, a white blanket of electricity pops and sizzles in the opening, keeping anyone from leaving. Jonah shouldn't be here; he should be halfway to Tunick's—to Zion's—with a decent plan on how to save his friends. *Run. Kids are free now.* He should be running back to Tunick's. He should be freeing the kids.

The room isn't a sphere, but instead like the inside of pyramid, pointed at the roof with straight walls radiating to the ground. Symbols are carved everywhere, including on the floor. All along the base of the room is one of the long white objects—the actual portal device—similar to the one that took Kip. Jonah knows they're going to ask him to figure out how to start it, but he's no demic. He can't find hidden patterns and put together formulas.

"Now what?" Jonah asks.

Hess spins on her bare heels and studies the walls. "I'm looking for something… This one certain one… But it's not…"

Jonah waits for something to illuminate in his eyes, or for the verve to point out a group of symbols, but all that comes is a shortness of breath, along with a wave of exhaustion. When was the last time he ate something? He sits in the middle of the room and holds his stomach.

The boy jogs around the perimeter pointing his gun at Jonah, his head bobbing up and down, his free hand fumbling over symbols at random.

When he was in the sphere, Jonah got an overwhelming sense of safety and the feeling that he was supposed to be there. In the pyramid, he feels absolutely nothing.

"Okay, kid," Hess finally says to him. "Do your thing. Work your magic."

Jonah laughs. "I don't have a *thing*. There is no magic. I have no idea what these rooms are all about. I don't understand portals. You've picked the wrong kid to follow."

"Listen. I know you're not going to believe me, but we're actually on your side here," the boy says. "We don't want Tunick to get to Peleus for many reasons. We want the ship for ourselves to get to a different continent."

Hess stiffens her shoulders and looks away.

"Wait. What ship?" A second later, it hits Jonah. "You guys didn't crash here, did you? You landed here, and now he needs the energizer to power up your ship from Thetis."

"Well, *that's* out of the bag," Hess mutters after taking a long drink from the canteen hanging from her waist. "We want the ship for ourselves. We want to get to another continent here on Achilles."

Jonah presses his thumbs into his sockets. "This is unbelievable. I need that ship to get to Thetis, or I'm going to die. Where is it?"

"We don't know," Hess says.

His eyes begin to throb and he squints straight up into the pointed center. "How do you lose a spacecraft?"

The boy presses a squiggly symbol above his head and sighs. "That's not exactly our finest moment. After we arrived here on fumes, on one of the first nights we were here, we *very stupidly* let Tunick cook everyone this huge dinner. Needless to say, we were all vomiting and sick and totally incoherent that night, and he used that time to move the ship, wasting the rest of its fuel. He showed up back at camp five weeks later—much to our surprise, I must say, because we assumed he was dead—and he refuses *to this day* to confess to knowing how the ship disappeared. We've been looking for it, off and on, ever since. So has another guy who has split off from everyone here and gone rogue, a guy named Armitage Blythe. Everyone has their own plans."

"I saw Armitage last night." Jonah waits for a response, but neither flinches. "How the hell are we going to find your ship on a moon this size? It could be on the complete other side of Achilles."

"You really *are* stupid, aren't you?" The boy laughs. "You must not have gotten a good look when you were going down in flames up there because you're on a piece of land roughly half the size of Australia. *And* we're more isolated. So our search area isn't that big, but you're right, it's big enough. Several of us are on the east coast right now, half-looking for the ship, half-exploring. That's what Portis's sister, Blage, was doing. Hess and Lark and a few others like me try to stick close enough to Tunick without him feeling too threatened, not only to see if he'll lead us to the ship, but also just to keep an eye out for him."

"An eye out? *For* him?" Jonah is exasperated. "Are you serious? That guy just murdered over a hundred people and you're looking out *for* him. That's sick. That's unbelievable."

Hess points her gun at him. "All that just happened, remember. The murdering stuff is new for him. We've been trying to protect him from himself, as much as we could. We owed that to him after what he did for us on Thetis."

"Wait." Jonah stands and points a finger at her face. He doesn't care if she has a gun. "If you saw us crash and Tunick told you what was going on, then why didn't you come and warn us? Come and *help* us? Holy shit, you guys could have stepped in at any point. You just let him kill us. You just..."

Hess exhales. "Lark felt it was best for us to stay out of it. We put it to a vote."

"You *voted* whether or not to save us from being murdered by that asshole maniac back there? Jesus Christ! And now you want *my* help in here? How dare you ask *me* to help *you*?"

"We're stepping in *now*," she says. "We're telling you *now*. We didn't realize Tunick was killing anyone until just a short time ago, when we started finding the bodies."

Jonah stares at a circular symbol with two lines intersecting over it. "You could have saved so many people."

"Did you know you were on Tunick's list? That he chose you?" the boy asks.

"Whatever that means." All this talk is getting him some answers, but it's also getting him nowhere. He has to leave. He has to get that force field in the entrance to disappear.

Hess sets her hands on her hips. "The day after the crash, he dropped in at our camp and said he picked out some of the kids at the beach to go with him to Peleus. He went on to describe them at length. He described you, in particular. He chose you."

"Well, he unchose me."

"Probably because you didn't take to the verve," she says. "Messed up his plans. Messed up his *plants*, rather."

"So was that a verve plant in your hand when you saw us in the jungle?"

"I had *just* found it. Didn't even get the chance to shuck the seeds. We try to find what we can of the plant ourselves, destroying and burying it. But we also keep a little to trade with Tunick when we need something from him."

Jonah thinks of Armitage last night, carrying two huge bunches of the same plant. Either he's addicted, too, or it's for Tunick, as a gift, bribe, or deterrent. Jonah wonders if Armitage, Paul, and Ruth found Tunick's cave last night, if there was a battle, if any of his friends were killed. He pictures Aussie lying on the floor, taking her last breaths. He's wasting too much time in here. He has to get this portal working so he can get back to them.

Jonah staggers to his feet. "What exact symbol were you looking for?"

"Looks like an octopus with a box on its head." Hess sighs. "The times we've used that one, the portal sucked one of us up and then let them somehow float over the moon, showing them things we would never have found on our own. Locations of food and shelter and other things."

"We can always use more food," the boy says.

The three of them circle the room, and that's when Jonah spots a hollow diamond with a single square inside, just like the one Kip focused on. It's near the opening. He checks the opposite walls like before, but to his chagrin, they're not there. He scans the ceiling. Not there, either. No pattern. No formula. As the other two argue over a couple of flower-like shapes near the top of one of the walls, Jonah walks into the middle and looks down at the floor, and it's then he spots Malix's worst nightmare: three circles inside a C. It's not carved as deeply as the other symbols, which is why he didn't see it earlier. He places a shaking hand over it and hesitates. There has to be a reason Tunick carved them into those adults Malix and Sean found.

Hess and the boy continue to discuss the flower-like shapes while Jonah stares at the symbol below his hand. Do the three circles represent something? Maybe they're Achilles, Peleus, and Thetis? Maybe they're for three people? Jonah then thinks about his dad, his mom, and himself, the three members of his family. But what does the 'C' mean? It could be a curved hand, about to crush the circles. He stands up straight and scans the walls, finding the same shallow symbol carved three more times. It's the only pattern he sees.

"Just try it and see what happens," Hess whispers to the boy who scratches at the flower above his head.

Whatever happens, happens, Jonah tells himself. He's going to die soon anyway. He drops his hand to the floor and digs his fingers into the three circles. Sure enough, they pulse and then begin to rotate within the C.

Hess shoves the boy out of the way and jumps to press the flower on the eastern wall. Jonah backs away from the moving circles on the ground and then casually walks toward the entrance, his heart pounding in his throat. He digs his fingers into the three circles, watches them move, and then he walks to one on the next wall, touching it, starting it.

"What are you doing?" the boy asks him.

"You figure something out?" Hess asks.

"Um," Jonah says, touching another one of the symbols. Once it activates, he marches right toward Hess, shrugging his shoulders. "I don't think so. What are you guys trying?"

The two turn to look up at the flower as Jonah reaches the last C with circles. As soon as he touches it, the circles rotate and then glow green. He spins around to see that all the circles he's touched in the room are now glowing green. He runs into the middle of the room and waits.

"Hey!" Hess shouts. "What's happening?"

The long white object running along the base of the pyramid comes to life. The milky material begins flowing clockwise, and a faint white energy field appears at the ceiling.

"What'd you do?" the boy yells at Jonah. "Which one was it?"

"I don't know exactly," Jonah says. He doesn't know if they believe him, but it doesn't matter; the portal is working. If only he knew what he was going to do next.

Hess runs her hands through her hair. "What do we do?"

The boy pushes past her in anger. "I knew we should have brought Lark! Now it's all screwed up!" He aims his gun at Jonah's face. "What did you push? Which ones? Tell me."

Jonah puts his hands in the air. He wants that gun so badly it takes everything for him not to reach for it. "I haven't touched a thing. I swear."

The white object speeds up. An eerie glow floats off its milky material and then disappears. There's a new energy in the room, and the walls begin to bend inward at the top. Red dust clouds the ceiling, mixing with the white force field.

"Screw it. You're going in, then," the boy growls at Jonah. "You're taking the plunge."

"Just wait," Hess yells above the noise of the room. "Let's think about it for a second. We can't waste it on him if it's a good one. What if he… Like the time with Ronald? We'll miss our chance."

"Well, but what if it's like the time with the twins?"

Hess drops her head and nods. She then raises her gun at Jonah. "See you on the other side, kid."

Jonah looks over his shoulder at the speeding white object. A voice inside his head tells him the symbol was the wrong one to touch, it tells him to leave, to not let them put him on that thing. But there's nowhere to run.

"Go!" the boy shouts. He moves to the left, and Hess breaks off to the right. There's no way to escape their lines of fire. If Jonah attacks him, she has a direct shot, and vice versa.

"What happened with the twins?" Jonah asks, trying to buy some time. He hopes the room will crack open and a new way out will appear.

"They walked back into our camp a day later," Hess mumbles. "Inside out."

"We had to kill them," the boy says.

The walls above them continue to bend inward. Red dust settles over all their heads and shoulders. Jonah imagines what he would look like with his skin missing, his muscles exposed.

"Turn around!" the boy shouts. "You ruined it. After all this time trying to find another one…and you ruined it somehow. You have three seconds. One."

Jonah turns and walks toward the wall. His eyes scan every symbol, looking for a sign. He tries to summon another vision from the verve, but none comes. He stops just steps from the white object speeding near his feet.

"Two."

He looks over his shoulder. He looks for Dr. Z. He looks for Tunick. He looks for his dad. He looks for someone, anyone to stop this. Somewhere Kip could be lying in a cave, his body flipped inside out, blood pooling all around him.

There's shuffling behind him, and the boy's voice comes closer. "Three."

Jonah ignores him and bends down to pick up a fist-sized rock. He tosses it onto the object, and the rock goes shooting along the base of the room like a ball on a roulette wheel.

"I said…" The boy's hand reaches Jonah's shoulder and tries to shove him forward, but Jonah's snatches his wrist and yanks the boy onto his back. The gun fires. The ground spits dirt next to Jonah's foot. Hess shouts something. There's another gunshot. And then Jonah pivots and whips the boy over his shoulder, tossing him onto the white object. With a howl, he sails down the room, and just before he reaches the end, the rock Jonah tossed a few seconds earlier drops from the ceiling, causing Hess to turn around. It's all Jonah needs. He dives for her torso, plowing her into the ground just as the boy meets the final few inches of the object. He disappears without a sound. The portal has its body. Within seconds, the force field covering the opening pops and disappears.

"No!" Hess screams under his weight. Jonah locks her neck into his armpit and straightens her arm, then slams her elbow over his thigh. She howls and the gun skids away. A moment later, it's safely in his hand.

"Get up," he demands. "Now."

"You probably killed him," she says.

"He killed himself."

"If that's what you need to tell yourself."

"I don't care about that kid, just like you don't care about me and my friends. Now, it's time we visit Tunick," Jonah says. He aims the gun at her flat nose. "Take me there. Now."

"Only Lark knows where he is. I swear. Only Lark knows."

"Then take me to Lark! I'm sick of this shit!"

Hess turns and walks outside, and Jonah follows safely, but closely behind, knowing she could have traps set like Tunick. Silently, they push through the narrow space between the porcupine trees and edge around the bloody clearing. Then they're in the jungle, tramping through sludge, scaling boulders, climbing hills.

Jonah keeps the gun on her back the whole time, more alert than he's ever been in his whole life. When he meets Lark, he's going to punch him in the face for everyone who's died. And then he's going to demand that he take Jonah straight to Tunick.

A wide, shallow stream appears, and they stop to rest. Jonah leans back and examines the bottom of his bare foot, how tough the skin has already gotten. He unties his other shoe and tosses it into the middle of the stream, where it stands straight up on a submerged rock.

On the other side of the bank, Jonah spots a tall flowering plant with circular leaves. The vervoluptis. He launches himself over the stream, all the while keeping the gun trained on Hess, who stands up to watch. The plant rips from the ground easily, but as he examines it, he can't find any seeds. He fumbles through its thick roots, but there's nothing there either.

"It's a dud, huh?" Hess says. "Sometimes they're empty."

In anger, he breaks the thick stem over his knee, and that's when he sees a short row of white seeds lining the inside of the stalk.

"Well, good for you," she mumbles.

He shucks them into his pocket and jumps back to the other side. Jonah doesn't know what he plans on doing with the verve but thinks it's a good idea to have them.

They reenter the jungle, and after a dozen steps, he hears voices deep in the trees. Hess tenses and then steps on a small branch, snapping it loudly. "You make another sound and I'll shoot you," he whispers. He forces her to pick up the pace, circling to the right as a harsh female voice complains about something. Through some bushes, Jonah sees a few pairs of bare feet, and then two small pairs of mismatched shoes. Hess ducks and tries to sneak away, but Jonah grabs her upper arm and tightens his grip.

He shuffles himself and Hess to the left until he can see all their faces. He's so stunned that he nearly falls backward into a row of thorns; with two older girls and one huge boy are Vespa and Brooklyn.

CHAPTER SIXTEEN

VESPA LOOKS LIKE SHE HAS JUST ROLLED OUT OF A BOXING ring; she's bloody and pale, stretching her jaw back and forth. A deep yellow bruise covers her swollen cheek. She takes a half step forward and stumbles, and the boy—a huge truck of a kid with the sides of his head shaved—catches her around the waist and ducks his head under her arm. Jonah holds his breath and moves closer, pulling Hess along with him. He can't believe she's here.

"Whoa there," the boy says to Vespa. He has the pointed face of a wolf, with deep-set eyes and a long, flat chin. Two ropes encircle his neck, buoyed with gems and black and white rocks. A large brown pouch sticks to his massive back.

"I'm fine," Vespa groans, pushing the hand off her waist. "Seriously. Get off."

"What's he doing? What happened?" Brooklyn spins in her giant white T-shirt. There's a huge bloodstain on its front, and it splatters up and over her shoulders. Jonah takes another few steps forward, but then stops when he sees how Brooklyn moves toward

Vespa with her hands out in front of her. She doesn't seem to be hurt. It's not her blood.

"I'm just feeling a little woozy," Vespa announces as she grabs one of Brooklyn's outstretched hands and pulls her into a hug. They hold each other closely, but it's an awkward exchange where Brooklyn steps on Vespa's feet and doesn't seem to know where to lay her head. Jonah watches to see if they whisper in each other's ears, if they have a plan, but they separate without so much as a mumble.

"I'll go look for them," one of the older girls says.

"Be quick," the other responds. She's tall, with narrow shoulders and a braid of long brown hair. A thick band of purple runs from temple to temple, over her eyes and nose like a superhero's mask. A long wooden spear leans in her hand, its shaft lined with sharp shards of amber-colored stone. Like the others, she's dressed in dirty rags. She turns and gently pushes Vespa toward the boy, and he directs her into the shade and out of Jonah's sight. "See what else you can do for her," she says to him. "And keep asking her about the energizer."

There's something familiar about her voice, Jonah thinks.

The other girl, a stoic and muscular young woman, with dark skin and a cloud of black hair, takes Brooklyn's open hand and leads her after Vespa. The demic stumbles into the shade.

Sweat covers Jonah's gun. It suddenly feels too light, or simply not enough. He releases Hess and picks up the first thing he sees: a flat white rock the size of his forearm. It's heavy in his hand, even in this gravity. He just hopes it's enough to take out the huge wolf boy. Jonah points the gun at Hess and demands that she stay there, and then he creeps forward, light on his feet. The trees ahead look perfect for climbing. Perhaps he can get the drop on them.

He moves to a nearby tree, and then another, all the while keeping Hess in his periphery. What happened to the girls? Where did all that blood on Brooklyn's shirt come from? Finally, from about twenty feet away, he finds Vespa lying on the ground, chewing on a thick root. He didn't realize until that moment how much he actually missed her.

"So you're Jonah, then?" a voice comes from his right. He turns to see the girl with the purple mask and spear, and his brain fires with options: shoot, throw the rock at her and run to Vespa and Brooklyn, play dumb, play coy, surrender, or fight. In the end, Jonah points both the gun and rock aggressively at her and sneers.

"Who the hell are you?" he asks.

"I'm Lark."

He pauses; he figured Lark was a boy. Then he aims the gun at her face. "Let them go. Vespa and Brooklyn. Right now. Or you'll be sorry."

"Don't tell me how sorry I'll be. That's for me to decide." Lark steps closer and a large silver circle swings on a rope around her neck. The metal is like nothing Jonah has seen before; it's a greenish brown and practically glows, reflecting the white sunlight directly into Jonah's eyes. Lark smiles and places her empty hand on her hip. Jonah isn't fooled by her friendliness and takes a step to the side, the gun and rock tight in his hands. She mimics his moves and says, "We've been keeping our eye out for you, you know that? We knew you were in the area, but we're surprised to see you're not still with Tunick, verving your brains out."

"Vespa!" Jonah shouts over his shoulder. "You okay?"

Her voice is weak, but spirited. "Jonah? Jonah! Where are you?"

Brooklyn shouts, "Really? That you, Jonah?"

"The question is, are *you* okay, Jonah? I mean, look at those eyes of yours," Lark says, slightly dropping the top of her spear toward him. Her other hand remains casually on her hip. Where has he heard this woman's voice before?

He doesn't like the way her spear leans and her eyes squint, but what's more, he hasn't forgotten that Lark was the one who voted to let Tunick hunt them all down like animals. Jonah stares at the girl so hard he thinks he's going to trigger another attack in his eyes, and then he makes his way toward Vespa with the gun always aimed at Lark. "Stay away from me. You come near me and

I'll kill you, I swear. Tunick was killing people, and you left us up there to die."

Lark stomps through the grass, always giving Jonah a little distance. "I know it looks like that, but it's more complicated. We had our reasons." Then, in a lower voice, she says, "We were selfish. And we're trying to make up for it now. I actually tried to make up for it the first night you were here, but things didn't work out."

Jonah ignores her. He pushes through a bush of star-shaped flowers. The wolf boy and the tall black girl are on their feet, crude weapons in hand, but Brooklyn stumbles past them with her eyes shut, hands out. "Jonah?"

"I'm right here," he says. "Straight ahead. Open your eyes. What's going on?"

Brooklyn extends her arms and keeps moving forward. Tiny lacerations frame her face and a long gash runs along her left bicep, all of which shine in some kind of thick pink goop. Jonah jogs into her embrace, picks her up with one arm, and hugs her tightly. She smells terrible, like rotten fish and vomit. Lark stops advancing, and in Brooklyn's ears, Jonah whispers, "You okay? They friends or foes?"

"I don't know. They've been trying to help us."

Hess casually appears from the left and receives an evil stare from Lark. Jonah sets Brooklyn down and then crouches in front of her face. "What's wrong with your eyes? What happened? They do something to you?"

The small demic sets her trembling fingers on her eyelids and then painfully pulls them apart. Her eyes open and Jonah feels as if he's been punched in the gut. He falls to his knees and drops the rock from his hand. Vespa says something and so does the wolf boy, but Jonah only hears a hollow echoing in his ears. Maybe it's the verve, Jonah thinks. Maybe it's still in his system, messing with his mind. He blinks hard and counts to five, but when he looks back up at Brooklyn, he's horrified to see that the whites of her eyes are a deep, deep blue, and the corneas and pupils are also completely gone. They're just two blue marbles.

Brooklyn stumbles forward and wraps her arms around his neck. Jonah's brain goes blank, and he crouches there, frozen in shock. His heartbeat pounds in his skull. No. It can't be. She has it, too?

Vespa sits up and says, "It happened last night. About ten hours ago. She has the same thing you do. She told me the moment we left you all on the beach."

"They found it right after the wormhole," Brooklyn whispers. "I didn't tell anybody. I should have told you. I'm sorry."

Jonah sits and squeezes Brooklyn's bronze hand. He struggles to hold back a tear as he stares at his future self in the eyes, and he doesn't know what to say. What have others said to him? He can't remember. Behind Brooklyn, the boy shrugs off the handmade pouch and opens it up.

"We're trying different things to see if we can help her." He carefully brings out several folded leaves tied neatly with thin vines, and he smells each one before unfolding a dark red leaf. Inside is a neon yellow powder that looks like pollen. Jonah gets a whiff of it and knows immediately it's from the nose of a snout.

"Brooklyn," Jonah says. "You're...you're going to be okay." He knows it's stupid to say things like that, but he can't bring himself to say he's sorry. If he says that, it's like saying it's over.

"Who needs to see anyway?" she says softly.

He stares at her long face for another second before closing his own eyes, hoping to conserve the amount of sight he has left, as if his lids stop a clock when they're closed.

"I'm Krevlis, by the way," the boy says somewhere above him. "But everyone just calls me Krev."

Jonah clenches his body in annoyance. This boy is partly responsible, just like the rest of them. Jonah sees flashes from the crash: the black rock slicing through Daniel like a shark, Jonah jumping through the spear-like branches into Garrett's arms, all the bodies in the valley, the raging fire, and the snouts. And then he sees these four kids from Thetis laughing under a tree, eating fruit in the shade.

"Vespa?" he asks.

"Yeah, Firstie?"

With anger burning his tongue, he says, "They tell you that Tunick is actually Zion? That there is no Zion? Tunick is the one who killed everyone."

"Yeah," Brooklyn says. She finds his knee and rests her hand there. "They just told us that. We're more than a little pissed off."

"I'm going to kill that piece of shit, believe me," Vespa says. It sounds as if she tries to stand but gives up quickly. "The next time I see him, he's a dead man."

Jonah squints his eyes open and sees Krev mixing the yellow powder in his hand with a red slime he's scooped out of a cracked shell. The boy then walks over to Brooklyn and says, "Keep your eyes closed. I'm going to try something else."

Above them, Lark, Hess, and the other girl pass a canteen around, taking long gulps, wiping their mouths. Then, Lark pushes Hess away. "Where's Everett?"

"Um," Hess mumbles. "I'll tell you later. He took the long way home. He'll be here later."

"What *is* this?" Brooklyn asks as the boy smears the mixture over her eyelids with his fingers. It smells sweet and sour. Jonah doesn't say anything about the snouts, but he wonders if it'll stimulate her eyes like it did his knee.

"It's something that we found works for headaches and fevers. Just let it dry."

Jonah clenches his fist and slowly aims the gun at each of them. He and Brooklyn have a blood disease, not migraines. Hess circles around to Krev's pouch and digs inside, and behind her, the black girl rests her head on Lark's stiff shoulder. They hold hands and whisper, and then Lark softly kisses her cheek. Their affection relaxes Jonah for a moment, and he squeezes Brooklyn's hand again and then drops down next to Vespa. She lies flat on a patch of short grass and avoids his eyes. He doesn't know why he thinks it's okay to do so—maybe because of the hug they shared on the beach before separating, or because of their intimate conversation in the caves—but he begins to run his hand through her black hair, stopping to examine a bump here, a bruise there. She smiles and turns her body toward him, but when she finally looks up into his face, Vespa gasps and sits up.

"Your eyes," she says.

"I know," he whispers.

"How long until…you're like Brooklyn?"

"How bad is it right now, Jonah? What are your symptoms?" Brooklyn asks.

He turns to Brooklyn, who has one eye coated with the slime. "I've been nauseous off and on and passed out earlier, and then I had some pretty bad pain in my eyes about an hour ago. Felt like needles. Like a thousand needles."

"Yeah," she says. "That was me yesterday."

Everyone grows silent.

Vespa gets up and offers her hand to Jonah, pulling him violently to his feet. "We have to get you two to Thetis for treatment. Like, immediately. Now how are we going to do it?"

Lark breaks away from the other girl and says, "You don't *want* to go to Thetis. That's the thing. You *want* to stay here. That's what we were about to tell you."

"Don't tell me what I want to do. If we stay here, my friends *die*," Vespa says, pointing to Jonah and Brooklyn. Her color is coming back, Jonah notices. Instead of stretching her jaw, she's clenching it.

"You go to Thetis and you're all dead," the other girl mumbles.

"What do you even care?" Jonah points the gun at the girl and closes his eyes to conserve his sight. "You don't care if we die. You've already proven that. You could have come to us *the first night* we were here! You could have warned us about Tunick and his brother and told us everything we needed to know to survive here, but instead you *voted* to hide in the bushes like a bunch of asshole cowards and then you watched us die. So *fuck you*, whatever your name is."

Something cold and sharp immediately touches Jonah's chin,

and then it scrapes harshly down his throat. He peeks open his eyes to see it's Lark's shard-covered spear. She rips the gun out of his hand and tosses it to Krev, who drops it into his bag.

"Her name is Camilla," Lark growls. "And if you ever talk to her like that again, I'll gut you like a potbellied gloomer."

"Lark," Camilla warns. "Please. I can speak for myself."

Lark keeps driving the gems into Jonah's throat, and he's just about to slide to the side and try to get his hand on the spear when Vespa punches it away from him. Lark loses her balance and stumbles forward, and Vespa stomps her shoe down on the middle of the shaft, breaking it into two. The girls lock arms, Hess shouts, but Jonah is able to get between them. If anyone from his group is going to fight, it's him. He's been through enough in the past two days, been lied to enough and seen enough blood, to make him want to fight all four of them. Jonah shoves Lark back into the other three and squares off with the whole group, hoping his eyes hold out long enough for him to do some damage. Then they'll find Tunick.

"Jesus. Everyone relax." Krev laughs. "Just take a breath and relax." He crouches in front of Brooklyn's face, admiring his sloppy work that covers her eyes. "What we need to do now is talk about the ion fuel cell container that was on board your ship, the energizer you guys were transporting to the colony. We need to find it before Tunick does. Where is it?"

"Just tell us," Lark says.

"Vespa," Brooklyn says as she leans blindly into Krev's face. "Aim for that purple stuff on her nose you were telling me about. Sounds dumb."

"It *is* dumb," Vespa says.

"We're *trying* to help you," Lark snaps. "Can't you see that? We're giving you our medicine. We're keeping you alive. But if you want to fight, I'll fight. I don't have a problem with that. But I can understand why you're angry. I get it, okay? You have to believe us, we didn't know Tunick was hunting people down. We were just trying to stay out of it. I even tried to step in the first night. When Tunick set part of the ship on fire."

It hits Jonah. The woman's voice he heard after they saw the cook and the professor down in the jungle, the one he and Vespa chased to the burning Support Module—that was her. "I heard you. You were yelling that night. Vespa, that was her."

"You're right," Vespa says.

"I tried to help, but Tunick got the drop on me and pulled me away. There was nothing I could do anyway. I stepped in to help you, though."

"Bullshit. You could have done more. You could have come back. You stepped in because you thought Tunick was about to lead you to your ship," Jonah says. Lark's eyebrows furrow and connect, and he watches as she struggles to choose her next words. It feels good to silence her, if only for a second. She finally looks at Hess, who averts her eyes.

Camilla places a gentle hand on Lark's wrist and looks at Jonah. "You're right. We want to find our ship. We want to find it so we can get to another continent here on Achilles. And once we're there, we're going to destroy it."

"What?" Vespa roars. "If there's a ship, then we need to get these guys to Thetis. *That's* what's going to happen when we find the ship."

"Definitely. That's our ship now," Jonah says.

Camilla clears her throat. "I'm sorry, but I need you to listen to us carefully. If Thetis finds us—and they will eventually know that your ship has crashed here—they'll finish what they started. They'll kill us all."

"But I have to get to Thetis," Brooklyn says from the ground. Her words come out soft and breathless, and they float around the heads of the splitters like clouds. The four look down at the small girl whose eye sockets are crusted over with yellow discs; Krev flexes his jaw casually, and Hess fumbles her fingers over the handle of her weapon, but that's it. Jonah feels a new surge of adrenaline pumping through his body, spreading over his scalp.

"We'll get you there," Vespa says.

"Absolutely, Brooklyn. We're going," Jonah adds. "Don't listen to these guys."

Vespa moves to stand over the demic. "And we're going to find Tunick along the way and beat his face in. I promise."

"We sure are," Jonah says. "And these assholes are going to take us to him right now."

Suddenly a series of blue flashes appear above the western trees.

"Go!" Lark shouts. "Now!"

The splitters don't hesitate; they pick up their things and run after the lasers. Jonah and Vespa look at each other. He steps in the opposite direction at first, but Vespa grabs Brooklyn's arm and follows the four leaping into the jungle.

"What's happening?" Brooklyn asks.

"Someone's shooting LZRs in the air, toward the beach," Vespa says, pulling her along. "Jonah! Come on! Before we lose them."

"Who cares about that right now?" Jonah asks, picking up the white rock. "We have to get to Tunick! We've escaped, let's go."

"I bet that *is* Tunick. And we can't let those guys destroy the ship. They're as much of a threat as Tunick is now. Come on!"

"Right. I say we follow them," Brooklyn says.

Jonah growls and takes a few more steps in the other direction before spinning around. The lights continue to zip above the trees. He grabs Brooklyn's hand and runs.

Vespa spots a worn path, and they catch up with the splitters after a few minutes. There's an explosion far up ahead, and three streaks of blue LZR-rifle fire show through the slits in the canopy. Jonah lowers his head and readjusts his hold on Brooklyn; they can't be more than a few minutes away. Hess slashes the jungle apart with her machete, Krev pumps his fists holding two short amber blades, and Camilla wields a stick with a thick axe-head tied to it. Vespa looks back at Jonah, her green eyes flashing in the setting sun.

"We almost there?" Brooklyn asks.

"Almost." He slashes his rock across a passing tree trunk, and it explodes into a thousand shards. "Shit."

Suddenly there's a deafening thumping up ahead; something large pounds against the ground like thunder. It's a familiar noise, he thinks, but can't place it. Then Hess skids to a stop and flattens her back against a tree.

"Pitchers!" she screams, closing her eyes.

Lark grabs Camilla and presses her into the back of a tree. "Against the trees! Now!"

Up ahead, Jonah can see the tops of bushes whipping wildly back and forth and small trees snapping and toppling. Then the ground begins to quake. A rushing sound fills the air. Krev hides behind a huge tree, but Vespa, to his horror, keeps running ahead.

"Vespa!" he yells.

The noise comes rumbling closer, trees and bushes just thirty feet ahead crunch and fall, and then between the leaves he sees the shining wet skin of a giant black creature. It's the hoppers, and he remembers how they threw themselves out of the water, arching high in the air before flopping onto the beach. Thousands of them gathered on the tide line before scurrying up the sand, disappearing in the jungle. That's what's happening now. He's on the other side of it.

Jonah throws Brooklyn at the base of a wide red trunk and then jumps on top of her. He thinks of Vespa as the creatures herd past him, forcing their enormous bodies into the jungle. Water sprays off their skin, covering Jonah's head, arms, and back. And then, just as soon as it started, the last ones pass, and the thunder moves further into the island. Jonah stands with Brooklyn and quickly finds Vespa huddling under a boulder. She's okay.

A shout comes from the beach, which they can see slivers of now. Jonah turns to Krev. "I need a gun. A weapon. Anything. Something. Now."

The splitters look at each other and no one moves.

"On your back," Vespa says to Lark. "You have a knife back there. Give it to him. Now."

"Fine," Lark says. She pulls out a broad amber knife from under the back of her shirt, a blade curved at both ends. It's warm in his hand. He nods at her, and then plows toward the ocean.

"Wait for me!" Vespa shouts.

He bursts through the last wall of trees and kicks off the lip of the jungle. With the double-bladed knife tight in his grip, Jonah leaps more than thirty feet over the sand, clearing a pack of hoppers lazily sleeping in the sun. Far to his right lies Ruth, her arms and legs awkward around her, her rifle broken to bits. Paul sits nearby, dazed and rocking back and forth, his hand pressed to a long gash on the top of his shaved head. And several feet from him, spread out in a rainbow of pieces, are the remains of Armitage Blythe.

"Paul! Paul!" Vespa shouts.

Paul squints at the trees, and when he sees Vespa padding across the beach, he wobbles to his feet, rifle in hand. The Fourth Year stumbles forward and then aims his weapon at the approaching Vespa.

"Don't shoot!" Jonah shouts as he speeds in their direction, the knife cutting the air at his side. "No!"

Paul swings the rifle toward him, and Jonah doesn't hesitate. He flings the knife with all his strength. The Fourth Year trips and falls forward, burying the barrel into the sand. The knife misses him by inches. Vespa reaches the cadet first and cradles his bleeding head in her sunburnt arms. She flips him over on his back.

The cadet's eyes are glazed over, pointing in different directions.

"Where's Tunick?" Jonah shouts.

"Paul? Can you hear me? What happened?" Vespa asks.

Paul tries to lick his cracked lips and then says, "They tricked us. They got the ion container…the energizer. We had it. Armitage had it."

Lark jumps and skids on her knees into the circle, covering Vespa and Paul with a slow wave of sand. She looks at Jonah as the others catch up. "What's happening? Where's Tunick?"

Jonah looks from Armitage to Paul, and then back at

Armitage. He grabs Brooklyn's hand and pulls her slightly away from the crowd.

"Jonah? What's happening?" Brooklyn asks. "I need to know what's happening."

"Where's Tunick?" Lark shouts in Paul's face. "Where did he go?"

"Back up!" Vespa warns.

Paul's eyes flicker and then close. Krev places a canteen to the cadet's lips, and instead of water, a milky white liquid flows over his chin. The splitters then pull back and watch as Paul's eyes flicker open with the drink. Vespa begins to wipe away the blood seeping out of his head. It smears over his stubble, his cheek, his ear. Jonah looks away, and that's when he sees them on the horizon, over hundred yards away on the sea.

Jonah wheels around and grabs the scope of Ruth's broken rifle. Aiming it over the water, he sees a crowd of people bobbing up and down on a raft. He can make out Tunick and Hopper. He sees Michael, Aussie, and Malix, but the others on board are just shadows in the setting sun. And tethered to the raft of people, alone on its own raft, is a long orange cylinder. The energizer.

"Brooklyn," Jonah whispers.

Lark suddenly lunges forward and slaps Paul hard across the face. "Which way did Tunick go? Hey! Which way did he go?"

She goes to slap Paul again, but Vespa snatches her wrist and bends it over, driving Lark onto her side.

Camilla places her axe to the back of Vespa's neck. "Watch it, bitch! Let her go right now!"

Brooklyn tugs on Jonah's arm. "What's happening?"

The cadet releases Lark's wrist, and as Vespa and the others argue, Jonah looks through the scope again. The kids are rowing frantically away from the shore as Tunick keeps jumping up and down. *Where are they going?* His mind clicks and flashes to Tunick's hideout, the spoiled meat hanging on its line, the symbols and scrawled writing on the back wall. Jonah then thinks of the childish drawing of a bat-like creature standing at the bottom of a deep pit, its head and wings sharp and robotic. There's something about that drawing…

It hits him so hard it's like he's falling from the sky onto Achilles all over again. That drawing. The robotic-looking bat isn't a bat; it's the ship. And that pit… Jonah grabs Brooklyn's arm, pulling her toward the water.

"I think I know where the ship is."

"Where?"

"The island. At the bottom of the canyon."

Brooklyn's blue eyeballs vibrate with anxiety. "How do you know that?"

"Jesus, we were so close to it. It's at the bottom of the canyon we slid down to hide from the storm. It *has* to be there. I saw a drawing of it on the wall of Tunick's cave." His mind stops and then starts up again. Brooklyn squeezes his hand so hard his knuckles pop. "The top of the canyon was black and charred at one spot, I don't know if you saw that, but it must be from the ship's boosters… And when we were all sliding down, I remember seeing something shine near the bottom. I can see Tunick and the others right now. They're on a raft heading that way. With the energizer."

"Holy shit, Jonah," Brooklyn whispers. "So, what do we do?"

Before he can speak, Krev pushes past him and points across the water. "There! There he is! And he has the energizer! Lark, look."

"Move! Now!" Lark shouts.

The splitters immediately spin and take off for the jungle, none of them saying a word to Jonah and the girls. In seconds, they disappear in the trees.

"Where are they going?" Brooklyn asks.

Vespa and Jonah look at each other. Neither knows what to do. Jonah then pulls Paul's rifle out of the sand. He picks up the double-headed knife and stuffs it halfway into his pocket, and when he does, he feels the tiny white seeds pressing up against his thigh. He thinks of Tunick and the first time they met on the island. And then he thinks of the reef stretching over the water.

"They're going to the reef," Jonah says. "The splitters are going to the island. That's where the ship is."

"Well, shit. Let's go, then," Vespa says.

The three enter the jungle and run along its edge as fast as their ravaged bodies allow. Jonah tells Brooklyn when to jump, when to duck, when to hold on tight. His mind races as fast as his feet.

"Where are your rifles?" he huffs as Paul's gun bounces on his back.

"We lost them," Brooklyn says. "We were trying to climb a cliff and we fell and we lost them."

"I don't want to talk about it," Vespa growls.

"But whose blood is that on your shirt, Brooklyn?"

"We met a bear kind of thing," she says.

"With horns on his face," Vespa adds.

"And we killed it and ate it," Brooklyn says.

"And I got as sick as hell."

The needling behind Jonah's eyes returns and intensifies, as if someone were trying to scoop his brain out through his nostrils with broken glass, and he has to close his lids every few seconds just to keep his feet moving. His knees, though, begin to buckle. *Not yet*, he thinks. *Just give me a couple more hours. That's all I need.*

After another ten minutes, after the sun has ducked halfway below the horizon and streaked the sky purple and gray, the three of them lie flat on their bellies on the sand. Jonah can still see, but things look grainy, and whites and yellows glow like ghosts. He and Vespa stare at the skeletal reef rising out of the water, winding its bony way across the ocean.

"Where are the splitters?" Vespa asks. "No way they got that far ahead of us."

"We're wasting time just lying here," Brooklyn says.

Jonah presses the riflescope to his needling eye, scanning the reef. He then rotates and looks back over the water to see if he can spot Tunick and the energizer, hoping they're still far away from the island and the ship. Instead, he finds the splitters rowing frantically across the sea.

"*Shit*," he says. "Lark and Hess have their own raft. And they're halfway there."

Jonah aims and fires, blasting a row of blue lasers over the water. His shots don't even get close to the splitters. They're too far away.

"Let's go," he says, jumping to his feet. He races toward the water, Vespa pulling Brooklyn right behind, but just as his toes touch the sea, Jonah's vision fades to a couple of bright pinpricks, and a second later, he can't see a thing. Blackness.

He's blind. It's over. His heart pounds in his ears, and he can feel his lungs gasping to come up with the air he needs to call out to the girls, but then there's a quick flickering in his eyes, and his sight bleeds together. After a second of blindness, he can see again. Vespa and Brooklyn have already entered the water.

Jonah pulls himself onto the reef and begs his eyes to keep working.

After just a few seconds, Brooklyn wrenches her arm away from Vespa and drops to her hands and knees. "I'm going to slow you down too much. You guys just go." She then starts crawling along the skeletal coral. "Seriously. Leave me here. I'll get there. It's just going to take me a while. Go!"

Jonah doesn't miss a beat; he reaches down and picks her up, swinging her onto his back. He then hands his rifle to Vespa.

"What the hell are you doing?" she asks. "Leave me."

"Just shut up. You weigh practically nothing here," he says, pulling her arms over his neck. "You're like a backpack. Just don't choke me."

And then they're off, speeding over the glowing reef as Peleus brightens overhead, and as Jonah's eyes adjust, he wonders what life is like up there, and if someone is about to find out. Brooklyn's tiny breaths huff and echo in his ear, but she doesn't say a thing except "okay" and "uh huh" and "thank you" as Jonah prepares her for jumps, stops, and turns. He considers telling her about his momentary blindness, his preview of what's to come, but instead he keeps his mind on Lark, Tunick, and everyone else who might be waiting for them on the other end.

CHAPTER SEVENTEEN

THE ISLAND GROWS LARGER AND LARGER, TALL WITH SHADOWS and wide with trees. The reef worms left and right, sometimes skimming the water and at other times rising several feet high. After a dangerously sharp turn, it looks like it's just a straight road to the shore, and Jonah finds another wind, a wind above his fourth wind, a wind stronger than the supposedly unreachable fifth. Even with Brooklyn swinging from side to side on his back, and his grainy vision becoming more and more sensitive, he feels like this is the moment fate has kept him alive for. This, right now, is why his dad shoved him underneath the dresser during the earthquake, why he survived all the foster homes and then the crash. Maybe he was always supposed to save Brooklyn. That, and stop Tunick.

Vespa squeezes past them, tightrope-walking the edge of the reef, and then she bounds ahead, rifle out. The reef finally comes to an end, and the silvery beach looks eerie in the moonlight. Vespa speeds up and launches herself high into the air, and she lands softly on the tide line.

"Okay. Here we go. This is where we get off," Jonah says. "Hold on."

"Please stick the landing," Brooklyn says into his ear.

He leaps high above the water, and when his feet hit the beach, he gently shrugs Brooklyn off his back. There's no one in sight, and the three of them pad up the beach, heads down.

They reach the base of the canyon in good time, pushing through choking leaves and thorny thickets of bramble. As Jonah looks for the best way up, Vespa covers the wind-blown jungle behind them. Then they begin to climb. Jonah, half-blind, pushes Brooklyn above his head and she sluggishly makes her way up. Then his hands stumble over some cracks, and he's on his way, too. They reach the outer lip of the canyon, and a faint glow radiates from the center of the chasm, and it floats up in shards in Jonah's vision until it melts into the night sky.

"We're here," Jonah says.

"So, we're just going to slide down again?" Brooklyn says, coughing. He can hear the fear in her voice, and if it weren't for the urgency of the moment, he'd second-guess it himself.

"Just like before," Vespa says as she stands on the lip of the canyon, the rifle rammed into her armpit.

Jonah crawls with Brooklyn to the edge, and when he squints downward, he sees a blurry oval spacecraft at the very bottom of the canyon, almost a half-mile down. Yellow floodlights illuminate its base, and all around its hull, windows glow white like fire. His eyes cringe and plead with him to close, but Jonah can't stop staring.

"It's down there. It's really there," Jonah says to Brooklyn. "We can see it."

The demic finds his wrist and squeezes it weakly. Then she coughs, and he sees blood in the corners of her lips. No more waiting. He shoves his thumb and index finger into his eyes, giving them one final moment of pressurized relief, and then he dangles his legs over the edge. Vespa does the same.

Jonah reaches back for Brooklyn, but she recoils and says, "I–I–I'm going to stay here. I don't feel very good. Something's wrong."

Vespa and Jonah look at each other, and then at the ship. The Fourth Year nods and says, "Just don't go anywhere. Promise us."

"I promise, as long as you rip off a piece of Tunick's beard for me," she says.

"We'll be right back," Jonah says. He pulls out the double-edged amber blade from his pocket and squeezes its handle.

"You ready?" Vespa asks Jonah.

"Yeah."

She stares directly into his face. "No matter what happens, Jonah, I'm happy I got to know you. I can act like a jerk and be all tough and whatever, but that's only because it's been a long time since I've met someone who seems to care about other people. Like how you care about Brooklyn and me. I think you're really great, Jonah. Thank you."

"And I—" Jonah starts, but Vespa leans far back and shoots her rifle deep into the jungle behind them. Trees explode and the landscape catches fire, spreading the flames north.

"Just a little diversion," she says. "Now let's go."

Rifle drawn, Vespa plunges silently downward, and Jonah follows. Their backs scrape and bounce along the bowl of the canyon. A swirling wind pushes on their shoulders and they travel faster than before, pulling blankets of rock with them. The lights below grow brighter, forcing Jonah to close his eyes for just a moment, and that's when they meet their first ridge. Vespa stops, but Jonah's knees buckle. He stumbles, pitches forward, and dives headfirst far away from the wall.

Jonah flits and floats from side to side in the canyon like a dead leaf, his arms and legs stretched out wide, his jumpsuit billowing around him. Maybe Vespa yells for him, or maybe the noises in his ears are just life-flashing memories; it's all so loud and bright and confusing. He's a quarter-mile down now, and the ship starts to come into focus. It's four or five stories tall, white with black stripes on its wings, and Jonah thinks he's going to slam right into it when a powerful gust of wind whips him far out of the middle, bashing him into the canyon wall. He slides headfirst, his chest grinding into the rock. A narrow ridge suddenly rushes upward, and at the last second Jonah turns his body sideways. He stops and coughs and coughs and coughs until his lungs catch up to him. When he opens his eyes, he sees a fuzzy black circle high above him, the night sky so far out of reach he thinks he may never stand under it again.

It takes a moment for Jonah to unravel the noises echoing below as human voices, but soon he can hear Lark shouting. Tunick shouts back, something about verve and payments. Jonah pulls himself to the edge of the ridge and watches blurry shadows circle each other in the ship's floodlights.

"You know this is my duty!" Tunick screams from somewhere near the base of the ship. "You know these are my orders!"

Jonah sits and flattens his back against the wall, the double-headed blade scraping along the ridge. He takes a deep breath and whips his head up and around to find Vespa, but she's not there. She's not anywhere. Knowing she wouldn't wait for him, Jonah runs to his right, but he doesn't get ten feet before a blue laser blasts a section of rock inches from his face. Shards cut into his cheek, neck, and chest, and he twists away from the edge, covering his head. The shot came from behind.

A familiar voice then echoes out of a cave: "You should have just listened to Tunick, Jonah."

Jonah narrows his eyes into the darkness. The white lights of a rifle barrel float just inside the cave. Then an outline of a boy begins to exit the shadows. He walks awkwardly, the insides of his feet sweeping the floor, and after a few more seconds, Jonah sees the bushy brown hair of Richter, the hacker who was sucked away from the cave entrance. Jonah can't believe he's still alive.

"Richter?"

The boy shoots again, and then he ducks back inside the cave, slumping in the shadows. Jonah flattens himself against the wall and watches the barrel of the rifle bouncing back and forth before steadying an aim right at his head. Without thinking, Jonah turns and throws the double-headed knife as hard as he can at the boy.

He doesn't see it connect, but he hears it; the sickening, suctioning noise echoes inside the cave.

Jonah falls to his knees and takes in a deep, sucking breath. His lungs flex and harden and he can't exhale; it's as if the organs don't know what to do with the balloon of air pressing against his ribs. He can't believe he just killed someone. A boy younger than himself. He knew it was a possibility, but he didn't know it would happen so soon, like this.

Richter comes forward with the glistening knife buried in his stomach. He slumps and wobbles side to side inside the mouth of the cave, and Jonah finally releases a long burst of stale, suffocating air. The hacker takes another step and then tips forward, but instead of falling onto his face, Richter's feet begin to rise above the ground. He's…floating. Jonah smothers his eyes with his knuckles and takes another look. How is that possible?

Richter's feet rise another few inches, and Jonah doesn't know if he should run and tackle him, or if he should turn and hide. But then the hacker suddenly drops flat to the cave floor, limp like a rag doll. The white lights of the rifle, however, somehow continue to float in the shadows. Then, to Jonah's shock, another outline of a boy forms, this one lean and tall. The figure steps completely out of the cave, and all Jonah can focus on is the blond hair and the bruises on his face.

"Sean?" Jonah whispers.

"Yup," the cadet says. "Really surprised to see you here after everything. You made it pretty far, Jonah. Pretty far. But then again, it helps that I purposefully didn't shoot you last night in the jungle, right? I could have blown your head off, but Tunick wanted you alive. But I clipped that fat Bidson kid pretty good. Heard he didn't make it."

Jonah looks from Richter to Sean, from Sean to Richter. What's happening?

"Oh, I found this guy all smashed up on the floor down there. Made for a handy good shield," Sean says. He flips the hacker over with his foot. The knife sticks straight up into the air. "One of you guys push him over the edge, or what? That Brooklyn girl do it?"

"What are you doing here? What's going on?"

Sean clicks on the barrel's flashlight and shines it on Jonah's face. "Well... Holy shit, Jonah. Your eyes look *insane*. You know that, right? You know they're completely blue? Jesus. Can you even see me?"

Jonah turns his head and makes himself into a ball. "Ruth said you were dead. You drowned."

"She thought I did. I know how to swim, though, *smart boy*."

"So, *you're* the traitor? You're Tunick's brother who made us crash?"

"I am," Sean says matter-of-factly. "I am the poor brother left behind on Earth with momma."

"You killed so many people. You...you're not some poor brother left behind. You're a piece of shit."

Sean rushes forward and buries the barrel of his rifle into Jonah's chest, right where his clavicle bones meet, and he pins him to the ground. He then crunches down on something in his mouth, and Jonah knows it's verve. "I killed a lot of people, but not everybody, right? Right, right? Not *all* the kids. We were sure to take care of all the adults, though. Couldn't have them around, doing to us what they did to Tunick and the others on Thetis. I don't know if you heard the story yet, but Thetis is *fucked up*, Jonah. It's so fucked up. So we're going to Peleus. I'm sorry to hear you can't come with us now."

Jonah stares up at Sean and thinks back to the first night on Achilles; how the cadet helped at the makeshift hospital, bypassing the adults to give water to the kids; how he was so focused on finding the energizer; how his face was yellow and purple with bruises, as if he were in a fight. Did the flight crew do that?

"Now what?" Jonah asks. The barrel is hot against his skin. Adrenaline pumps into his bloodstream like never before, and for the first time in a while, his eyes focus without pain. *Maybe this is their last moment before shutting down completely*, he thinks. He drags a leg into a fighting position, but Sean stomps on his heel, holding it down.

"Now, we take Aussie and Michael and Hopper and the others with us to Peleus where Tunick gets his new orders. And you die now, too. Just like—"

A flash of blue light zips over Jonah's head and explodes through Sean's shoulder like a bolt of lightning, blowing him backward in a cloud of red mist. Jonah lies there paralyzed as Sean's rifle falls into his lap. Jonah spins around to find a black speck sliding down the opposite wall of the canyon. When he looks through the rifle's scope, he sees Vespa, her weapon lit and aimed at him. She's moving fast.

Jonah rolls onto his stomach and peers down over the ridge. A blue laser skims his hair and splits the rocks above him, raining boulders all around. The ridge to his right explodes, and a huge section slides down the wall, cutting off the entire direction. Another laser hits his rifle, spiraling it out of his hands in a thousand scalding pieces. Jonah has no choice but to run toward Sean's cave. He jumps over the cadet's body, still in shock that it was Sean who betrayed them. All for a drug. All for his crazy brother who thinks aliens give him orders. He watches Vespa reach a ridge and wave at him, and then she disappears into a cave.

He makes his way to the back of his cave where it's pitch black, and he walks right into a wall. Something in his pocket pushes into his thigh. The night-vision specs. Sean's night-vision specs that Ruth gave him. Jonah slips them on and takes a deep breath, bracing his eyes for the brightness, but the pain is minimal. His luck is short-lived, though, when there's no tunnel to be found.

He walks back to the entrance and spots another cave on the other side of the canyon, but how can he get there after the ridge was blown away? He then notices that a narrow section of the opposite canyon wall leans inward on the left, cutting the distance between the two sides to maybe just fifty feet. There's a ridge over there, a bit farther down the wall, and several caves connect with it. Jonah bets one of them has a tunnel to the bottom. He has to jump.

"For Brooklyn," he whispers. "For me." Jonah backpedals into the cave. With a lump in his throat, he yanks the amber knife out of Richter's belly and stuffs it into his pocket. When he touches the back wall, he counts to three and then explodes forward like a rocket. The mouth of the cave charges at him, growing larger and larger until he's just a few feet away from the ridge, but then something blocks his path. It's Sean, his arm dangling and twirling from just a stretch of skin, and he lurches at Jonah with an insane look in his eyes. The verve has taken over.

At the last moment, Jonah fakes right and then darts left, never slowing down. Sean swings at him with his good arm but misses, and when Jonah's feet reach the ridge, he leaps.

Wind plugs his ears and pushes on the backs of his legs. He whips his arms at his sides like helicopter propellers, doing whatever he can to clear the distance. The opposite wall keeps coming toward him. When he makes it halfway across, he pumps his legs straight out in front of him and leans back like he's on a playground swing. Blue lasers split the air around him, but the ridge gets closer, closer, closer, and he tucks himself into a ball and begins to flip upside down. At the last moment, when he knows he's not going any farther, he unfurls and blindly reaches out his arms. His fingers touch stone and grind against it for several seconds before finding a grip. His body slams against the wall, and his shoulders are in agony, but he stops falling. He opens his eyes to find himself hanging from the ridge. He just leaped fifty feet.

Amazed, he pulls himself onto the ridge and rolls into the wall. He stands and looks back across the canyon, and to his shock, Sean comes flying out of the cave with his arm flopping at his side. He jumps. The cadets lock eyes as Sean sails into the middle, but when the boy travels another dozen feet, he begins to plummet. He opens his mouth in a tortured, silent scream, and then he hits the wall far below, face-first, snapping his neck so far back that his skull nearly touches his waist.

Jonah turns and sprints into the first cave he sees. Luckily, there's a tunnel at the back, and as soon as he enters it, the path steadily declines. With the double-headed blade now in his hand, he moves faster and faster toward the bottom of the canyon. He wants to yell for Vespa but stops himself. Dozens of tunnels begin to appear on either side of him, sometimes directly above his head. They're only a few feet in diameter, and sticking halfway out of them are pulsing white sacs lined with thick veins, dripping with clear liquid. They look like living, breathing balloons. Like eggs. He hurries along with his shoulders sideways.

The tunnel winds like a circular staircase. The floor is perfectly smooth and wide, and Jonah realizes this section is manmade, different from the rest. The tunnel flattens and a light that seems as bright as the sun appears at its end, and whatever reprieve his eyes had leaves as fast as it came. The needles are back, but now they're two-foot spikes. Jonah rips off his specs and fumbles blindly along with his hands on the wall.

A high-pitched whirring comes from the exit. There's shouting. He thinks he can hear Tunick. He definitely hears rifle fire. Then he hears something that makes his stomach drop: an engine roars to life like a marauding lion. The ship, Jonah realizes. It can't leave. Not without Brooklyn. Not without him and Vespa. Not to Peleus or to the other side of the moon. He rams a palm into his eye and staggers toward the lights. It can't leave. It can't.

A thruster whines and coughs until it's a howl, and a smoldering heat pushes past Jonah, turning the tunnel into an oven. More rifle fire. More engines whining and coughing and howling. More heat. He tightens his grip on the knife and steps out of the cave, forcing his eyes open. Everything's a blinding yellow for a few seconds, and then blobs of orange painfully start to form. An invisible hand slams into his shoulder, and he spins and falls in a whirlwind of sound and color. Someone yells above him, but the voice blends in with the engine noise.

"Don't leave!" he shouts, but he can barely hear his own voice.

Vespa's voice barks into his ear: "I'm going to try to get inside it!"

"Wait for me!" Jonah shouts, but he knows she can't hear him.

Her hands are on his back and he tries to straighten up, to show her he's okay and ready to fight, but she must know he's either blind or in too much pain, because she pushes him back into the mouth of the tunnel. He staggers two steps inside before something rams right through his shins and his legs are swept out from underneath him. He falls on his face, and then something as large as a dog skitters over his back with what feels like several spiked feet. More come, their feet digging into Jonah's back and legs, and he finally rolls to the side of the tunnel and flattens himself against it. He cautiously pulls the specs up to his face and gasps.

A wave of giant white spider creatures race down the winding path, their matted fur dripping wet, their mouths cluttered with tusks that curl at their tips. The white, pulsing balloons, he knows, have opened. The creatures crawl over each other to exit the tunnel first, giving Jonah no choice; he turns and runs back onto the canyon floor where the heat is so intense he can feel parts of his jumpsuit melting. He dives to the right, against the wall, and squints up to watch hundreds or thousands of the spiders exiting every cave lining the bowl of the canyon. They climb straight up the sides toward the top ridge, and he yells out for Brooklyn, as if he could actually warn her, but he can't even hear himself.

The yellow floodlights click off from the middle of the floor, and the air pops in his ears. Where's Vespa? Jonah directs his attention to the ship. It's moving. It lifts a few feet off the ground, its thrusters dissolving the growing space below them into waves of heat and mist. Several fires come to life on the canyon floor. Jonah screams. His eyes scream. His body screams. The ship rises a few more feet, and then like an elevator, it slowly climbs to the top of the canyon.

The spiders speed upward even faster, as if the glowing ship were their queen, and some actually spring from the ridge to grab a hold of it. Each one misses, though—the ship must be too high—and they fall wildly with their legs waving. Then either the swirling wind blows them back to the canyon walls where they start to climb all over again, or they drop all the way to the fiery floor, splitting open like melons. Jonah ducks back inside the cave to avoid being smashed, his neck still straining to watch the ship.

Jonah grips the edges of the entranceway. The ship hovers a little higher and gets a little blurrier. The spiders stop jumping for its hull. And then in a column of flat red clouds, it's gone. Everything is numb, even his eyes. He stands there and waits for the ship to come back, or even to circle around, but the red clouds simply separate and fade away.

It's over. He's going to die here. Any hour, he's going to cough blood like Brooklyn, and then he's going to waste away on a moon he was never supposed to step foot on. If only he had his sheaf. If only he could see his parents' faces one more time. That's what he's going to do, he decides right then and there. He's going to go back to the crash site, find his sheaf, and then go blind staring at a life he never knew. Then he's going to die.

Fire and dead spiders line the canyon floor. Just in front of him, one of the creatures has landed halfway into a crackling line of flames, its spindly front legs crisping and curling down into its smooth belly. Jonah stares dumbly as its abdomen catches fire. He then drops the knife and turns sluggishly around into the darkness of the tunnel. Is Vespa on the ship? What happened to Brooklyn up there? Is there any way she survived?

Vespa's voice rings out on the canyon floor, stopping Jonah in his tracks. He grabs the knife and sprints past the burning spider. Where is she? Is she still here?

"Vespa!" he shouts. "VESPA!"

He runs back and forth until he sees them. Inside a dwindling ring of fire, there, with his back to Jonah, stands Tunick, looking up into the sky. He's black with soot, his whole body shaking with raging disbelief. Under his foot lies Vespa, her hands wrapped around his ankle.

Jonah forces his eyes all the way open—he's done with the

pain, he's pushed past it—and he charges with the amber knife. Tunick never sees him coming; Jonah leaps and hooks one blade deep into the man's side, and then rips the knife back with the other end. Tunick stumbles forward, and Vespa pulls up on his ankle at the same time, tripping him to the ground.

Tunick flips over and sees Jonah. A crazy smile comes to his face. "Smart boy. I knew you'd come back." He winces as he examines the long L-shaped wound under his ribs. Blood crawls down his side and over the small green sack on his hip. "Where's my little brother, Sean, smart boy? Tell me he made it on board. Because if he didn't, we're all dead, dead, dead. Earth, as well as everyone on it, is dead. That's what they told me. That's the plan."

Jonah opens his mouth. Maybe he'll tell him Sean *was* on board, that he closed the door himself, making sure his brother was left behind. He could tell him Sean secretly hated him and never believed he could talk to a race of alien ghosts. That he went to all these lengths just to see him suffer. After all, Jonah thinks, wouldn't it be appropriate if Tunick never knew the truth?

"That traitor Sean is your brother?" Vespa asks. "I shot him. He's dead."

Tunick twitches, and then as if by instinct, he puts his fingers into the green sack at his hip, but his hand goes right on through the bottom. It's empty. The bag is ripped. He starts to laugh, but it turns into one continuous soul-draining wail. Then he stops and wheels around and around as if someone has said his name. He stammers at a section of the sky, "I'm sorry, I'm sorry! Zion, I can still do it. No, I can. I can do it from here. We don't need Peleus. We don't. Please!"

Jonah adjusts his grip on the knife. He's sick of Tunick's insanity. They have to finish him off before he gets another wind. At that moment of clarity, Jonah's eyes pop with what feels like tiny detonations. It's something he hasn't felt before, a pain he doesn't know how to push past. He watches as Tunick searches the ground feverishly while still mumbling over his shoulder. Vespa rushes over and kicks him so hard in the wound that his body lifts a few feet off the floor.

"Don't you get it? It doesn't matter anymore! You idiots just killed us all!" Tunick wails. He gets to his feet and swings for Vespa's head, but she ducks and drives her fist into his chin and a heel into his gut. He merely steps backward, right to the edge of a fire that has found new life. Her blows hardly faze him. Who knows how many verve seeds are pumping through his blood?

His eyes pulsing in pain, Jonah stands next to Vespa and points a blade at Tunick. "Are we still free? Do you still want us to run? Because I'm never going to run again. Because of you and Sean and your stupid hallucinations and *all* the rest of them, I'm the furthest thing from free. I'll never be free."

Jonah lunges with the knife, but as he does, his vision disappears. It just shuts off, as if someone has thrown a switch. There are no shadows, no blurry figures. There is also no pain. The moment it happens, Jonah knows it's permanent.

The knife is knocked out of his fist, and an invisible hand grabs the back of his neck. He's pulled forward, and then Tunick's bony knee hits his sternum. Jonah's suddenly on his side, dirt coating his lips, feeling absolutely weightless. It's like he never left his launch seat, and he's still in the module, hanging above the spear-like branches of the twisted tree.

"And *you*," Tunick growls. The ground next to Jonah's head comes alive with circling footsteps. Vespa grunts and growls. A great struggle happens above him. Flesh hits flesh. Something rips. Vespa screams in pain and Tunick laughs. And then Vespa gasps for air, as if she's being choked.

"Stop!" Jonah shouts. He rolls onto his back, trying to work through the throbbing in his chest. Vespa gasps louder. The ground scrapes more frantically, and Jonah can picture her heels kicking for a grip. *No*, he thinks. *If anyone survives this, it's Vespa*. Jonah rolls toward the noise, and when he does, he feels several small objects pressing into his leg. He digs his hand into his pocket and pulls them out.

"Tunick!" he shouts, waving the seeds above his head. "I've got verve! Come get it!"

The struggling stops, and Vespa gasps and coughs. He hears Tunick rushing at him. Jonah listens for the nearest patch of fire and tosses the seeds right for it.

"NO!" Tunick roars, running in the same direction.

And then Vespa belts out a scream, and Jonah hears flesh hit flesh, and then something falls into a crackling fire.

Tunick's screams are indecipherable. Jonah knows he's in the fire, maybe tangled with a spidery corpse, and he's not only feeling pain, but he knows he's going to die from it.

"Enough!" Vespa barks. A blade scrapes against the ground, and then a few seconds later, the man's screams abruptly stop, and all Jonah hears is the fire and the wind and his own heart beating in his throat. A small hand falls on his forehead, and then Vespa's face is on top of his, temple to chin. He doesn't move. He feels her lips brush his cheek and listens to her breath slow down until she calms herself enough to say, "He's dead. Let's go."

CHAPTER EIGHTEEN

THE TUNNELS SMELL OF SMOKE AND SOUR EGG SACS, AND THE walls are hot to the touch. Jonah holds Vespa's elbow as she tells him how the seeds landed right at the edge of the fire. All she had to do was kick Tunick in when he crouched down. "He still somehow got to his feet. He walked toward me, completely on fire, and so I stabbed him in the heart with your knife. And then I twisted it." Her voice isn't celebratory or proud. It sounds like she's come to terms with what the ship leaving means for not only him and Brooklyn, but also for herself. This is her future. This island. This continent. This moon.

They worry about Brooklyn, how fast it will take them to reach her. That's if she's still there. If she wasn't trampled and killed by the spiders. Vespa picks up the pace and Jonah asks, "What about Aussie and Michael and Portis? And what about Hopper?"

"They're on board," she says, huffing. "That asshole Hopper was the first up the ramp, the coward, and Krev was right after him. Lark and her girlfriend made it, too. They were all chomping on verve, fighting me, fighting each other, fighting Tunick, who was going crazy looking for his brother. *That piece of shit, Sean.* I can't believe a cadet would do that."

Jonah doesn't respond. He doesn't understand the ties that bind families; he never will. That kind of love and bond has forever been absent in his life, and it will surely remain absent during these final few days he's alive.

"There were others down there, you know," Vespa says as they jog down a new tunnel. "Other kids from Thetis. They got on board. About five or six or seven of them. I never even saw them until they bolted out of the caves and ran up the ramp like a bunch of rats. I shot one in the leg, but I didn't see what happened to her."

Jonah pictures Hopper, Aussie, Portis, and Michael in their seats, rocketing to Peleus or the other side of Achilles with a bunch of addicts, maybe with Portis's sister, too. Are they happy to have been chosen for the journey? Are they laughing with Hess and Krev and the others at the opportunity of a new beginning, or are they frightened beyond belief, hoping to escape the moment they have a chance?

"Maybe Aussie and Michael will come back for you," Jonah says. "Maybe they'll steal the ship and come back here to help. Maybe even Hopper will come. You never know."

"Yeah, maybe," she says. Then, after a long pause, she asks, "How are you feeling?"

Jonah doesn't answer right away. He takes a moment to assess his body, to feel every cut and bruise and broken bone. His shoulder wound burns as if an animal were feasting on it. One, maybe two, of his ribs are broken. Something is terribly wrong with his left knee. He feels run over. Crushed. Wrecked. And on top of it all, he feels absolutely and utterly hopeless. "I'm okay," he whispers. "Just a little tired."

"And your eyes? You're totally blind now?"

"I think so."

She squeezes his hand. "I'm so sorry."

Outside, Jonah feels the cool wind and hears fire raging in

the distance. The smell of smoke permeates the air. So much for a diversion.

"Where are the spiders?" he asks.

"I don't know. Not here. I don't see them anywhere."

They slowly circle the base of the canyon, going in the opposite direction of the fire, looking and yelling for Brooklyn and anyone else left behind. Then Vespa sits him down next to a tree and gives him the knife, and she bounds upward to check the ridge.

Jonah sets his head against the bark of the tree. It's rough like sandpaper but molds to his skull like a pillow. He can't help but notice the smell of the tree; it's smoky yet intensely sweet, and in a daze he wonders if it's some kind of fruit tree, or if it's drooping with giant tropical flowers. He pushes away from the trunk of the tree and looks up at its branches to see if it actually has fruit or flowers but…nothing. Just blackness. He forgot. He punches the ground and then digs his knuckles deep into his sockets, forcing his eyeballs this way and that, hoping to ignite something, to somehow reconnect the wires, but when he pulls his fingers away, there's just nothing. No real pain. No sight. Not even a floating white circle from the pressure.

What else can he do? Is there anything else he can try? He rocks himself forward and attempts to stand but gives up, and instead he replays the scene of Sean trying to make the fifty-foot leap. He sees the cadet's wrenched face, the way his arm flaps every which way above him like a punctured kite. He sees Tunick running along the reef. Tunick sitting in front of the fire. And then his mind wanders to Manny's thumbs unclasping his belt in the module. The boy falls. Then he sees his own narrow escape through the branches. Garrett. Dr. Z. The snouts. The professor hanging from the tree. *Run.* He ran. And this is where he is.

But then, for the first time, Jonah recognizes something; an odd thought squeezes through all these flashing scenes of death and panic and betrayal, and it expands and rushes over him, coating his entire body with warmth. Even with all this, the disease and the blindness and the crash and the constant fear if he's going to survive the next minute, he realizes that some of these people from the past four days actually cared about him. Not in a pitiful way, either. Not because he didn't have any parents or he lived on the streets. They seemed to genuinely care about him in a way someone is supposed to care about a friend or a brother. He *did* make connections. Aussie and Brian. Definitely Brooklyn. Dr. Z and Garrett and Michael. The faces circle his mind and then Jonah holds back a sob when he thinks about how Bidson sacrificed his body for Jonah's escape. And then there's Ruth, a girl he didn't even want in his camp because he thought she was insane, and here she kept him safe on the other side of that boulder and gave him the glasses. And Vespa. Vespa, Vespa, Vespa. She not only saved him countless times, putting herself in danger to keep him alive, but unless the disease has totally eaten away at his brain, he thinks she might actually like him. That's never happened with a girl before. Maybe Achilles didn't only take. Maybe it gave a little, too.

These feelings fade, though, and Dr. Z's words come back to him from the night at the makeshift hospital: "No one is happy in this galaxy right now, I assure you."

The whole colonization effort from Earth sounds like a failure. Thetis, if he can believe anything the others said, is a failure. Achilles is forever ruined, after all the misery and death here. No human was meant to go through that wormhole.

Then, over Jonah's right shoulder, he hears a low buzzing. It's soft at first, like a swarm of bees, but soon the buzzing grows louder and louder until it's so loud it feels like it's coming from inside his own head. His teeth rattle. His tongue rolls back into his throat. Just when he thinks his head is going to explode from the pressure, the buzzing slows into something that feels electronic. It breaks into a repeating pattern of static. Fearing it's one of the spiders or something worse, Jonah feverishly pushes away from the tree and stumbles into a boulder. He scrambles over it and crouches into a ball, waiting for the noise to disappear, but the buzzing follows him, popping and changing pitch. Jonah stands and swats his arms wildly over his head, hoping to kill its source.

"Get away! Go!"

The static consumes him. And after a few seconds, it paralyzes every muscle, leaving him standing still and helpless. Through his blindness, he sees a speeding line of glowing symbols and upside-down numbers. They're green, blue, and white. The line repeats over and over behind his eyes, and it's mesmerizing. The numbers then flip over, and the symbols crash together in a dazzling display of colors. And that's when he first hears the voice.

"*It's you now.*"

Jonah chokes at the sound of it. The voice is demonic, gravelly and robotic, and there's no denying it's coming from just a few feet over his head. Whatever it is, it's floating over him like a ghost.

"*It's you now,*" the voice repeats.

"Tunick? Tunick, is that you?" Jonah pleads. He's suddenly able to move again, and he punches at the air, but his fists touch nothing, and he trips headfirst into a thick shrub. He thrashes in its sharp branches, rolls and bites and claws his way back toward the tree, and then he flips over shouting, "Vespa!"

"*It's you now.*"

The voice follows him as he circles the trunk. He finds the amber knife in the ground and slices in every direction. The voice chases him, repeating itself several more times. A new line of symbols and numbers appears in his head, and then the floating voice says, "*We need you. You need us. We need you. You need us.*"

"What? Stop! I don't need you! Who *are* you?"

"*We need you. You need us.*"

Jonah falls to the ground and covers his head. "I'm hallucinating," Jonah mumbles. "I'm just sick. I'm dying and I'm hallucinating and my brain is…"

Another line of upside-down numbers zips behind his eyes. More symbols crash together. There's a pulsing cloud of static between his ears, and the next sentence sends a series of chills down Jonah's spine.

"*We choose you now.*"

"No! Please, stop."

"*We choose you now.*"

"Stop it! Vespa! Where are you, Vespa?"

Jonah stuffs his fingers in his ears, but it doesn't make a difference. The voice booms inside his head: "*WE CHOOSE YOU NOW. EAT THE SEEDS.*"

The words paralyze him. He knows it's not Tunick. It's not anyone.

He wants to believe that the voice is coming from another cadet, that someone's trying to scare him, or maybe it's one of the splitters left behind, but he just can't convince himself. The voice is too strange, too unworldly. His only hope is that it's all a hallucination. *It's* not *an alien ghost*, he tells himself. That's impossible. Tunick was crazy. Wasn't he?

"Who is this?" Jonah finally asks in a shaky voice.

"*We are Zion.*"

The answer propels him into a dizzy frenzy, and he jogs in a blind, stumbling circle, unsure of what to do. Jonah leaps into the air, determined to destroy the voice. He jumps what must be over ten feet straight up, but his knife connects with nothing but the sky. When he lands, his ears pop and hiss, and a new line of incoming symbols and numbers stops and disappears, leaving him alone in the dark with his blindness.

"Zion?" he whispers.

There's only silence. The static cloud he felt so strongly just seconds ago has lifted. Jonah waits a moment and the only thing he hears is his own heartbeat. Then he crumples to the ground in exhaustion where he falls asleep.

• • •

"Jonah?"

The sound of his name wakes him, and he feels the weight of a hand on his ankle. He blindly pushes away, swatting the air and growling. His neck crashes into a tree and he lifts his legs to kick whoever it is.

"Hey, hey, hey. It's me, Vespa. Relax."

It takes him a moment to believe her, to find comfort in her presence. "Vespa? Where were you? Didn't you hear me yelling?"

Vespa sits down next to him. "I was looking for Brooklyn. You know that. And no, I didn't hear you yelling. Why? What happened?"

"I think I heard…" He doesn't know what to say. That he thinks he heard what Tunick heard? That an alien ghost spoke to him through numbers and symbols from inside his head? The more he replays the events, the more he convinces himself he imagined it.

"What did you hear?"

"I…thought I heard someone talking to me," he admits. "I think I'm getting sicker. I think I'm going crazy."

"Jonah, I can't find Brooklyn anywhere. She's gone. I feel awful. I don't know where she is."

Jonah sits up straight. "She has to be here somewhere."

Vespa puts a hand on his chest. "You saw those spiders… I'm worried that one of them…"

He pictures his friend trampled by the spiders on the ridge, or hanging from one of their mouths. "So, you think…you think she's dead?"

"I think we're all dead," she says. It sounds like she's been crying. "Come on. Let's get to the beach. This entire island is going to be burnt to a crisp in less than an hour."

Soon, sand slips through Jonah's toes. As they walk in silence, the voice from earlier bubbles in his mind, but it's getting harder to replicate. It must have been a nightmare.

Vespa gasps.

"You see Brooklyn?" he asks.

"Jesus," she whispers. "No, I don't see her, but there *they* are. Way far out there on the water, those things are bobbing up and down."

"What things?"

"The spiders. They're all holding onto each other. Like a huge white blanket. It's kind of… This is going to sound weird, but it's kind of beautiful."

He sighs and squeezes Vespa's hand. It's a nice thing to hear. In fact, it's almost overwhelming to hear. Somehow, there's still beauty in all this chaos, even if he can't see it. Those things are out there, just trying to survive, possibly crossing an entire ocean as one. Some will probably die, but others will keep swimming.

"Vespa?"

"Yeah?"

"Promise me you'll get off this place."

"I can't promise that," she says, dropping his hand. "That's a stupid thing to ask, Jonah. That's like me asking you to promise me that you'll see again."

Jonah opens his eyes, but it's as black as it is when they're shut. "Well, I'll keep trying to see. I'll keep opening my eyes until the moment I die, okay? I promise. So if I can do that, then you can keep trying to get off this moon, or at least promise me that you'll just keep going. Like, keep living. Do something here. I don't know what. You said your life was kind of shitty back on Earth, just like mine was, and that you volunteered for Thetis because you wanted to see the one thing that was able to ruin your dad's life, and yours."

"And here I am," she says. "It's still ruined. It's beyond ruined."

"Well, maybe it is today, and maybe it'll feel like it's ruined for a while, but maybe one day it won't feel like that. And then, I don't know, maybe the discovery of Thetis will be worth everything."

Her arms are suddenly around his waist. The hug is tight and dizzying, and he can feel the heat of her body on his chest. She rests her cheek on the bottom of his neck. Vespa will keep going, he thinks. This is her promising without having to say it.

Vespa then gasps and ducks out of his arms. Before Jonah can say a word, she shouts, "Brooklyn! Over here! Oh my god, it's Brooklyn! To your left!" Then, to Jonah: "I can't believe it. She made it. She's walking out of the jungle right now."

Brooklyn yells something back, and he can hear Vespa racing

off toward the smoke and fire. Jonah lets out a sad laugh. Even if he and Brooklyn die from the disease, she'll have them for a little longer. And maybe there are more splitters in the jungle. Maybe there are others. Maybe Vespa will be okay.

Suddenly there's a whooshing sound high over his shoulder. At first he thinks it's his nightmare, the alien voice returning, but it's different. It grows steadier, louder, and Jonah realizes it's man-made. *It's the ship*. It's Aussie and Michael and Hopper. They've come back.

Vespa runs back toward him screaming. She grabs his arm and swings him in a wide circle. "Oh my god! Oh my god! They found us! Hey! Hey! Right here! Right here!"

The noise grows louder.

The whooshing turns into a wall of noise.

"Help!" Brooklyn yells nearby.

Jonah pulls Vespa toward him and finds her smooth head between his hands. "What if they're back to kill us? What if that's why they're back! Because of Tunick?"

"But they're not back!" she yells. "It's not them!"

The wall of noise lowers from the sky until it feels as if it's right in front of him, just a few dozen feet away, and his mind goes as blank as his eyes. A blast of air flaps his melted jumpsuit around his body. He falls to his knees and finds Vespa's ankle. He rips her down to the sand. "Who is it? Who is it, then?"

"It's..." She waits. A high-pitch whirring screams, and then it pops and slows down. "It's..." she says again. He's suddenly warm. Is he in some sort of light?

"Who?" he shouts.

"It's...it's Thetis."

Vespa's words march back and forth behind his eyes. Her small hands hook under his arms, and she pulls him to his feet.

His first instinct is to think of Tunick and to run, to run into the water and swim all the way to the spiders and hold on and float where they float. After everything he's heard, even if half of it was rooted in truth, Thetis is a death trap.

Jonah stumbles in the opposite direction of the noise, knowingly walking toward the fire. Tunick and Lark and everyone escaped for a reason, he's sure of that now. And you don't escape if you're happy, and you don't escape just for a drug. Something else is happening on Thetis, and he thinks it might be better to just die now. To die here.

But then he hears Brooklyn's voice cutting through the noise. She's celebrating with the others. She's been through everything he has, even worse, and she still sees Thetis as her salvation, a place with a cure. Could she be right?

"Kip?" Vespa says. "*Oh my god.*"

"What?" Jonah begs.

"He's on the ship. He's in the window. Kip's on the ship!"

"How could he be…"

Brooklyn laughs in disbelief. Then she starts to sob. "He can't be here. You said he…"

Vespa shouts, "The portal must have sent him to Thetis! He brought them here! He brought Thetis!"

Jonah pictures the pink-haired demic waving in the window, and he feels a smile cross his lips, but then, to his horror, the buzzing static from the jungle returns to his ears like a tornado, this time quicker, louder, more aggressive. The symbols and numbers bounce behind his eyes, and then the demonic voice booms and flattens him against the sand.

"*We choose you.*"

"Please stop," Jonah pleads.

"*EAT THE SEEDS.*"

Jonah starts to cry. Then there's another hissing sound from the ship and Vespa is on top of him, her arms wrapped around his neck. "We need help! We need medical attention! Her and him right here! Over here!"

Vespa hugs him tightly as a man from the ship shouts back. Jonah can't hear what he says over Vespa's cheering; the buzzing voice still echoes in his skull. She yanks him to his feet and pulls him forward.

"What's your name?" a man shouts in his ear. Jonah can smell him, the soap on his skin, the mint from his mouth.

He's afraid to answer.

"He's Jonah!" Vespa says. "I'm Vespa Bolivar. We're cadets. Everything's fucked up."

"We're aware of the situation." A thick arm slides under Jonah's armpit. He wants to wrench himself away, but he doesn't know what direction he'd go. He hears Brooklyn say she's blind. He hears her say that he's blind. Someone pats his back and in a few steps, his toes touch something cold and metallic.

He's escorted up an incline. The air changes and cools, and the noises fade into a series of whirs and hums and beeps.

"Vespa?" he asks over his shoulders.

"Right behind you, Firstie!"

"Brooklyn?"

The demic laughs and coughs somewhere behind him. The man holding him up veers him to the left. He's dropped into a vinyl seat that pulls on his sweaty skin. "Stay here."

Before Jonah can move, safety belts are clicked over his lap and chest. It causes him to panic and he whips his shoulders up and down until Vespa grabs his hand and sits down next to him. Her sigh is louder than anything on board. "We made it. We fucking made it."

"But is this a god thing?" he asks. "Should we stay or get off? What do they look like? Does it look like they want to help us or like they're going to hurt us?"

"Help us, Jonah. They're already treating Brooklyn. It's over. We're going to Thetis."

"We are?"

"Yes."

Jonah hears Brooklyn coughing and whips around as if he could spot her. A man and a woman mumble, and Brooklyn agrees to something. Vespa says, "They're putting a mask on her. They're putting her to sleep. It's okay."

"Everybody please take a seat," a man says. "We're happy we

found you. We didn't know if there were any survivors. We're very sorry all this happened."

"What took you so goddamn long?" Vespa asks.

"We got here as soon as we could," the man replies. "I wish we could have gotten here sooner. Believe me."

Jonah hears the engines come to life, and the ship begins to rumble. Vespa rests her head on his arm. He leans back in his chair and lets his mind clear. The smell of food wafts by his face and he opens his eyes to the blackness. He'll always keep his eyes open. That's all he can do.

END OF BOOK ONE

ACKNOWLEDGMENTS

THE IDEA FOR *ACHILLES* STARTED TAKING SHAPE IN 2011, AND back then it was simply called *The Space Crash Book*. And here's a little secret of mine: I've never actually crashed anything in space. Heck, I've never even *been* to space, if you can believe it. I know! Okay, that felt really good to get off my chest. Burden, lifted. Finally.

So, I'd first like to acknowledge the space experts (who have also not crashed out there, thankfully) who sat with me and listened to my ideas and told me I had some interesting takes, but then would lean in and say, "In reality, it would be more like..." Thank you to Glenn Law, a systems director in the Civil and Commercial Launch Projects Group at Aerospace who not only helped me figure out the structure for the Mayflower 2 ship in the book, but also for inviting me to watch a Mars rover launch from the control room in El Segundo, an experience I'll never forget. Thank you to NASA's Jerry Miller who talked to me about gravity and moons and the mysteries of the galaxy. And a big thank you to Werner Däppen, Professor of Physics and Astronomy at USC, who entertained my ideas with passion and humor before getting down to the theories of black holes and space travel. Also, thank you to my friends Mark Wind and Nancy Profera for introducing me to some of these experts.

So many people have my deepest gratitude for their hard work and support while putting *Achilles* together:

To my literary agent, Wendy Sherman, for taking a chance and diving into the Young Adult book world with me years ago, for always talking me down when I get upset or too excited about a certain email or meeting, for protecting and supporting me during my ghostwriting days, and for being professional at all times and becoming a secret role model to me as my writing career moves forward. *Achilles* would not have a leg to stand or crash on if it weren't for Wendy, and I can't thank her enough.

To Jaime Levine and everyone at Diversion Books for getting excited about *Achilles* and holding my hand through the edits, for listening to my ideas and gracefully steering me in the right direction, and for the guidance on the two sequels I'm currently tearing my hair out over. I am lucky to have Diversion on my side and wouldn't want to be anywhere else.

To my immediate family, and bear with me, there's a lot of them: my parents, Bill and Rita, for supporting me in more ways than one and respecting my passion for writing; my siblings, Eric, Alan, Sara, Brad, and Matt, for sharing their excitement or opinion on whatever silly things I've published over the years; my in-laws, Kristin, Gabrielle, Matt, Chris, and Sarah, for always asking how my writing is going without their eyes glazing over; my Uncle Ron, for showing more genuine excitement for me than I deserve; and to my daughters, Veronica and Juliette, for sneaking up behind me to hug my neck while I type away and for begging me to tell them in great detail what happens in *Achilles*, which helped me better mold the story while surely giving them nightmares for years to come.

To my friends for listening to me complain and blather on about whatever I'm writing at the time, and for telling me to keep going, especially: Tarek Said, Sean Widman, Michael Loomis, Dan

Freeman, Karah Woesner, Mike Gilpin, Tyler Stoddard Smith, Julie Mosiello, Brett Krupp, Joel Hagen, Alea McKinley, and Hanna Kahn. And a particular thank you to Joe Andosca, for listening to me for hours on the phone and brainstorming with me, only to have him shoot down one idea after another by saying something like, "If you've ever seen *Star Trek II: The Wrath of Khan*, they did something similar where..." Joe truly helped shaped *Achilles*, and if there's anything in the book you have problems with, I'm going to blame that section on him.

And finally, to those who have picked up a copy of this book, thank you so much for reading. It's humbling to have someone spend their time swimming around in the world I've created. I promise that if I ever visit outer space, or if I crash anything out there, you'll be the first ones I tell. Unless I die in the crash. Then you'll probably read about it online or something.